Room 3

Jonathan D Allen

ROOM 3
A Qwendellonia Book
PRINTING HISTORY
Qwendellonia First Edition/October 2012

Cover art by Ryan Bibby (http://novelbranding.com)

For more information, contact the author at crimnos@gmail.com
or visit http://jonathandallen.com
ISBN-13: 978-0615603919
ISBN-10: 0615603912

Praise for The Corridors of the Dead:

"This is a curious and compelling story about the existence of parallel worlds in a 'Multiverse' and the very unusual heroine and her friends, who have set off on a mystical, freakish quest to save the world. The only question is which world in the Multiverse will Matty save?" – Martha Bryce

"While this type of book is not what I usually read, I was drawn to this book. It was so hard to put down. The author has created wonderful characters that just draws the reader into the book. This is an author to watch for, I believe his future books will quickly become best sellers." – KYBunnies Books

"CORRIDORS OF THE DEAD was my dark and compelling companion…(it) pulled me aside in spare moments. When I put it aside for more pressing needs, it lay waiting in the shadows, whispering. It called me back to its well-crafted and fantastic world of mysteries, shifting dimensions and angels from Hades. Now I'm waiting for the second book in the series! Please Mr. Allen, write faster! I'd like to know I have your next book waiting for me, calling me aside for more amazing thrills and chills." – Sandy Signing In

Dedicated to Rob, one of the craziest guys I've ever known.
Keep dreaming big.

Thanks, first and foremost, to beta reader and fellow author Marie Loughin for going way above and beyond in helping this book to take shape. Thanks also to fantastic cover artist Ryan Bibby, a fellow traveler on the way of the Beam. Thanks also go out to dedicated beta readers Mary Allen and Aleta Best and Editor Shelly Burnett for their efforts. Thank you for making this possible.

The dream is a little hidden door in the innermost and most secret recesses of the soul, opening into that cosmic night which was psyche long before there was any ego consciousness, and which will remain psyche no matter how far our ego-consciousness extends.

C.G. Jung, "The Meaning of Psychology for Modern Man" (1933).

April: Wake up Dreamer

April 10th

Here I am, alone again, an alien in an empty motel room somewhere in Texas, listening for footsteps outside the door. Someone on the outside might think I waited for an eager lover who'd taken a few hours away from his wife, or even my own people, beamed down from the mother-ship. Good guesses both, but you'd be wrong. Instead, I'm waiting for death. Maybe worse than death; I admit my imagination escapes me a little with these things.

I do hear footfalls, though, and every time I hear them, I'm almost positive that the Organization has found me and is ready to take what they think is theirs. Some nights I wonder if they're right. Maybe I should be their property. Maybe I overstepped my limits by escaping them and coming to this weird world that seems so familiar and yet so damned alien at the same time.

The central question of my existence, or anyone's existence if they really think about it – if someone creates you, do they own you? Does that mean they can destroy you, too, like the parent who brings you into this world and can take you out again? It sounds absurd but don't be so sure about your own answer if you've never found out that your entire existence is a lie.

Okay, they didn't create me. Not really. They only shaped me, and God knows what they'd do if they got their hands on me again. Maybe killing me would be too nice. They have worse things to do to a person.

On the other hand, I suppose freedom in itself is a sweet and noble goal, but can you call holing yourself up in a motel room and jumping at every sound freedom? Sometimes I wonder if I've replaced one prison with another, though this prison is a lot safer and comfier than the one where I had to ingest mass quantities of drugs on a daily basis.

I feel like I'm losing my mind an inch at a time. Don't get me wrong, I never thought life on the run would be easy, and Sam says things will be getting better soon, but come on. Things have to change; I just don't know how they could or will. Foresight has never been my thing.

I think that's where this journal comes in. Am I a writer? Not sure. My family tree includes a pretty famous writer, or at least a reasonable facsimile of one, and if my creator could do that, what else could she do? My memory tells me that the last journal I kept ended about the time I turned 13 and discovered boys, but I can't trust that period of my life.

It doesn't matter. In the end, like most folks who put pen to paper, I have a story to tell. A weird, poisonous story that hangs on me, dragging me down any time I start to feel I might be a normal human being, but no story is perfect, right? It's time to get rid of it. Maybe it'll be like passing a kidney stone: excruciating but necessary.

Nothing can be normal until I get this stone out of my system.

=======

The story starts one night at a little bar in Boston. It also starts with a guy named Bloch. Big slab of a man and a real sweetheart, at least until he acknowledges your existence. My memories happen to solidify on that night, but I still haven't figured out how much of it is fact and how much fiction. Does it matter? Everyone's memory sucks in some way. At least I have a coherent narrative.

Memory tells me that I had been a bartender and a performer - sing on the weekend, sling beer during the week. Not glamorous, but there are a lot worse ways to make a living. I had the "good" fortune of living in a hellhole just down the block from the bar. Its proximity to the bar was a blessing and a curse. I didn't own a car, so walking wasn't such a big deal, but I also got off in the wee hours of the morning, so I had to cut through a not-so-great neighborhood all on my lonesome.

It might have been a Wednesday. Or maybe a Tuesday? I don't know if the fact that I can't remember is a sad statement on the human condition or a glitch in my upbringing. Maybe both. The important thing is that I was there, on the street, and more than a little tired. Back-to-back shifts, some mean drunks; nothing unusual but still, worn out. Unfortunately, that meant I had dropped my guard. A girl can only handle so much in one night.

This voice from just up the sidewalk broke into whatever thoughts rattled around in my head.

"Hey, excuse me. Can you help me?" he said.

I paused, mid-stride. I had gotten my share of catcalls on that street, even at that hour, and while you never get comfortable with it, you can at least stomach it after a while. Asking for help, though? In this neighborhood? That seemed dangerous.

It didn't help that he was a big guy - most people would think he packed a layer of fat under that black leather jacket, but that would have been a mistake. I had dealt with enough bouncers in my time to tell he was a wall of solid muscle. I wondered how I couldn't have noticed the behemoth standing there.

Weren't paying attention, as usual, I thought.

"What can I do for you?" I said, careful to keep my distance.

He motioned toward his car, a red, compact thing parked just off the sidewalk. He – or someone – had popped the hood open. "I'm having trouble getting my car going."

"I don't know anything about cars." Pretty straightforward, right?

He cocked his head. "Hey, don't I know you from somewhere?"

Did he? He could have been a patron at some point. "Maybe. I don't recognize you."

He nodded and wagged his finger at me. "Sure I do. From Sully's. You sing, right?"

I might have blushed. I did get a little rush of adrenaline with the recognition, and it might not have been the best thing for me. But still, a fan, maybe? Who could resist? "Yeah. That's me." I got a little closer to him without even realizing it.

"Right. Love your stuff. Anyway, I don't need you to fix it. I forgot my phone, I was wondering if you'd let me use yours."

Anything for a fan. I reached into my purse, pushing one of my annoying curls out of my face with my other hand. Did I mention that my hair is the bane of my existence? I should. "Sure. You know how to use one of these?"

He took my iPhone. "Yeah. Hey, thanks. Kelli, right?"

I nodded and glanced around the sidewalk and street. I didn't know, there might have been other fans there, or people who saw that I might be a famous person. They needed to see this.

Not my smartest move. I heard him move an instant before I had time to turn my head, by which point he'd already sunk the needle into my neck. You'd say that's bad, and you'd be right. Pain shot up to my head and down my shoulders, followed by a rush of warmth and the taste of licorice in my mouth.

Panic washed over me. "Hey, you…" I managed to get out. Nothing else. Everything went dark.

=======

My body felt strange. Disconnected, as if gravity had lost its grip. I opened my eyes slowly, my fuzzy mind trying to piece together what had happened. I remembered Bloch, and the jab of the needle…

My eyes completely opened at this last, my mind struggling to connect his action with my current situation.

I understood in a moment, though I didn't – couldn't – fully comprehend the situation: I floated, head up, in water, my feet bound to unseen contraptions anchored below me.

Oh my God oh my God, I thought. *Breathe.*

My mind didn't register that breath already pushed through my lungs, so I panicked, kicking and hitting something hard that I couldn't quite see, out past the water, or maybe inside the water. I couldn't tell.

The only clear fact? I wouldn't be moving anytime soon. Panic increasing by the moment, I reached for my face and found a rubber mask strapped across my nose and mouth.

You're breathing. It's normal air. Calm down.

A blob that looked something like a human face appeared at the edge of the water, and my sluggish brain put it together at last: I floated in a giant test tube. It set me off again. I tried to scream at the blob of a person, pounding at what I now recognized as glass.

The blob took a step back and made a motion that I couldn't quite interpret.

Warmth spread from my right wrist down over my body, followed by licorice, and I went out again.

=======

I snapped awake in a bed, an overhead light shining into my face. Recoiling from the photons stabbing my eyes to death, I tried to cover my face, but my arms - along with my legs - had been restrained, cuffed into place on either side of the bed.

If you like the idea of restraints, you could get used to it. Maybe even enjoy it.

I never got used to it.

A cultured, feminine English voice spoke from somewhere outside the light. "She's awake."

Another woman spoke, from the other side of the room. "Give her some room to breathe." Her voice sounded like she'd gargled with whiskey for a few years.

I heard footsteps as two - maybe three - people stepped away from me.

"Cover my eyes," I said.

The Englishwoman snapped her fingers. "Please. Get the lights."

A guy with a thick Jersey accent answered her. A man of many words. "Right." A click, and the lights went out.

I silently thanked a few deities, trying to push my fear out of my mind. Not very successful at that last one. "Where am I? Who are you?"

A hand touched my arm, and I jerked against the restraints. "Don't touch me, don't you touch me."

"Stay where you are," New York said to someone that I

couldn't see.

"Please, do calm down." Englishwoman again. My eyes had recovered somewhat from their rude assault, at least enough to make out the woman's outline in the dark. It wouldn't be fair to call her fat. Solid? Yeah, that's a good word for it. She had pulled her hair up into a severe bun, the kind you go for when you want maximum evil effect.

I jerked my head from side to side, trying to pick out details of the room through the dark. I thought I saw a closet somewhere off to my right. Soft yellow light pouring through the cracks, of what must have been a door just to its left. It took me another second to figure out the weird dark spots in the light came about because of a big shadow standing in front of the door.

I tasted fear. "Where am I? Who are you?"

"Shh," the Englishwoman said.

I struggled with the restraints again. "Answer me."

Whiskey woman spoke again. "She can't calm down; can't you see what you're doing to her?"

"Be quiet," New York said.

"Fuck you, Zito. Let her loose."

A slapping sound, and the other woman went quiet. I tried to crane my neck in the direction of her voice, and I could make out her body lying prone on the bed, a short, puffy-haired guy standing over her. Zito, I presume.

"Told you to shut up," he said.

The fear in my throat blossomed into full-on panic. I kicked and pulled, trying to break free of the restraints.

Footsteps rushed toward my bed and a single calloused hand touched my throat. "Stop. Do it again and I'll hurt you worse than I hurt her," Zito said.

I handled the situation with all the dignity that I could

muster after my miserable night. "Please don't hit me. I'll do anything you want."

Englishwoman answered me. "Of course you will, dear. We're counting on it."

"Who are you?"

I still couldn't see her face, but her features crinkled, so I imagine she tried to show some emotion, though not very well. I tried to calculate her age based on the wrinkles. Mid-30s? Mid-40s? From any one second to another it changed.

"You may call me Ms. Maple. At your service."

"Why did you take me?"

"You're a very special one. Very special indeed," she said.

Damn my dysfunctional brain. For half a second I got a little thrill; me, special. Hadn't I always wanted something like that? I corrected that thought pretty quickly, though. Okay, fear corrected it. Same thing. "What do you mean?"

She patted my arm. "We brought you here to help us."

I cringed, but the thought of Zito's threat brought me up short. I didn't *dare* pull away. "With what?"

"You'll see."

"We done here? Senior's paying Barren overtime for this. We need to make sure she's the right one." Zito said.

Maple turned her head. "I am *quite* aware of the situation. Please do remember your place."

"Uh. Yes, ma'am. Sorry."

"Bloch."

That's when a new voice spoke. Well, not quite new to me. I sure as hell recognized it: my friend from the street, the guy with the red car and the syringe. "Yes?"

He moved, and I realized that he had been the shadow by the door. Who would have guessed? I also realized that the man scared me shitless; that should have been a little easier to guess.

Another surprise, though: I shrieked a little without even meaning to.

A hand flashed out and slapped my face. "I told you to calm down, and I meant it," Maple said.

Some Englishwoman. I went silent.

Maple spoke. "Take her to Room 3, please."

"Absolutely," Bloch said, and came close. I didn't need to see him. I could feel him in my nerve endings, in the way that my body tensed against my bindings.

He leaned down over me. "Listen, that whole thing in Boston wasn't personal, okay? Just business."

"Yeah. Business," I said. I worried. Did that sound sarcastic? It might have. I winced, waiting for another slap.

Bloch nodded. "I get it. It's not business to you. But what's done is done. I'm going to set you loose, and we're taking you out of here, okay?"

"I told you to move her, not counsel her," Maple said.

He glanced over his shoulder at her. "You do your job and I do mine."

"The impertinence…"

"You want her moved or not?" Bloch said.

She said nothing, and he turned to me.

"I'm going to set you loose. I don't want to hurt you, but if you try anything funny, we're going to have to. You understand?"

I didn't figure bravery would get me anywhere. Well, other than abused, and I wasn't looking to go there anytime soon. I nodded.

"Good. I'm glad we have an agreement." He reached for me and I steeled myself, screaming at my body not to recoil or pull away this time. My body surprised me by obeying. A key slid into the lock on the restraints, and a few moments later he had freed me from of the cuffs and bindings.

"Can you stand up?" he said.

I didn't want to say too much. It seemed too risky, so I pushed myself up on the bed. My head swooned, the dark room spinning around me. I put one hand to my head. "I don't think so."

He motioned toward Zito, keeping his eyes on me. "We're going to help you up. You know the drill. Do anything funny…"

"Got it," I said.

Zito joined him. "He means it."

My traitorous little body got away from me again, and I snapped, "I said that I got it."

Again, I waited for the slap that never came; instead, they just reached for me.

Zito brushed one of my tits. I know, classy guy, right? I had to swallow the drive to slap him.

They helped me ease off of the bed. For a second I thought the world might stop spinning, but I should have known better; it returned, and I almost tipped over with its strength. I leaned hard against Bloch and he pushed back, keeping me upright. Hell of a guy.

"Okay, one step at a time. Taking it easy," he said.

Like I had any other choice. I took a hesitant, shuffling step forward. "What's Room 3?"

"You'll find out soon enough," Zito said.

That was clear. I took another step.

Bloch spoke up. "Don't be such a bitch. Of course she's worried. Girl can't help it."

Like I said, hell of a guy. Another step.

Zito laughed. "You getting all soft on me here or what?"

Another step, and we stopped in front of the door. Zito opened it, and the warm orange light of the new room hit my eyes. I struggled to clear my eyes, shaking my head this way, and then that, but I couldn't comprehend much of what I saw beyond that door.

"I'm doing my job. There's force, and there's sadism. You cross the line, my friend," Bloch said.

"Yeah? Fuck your mother."

Bloch said nothing, but I felt his body tighten against mine. Something in my brain must have short-circuited in interpreting it, because I could have sworn that he planned to attack me. I took an involuntary step backward, and the room pitched over, my brain swimming.

"Whoa, now," Zito said. They caught me, trying to get me upright. They overcompensated, though, and I started to go forward, my arms flailing. I thought of some of the drunks that had stumbled out of the bar. I must have been a sight. Bloch caught me this time, and the two dragged me through the door, my feet dangling and scraping on the floor.

I fell sideways, almost hitting the ground before Bloch pulled me up. "Jesus Christ, be careful," he said.

During all this fun, drunken swaying, I caught a glimpse of the door to our room. Someone had taped a black, plastic 1 to it.

I thought to ask a question, but had already lost control of those functions.

The pair shuffled me across the front room, one step at a time. Given my drugged state, it might not be that surprising that I don't remember much more than those two manhandling me. I remember a glimpse of a door labeled with a plastic 2, but that could also be my mind playing tricks on me.

I *do* remember when door 3 swam into my vision, though.

Hard to forget that. It looked innocent enough, not so different from door 1, but strange, multicolored lights poured out through the crack between the floor and the bottom of the door.

My heart skipped a beat – I felt it – and I took another one of those hesitant steps backward. It might have been a traitor, but my body had had enough. It sensed what my mind didn't understand and wanted no part of it. I wish I could have listened to it, but I didn't have a choice in the matter.

"Oh, no. Not now," Zito said, and pushed me forward. "Come on."

Bloch opened the door on a low-lit room, and they dragged me through. My body kept fighting, though, credit to it. I dragged my heels and tried to pull away from them, desperate to get away from whatever fresh hell I feared they might unleash on me next.

A small, chubby black guy with Harry Potter glasses waited on the other side of the threshold.

"Good evening, Ms. Foster," he said, and stepped to one side, revealing a large, yellow contraption in the middle of the room. It looked like a dentist's chair crossed with a torture machine, a big, reclining thing bolted into the wooden floor. Wires and straps hung from its side, along with a steel swing-out tray to accommodate some strange, silvery tools

My stomach turned to liquid. "Come on. Can't we talk about this? I need to go to the bathroom."

"Boy, never heard that one before, huh, Barren?" Zito said, and the two dragged me over to the chair.

They tried to push me into the chair, and I resisted, bracing my feet against the base of the thing.

Something heavy hit the back of my head and my vision doubled. "None of that," Zito said from the end of a far tunnel.

My strength sapped, I let them push me into the seat and

started pulling the straps over my limbs. I inhaled the rich leather of the straps, my head spinning with fear. Visions danced through my aching head: the dentist's drill, bamboo under fingernails, strange devices that picked at and opened up flesh.

Zito's stinking breath swept over me as he reached over the body, securing the last of the straps against my chest.

I stared at the worn wooden ceiling, hoping that it would be over soon, but I couldn't even succeed at distracting myself, for someone had hung a big ball of multi-colored lights over the chair, dangling from the ceiling like a tacky Christmas decoration.

Zito's hand brushed one of my breasts as he withdrew. I tried to pretend that it had been accidental; a voice in my head told me that I should know better.

"What are you doing?" I said.

Zito and Bloch stepped back, and Barren came forward, that serene smile still on his face. He held a syringe in one hand. Its barrel had been filled with a clear liquid - no, not quite clear; particles drifted through it, catching the light from the ball overhead.

Barren lowered the needle toward my arm. "Don't worry. We're paving the way to the future."

=======

I think that's enough for tonight. As much as I'd like to talk about the torture of that first time in Room 3, it's late, and I don't think I'm ready to talk about it. Maybe not ever. Disappointing, but what can you do? There are wounds and then there are *wounds.* No need to pick at those kinds of things.

More tomorrow, if I'm still here.

April 11th

Still here. I didn't expect Sam to come and sweep me away to a castle in the sky or any such nonsense, but anything would beat sitting around waiting for my own death. At least I have my memories. Oh, wait, I can't even rely on 90% of those, either. Maybe my good looks?

It didn't take long for me to figure out that I wasn't the only woman who lived in Room 1. My first clue should have been the woman with the whiskey voice, but they scrambled my brains a little bit that night and I didn't remember her presence for a little while.

Not that I could have ignored her for long; she wouldn't, or maybe *couldn't,* let me be alone, no matter how much I *wanted* her to leave me alone. The perils of being stuck with a helper bee.

That first trip to Room 3 wasn't the greatest thing I've ever experienced. I came out of it dizzy, nauseated, and numb, which might normally have been a lot of fun. Maybe it's just me, but I don't think it's quite the same when a bunch of scary strangers strap you down and shoot you full of those drugs. Either way, the results make it hard to put your best foot forward when meeting and greeting new friends, so of course I wanted nothing to do with anyone. I wanted my bed (well, and the toilet) and solitude.

Try telling Whiskey Voice that, though. I found myself exhausted and out of it, unable to pay more than a few seconds of attention to my surroundings, let alone vocalize something like that.

She introduced herself as Regina, "but only my mom calls me that. You can call me Gina." She pulled my blanket over me and tucked me into bed. It didn't take her long to cross the room and start mixing a small bit of powder into a glass of water.

I tried to ask her what might be in the powder, but my voice still refused to work.

When she leaned over me, I decided not to fight, letting her pour the whole thing down my gullet. What more damage could it do? And hey, it helped, too, just not quite the way I might have thought. It made things better, sure, but it didn't take the pain away so much as make the pain seem like it happened to a woman on another planet. Had I known then what I know now, I probably wouldn't have let her give it to me, but what can you do?

I should have been annoyed, but even once I'd come down off the high I couldn't feel angry at her. That sums up the Gina Experience, though. She had her problems - hell, a *lot* of problems, but who doesn't? For that matter, who *wouldn't* have a problem or two in that place? She managed to rise above all her damage, though, in ways that continually surprised me. She could be so wholesome, give you the shirt off her back, but you could see the beast inside her eyes, waiting just below the surface.

My subconscious is a sucker for that kind of duality in a person, so it gave her an almost otherworldly pull.

She had a way of making you want to overlook her problems - no, scratch that, you *had* to overlook her problems because doing otherwise would be a mortal sin.

I didn't know then about the way that addicts can draw you in.

There's another truth, though: I *needed* Gina. Not in some psychosexual way, but all the same I needed her presence. She alone kept me from going crazy during those difficult early days. That first day after the trip to Room 3 just about did me in. Her little "remedy" only went so far, and she didn't have any more on hand. Once it got out of my system, the side-effects came roaring back, and they were pissed. The reasonable response was lying in bed for a few days, pissing and moaning about my fate. If not then, after my brutal kidnapping and torture, then when could I do such a thing?

Never. Not so long as Gina was around. She would have none of it.

"I didn't get to sit around, mope, and blame myself for any of this, and neither do you," she said right before she wrapped one arm around me and lifted me out of the bed. That little move almost resulted in me vomiting on her shirt, but I managed to keep it down. She waited for me to get my equilibrium and then started shuffling me around the room as if I were her personal marionette. She helped me put one foot in front of the other, the whole time filling my head with details about her childhood in Alabama that are lost to time.

We played that game for a week or so. I would start getting better and the people of the Organization (so dubbed by Gina) couldn't have any of that, so they'd return and take me to Room 3 once again. Sure, Gina sometimes took the trip, but she seemed to have gotten over the hurdle of her head turning inside out. When they brought me back out, it would be time to start the dance all over again.

After a while, my body must have adjusted to the drugs. At some point I started getting up under my own power, though I couldn't say when that began to happen. Week two or three, maybe. I started pacing off the corners of the room, memorizing every nook and cranny, figuring they might come in handy should I get a chance to escape. That backfired, though, because at some point I stopped seeing the little details, like the cracks in the old wood or the layer of grime on the single plastic window.

Gina told me what she knew about the place during what I now see as my personal rehab sessions.

One evening stands out as particularly crazy. She had been back from Room 3 for a few hours, lying on her side, staring into space dead-silent. All of a sudden she popped up from the bed and started pacing.

"What do you know about the people that took us?" she said, never breaking stride, never even looking at me.

"Nothing more than you do."

She put her hand to her chin. "Right. See, way I have it figured, the CIA hired those monkeys, Zito and Bloch, and they got Maple from…I don't know. Chiron Beta Prime, maybe."

"So we're being held by the CIA, assisting aliens?"

She stopped, looked at me at last, and grinned. "That's just crazy. It's the aliens helping out the CIA."

"Right. Of course."

I lived for those talks. The crazier her theories got about that place, the better I felt. I suppose it helped to believe that our suffering contributed to something larger. It's weird; it almost felt like an innocent time, even with everything that had happened to us, even with the crap that they dealt out to us.

Even with her store of knowledge, Gina couldn't avoid the abuse any better than I could. Reason and intellect had little to do with avoiding their abuse. Take the afternoon when Maple got a bug up her ass about how we were folding the towels.

Could we have done a better job? I suppose, but come on – were we really in boarding school?

Apparently so, because she picked up a half-dry white towel

and came at us, snapping it, screeching "unacceptable" over and over. You don't think a towel could do a lot of damage beyond some stinging welts, but she managed to catch Gina just right on the cheek, slicing it open.

Gina didn't let that get to her, though. Her knowledge might not have prevented the beatings, but it did help her deal with them.

"Kelli," she'd say, leaning against the wall with her arms crossed over her chest, "I've been through a lot. Seen a lot of things I shouldn't ever have seen, and I figure there's one thing I can control – myself. Can't control the circumstances, sure as shit can't control other people, but I *can* control how I react to things."

I considered pointing out that she didn't even have control of herself, given her crippling addiction to heroin, but would that help either of us? Not really. I let her go on.

"When they hit me for not moving fast enough, I think about how my momma would whip me for messing with the neighbor boy. Turns it into love, you know?"

Sure, it made sense in that whole psychosexual thing I mentioned earlier. Turn the pain into love. Why not? All right, truth, I didn't follow, but I still took what I could. Bottom line, I needed a way to reframe their actions. I tried to remember my folks when they hit me, but that made me angrier. I tried to think of lovers (real or imagined) before they shot me up. No real luck there. In fact, I never quite got to where Gina lived (and let's be honest, she had her own crutch to help her get there), but after a while, I did okay for myself. Thinking about personal growth through pain – the ways that I had grown from adversity - helped a bit. For a while there, I almost felt normal; as normal as anyone in that place *could* feel.

I didn't quite understand why the Organization would keep

a junkie around, but at some point Gina told me that they had known about her addiction right from the beginning. They must have figured that the addiction was worth the trade-off, since she could do great things in Room 3. Things that I didn't understand yet, but they must have been pretty great. Would you feed a junkie's habit willingly? I know I wouldn't.

So the Organization kept her stocked with horse. They had a standard ritual: Zito or Bloch would come in, once in the morning, once in the afternoon, carrying a fat syringe. She'd lie on the bed and skin-pop, they'd leave, and she'd check out for a while. It seemed to work for her, and I won't lie, I considered asking for some myself on more than one occasion. It at least seemed like a way to escape and, hell, maybe even enjoy myself. At some point, though, I caught on to the real reason they kept giving her fixes: it was a pretty effective way to keep her in chains.

With such a surreal situation, the heroin seemed pedestrian. I never quite got used to rooming with a junkie, but the junk just didn't seem so important in the big picture. At least, until it *became* important. I have no idea which day it happened, and I hate that. She had been pacing for a little while, hand to her mouth, cursing Maple and Zito under her breath.

"You know they're using you," I said.

She turned on me. "You think I haven't figured that out? I'm not a moron. But what choice do I got?"

I admitted that I had no idea, and she kept on going.

"For me, it's survival. For them, it's usefulness," she said. "My work - stuff - you know, it's worth more than what they're putting in for the junk, you can be damn sure of that."

Figuring she might be a little more vulnerable and thus willing to talk at last, I tried to pry some more information from her. "What are they having you do in there, anyway?"

By God, she answered. "Write. I mean, not in real life, you know. It's the visions. They send me over there, or into my head, or where-ever, and I have to write what I see."

I held up a hand. "Come on. You're screwing with me, right?"

She said nothing.

"I've seen some weird in Room 3, no doubt, but you're not going to convince me it's anything other than my brain swimming in sludge."

She started pacing again. "We're not talking about this again."

Worked for me. "Fair enough, but will you *please* sit down? You're making me nervous."

"Can't. Need a fix." She tapped one foot. "Where are they? They're usually here by now."

"How can you even tell?" I said this because time in the cabin just didn't work the same as it worked anywhere else. Some days the sun rose and stayed suspended in the air for what seemed like days, and then the night would pass you by in minutes. Real mind-fuck material. I'm sure the Organization loved the advantage that it gave them over us – one more bit of ammo in their arsenal.

Gina sighed. "Trust me. I just can. Body tells the truth, girl."

"If you say so."

She went to the door and knocked. "Hey, where are you?" Nothing too rude. She might as well have been asking when dinner would be coming. She even waited for them. When they didn't answer, she steepled her hands together at her chest. "Come on. Just a little bit. You can't do this to me, it's not fitting."

A long pause. More silence, and her veneer cracked: she slammed a fist against the door and howled. I'd never seen her so violent. It put me on edge, like I hadn't quite felt in weeks.

You know how sometimes you can just sense that a violent, rapid change is coming? If not, it feels like you're tipping over an edge and about to fall, screaming. I shuddered as that sensation consumed me.

She shouted again, pounding on the door one more time. "Come on."

More silence, but that over-the-edge feeling intensified; anxiety crept up my throat. "Maybe you shouldn't..." I said, but trailed off.

She shook her head. "No. These assholes knew what they were getting into. They *owe* it to me."

I didn't answer; what could I say? Once a junkie's zeroed in on her fix, you just get out of the way. I pushed myself into the corner of my bed, waiting for the hammer to drop.

When the hammer did arrive, it didn't quite sound like I had expected. Rather than a violent burst through the door, we just heard a soft voice.

"Ms. Tolleson, this is not the way to get what you want," Maple said.

"Fuck you. Where's the junk?"

A pause. "You are to no longer receive your doses."

Gina became a statue, her eyes bulging. I don't think she could quite grasp what she heard, or if she did, she refused to acknowledge it. The seconds drew out forever. Finally, she spoke in a hushed tone: "What are you trying to do to me?"

"We are thinking of your health."

She scratched one arm. "You have *got* to be shitting me. You really think this will make me healthier?"

"In the long run, yes."

Gina flipped her middle finger at the door. "Don't try to lie to a liar. How can you look yourself in the eye, after all I've done for you?"

"You have done so for yourself." The door muffled the Englishwoman's voice, so I couldn't attest 100% to what I heard there, but I swear she had a hint of smugness.

"I won't go cold turkey. You can't make me," Gina said.

The knob clicked, and the door swung open, creaking on its hinges as it went inch by inch. Maple took a single step across the threshold, and behind her came Zito, Bloch, and a tall, pale white guy that I'd never seen before.

Maple gave Gina what might have been the fakest, toothiest grin I'd ever seen, tilting her head. "We can make you do what we wish."

Gina took a step back. "Wh-what's going on, fellows?"

"All will be well." Maple snapped her fingers.

Bloch and the big pale guy each took one of Gina's arms and dragged her toward the bed. Gina tried to fight back, but withdrawal had already sapped her strength. It reminded me of a bar fight that I'd seen (or thought I'd seen) between two bouncers and a dweeb from Harvard – he had lasted all of five seconds, too.

"What are you doing?" she screeched.

Maple produced a syringe. "Be calm, my girl. Be calm."

Just the sight of the syringe put Gina at ease for a few moments. I'm sure Maple counted on that, too. It gave Bloch and the pale guy the time they needed to get Gina flat on the bed and start slipping the cuffs on her wrists.

The cuffs on her hands snapped her out of the momentary daze. She came to life, her eyes on fire. "Don't you fucking touch me."

Bloch held her now-twisting right wrist in both hands, clamping the cuff closed. "Come on. Nobody's here to hurt you.

We're on your side."

Gina didn't agree. She wrenched at the cuffs, howling and kicking. "This is bullshit."

All this had tied my stomach into knots. No kidding, I'd thought that might be exaggeration before, but it felt like my intestines looped in on themselves. I kept hearing what sounded like my mother's words, ringing in my ears over and over:

Never neglect a friend in need, no matter what. You never know when it might be you who needs the help.

My instincts – you know, the ones tying up my guts? They told me to do the exact opposite. Instincts' very loud and insistent voices told me to run and hide in the farthest corner while the thugs did what they came to do. My mother's voice only just shouted down that instinct.

Compelled, I slid forward on the bed, not even sure what I would do once I got to her. Maybe kick the guys in the nuts?

Zito spotted me and took care of whatever move I might have made, stepping between me and the battle. "Ah, ah. No interrupting the process."

"You can't do this to her," I said, but I backed up all the same.

He scoffed. "Can and will."

I glanced over his shoulder. The two large men behind him stepped away from the now-bound Gina, watching Maple tap the syringe.

Gina's eyes bugged out of her skull. "What's in there?"

Maple smiled at her, ever the saint. "Our very own cocktail. Don't worry; it's just a little something to calm you."

"What is it? Methadone? Subox?"

Maple sighed. "As I said, our own cocktail."

Gina shook her restraints, snarling "fuck" at the

Englishwoman.

Maple raised an eyebrow. "I'm sorry, truly I am, but we're no longer allowed to provide you with your drug. Orders from above."

Gina made another rough noise, sounding more feral animal than human, but before she could summon any more real words, Maple bent over, jabbing the needle into her vein. She pushed the plunger, delivering the "cocktail' as quickly as possible.

Gina squealed and Maple stepped away, pocketing the syringe.

In moments, Gina started grunting and shaking all over, her body twisting and jerking.

Maple watched for a moment, her face contorting in horror. "Bloch, Samarta," she said.

The big men took hesitant steps forward, glancing from one another and then to her. "What do you want us to do?" Bloch said.

Maple took a step backward, hand to her mouth. "Get Barren. Quickly now."

The big pale guy, Samarta, bolted from the room, the door slamming shut behind him.

I swallowed my nausea, jumped up, and rushed to Gina's side. Nobody tried to stop me this time. Even Zito stared in abject horror as Gina foamed at the mouth. "What the hell did you do to her?" I said.

Maple took another step away from Gina. "I didn't –"

The door burst open and Barren entered, leading the charge with Samarta close behind. I wondered if Barren had made the "cocktail" that had been shot into Gina. If he did, he could fix this, right?

Barren looked to Maple, his mouth tight, his eyebrows

drawn. "I told you not to give her the full dosage."

"I didn't mean to do this. She fought us."

"Come on. Uncuff her. We have to roll her on her side."

Bloch and Samarta moved and I rolled off the side of the bed, letting go of Gina's spasming hand. I backed toward the far side of the room, near the door, chewing on a fingernail.

The blocks of meat fumbled with the restraints, freeing her. They rolled her on her side so that she faced me. Her mouth hung open, her seizures had slowed, and her eyes were going glassy.

I bit harder on my fingernail, ripping the edge off. Don't leave me, Gina. Please. I don't know what I'll do if you go.

Barren produced a syringe from inside his white lab coat and went to Gina's side, bending over her. I'm not sure whether he meant to do it, but he blocked my view of what must have been her dying eyes.

He meant to be merciful, but I felt a flare of anger. She needed to see a sympathetic face in her last moments, not his. I stepped to one side so she could see me and I could keep an eye on what he did.

He bit his lip and touched her neck. "Goddammit," he muttered, and rolled her on her back again. He tilted her neck and leaned his ear over her mouth.

"Goddammit," he said again, and cleared the foam from her mouth. He went to her mouth and started breathing into her, making her chest rise and fall.

I clenched my fists at my sides, rocking with each breath from Barren. "Breathe, Gina. Come on. Breathe," I said.

Barren put his hand over her chest and started pumping, glaring at Maple all the while. "This is why I told you we needed a defib machine."

Maple looked away. "The Senior refused to approve it."

"If the Senior wants to keep his precious 'assets' alive, he damn well needs to do *something*." He felt for her pulse, didn't like what he found, and started another round of breathing into her mouth.

I felt a presence at my back and turned, looking up into Samarta's pale face. I know I should have felt horrified that he'd snuck up on me like that, but…I wasn't. Call me crazy, but having the hulk of a man so close calmed me a little bit.

I think his goal was calming me, too. "I am sorry," he said.

"Not your fault," I murmured, and looked to Gina, watching Barren labor over her, my heart going colder with every moment that she didn't wake. He worked on her for almost ten minutes, cursing his colleagues between breaths. Maple said nothing in response, drifting closer and closer to the door. Her face had almost reached the same pallor as Samarta.

Give the guy credit, Barren wasn't one to give up. I wondered whether he believed that he could beat life into her. I *wished* that he could, but the ache in my heart told me that wasn't going to happen.

Tenacious or not, even his hope vanished at some point. He leaned over her body, supporting his weight on both elbows. A sheen of sweat glowed on his forehead, and he gasped for air. Everyone else in the room had fallen silent, shell-shocked, and unable to move.

At last he looked at his colleagues and said, "I hope you're all happy."

"We aren't. We don't have to be," Bloch said.

Zito nodded. "The Senior gave the orders. We just did –"

"What you were told. Right." He straightened up, hands pressed to the small of his back. "Oldest story in the book."

My mind raged. *How could they?* I wanted to fall over her

body and wail. I wanted to pick up where Barren left off and try to pound life into her.

I wanted to grab whatever syringes remained and kill them all.

As innocent as it might have sounded, the last thought changed something inside of me. I don't mean that in a "finding enlightenment" way, either. I felt something overloaded and rotten break in my head, my fear and anxiety disappearing into a dark hole somewhere deep inside of me.

You know why? It wasn't the anger, though that would be a good guess. Grief would be a good one, too, and I'm sure it played a part, but that wasn't just it. I knew then, for sure, that these assholes had no grand plan, no matter what they claimed. They hadn't killed Gina for maliciousness or some grand cause. No, they killed out of stupidity and carelessness. I had feared them when they seemed to be gods or demons. Now I saw them for just what they had always been: stupid, flawed beings.

I glared at Maple and started toward her. I would have torn her throat out if I'd gotten the chance, no doubt about that. I would have done it and enjoyed it. To our mutual good fortune, Samarta had control of his emotions and restrained me, squeezing my shoulder.

I strained against him, trying to break away. Failing that, I hoped that I might be able to kill Maple with my eyes. "You killed her, you bitch, how could you?" It was supposed to be English, but I admit it sounded a lot more like the noises that Gina had been making. I practically vibrated with rage; I felt like I should be able to run through walls, breathe smoke.

My venom knocked the distant, slack-jawed look from Maple's face. Her jaw muscles tightened, and she turned a cold stare on me. "You couldn't possibly understand."

"Understand what? That you're a careless murderer? I don't need to know anything else."

"Patience," Samarta said from behind me.

Patience? What is that supposed to mean?

Maple's lip curled. "Think what you will. We did what we could."

Barren roared. "Enough. A woman is dead. Show some goddamn respect."

We stood that way for a moment, Maple, Bloch, and Zito on one side of the bed, Samarta and me on the other, with Barren standing between us, looking very angry and exhausted.

At last Maple sighed and waved toward the bed. "Zito, Bloch, please do take care of her." She glanced at Barren. "And be respectful."

"Please," I said.

She crossed the room and stood before me, glancing up at Samarta for a moment before she met my eyes. "You. Back in your bed. I hear another word out of you, and we'll be forced to take drastic measures. Wouldn't want that, would we?"

"You bitch –" I moved toward her again, and Samarta restrained me. I heard that word in my head:

Patience.

I had no way of knowing whether the big guy had a plan. Maybe he didn't have to. Maybe all he needed to do was remind me that I couldn't get past these people on my own.

I looked to the floor. "No. Wouldn't want that."

"Very good. I knew you could see reason." She looked to Samarta. "We need to speak."

He moved away from me. Why had I listened to him without questioning? Why had I just let him put his hands on me without fighting, and why did I feel like he was already on my side?

I stumbled to my bed, sitting down hard. My heart hurt as I watched Zito and Bloch roll poor Gina into her bed sheet.

"Be good to her," I said.

The wind had even been taken from those two assholes. Bloch just said, "We will," and helped Zito carry her from the room. Maple and Sam watched them go, too, their hands at their waists. When they had left, Maple laid a hand on his arm and nodded toward the front room. He nodded and glanced at me, meeting my eyes once more.

"Leave her," Maple said.

I waved and looked away. "Yeah. Go."

He lingered for a moment longer, and then followed the Englishwoman out of the room. I lay on the bed and tried to fight back my tears. I wouldn't be very successful.

=======

Now I'm worn out. I thought writing this down might help, but so far all it seems to do is make me relive the emotions. Is that good? I'm not sure, but I'm also not sure that I could do much else. This journal demands that I write in it, and I do what I can.

Sleep now. More tomorrow.

April 12th

Surprising, I know, but I have many enemies. The most surprising is the identity of my worst enemy. It's not the guy who kidnapped me, though he has a special place in Hell. It's not the folks who held me hostage, either.

It's boredom.

Boredom didn't drive me crazy from the very beginning, but I kept hoping that, at some point, I'd develop a super-human resistance to the stuff, given how much time I'd spent in tiny, enclosed spaces.

Guess what? Not so much. In fact, it's the opposite. A hint of boredom makes me want to knock the walls down. Like today. Today was just filled with it.

I hadn't experienced much rain until the day I left the cabin. I know, my brain told me that I had, but my "memories" of rain had very little to do with the real thing. The first time I found myself caught in the rain, I held my hands out, squealing with delight. Then it soaked my clothes. Then it soaked through to my bones.

Then I didn't like rain so much anymore.

All this talk of dancing in the rain? Bah. I've found that to be one of the many times when people overrate this whole "real world" thing. Many things sucked about that place, but at least the temperature and weather never changed. I liked it. No snow. No cold.

Earlier this morning, flipping through crappy show after crappy show, I found myself wondering why I left at all. Why leave one cramped room for another, even smaller room? Sam keeps telling me to be patient, but it's hard to keep your head on straight. Yeah, no one is actively torturing me anymore, at least physically. But this mental stuff isn't much easier.

I sat down to write again, so I could remember just why I left that place. Put down the words, and maybe the memories of misery will stick with me.

=======

I spent a lot of time in that small room alone after Gina died. I spent some of it in Room 3, as well, and got familiar with my broken psyche. When I say broken, I mean it, too: something had changed inside me, and it felt like it might never return.

The next time they came to get me - maybe a day or two later, I'm not sure - I went right for Zito's face. I didn't do a lot of damage, but I did manage to track claw marks down his neck before Bloch pulled me off of him.

I didn't like that side of myself, but I figured it beat cowering whenever they came calling. Not that they came calling *that* much. Oh, sure, they stopped by every now and then to take me to Room 3, feed me, drop off new clothes, and take the old ones - one time they even brought me a sweet Korg keyboard, but I figured that I must not have had that "it' quality that Gina had possessed. Almost all of my time after she died ended up revolving around that room. Night and day, day and night.

That doesn't help too much with the misery factor, though. In fact, it reminds me that it's not too different from what I'm living right now, just that I had a sense of purpose back then. They didn't kidnap me just to kidnap me - there was a whole lot more to their motivations. I'm missing a sense of purpose now, and I hate waiting for Sam to give it to me.

Maybe telling my story gives me purpose; I don't know, but I do know that I need to talk about Carla, because the real story begins with Carla. Delusions of grandeur or not, I know that I'm just a tiny little cog in the grand majesty that is Carla's destiny.

I have no idea of the exact day or time that they brought her into my life. I know it was late; I sat at the keyboard, unable to sleep, plinking away at some random melody as I stared out the filthy window.

Zito burst through the door and stopped, glaring at me as I looked at him over my shoulder. He held a little black pistol at his side. The pistol had been a recent arrival, and it had changed things. I didn't dare take a punch at him after that, even if he did think he was the big man when he waved that thing around.

"Get on the bed. Face-down. Don't move," he said.

"What's going on?" I said.

"No time to debate this. Just do it."

I had a mind to protest further, but I liked continuing to breathe, so I did what he told me. I don't think he *actually* would have killed me, but would he have hurt me? No doubt. He'd have enjoyed it, too.

The cabin's front door scraped open and I heard someone dragging something heavy across the floor.

I'm not an expert on such matters, but I quickly figured out that had to be a body.

I turned my head just a bit, enough to see two big guys hauling a heavyset girl across the threshold. Taking my chances, I moved my head a little more, trying to catch a glimpse of her face, but her mess of curly red hair covered it.

I've written just about all I care to write about the first man carrying this poor woman, though seeing him *still* made me want to drive a thousand knives into his chest, even after months of getting used to the bastard's presence. Bloch. The guy who stuck me with the very first needle. One glance at him and I could see that they had most definitely screwed *something* up. This woman - or someone else - had gotten him right in the eye, leaving it all puffed up. No doubt he'd have one hell of a shiner the next day.

Couldn't have happened to a better fellow. I just wished I could have been the one to give it to him.

Barren was the second man. Where Bloch had no problem carrying the heavy woman, Barren seemed to struggle, staggering ahead one step at a time as they moved her.

Bloch sighed and shook his head. "For God's sake, be more careful."

"Yeah, don't want to damage the cargo. Senior would have all of our skins," Zito said.

Barren stared at the woman, refusing to meet their eyes. "Sorry."

If pressed, I'm not sure I could pick which one I hated the most at that moment. They all made such great cases for themselves.

The woman - Carla as I would soon learn - muttered something as they hoisted her on to the bed, but damned if I could make it out. I couldn't help but be impressed. As good caretakers they had of course drugged her like they had drugged me, but she still managed to dig through and get a word or two out. Maybe they hadn't given her the right dosage, her being larger and all, but I couldn't say for sure.

I slid my face onto the mattress. Hard-ass or not, broken or not, I didn't see the wisdom in jumping into this scene. Best to let them play it out; that is, unless something serious happened.

The truth? I probably wouldn't jump in then, either, but it helped to tell myself the lie. All I could do was say a silent prayer of thanks when they just unloaded her onto the bed and started slapping the restraints on her. It sucked, but it didn't require me to step in and stop them right away.

Once she had been trussed up nice and tidy, Zito leaned over me, his nasty breath wafting over my head.

Cottage cheese and something else. Pickles maybe?

"Help her," he said, sure to inject a dramatic pause here, "and you're dead."

"Try to stop me," I said.

He ran the pistol over the back of my neck. "I'd love to."

I shivered.

"That's what I thought," he said, and laughed.

Footsteps approached us, and the pistol withdrew. "Come on, leave her alone," Barren said.

Bloch chuckled. "Listen to this motherfucker."

"Yeah, what's up with that? You got something for her?" Zito's voice rose on the last word.

"Don't you think she's suffered enough?"

Barren. Months on and I still had no idea what to make of the guy. One minute he'd be shooting me full of exotic chemicals without so much as a hint of mercy, the next defending my honor. Those moments didn't make me want to forgive him for what he had done, but…maybe I didn't want to kill him outright.

Bloch and Zito? Those assholes deserved all they ended up getting.

Zito piped up. "What's wrong with you? Bitch is crazy."

"It's called compassion."

I heard Zito move, probably putting his arm around the guy's shoulder. "You pay any attention at all to what we're doing here? Compassion ain't the name of the game."

Bloch cleared his throat. "It is if it makes the job easier."

"Okay. Fair point. I'm glad you still got a heart - or at least think you do, anyway - but don't go screwing things up for the rest of us. You get me?"

A pause. I hoped that the silence involved Barren pushing the guy away, but I didn't hear any scuffling. "I get you," Barren finally said.

Bloch didn't say anything for a moment; I imagined him nodding. "Good. Now let's get out of here. I need some rest."

They didn't say another word. They crossed the room and left, slamming the door closed behind them.

That's when it occurred to me: I wasn't alone anymore. Even if they had completely knocked this girl out, I had someone to talk to on a regular basis.

I sat up in my bed. My heart pounded in my throat. I *needed* to get a look at the new girl, but Zito's threat stuck with me. I knew he wouldn't shoot me. He didn't dare.

Still…

The threat hung in my mind. What if they were watching, somehow? I leaned over, trying to catch a glimpse of her face. Sweat coated her face, making it shine in the overhead light. Sweat, and something else that I couldn't quite identify.

Ugh. Even if I had been broken, I couldn't just leave someone to suffer like that, even a newbie. I pushed myself up off of the bed and went to her side, leaning over her.

I kept my voice low. "You okay?"

She moaned again, and as she moved I could see the crap on her face more clearly. Someone - either herself or Bloch - had coated her face in a thick red muck.

"Assholes," I murmured, and went to the tiny little sink on

the other side of the room.

Lucky might not be the right word to describe Carla's situation, but she could have done worse for a roommate. I'd dealt with more than one passed-out drunk in my life, even ones who had bled all over themselves. I had a good idea of how to cool her off, if not wake her up.

I wet one of the rags that they'd so helpfully left hanging over the doorknob once upon a time (and never since replaced). I wrung it out and sighed, considering my situation. If I cleaned her face, they'd see that I had touched her. If I left her, I only had to deal with my conscience - something that I had thought dead right up until Carla arrived.

Not completely broken. I thought, and wiped at her face.

That stuff that came off her face resembled blood gone horribly wrong; it had a rusty color and a Jell-O consistency, thick and gooey. Could it be clotted blood of some sort? I might not have been an expert in the subject, but I had my doubts on even that hypothesis.

"Kelli, is that you?" she said, her voice thick.

I froze. How did she know my name?

Her eyes shot open and she grabbed my arm. No soft grip, either; she got her claws into me, leaving marks that wouldn't fade for days. "They're in the basement. They're all in the basement."

"Let go." I pulled at her arm, but like I said, she had a death grip.

"Don't go," she whispered.

"I won't."

"Promise it. Like you mean it," she said.

What else could I say? "Yeah, sure, I promise." Maybe I screwed up. I think I missed the class where they taught you how to handle a crazy person getting hold of you and making demands like that.

Those might not have been the words that she wanted, but they seemed to work. She nodded and released my arm from its death grip, laying her head on the pillow.

With my arm free, I realized just how tense and crazy the whole thing had made me. Rubbing my forearm, I stumbled to the sink, leaning over it.

They're in the basement.

Who was in the basement? Who - or what - could she be talking about?

She knew something. That meant that she might not just be a random victim; or, maybe her babbling came from getting knocked on the head?

That seemed more likely. She could be talking about any basement, in any place.

Still, she knew my name.

I went to my bed and sat on the edge, glancing at her from time to time.

She kept moaning and twitching in what I guess you could call sleep for what seemed like hours. I glanced over my shoulder at my Korg a few times, but I knew no more music would come out of me that night.

I surrendered and lay on the bed, arms behind my head, staring at the crumbling ceiling. Eventually sleep found its way, and my cares melted into dreamless sleep.

Next thing I knew, dirty sunlight streamed in through the streaked Plexiglas windows. I put a hand over my eyes and groaned. I rolled away from the sun and toward the new girl, managing to pry my eyes open just in time to see her stirring in her own bed.

"Good morning," I said, my voice full of gravel.

Her eyes popped open, finding me quickly. "You."

I propped myself up on one elbow. "So you *do* know me. Too bad I don't know you."

She shook her head. "I do? No, I…have we met?"

I suddenly had some doubts. *Had* we met, maybe in the bar? She had a South Boston accent, something I heard all the damned time, and something about her voice sounded familiar, but I couldn't quite place it. I racked my brain for a moment, but the damned thing refused to cooperate.

"Well, we met last night. When they brought you in," I said at last.

"Right. Maybe that's it. Who are you?"

I got up and sat on the edge of the bed, facing her. "The name's Kelli, but you already know that."

"Do I?"

"Yeah. You said it last night."

She blinked. "I did?"

I cocked my head. "You don't remember anything about last night?"

"No. I…" she closed her eyes, shaking her head. "Well…"

"Mmm. Looks like you remember after all. Remember *something*, anyway."

"Just impressions. Who are you, really?" she said. When she asked that, it sounded like *who ah yew.*

"Good question. Not completely sure I know myself. But I do know I'm your new roommate."

Her head swiveled, and I saw the room anew through her eyes: the cracked wood paneling, the big dark closet that seemed to open on eternity. "What? Where are we?"

"That's the big question. I couldn't tell you precisely."

The door opened, and Zito came stumbling right on through. He had big dark bags under his eyes, but you think that would slow down a champion of the world like him? Hell, no. He wore a broad, shit-eating grin. I guess they *would* have a lot to celebrate, what with bringing in the Big Find.

"Oh, fantastic, it's the welcome wagon," I said.

Zito hitched his fingers into his belt loops. "Shut your trap."

Maple came just behind him, bringing her stiff upper-lip frown along with her. She was a vision that morning, decked out in a red-and-white striped housedress, her hair pulled into what may have been the tightest bun I'd ever seen. I may have been imagining it, but I could have sworn the thing had pulled her face into a Joker grimace. She balanced a tray full of pastries and tea cups in her right hand. She could be a super-villain version of a 50's housewife – leader of the League of Evil Housewives.

She tutted at Zito. "Do please be kind."

"I'm the kindest guy I know," Zito said.

"Hm. Yes, we could debate that all morning, but we're here to greet our guest." She put the tray on the cedar dresser over by the door.

I rubbed my hands together. "It's about time you took care of us. Oh wait, are you going to spread the wealth, or is that just for our Guest of Honor?"

Maple waved at the tray. "Please do, help yourself."

I stood up. "About time you recognized my qualities. I *am* a lady."

Maple snorted as I grabbed a Danish and took one mind-numbing bite.

I'm not sure heroin would give me as pure a hit of bliss. I'm sure my knees quaked.

In the meantime, Maple sat down beside our guest of honor,

affecting a concerned look. "Good morning, Carla."

So now I knew the arrival's name. Like her voice, it tickled some distant, hidden part of my mind, but when I tried to grab hold of the fluttering thought, it vanished.

Carla tried to pull herself into a seated position, but the restraints held her in place, bouncing her against the headboard. She winced and croaked out, "who are you?"

Maple clicked her tongue. "Those things are so uncivilized." She snapped her fingers.

Zito gave me a sideways glance before he pulled a key from his pocket. He dropped it in Maple's hand and stepped back, crossing his arms over his chest.

"I do apologize," Maple said. She unlocked the shackles around Carla's legs and the handcuff on her left wrist.

Carla could finally pull herself more upright. She rubbed the raw, red spots on her ankles, wincing as she did so. "Please tell me who you are, and why you brought me here."

"We can talk about that in a bit, but for now, how much sugar do you take in your tea?"

I laughed around my Danish, putting a hand to my mouth to keep from spewing crumbs. "Sugar in her tea. Good lord."

Zito's lip curled. "Shut up."

"Please, both of you," Maple said.

Carla shook her head. "Right. Of course you're offering me tea. What else? One lump. Like the one on my head."

"Lovely." Maple rose and pushed past me, picking up the tray.

I swiped one of the teacups and swung it in front of her face. "You're not going to neglect me, are you? That would be ever so rude. I take mine with two lumps and some milk, thank you."

"You'll get two lumps from me," Zito said.

"That's original. You come up with that all by yourself?"

He tore the cup from me. "Get on your bed."

"Fine." I grabbed a doughnut before doing as he said – couldn't let him think he had *too* much of the upper hand.

"Very good." Maple picked up a dainty silver tong from the tray. "It's Lady Grey. I hope you don't mind. We just have to make do."

I raised my eyebrows at Carla. "Indeed we do. Trust me, you haven't seen anything yet."

Carla scratched her neck, looking from me to Maple, one eyebrow stuck in befuddlement. "Uhhh. Okay."

Maple laid the tongs on the tray, sat the tray on Carla's nightstand, and turned her toothy grin on me. I didn't like the glint I saw in her eyes. I felt awfully exposed and vulnerable, and slid back on the bed a bit. She swung her head to Carla. "I take it you've been speaking to our resident talent, Ms. Foster."

Carla couldn't have missed the nastiness hidden in that face. "Barely," she replied.

Maple introduced herself and Zito as she poured the tea. "It's lovely to meet you. I'm sorry it has to be under these deplorable circumstances," Maple said.

Carla held up her right hand, the one still secured to the bedpost, and showed her the cuff. "Why am I chained to a bed?"

"Those would be the deplorable circumstances that I spoke of." Maple sat down, straightening her dress down over her knees. "As for where we are, it's always been called Khesnaa B'khayea. At least as far as anyone here can remember."

"What kind of name is that?" Carla said.

Maple handed Carla her cup. "It's Aramaic. I have been told that Khesnaa means stronghold, or fort. B'khayea means life in Aramaic. So, Fort Life."

Carla blinked. "Aramaic?"

"I know, right?" I said.

Maple tittered. "Our organization is a tad…eccentric."

"Eccentric. That's one word for it."

Maple glanced at me, and then pushed on. "Would you care for a pastry?"

Carla pulled at her remaining cuff. "Not sure that's going to be possible."

Maple's hand hovered over the tray. "Oh, no worries, love, I'll feed you. I know you must be starving."

Carla eyed the tray, biting her lip. "How do I know you're not trying to poison me?"

I froze mid-bite, gazing into what might be the face of baked death. "Now that's a good question."

"Come now, why would we go to the trouble of bringing you here only to poison you?"

Carla shook her head. "I'm not an idiot. You beat me over the head and drugged me last night. You didn't seem super concerned about my, ah, well-being, if you know what I mean."

"A fair point, but were I in your position, I would suppose that we need you alive and awake."

"Guess I don't have much of a choice, do I?"

"Truer words were never spoken," I said, and worked hard to avoid the looks that both Maple and Zito shot toward me.

Carla cleared her throat. "How about that chocolate one?"

Maple looked to her. "Absolutely." She grabbed a napkin from the tray, pinching it between the tips of her index finger and middle finger, pinkie extended - as fancy as could be. She wrapped the napkin around the chocolate doughnut and lifted it toward Carla so she could take a bite.

Broken though I might have been, I wouldn't necessarily

have called myself a bitter woman. Angry? Sure, and rightfully so. Resentful? Who wouldn't be? But bitter – that was a line I didn't think I had crossed until I saw her feeding Carla like that. Sure, she got handled even rougher than I did at first and got the same drugs, but did I get the velvet glove and doughnuts when *I* arrived? No. It had been nothing but threats and crappy gray food for months.

"You know, you can stop play-acting that you're civilized. I think she can see the truth," I said.

Zito took a step toward my bed. "We want your opinion, we'll give it to you."

I stuffed the rest of the doughnut down, hoping to drown the bitterness with cloying sweetness. It didn't work, but can I get an A for effort?

Carla spoke up. "You know, I think I'm with our friend here. Some might say that a group who'd kidnap a woman –"

"Wo*men*," I said. "How you think I got here?"

Carla raised an eyebrow. "Okay, kidnap *women* is pretty far past civilized."

Maple leaned back, taking the doughnut with her. "Oh now, don't be like that."

Zito changed course, looming over Maple's shoulder. "We're a bunch of swell folks here. Your roommate will vouch for us."

Or else. "Uh. Yeah. We just have tea parties all day every day. That should be obvious," I said.

Carla raised her hands. "You're right. I'm sorry; I don't know how I could have been so blind. Maybe it had something to do with the punch to the gut, or maybe the drugs that knocked me out. Could have shaken something loose up there."

Maple looked over her shoulder at the little man. *Let me*

handle this, that look said. "No, no, dear. Of course you have a right to your feelings. That's not what I mean. You weren't supposed to be harmed. Surely Mr. Zito told you that?"

He shrugged. "I might have forgotten to mention it. Sorry about that."

Maple leaned forward again, feeding Carla another bite of doughnut. "We can debate methods all day long, but the point is that we never meant to harm you. For that, I apologize."

"Thanks, I guess."

"Mmm. Good. Now listen, dear. We require your services."

Here came the bitterness again, and I couldn't hold it back. "'Services', she says. Oh, unless you're talking about the kind of services whores give. They want to shoot you full of drugs and –"

Maple's toothy grin returned. I shuddered. "Ms. Foster, are we going to have to remove you?"

Zito nodded. "Wouldn't be a problem at all, you know."

I eyed him. I felt tempted to push the issue, but even my false bravado had its limits, and those limits ended at the feel of that pistol against the back of my neck. I never wanted to feel that again. "Nah. Won't be necessary."

Maple cleared her throat. "Ms. Foster. Do you want something else from this tray?"

"Could go for a cruller," I said.

Maple picked up the exact cruller I'd been eyeing and brought it to me. She then took Carla's cup and put it on the tray. "I *had* hoped things would be different this time."

"What's that mean?" Carla said.

Maple didn't answer.

"She was telling the truth about what you want to do to me, wasn't she?"

Maple sighed. "If you mean the involvement of drugs, then

yes, that is an…unfortunate requirement. But really, it's nothing as sinister as she'd make it out to be."

My mouth got me in trouble again. I couldn't help it, honest. "Oh yes it is."

Zito made a move for me, but Maple held her hand out, stopping him. "Not yet," she said.

He cracked his knuckles and started pacing behind her.

Maple turned to Carla. "You enjoy puzzles, don't you?"

"Uhm, sure."

She patted Carla's hand. "Really, that's all we want from you – we want you to solve puzzles. Does that sound so bad?"

Carla shifted. "What sort of puzzles involve shooting me up with drugs?"

Maple tapped her chin. I wondered what outrageous lie she might be cooking up. "Mind puzzles. Or you can call them thought experiments, if you like. They will transform the way you look at life, I promise you."

Mind puzzles. Right.

"You kidnapped me to solve puzzles," Carla said, after a lengthy pause.

"Think of them as a test. We're recruiting."

"You keep talking about 'we'. Who is 'we'? What's the name of your…you know, your 'eccentric organization'?" Carla said.

"You don't need to concern yourself about such trivialities."

"Trivialities?"

"Yes, trivialities. You have an amazing opportunity in front of you, but you're obsessed with the speck of dust in the corner. Look at the bigger picture."

Carla put her hands to her face. "The bigger picture is that you kidnapped me. I don't see much opportunity in that."

"I admit, at first our methods may seem brutal, but we are

trying to change the world here."

"How?"

Maple heaved a sigh and rose, carrying the tray to the dresser. "All will become clear. In the meantime, I ask you to have a little faith."

"Easier said than done," I said.

Maple turned on me. "Yet you've done it."

"I wouldn't call my feelings faith. You're familiar with survival instinct, right?"

She pursed her lips. "Yes. Well."

Zito looked to Carla, folding his arms over his chest again. "Foster's right. Maybe you don't need faith. Maybe you just need a good sense of self-preservation. Never know what might happen to you."

"Mr. Zito, *will* you stop acting like a thug?" Maple said.

"Hey, that's what they pay me for."

Carla looked from him to Maple. "Help me understand, here. I want to. How come she's not cuffed? Do I have to stay cuffed the whole time?"

Maple waved her hands. "Oh no, no. We're not that cruel. It was simply to keep you in place so that I could safely talk to you."

"The goon wasn't enough?" I asked.

"I'm here for *you*, baby," Zito said.

"You can't handle this."

He grabbed his crotch. "Why don't you come over here and try me?"

"That's real classy, you son of a bitch."

Maple stomped one foot on the floor. "Enough."

We both fell quiet.

She crossed the room to unlock Carla's last cuff, and Carla pressed herself as far back on the bed as she could. I think if she could have pressed herself totally flat against the headboard, she would have.

"You think I'm dangerous?" Carla said.

Maple reached for her. "You have no idea of your capabilities."

Carla recoiled. "What does that mean?"

"You will see." She stood back, hands on her hips. "I had hoped to welcome you with open arms, just this once. I apologize if you've gotten the wrong impression of us –"

"I think I get it," she said. "Kidnap me, I solve some puzzles, you turn me into a super-spy or something."

I piped up. "Something like that, only without any of that. It's mostly pain."

Maple and Zito ignored me, at last. I think they'd given up on shutting me up; I know I had.

"What if I don't want to?"

Zito shook his head. "Afraid that's not an option, sweetheart."

"Ease up on her, Zito. She's scared," I said.

"Stay out of it."

"Both of you. Enough," Maple said.

Carla narrowed her eyes. "Where are you from?"

Maple pursed her lips again. "I should think it's obvious."

"Well, yeah. I know a little bit about the world. I *assumed* England. Where in England?"

I would never claim to be privy to much of Maple's personality, but I had noticed one quirk up to that point: any personal question and she'd freeze up on you, even more than normal, and try to shut you down. This time wasn't much different.

She pursed her lips. "This is not about me."

"Please? Come on, you've got to tell me."

"I don't see why –"

"It'll help. Trust me."

Maple sighed. "Very well. London. Does that satisfy you?"

Carla took a long time to answer. At last she said, "What did your parents do?"

Maple threw her hands in the air. "Come now."

"Please."

"I refuse to answer that."

God love her, Carla refused to give in. She just took a different approach. "Did you like it there?"

"I liked it as much as any other place, I suppose. Is that *quite* all?"

Carla loosened up, just a little, unfurling her legs from underneath her. "I'm curious about you. We ought to get to know each other."

Of course Carla believed no such thing, and we could all see it, but she had them where she wanted them, relatively speaking. I figured let her put Maple back on her heels, if only in a small way.

For her part, Maple seemed to have given up on even denying Carla the knowledge she wanted. She just said nothing.

"You want me to shut her up?" Zito said.

Carla didn't give Maple a chance to answer. "You never expected to end up working in a prison, did you?" she said.

Maple's eyes widened. "This is not a prison."

"Say what? How is this not a jail? Once you guys leave, what's to keep us from running out that door?" Carla said.

"Locked door," I said.

"Of course." She smiled at Maple. "Let me guess, you were meant for something else, right? Some high-powered servant position, maybe? Nothing like this."

Maple snarled. "Where I was meant to be –"

"Is not the issue, right? Whatever helps you sleep at night. Anyway, do we get any entertainment in this place? TV? Internet? Gym?"

"This isn't Club Med," I said.

"Even prisons have TV these days."

Maple rubbed her chin. She must have been ecstatic to have the focus off of her for a bit. "No. But I don't see why you couldn't have a telly."

She might as well have stomped Zito's foot; he came to life, waving his hands at both of us. "What? How the hell you going to do that? If the Senior –"

She faced him. "The Senior *will* approve it. Do not overstep your bounds."

"That's what I'm talking about," I said. "You tell that piece of shit."

Maple whirled on me. "I have told you not to address me in that fashion."

I raised my hands. "Sorry."

"So, uh, what's my schedule?" Carla said.

Zito scoffed. "Ask Foster there. She has all the answers, I'm sure she'll be happy to fill you in."

Maple sighed. "We're leaving these two for now."

"Don't have to tell me twice," he said.

Carla held out her hand. "Wait guys. Come on. Can you leave the tray?"

Maple sniffed and picked up the tray, leaving without another word.

======

Once they were gone, Carla bounced off of the bed and stretched, twisting this way and that, her back crackling. "I appreciate what you did, there," she said.

I stared at her. I'm sure my mouth hung open, too. I just couldn't believe what I saw.

She raised an eyebrow. "Something wrong?"

"Well, not wrong. But you. Look at you."

"What about me?"

"I don't get you. You get drugged, snatched up, and brought here by complete, hostile strangers. Then you're told you're going to be shot up with massive amounts of drugs in a glorified jail in order to do…I don't know what it is we do, and here you are bouncing off the bed. You know what my first few days here were like? I wanted to collapse. I had no idea how to deal, but you're just fine and dandy."

She frowned. "Honestly? I don't think it's quite hit me what's going on here. It's like, I got in a car crash one time where I probably should have died, walked away without a scratch, but the other guy was pretty shaken up. I went to work the next day, no problem. Two days later, the whole thing hit me like a sack of bricks and I almost went comatose."

"So you think you're going to be a mess in a few days? Once everything hits you?"

"Maybe. My pop always told me there's no use worrying about what's done."

I picked a piece of fluff from my ratty comforter and tossed it to the floor. "Right, I hear that, but we're a long way from having anything done. Sorry about that."

"Kidnapping's done. I'm not going to get kidnapped again."

"I wouldn't bet all my money on that."

She stretched again. "Nothing I can do about that, either. No use being weak and worrying."

I put a hand on my hip. "So I'm weak, then?"

"No. God, I didn't mean that."

"Sounded like you did," I said, but I didn't mean it. I knew what she meant, but I felt a compulsion to get back at her for the way they treated her. Real asshole behavior, but what can you do?

"I'm sorry."

I admit, I probably wanted her to get up in my face or something, not be sorry about the whole mess. I felt bad. "Calm down, I'm just messing with you. No offense taken."

"Okay. I guess we've got to be good to each other, huh?"

"I guess."

"So, uh…where are we? Really, I mean."

I shrugged. "I don't think I'd put up with half this if I had even the foggiest of notions."

"Have they let you outside? Do you have any clue where we are?"

All questions I'd asked Gina. Her answers hadn't been any better. "I couldn't even tell you the last time I saw the sun. The real sun, not filtered through this crap." I waved a hand toward the windows.

"Ah, crap." She hung her head, and something jagged hit my heart.

She was doing just fine and you had to tear her down, didn't you? I wrung my hands. "Not that it's all bad. Just…not all good," I said.

"Do you know anything about their, what did you call it, organization?"

"Capital-O Organization, and they don't say *anything* about what they're up to. I've seen five people, tops. Not counting Gina."

"Who's Gina?" she said.

Oh. Right. "She used to be my roommate."

She glanced around the room. "I'm not your first roommate?"

"Nope. Let's hope you're the last, though."

"Where did she go?"

"Uhm, away."

She blinked. "Where?"

"You know. Passed on."

"I'm sorry."

"It's okay. I mean, not *okay*, but you know." No, she didn't. I didn't even know what I meant, other than for her to stop talking about it.

"What happened?" she said.

"I'd rather not talk about it. She died. That's all you need to know."

She approached me, sliding onto her bed, facing me. "I do, though. I need to know more. We're in this together. You see that, right?"

"Listen, *chica,* I'd love to see it that way. Truly. But I just *don't.* I mean, yeah, maybe we're together in a 'sisters-gotta-stick-together' way, but sticking together never saved Gina. In fact, it probably cost her more than I'll ever know."

Her face looked stricken. "Come on. The same thing could happen to me –"

I cut her off with one move of my hand. "Of course the same thing could happen to you, or me. They could come in here this second and waste the both of us if they wanted to. That's what I was trying to tell you – I don't get you bopping and shuffling around like you're the queen of England. Or New England, or where-ever."

"Boston," she said.

"I figured. Sounds like you got Southie running through your veins." I had to get away from those pleading eyes. Anything to get away from them. I stood up and went to my keyboard, running my fingers over the keys.

"Born and bred. Is that a *keyboard*?"

"Yes, ma'am. A Korg PA-800. It does the trick."

"What trick would that be?" she said.

"You know those 'mind puzzles' Maple mentioned?"

"Yeah," she said.

I pressed a key and held the note, letting it drone. "That would be the trick."

"They make you play music?"

"Sort of. When they shoot me up, I have visions, or dreams, or whatever. When I'm out…there, I have to work out the notes to a specific song. You know, play them, on this organ. Only I can't. I never can. The keyboard's supposed to help me."

"You have visions?"

I faced her. "Yeah. That's the nature of those 'mind puzzles'. The drugs make you see things."

That took the wind out of her sails. She drew her feet up on the bed and folded her arms over her chest. "So I'm screwed, then. I've never played a note in my life."

"You probably won't have to."

"What do you mean?"

"My understanding is that my 'puzzle' involves music because I'm a songwriter. Gina had to write a book or something. I don't know about you."

"I take it Gina was a writer."

"Among other things." I knew she'd drawn me out about Gina again, but I didn't see any other way to tell her this stuff.

"Listen, I'm sorry for getting all weird. It's just, Gina and I got real close, and when she passed away…you can imagine what happened to my brain." I went to my own bed, sitting across from her once again.

"Did they kill her?"

"Not outright. But they didn't help."

A moment of silence passed between us. I felt that we'd cleared a vague hurdle - something that needed to happen before we could co-exist as more than just women trapped in a peculiar predicament. A little more like what Gina and I had experienced. I wasn't sure I wanted to go there again, but I didn't know if I had a choice.

Once that appropriate moment of time passed - you know the one, it's just on the other side of awkward - she said, "Listen. Were you awake when they brought me in?"

"Yeah, sure."

"Did they do anything to me?"

"Like, sexual or…?" I said.

"Anything."

"Not that I saw. You *were* a mess when they brought you in, but I could see you'd gotten Bloch."

She chuckled.

"What did you do to him? I always assumed he was made out of a side of beef and couldn't really be hurt," I said.

She grinned. "Got him with my purse. He never saw it coming." She demonstrated her purse-swinging hand, giving a sweet right hook.

"Nice. What did you have in that bag, gold bricks?"

"Couple of hardcovers."

"Oh, you've got what my friends used to call the Granny Deluxe purse, then."

She cocked her head. "Where did you say you were from?"

"I didn't. But all around. I was living in Boston when they grabbed me. Why?"

"It's just weird. That's what we called those purses, too." Her face fell, and she shook her head. The thousand-yard stare followed. "That's the damnedest thing. I can't remember if I locked the door behind me when I came home, but I could tell you the name of the books in my purse by heart. People say it's ridiculous the things you remember when you're in a high-stress situation. I always figured that was crap, but now I'm not so sure."

"I wouldn't get too upset about it. Sure, I remember most of the things that happened the night they took me, but I couldn't tell you what happened last week. The brain's got ways of playing tricks on you."

"I suppose. How did they get you?"

I sighed and ran my hands down my legs. I hesitated. It wasn't the problem of telling her this stuff. I had no problem with revealing it. I just wasn't so hot on the idea of reliving it.

In the end, I decided her need outweighed my own need. Hardly the first time I'd made a decision like that, but it was another hint that I might not be as broken as I thought. I told her my story, trying to sugarcoat some of the more horrific parts.

When I finished, I walked over to the window, leaning against the sill and crossing my arms over my chest. "Wish I'd been more on my guard. That's what a girl's supposed to do, right? *Be ever vigilant,* that's what Momma always told me."

"Yeah. Is your mom still with us?"

"No. Lost her a few years back. Still miss her like crazy, though."

Her eyes went soft. "I don't think you ever stop missing

them. I lost Pops about ten years ago, right after I finished college. I miss him, even if he wasn't always good to me. He walked the Roxbury Parkway beat for 20 years."

"No shit? Wouldn't mess with Dad."

She laughed. "He was a tough son of a bitch who didn't take crap from anybody, including his daughter."

"Sounds like a hell of a guy," I said.

"Yeah, like I said." She shrugged. "Maybe I need to be tougher, too. Maybe I wouldn't be here if I was."

"Come on, you can play those games forever. Doesn't help anybody, including you."

"You're right. What can I really expect? It was after midnight on a Monday night, and I'd worked something like 14 hours."

"I'd imagine they waited just for that, so they had you how they like their women. Vulnerable."

She ran a hand through her hair. "How long *have* you been here?"

"You know, that's a funny question. I've asked myself the same thing. Time doesn't work the same here as it does in other places, I don't think."

She sat up straight. "What do you mean?"

So I got to explain that as best as I could. I hoped that I did it justice; she looked almost as confused as when I started, but she'd figure it all out soon enough. I finished with: "For all I know, I've been here a year."

"Does it *feel* like a year?" she said.

"Nah." I looked to her. "You know, you asked Maple what part of England she came from, and I got the impression she didn't answer quite right."

"Very sharp. No, she didn't."

"What part of England do you think she's from, then?'

She rubbed her chin. "Can't place it. Something's not right, though. There are just these little inconsistencies, you know?"

"I don't, but I'll take your word for it. How come you know so much about accents?"

"I taught language," she said.

"Get out of here. With that accent?"

"You got a problem with how I talk?"

I held my hands up. "Not at all. You teach at Harvard?"

She laughed. "God, no. I haven't lived up North for years. I lived in DC."

"Oh. What languages did you teach?"

"Russian and Spanish," she said.

"Good lord. I wonder if your puzzles are going to be some sort of foreign language that you've got to figure out."

"That'd make sense, wouldn't it? Listen, how do you do that, anyway? Prepare for the puzzles?"

I went to the keyboard, laying one hand on it. "This is all I've got. When you got here last night, I was playing with some chords and notes, trying to figure out what song the vision's trying to get out of me."

"Any luck?"

"Never. Every time I go in there it's the same damn thing. Have to play the song. Don't play the song. Fail."

She shook her head. "Go where?"

"Room 3."

"What's Room 3?"

I indicated the room; its plain brown walls, the closet, the door. "This is Room 1. Room 2 is next door. Room 3 is on the other side of the cabin. That's where they take us to solve the puzzles."

"What's in Room 2?"

Question of the ages. Gina hadn't even known the answer to that one. "Who knows? I think they store stuff in there, but I wouldn't swear to it. Hear them in there sometimes, but they've never opened it when I was out."

"Tell me about Room 3."

"Not much to tell." I ran my hands over the keys, trying not to meet her eyes.

"There has to be. Come on. Please."

Another time where her needs and my own crashed together. I'd learned to block out thoughts and memories of the place when I wasn't in there. Why would I want to dwell on awful shit when everything else was so damned awful? This time I didn't see the point in giving her information. I shook my head. "I don't want to talk about it. I'm sorry, but don't ask. You'll be learning a whole lot more about it soon. Sooner than you'd like."

"All right. I get that." She crossed her arms over her chest, pulling them tight against her body. "I don't like the sound of it, though."

"Good instincts. Anyway, you asked what I do to prepare? I try to have the song in my head, ready to go. Something like this." I sat down on the creaky wooden chair that they'd put before the keyboard and tapped a few keys, playing her a simple little chord progression.

She purred right after I plinked the last note. "That's pretty."

I glanced at her, raising an eyebrow. "Right. You don't have to kiss my ass."

She stood up. "I'm serious."

"Whatever. Just some dumb crap I came up with off the top of my head."

"You must be talented, then. Play me something you wrote."

"I don't know..."

"Come on, you've got to have something worth hearing, right? What genre do you sing?"

I looked to the keys. Explaining my music had always been the toughest part of it. Hell, artists just *do,* they don't explain. "It's R&B. They used to call it Quiet Storm. Never did like that term myself. Let's just say I listened to too much Sade when I was little. That make sense?"

She nodded. "Yeah, all right. I grew up with Sade, too. Wanted to be her, as stupid as that sounds for a fat white red-headed chick."

"Doesn't sound stupid to me at all."

She walked to the other side of the keyboard, standing between the window and me. She bent over to touch the keys, and I smacked at her hand. She recoiled, eyes wide.

"No touching the merchandise," I said.

She pouted. "Fine. Then let me hear what you play."

I exhaled a heavy breath, pushing the tension of stage fright out. "Not exactly the best setting, but all right. You got it."

I fingered the keys again, playing a piece that I'd written a few years back called 'Never Wanna Let You Go'. Optimal conditions or not, she caught the groove pretty quickly and started swaying, her body moving just fine for a big girl. She had rhythm, and moved on what passed for the beat, rather than the lyrics – not as common as I once believed.

I couldn't have hoped for more out of an audience of one. It helped me feel normal again, if only for a couple of minutes.

"All right, you work it, girl," I said.

"You better believe I will."

Of course, it felt too good to be true. I could never enjoy normalcy. Ever.

Two knocks on the door, beats that almost matched the rhythm of the music, mind you, and Zito yelled through the door.

"Time to take your medicine," he said.

I stopped playing and hung my head, pressing my palms to my closed eyes. "Ah, damn."

"What's that mean?" Carla said.

"I think you know." I swiveled in the chair and raised my head in time to see Zito swing the door open.

He leaned against the frame with one hand, shoving the other in his pocket. "What you playing there?"

"It's called 'None of Your Business.' I'd imagine you've heard it before." I said the words, but I didn't feel the conviction that should have been behind them. I just felt tired and a little panicky.

He stood straight and gave me a sarcastic clap. "Well played, it's a beautiful song. My soul weeps. Now come on. Get moving."

I sighed. "Do we have to do this?"

"You know we do. Are we doing this the easy way or the hard way?"

"What does the 'hard way' entail?" Carla said.

My knee flared as I remembered the last time I'd had to endure the 'hard way'. It had hurt for days. "Pistol butt to an extremity and then dragged out of here," I said.

Zito nodded. "Now come on, you moving on your own, or do I have to beat it out of you?"

I rose and crossed the room, glancing at Carla. "Don't worry. I'll see you in...well, you can never tell with this. Soon. I guess."

She frowned. "Are you all right?"

"I don't know."

Zito snorted. "She's being dramatic. It ain't all bad, and we'll have her back in a jiffy."

Anger pushed up through the layer of exhaustion coating my brain. "Have you ever done it, short stuff?"

"Doesn't matter what I've done."

"Then shut up when you don't know what you're talking about."

He grabbed my arm, squeezing hard. That would leave a mark. "I told you about correcting me. Now let's get moving."

He pushed me through the door and into the cabin's front room once more. Room 3 again, and nothing I could do about it.

I think that's where I stop for today. I'm almost ready to write about Room 3, but maybe not just yet. The rain is still falling, but it's dark. For whatever reason, I can only sleep once the sun is down these days. Maybe tomorrow I'll try to head farther into town, maybe get a drink. More on that later.

April 14th

Missed a day. Tragic, I know, but I didn't have much choice because Sam showed up in the middle of the night on the 12th. I hadn't gotten to sleep yet when he arrived; Room 3 still loomed large in my mind, an abscess in need of lancing.

I came to life as soon as the door clicked and swung open. I sat up on the side of the bed, wiping the sleep from my eyes, knowing Sam's shadow the moment it showed up in the door. "What's up?" I said.

He flipped the switch on the light by the door. "We have to move."

"What? Why?"

He glanced through the curtains. "There is a strange man in town, asking questions about us."

He didn't need to say anything else. I got up and started packing within seconds. It took less than 10 minutes to pack up the rental car and another 12 hours to drive to our new motel, ditching the car for another somewhere in the middle - I've completely lost track of where that might have been. It's better that way. I shouldn't write down exactly where we are in case someone finds this journal.

All I have to say about the new place, after a whopping half a day spent here, is that if the last place beat me over the head with boredom, this one may shank me in the back with it. Still, safety is safety, and we do what we must, right?

Without much else to say about this place, I suppose I

should pick up where I left off. Two days ago I still didn't know if I felt ready to write about Room 3, but the last few days reminded me that a physical threat still means a lot more to me than facing a few bad memories, so I'm going to give it a shot.

=======

Barren elbowed Zito to one side. He held a cotton wipe in one hand, using it to clean the point of a nice, big syringe full of clear liquid. In any other situation, without the syringe of course, you might have taken him for your common middle management drone, but here he got to play mad scientist. He acted like he didn't enjoy it at all, but I had to wonder.

Zito had just finished strapping me into the big chair, and so Barren waved him out of the room with a few muttered threats. Zito groused, as he should, but shuffled off after a moment. Barren laid the syringe down and put his elbow on the flip-out tray. "Hello, Ms. Foster. How are you this morning?"

"Same as always." My teeth chattered against my will.

He cocked his head. "Can I help with your anxiety?"

"Letting me out would be a big help," I said. Can't blame a girl for trying, right?

"Don't be absurd. You know I can't do that. What I can do is give you a sedative. We have plenty in stock." He gave me a smile and swept his arm toward an old glass cabinet on the other side of the room.

Tempting idea; put an untested sedative on top of an untested hallucinogen. It would certainly be an interesting way to die. In the end, stupid though it may ultimately prove, I shook my head. "No thanks."

"Your choice, but they're always available." He leaned over me, clearing the hair from my eyes. "Any changes since the last time we met?"

I averted my eyes. "You moved somebody new in. That's a change, I reckon." I strained against the straps.

He laid a hand on my arm. "Please try to stay still. You have no new insight as to the nature of your…problem?"

"No."

"Have you been practicing?" he asked.

"Of course I've been practicing. You telling me those people can't hear me?"

"Now, now. No need to be hostile."

"Not hostile. Just wonder if they want you to hurt me," I said.

"Of course they do." He wrapped a blood pressure cuff around my arm, pumping until I wanted to scream for mercy.

When he loosened it, I shot him daggers. "Does it have to be so tight?"

"Just a matter of procedure." He ripped the thing off and threw it on the tray, and then he pulled a little flashlight out of his pocket. He bent over and checked each eye.

"Please. You've got to help me," I said.

"I am trying to help you. Just relax."

"Let me strap *you* down. We'll see how *you* relax."

He sighed and pocketed the flashlight, writing something on a notepad.

"You reporting me to the Senior?"

He ignored that. "Do you remember what happened last time?"

"Same as always. Three notes and I was out."

"Mm, yes. We had hoped you would make better progress

by now," he said, not looking up from the pad.

"I'm sorry I can't perform better when I'm held against my will and drugged up. Maybe your new star will do better than me."

He stopped writing and looked at me over the top of his glasses. "We'll be altering your dosage today."

Sweat beaded my forehead. "What's that mean?"

He swabbed the inside of my arm with an alcohol strip. "We'll be increasing it slightly. The visions may increase in intensity."

I twisted my arm a little, but he clamped down. "You really have to do that?" I said.

He sighed and picked up the syringe. "I'm afraid so."

"Come on. Haven't I been through enough?"

He paused, syringe held mid-air. "I'm sorry, but we have to do this. You'll understand one day."

He was right about that. One day I would understand. Wouldn't like it, but I would understand. I didn't know what to say, though. How do you argue with someone who believes that torture is doing the right thing?

Answer: you don't.

He shook his head and moved the syringe toward my arm. "Now just a pinch."

Pinch, my ass. It felt like the world's biggest wasp had stung my arm. He pressed the plunger, injecting the full dose into me. I tasted something metallic and instantly became more aware of the air rushing into my ears.

I summed it up the best I could: "Whoa."

He patted my shoulder. "That's good. Just relax." His voice echoed.

"Don't have a choice…" I said. I couldn't manage much

more.

The next moment, the colors in the ball of light over my head kaleidoscoped, twirling into a brilliant mass that hung in mid-air. It expanded and the walls of the room melted away. Soon the chair went with it, taking its bonds, too. I stepped off of it before it vanished altogether, rubbing my wrists.

I gazed around me, getting my bearings, though I pretty much knew what I would see. As always, I stood in a giant crop circle in the center of the world's largest field of corn, the sun beating down on me. I turned to look at the chair, but it had melted into the ground.

Something rustled in the corn. I whirled, but I knew who it would be before she even appeared. She always found me. "Mimi?"

A little girl appeared from between the rows, pushing the bottoms of the stalks apart. She had blue eyes, dark brown hair, and a smile that could just melt your heart – the kind of smile that never, ever survives into adulthood.

She cocked her head. "How'd you know my name?"

She always asked me that.

"We've met, but I've told you that before, too."

She put her hands on her little hips. "How come I don't remember you?"

"I think it's this place. It always makes you forget."

"I don't like that."

I looked around. "I don't like it much, either. But don't worry about it. I'm here."

Wheels turned in her head. "But *why* are you here?"

No clue how to answer that one. "You're looking for something, right?"

She nodded.

I leaned down, putting my hands on my knees. "What are you looking for, sweetheart?" I already knew the answer, but this had gone down a certain path forever, and the show had to go on.

She rubbed her eyes. "Cici's gone. I can't find her."

Cici. The girl forever searched for Cici. I had no idea if she even existed. "Now where did you last see your sister?" I said.

Her eyes widened, like I'd shown her the secret of the universe. "We *did* meet, didn't we, that's how you know about Cici?"

I nodded. "Where did you see her last?" Knew the answer to this one, too.

She pointed over my shoulder. "There."

I knew what I'd see when I turned. I'd seen it so many times that I'd even started to see it in my dreams. It didn't matter, though. Every single time I turned to gaze on it, it knocked me on my proverbial butt: an enormous, gnarled tree, soaring up into the sky. This wasn't just any tree, though. Somebody had carved a wooden organ out of the trunk, with two levels of wooden keys and wooden pipes rising out of the higher reaches.

The largest keyhole you've ever seen had been connected to that organ, its details carved right into the trunk, between the keys and the pipes.

"She's locked in there, isn't she?" I'd lived this nightmare so many times I had lost count, but this little detail got my heart pounding each time. To be locked away in solid oak, unable to escape –

"How do we get her out?" Mimi said.

That question. Always that question.

"I think we have to play the right notes to open the lock and get her out," I said, but I couldn't be certain.

Mimi's brow furrowed. "Do you know what to play?"

I sighed. "No. But I can try." Endless tries and just as many sleepless nights, and I hadn't come any closer to figuring out the song than the first night that they put me under.

"Oh, please, you have to. She can't live for long in the tree."

"I know."

I strode to the tree and stood before it, holding my hands over the wooden keys. I'd only ever seen organs in magazines before I started having this vision, and while you might think that it's similar to playing a keyboard or piano, there are some key differences that had been throwing me off from the very beginning, and I couldn't afford a single mistake.

I swallowed hard, stared at the carved wooden keys for a moment, and then glanced at Mimi.

She gave me a lopsided smile and a tentative thumbs-up.

Ringing endorsement.

I leaned over the keys. Did I feel ready to go?

Not at all, but might as well get this over with.

I played the portion of the first verse that I had worked out. The notes sounded clear as always, if a little bass-heavy. My stomach tensed as I played, approaching that dreaded unknown section.

My fingers froze when I reached the end of that first verse. I knew that if I could just get the first few notes of that next section started, the rest would flow from me. The damned thing had gotten backed up in my soul - could that be a bridge, a chorus, or something else entirely? There should be lyrics, too, but they refused to come to mind.

"A Minor?" I murmured, and hit the key.

Mimi groaned behind me. "Oh no, missy, oh no."

I turned to look at her. "What?"

She didn't need to answer; the answer came from overhead.

It came as a great *whoosh* from the leaves caught fire, spreading into a curtain of red and orange that filled the sky above me. I screamed and fell backwards, but in those few seconds the intense heat had already baked most of my skin. My nerve endings blazed – I couldn't imagine such pain, it had never been so bad, not ever. I could feel my eyelids melting down over my eyes, darkening my view of my arms and the nightmare unfolding on my flesh.

I screamed and screamed as the world went dark. My world became nothing but pure, unending pain.

======

Barren shouted from the end of the long, dark tunnel. "Ms. Foster. Ms. Foster!"

I found myself back in the chair, my vision restored. The burning tree overhead had turned into that weird ball of light, and I found myself surrounded by warm light rather than flame and agony, but my body didn't care. It kept on screaming, the nerve endings on fire.

Barren put a hand on my forearm and I jerked in the restraints, making the chair squeal underneath me.

He held my arm gently; the pressure soothed my skin. "Ms. Foster, please. Calm down. You're with me now," he said.

The rest of my nerve endings caught up with the point where he held me, and the agony began to fade. I gasped. "Jesus Christ. That was the worst. It's never been that painful."

"It's over now. You can relax."

"No, I can't. Not ever. How could you? How…" I felt the pain coming on again and all my muscles tensed.

Barren snapped his fingers twice in front of my face. I don't know what that sound did, but all the muscles in my body eased at once, and I slumped into the chair.

"Are you okay now?" he said.

I shuddered. "Not okay. But better. Why did you do that?"

He might be smart, but he sure didn't understand women. When he put a hand on my shoulder, no doubt thinking he would comfort me, I recoiled, pushing as far away as I could. He took a step back and raised his hands, showing me his palms. "It wasn't my idea. They intended it to be a learning experience."

"I'm so glad to hear it wasn't your idea. I hope that helps your conscience, you...monster." It felt lame, but I couldn't come up with a more fitting word. "You wanted to see if the pain would make me solve the puzzle?"

His eyebrows knitted together. "You must believe me."

"You think I care? You think it's better that you were just following orders? Does something about that sound familiar?"

He frowned. "There's no need to be hostile. It was just a vision."

Anger flared in my chest. *Son of a bitch.* I fought against the restraints with every bit of energy in my body, but I just didn't have enough. "Tell you what, how about I strap you into this chair, see what *you* can learn? I can jam the drugs right into your eyeballs, if it'd help."

He cleared his throat and strolled to the door. "Right. I think that will be all for today." He knocked once on the door.

"Hey, listen, no hard feelings, but if you touch me again, I'll take your balls."

He turned to face me; I could see him out of the corner of my eye. "I understand that you're angry."

"This isn't the beginning of angry. I'm saving that for the assholes who sign your check."

He knocked on the door again, harder this time.

I chuckled. "You're scared, aren't you? Have to get the hired help to take care of me."

"Don't be absurd." His voice said that, but the extra step back against the door said something else entirely.

The door cracked open and Samarta's head appeared. "Is everything okay?" he said. My nerves started to ease the moment I heard that deep, velvety voice. Sam and I had gotten closer since that first night. Nothing major, just a chat here or there when both of us were feeling lonely, but enough that I'd probably call him a friend. I think. I hoped he felt the same, but I couldn't be sure.

I could be sure, however, that he would protect me if Barren started acting up.

The mad scientist in question adjusted his glasses with a shaking hand. "Everything's fine. It's time for Ms. Foster to return to her room."

"Got that right," I said.

Samarta pushed the door open. "Very good." He walked toward the chair, his heavy footsteps rattling my bones.

I gave him a lopsided smile, the best I could manage. "Howdy, Sam."

"Good evening." He pulled a key chain from his belt, zipping it out as he bent over me.

"You going to protect Barren from me?" I said.

He hesitated, and I realized that I'd never been quite so close to him, or if I had, I certainly had not paid this much attention to his body. Seeing him up-close, though, that large body flexing as he worked at my restraints, I couldn't help but notice that Sam was *ripped* under his goofy-looking starched white shirt. He smelled good, too, like he'd taken a bath in an exotic potpourri before he came to…work, I guess you'd call it?

"I was not aware that he needed protection," he said.

"Oh, come on. You know I'm a tiger. I could strike at any moment."

"Of course." The shadow of a smirk crossed his face. He was an odd one; no doubt about it, but something about him put me right at ease. "I suppose I will protect him, if that is required."

"Just get me out of here. Please."

"That is my job." He released the restraints, freeing me at last.

My body surprised me. Even with how I felt about the big guy, it had other ideas for self-preservation. A surge of adrenaline rushed through me, and I had to resist the temptation to jump him and choke him. I shook my head and pinched the bridge of my nose.

He cocked his head and offered a hand. "Are you sure you are okay?" His ice-blue eyes met mine, and any resistance melted. Those eyes were pretty much unnatural, and most definitely unfair.

I touched the back of my head. "Uh. Yeah, just…little headache. I'll be all right." I said. At least, I think I said it. I have to admit my brain had traveled off to some distant land when he took my hand and helped me out of the chair.

"I am glad," he said.

Barren cleared his throat. "Can you please take Ms. Foster to her room?"

He took a step back. "Yes. Of course."

Thank God that broke the spell. "Right. Take me now. Wouldn't want to hold up our good friend here."

Sam blinked, and then nodded. "All right. Yes. Let us go."

He held the door open, and I left Room 3.

April 15th

As suspected, this town is even duller than the last. Last night I all but begged Sam to drive me into the nearest city, but he insisted that it was a terrible idea, and refused to back down. Typical. I know it's silly, but sometimes I wonder what it would be like to have a normal boyfriend, the kind that would take rides into town with you, hold your purse, and generally not involve the constant risk of painful death. Call it a dream.

Joke's on me. Neither of us is normal, and our days sure aren't normal. They'll never be normal, not as long as The Organization has its hands in so many things.

Wow, reading that, it sounds like the ravings of a paranoid schizophrenic, but I have to remind myself that it's also true. Maybe as I tell more of the story it will become clearer and easier to remember the one thing that Sam keeps telling me: there is no such thing as too paranoid when you come from our world.

I spent the day watching Sam's collection of Seinfeld DVDs for the fourth – or maybe fifth – time. I should be sick of them, but it's my way of keeping Sam close, even when he's gone. About halfway through Season 2, I started feeling the itch to write some more. No amount of watered-down beer could drown the impulse, so here I am again, and ready to go back to the Khesnaa.

=======

Hard to say if she felt concern for her well-being or my own, but Carla had just about paced a groove into the floor by the time I staggered into Room 3.

Once I had gotten inside the room and the door closed behind me, I just stood there for a moment, wobbling a bit as exhaustion washed over me.

I noticed that the sun outside of the filthy window had dropped about three-quarters of the way through the sky, which should have put the time somewhere in the late afternoon.

My time in Room 3 had felt a lot longer than a handful of hours. "How long have I been gone?" I said, slurring a bit.

She stopped pacing and raised an eyebrow at me. "Couple of hours, at least. Hey, are you okay?"

I waved a hand. "Just fine." I stumbled over to my bed, where I flopped down, covering my eyes to shut out the light.

She approached the bed. "Are you sure you're okay?"

"Fantastic."

"Did you make any progress?"

I could feel her hungry eyes boring into me. I rolled over on my side, trying to get away from them. "Take a guess."

She didn't say anything for a minute. "You think they'll get me next?"

"Couldn't say." I know, bitchy of me. I probably should have felt sympathy for her, but at that moment I found it hard to feel much of anything.

To my never-ending frustration, Carla seemed to have gotten her major in Not Getting the Point, because she circled around the other side of my bed, standing in front of me again. "Come on. You have to know."

I sighed and rolled over again, burying my face in the pillow.

"Did they ever take Gina right after you?" she said.

I wished for a blunt object to shut her up. "I guess," I said into the pillow.

"But they wouldn't take me on my first day."

I looked over my shoulder at her. "Is that a question or a statement?"

She scratched her arm, her eyes wild. "Both."

I put my head down and closed my eyes. I didn't find darkness, but instead Mimi standing under the tree, that bright little face staring up at me. I gave an involuntary jump and opened my eyes again. "Then I don't know, either."

"Do you –"

I looked at her over my shoulder again. "Jesus Christ, Carla. Come on. Give me a minute here."

She turned away, crossing her arms over her shoulders. "I'm sorry, I'm just freaking out here."

At this point, I probably deserved a medal for putting up with this nonsense, but I took it one step further and bit back a sarcastic reply about what I'd just gone through. "Listen. Don't freak out. Yeah, it sucks, but they're not going to kill you," I said. At least, I didn't *think* they would kill her.

"Promise?"

"Come on. You know I can't promise that."

"Right. Of course." She ran a hand through the tangled mop of her hair.

"Wish I could tell you something better." I needed to get her mind out of the fear trap, if only for the sake of my own sanity. I said the first thing that came to mind. "Hey, have they brought dinner yet?"

"About an hour ago."

"Typical. Didn't bring enough for me, did they?"

"No. Barely enough for me."

Interesting. That meant they had already begun to cut back on her food. A reaction to her behavior or some other form of control? I wasn't sure. I started to say something, but a knock at the door interrupted me.

Carla's eyes darted from me to the door, and she shook her head. "No…"

"Calm down. It'll be fine," I murmured.

"You don't look fine," she said.

Maple spoke from behind the door. "It's us. Do please make yourself decent."

I didn't give Carla a chance to speak. I lifted my head from the pillow and shouted, "We're fine."

The door swung open. Zito and Maple stood in the doorway, and my heart sank. Room 3 had always been inevitable for Carla, but deep down, I thought that they might give her a night to get used to the place. They hadn't done it for me, but she seemed to be special to them. Irritating or not, she didn't deserve that.

I sat up and glanced at her. That glance told me everything I needed to know: she had gone pale.

Maple gave her a *good courteous woman* smile, nodding her head. "Good evening."

I rubbed my face with one hand, trying to shake away the cobwebs. "Aren't you up past your bedtime?"

"Such a clever girl." She looked at Carla, raising an eyebrow. "Speaking of clever girls, they're ready to see you now, Ms. Summers."

Carla took a step toward the window, raising her hands. "I don't want to go."

Zito stepped forward. "You don't exactly have a choice in

the matter, chubs."

"I do. You're going to have to drag me out of here," she said. "I can choose that."

Zito sighed and looked to Maple. "The usual?"

She shrugged, clearly broken up about the whole thing. "Do what you must."

He took another couple of steps toward Carla, and she cowered against the window.

Then something happened that I didn't expect or understand. Something deep inside of me, in the part that wasn't broken yet, flared up, and I jumped up off of the bed. I wobbled a little, but managed to get between the two of them, hands up to stop him, steady enough to make the little prick take a step back.

"Out of the way, Foster. This doesn't have anything to do with you."

"Come on. Give the woman a break. She just got here," I said.

He put a finger to one ear. "Excuse me? Did I hear you right? Because sometimes I wonder if I'm going a little deaf in this ear."

The tone of his voice gave me reason to take my own step back. I didn't know exactly why I wanted to defend her. I barely knew the woman and she had annoyed the living fuck out of me, but I had practically thrown myself in harm's way for her.

I didn't think it at the time, but I suspect I didn't want to witness another Gina incident. In that sense, I acted in self-preservation, like stopping him saved me, too. I didn't quite get it at the time, but it would make sense much later on.

In the meantime, I had to live with the decision, so I figured why not go all out? "You…you heard me," I said, a little hitch in my voice.

"That's what I thought I heard." He reached into his pants pocket, no doubt going for the pistol.

Maple put a hand on his shoulder. "Mr. Zito, please."

"Shut up, Maple, I got this."

She cleared her throat. "Excuse me. Did *I* just hear *you* correctly?"

I chuckled.

He stepped aside, looking at the floor. "Uh, I mean. Sorry."

"I thought so." She stepped forward, taking his place, and gave me a grandmother's smile. "We won't hurt her. Promise."

Now, Maple might have been the one in charge, but I felt I could handle her a lot better than the little man. I crossed my arms over my chest. "Are you planning to give her the same dosage you gave me earlier?"

She didn't even blink. "Her treatment is none of your concern."

Carla put a shaky hand on my shoulder. "Maybe I should just go with them."

Zito nodded at me. "Listen to the lady. You don't need to get involved."

"I'm already involved." I hoped I sounded a lot braver than I felt.

"This doesn't end good for any of us. Come on. You've got to see that."

Carla slipped between us, looking at me. "Please. Let me go. I can handle this one myself."

I exhaled. "All right. But don't let them give you any more than the minimum dose at first, okay?"

"What is the minimum?"

"Just insist on it, okay? The black fellow you see - tell him minimum dose, no more. Got it?"

Zito twirled his finger. "She's got it. Now why don't you get back to bed? Relax. Take a load off."

I backed away as he took Carla by her upper arm, leading her toward the door.

"You take care of her," I said. Lame, but not much else I could do.

"Why do you even care?" Zito fired back.

"Gina."

I wish I could have seen the look on his face. All he said was, "whatever," and they disappeared through the door, leaving me alone with Maple. We looked at each other for a long moment.

"She's familiar to you, isn't she?" Maple said.

I jerked. "What? I…no. Not exactly. But…"

She smirked. "I'm sure it will come to you in time. Oh, yes. You must be hungry." She reached into her apron, producing a wax-wrapped sandwich. She handed it to me.

"What is this?" I asked, pulling at the wrapper.

"I told you. Your dinner."

"You couldn't bring me chips or anything to go with it? Maybe a Coke?"

She sniffed. "I apologize. I didn't realize I needed to consult you."

"Something to keep in mind." I lifted the top slice of bread and groaned. "Egg salad? Come on, I hate egg salad."

"Maybe I can prepare something better for you once you start producing for us."

"You're so sweet," I said.

Her face drew up in the ugliest sneer I'd ever seen. "You have no idea who I am."

"I don't, and that's probably for the best." I put the sandwich back together and took a bite.

"Or who you are," she said.

I stopped mid-chew. "What's that mean?" I asked around the sandwich.

She just kept giving me that sneer for a long time, and then said, "it means nothing. Enjoy your dinner."

"No, get back here, you – "

Too late. She left, the door swinging shut behind her.

"Yeah, well, fuck you too," I murmured, and sat down on the edge of the bed to eat her smelly egg salad sandwich.

======

I stood below the tree again, swaying in the breeze that blew across the field, making the corn whisper in voices that remained just outside of comprehension. I didn't know how I got there; I couldn't remember going to Room 3. That's when I realized that a lot of other things were different, too. I had never found myself right beneath the tree from the beginning. I always had to meet Mimi and hear Cici's story.

Always.

But I found myself under the tree all the same, staring up into its expansive branches, watching them ripple in the wind.

"You think you can do it, Ms. Foster?" Mimi asked from somewhere off to my left side.

I shivered, looking to her. She stood at my side as usual, hands behind her back, little eyes boring into me.

"I don't know, sweetheart."

"You have to." She looked from me to the organ, her eyes rimmed with moisture.

Tears? Haven't seen her cry before.

I followed her gaze to the organ. Somehow the keys had expanded into four rows, the keyhole expanding to the size of Mimi's body. The site made me nervous. "I haven't done it yet," I said, my palms sweating.

"I believe in you."

I glanced back at her. "But every time I try, I fail."

She folded her hands, one over the other, at her waist. "Just remember the song. Let your fingers feel the truth."

I cocked my head. This wasn't how Mimi normally talked to me. I didn't know what to make of it. "You know me, don't you?" I said.

"Of course I do."

"You never remember me."

She smiled. "Some might say that means I'm a project of your subconscious, but I'm a child, so what do I know of that?"

I shook my head. "What did you mean when I said I'll feel 'the truth'?"

She giggled. "The real thing. It's playing hide and seek."

"What do you mean? I don't get you."

"Don't you?" She pointed at the keys.

"What do you mean?" Nothing appeared to be different at first, but within a moment of watching, something changed. My brain didn't quite understand what I saw at first, but then it clicked: the keys themselves were changing, morphing from a darker wood to a brighter wood, and then back again. Something clicked in my head. I might be slow, but when I get it, I get it: This was the sequence of keys in the song; the answer to the whole shebang, from verse to chorus and back again.

"How the...?" I said.

"She must be freed before you can live."

I watched the keys, mouth hanging open. "I can't keep up."

"The answer is coming."

"But I can't –"

She shushed me. "Be patient. You don't have to be afraid."

I looked to her. "Who are you?"

She smiled and touched the side of her nose.

======

The sound of a slamming door ripped me out of that world. I snapped awake, suppressing a shriek, or at least trying my best to suppress it. A muffled noise squeaked out, and I covered my mouth.

I hadn't exactly hoped to hear Zito's voice. "That's right, you stay quiet," he said. I rolled over and faced the door, where his outline, along with Bloch's, stood at the threshold, their lumpy shapes haloed by the light from the front room.

"What's going on?" I said. My eyes insisted that I had returned to Room 1, but my brain still showed me the keys, pulsing as they fired off, note by note, lighting up the darkness.

"Geez, I just told you, stay quiet." They dragged a large dark form between them: Carla. She must have taken her first trip to Room 3 about as well as I had. They dumped her on her bed and stepped back.

"She won't be bothering you again tonight," Zito said, and laughed.

"Come on, let's get out of here," Bloch said.

"Sure. You buy the beer tonight."

"Whatever, man."

I closed my eyes and waited for them to leave, slamming the door shut behind them. Once they were gone, I jumped up from the bed, turned on the overhead light, and went to her, my mind very much on what Gina did for me that first night.

"Jesus, what did they do to you?" I whispered. Her eyes had rolled back in her head and a trail of drool ran from the corner of her mouth. Room 3 had wrecked me, no doubt about that, and it had wrecked Gina too, but I'd never seen anything like this. Would they have wiped her mind out? *Could* they? I suddenly realized just how much I didn't know, and it gnawed at my gut.

I wiped the drool from her mouth with my fingers and rubbed my hands down on my jeans. I wished I could do more, but I knew my limits. I stepped back and watched her. Every now and then she'd twitch or moan, and my heart jumped each time.

I don't know how long I watched her like that. Felt like hours. I might have done it all night if it hadn't been for four knocks at the door, two rapid, two short.

Sam.

I went to the door and cracked it, looking through cautiously. "Who is it?"

Samarta's eye appeared in the space, his face expressionless. "It is me."

"I was beginning to think you weren't here tonight."

"I have been here, but it has been difficult with Maple present. She has left. May I come in?"

I opened the door. "Please. I think they might have broken her."

His beautiful, thick eyebrows furrowed. "What do you mean?"

"Just come in and look."

He went straight to her, leaning over her. He touched her forehead, frowned, and then crouched by the side of the bed. He looked to me and shook his head, hands at his mouth.

"Well?" I said.

"What have they done to her?"

I joined his side, standing over him. "I don't know. They brought her back from Room 3 like this. I didn't know what to do with her."

He felt her head and cheeks. "She is burning up. I have never seen a reaction like this."

"Me neither. Not even with Gina. You have any idea of what we can do for her?"

He considered her. "Have you given her water?"

Pretty obvious, right? "Oh, duh. Good idea." I went to the sink and filled one of our little plastic cups.

He rose, and I could have sworn he watched every little move I made when I crossed the room back to him. "You were panicked. You could not think of everything," he said.

"Sure, keep on telling me that."

He took the cup with one hand and lifted her head with the other, glancing back at me. "Help me, please."

I moved in next to him, all too aware of his warmth near my side. I slid my hand under his, cradling her head, and lifted it toward the cup. He pulled his hand from her head quickly, glancing at me for a moment before he put the cup to her lips, nice and slow, gentle as could be.

It took a second of pouring, but she came to life, choking and spitting, the water flying all over Sam, who took it without even flinching.

Her eyes were wild as they rolled around the room. "Where am I? What happened?" she said, and then started coughing.

I let go of her head. "You're all right. It's just us."

Her eyes focused, and she saw Sam for the first time – really saw him. She recoiled. "Who are you?"

I put a hand on his shoulder. "This is Samarta. He looks after both of us. Don't worry, he's a good guy."

He nodded. "I am the night watch. Do not worry."

"Can't help but worry," she said, and coughed again.

"He'd never hurt a fly," I said.

He looked to me. "That is not quite true, but I would never hurt either of *you*."

She squeezed her nose and coughed again. Her eyes were bloodshot when she opened them. "That was horrible. Is that what they've been doing to you?"

"I don't know. What did they do? Did you tell them to give you the smallest dose?" I said.

"I did. That guy –"

"Barren."

"Yeah, Barren. He told me not to worry. He was going to give me the lightest dose he could."

Sam rubbed his chin. "Barren is many things, but he is not a liar. Something strange is afoot here. Are you okay now?"

"I guess. How long was I out?"

"Hard to tell," I said.

She sat up, eyeing me. "That didn't feel like what you described at all. I thought you said I'd be solving some sort of puzzle?"

I blinked. I sure had said that, and didn't have a reason to believe anything else. "You didn't?"

She shivered. Sam reached for her, and she pulled back, hissing. "Please. Don't."

He pulled his hand back. "I apologize. I did not understand."

"It's okay. Just don't do it again." She looked at me. "No. No puzzles."

"Well, I never said I knew for *sure* that you'd be solving puzzles. That's just what Gina and I had to do." If she hadn't solved puzzles… "Why? What did you see?"

She wrapped her arms around her chest. "I don't know. He shot me up, and I passed out, or…well, something like that. It was dark at first, like…I was awake but not, at the same time. I couldn't tell much about the place, so I tried to walk in one direction, and then another, but I got nothing. Then suddenly, all this light, everywhere, like God said 'let there be light'. It blinded me. It didn't matter if I closed my eyes or put my hands up, I couldn't block it out. That's when I realized I was floating in space, staring into the heart of something big and bright, like a star. I freaked out at first, because I had gotten too close, but I didn't feel any heat after a few seconds so I stared right at it, trying to figure out how this had happened. The weirdest thing happened then. I felt like it was staring back at me and we had something in common." She rubbed her throat. "Could I have some more water?"

Sam nodded. He seemed glad to have something to do. "Absolutely."

I spoke. "So you did have a vision, just without anything to solve?"

She shook her head. "More like a dream."

"Sometimes my visions are like dreams, too. Sometimes I even have them when I sleep, without the drugs. I had one tonight, as a matter of fact."

"That's weird." She took the cup from Sam and took a deep drink.

"Is that all you saw?" he said.

She smacked her lips and sighed. "Nah. After a few seconds of staring at the light, I realized it wasn't actually a star. I mean, it *had* been, but suddenly it wasn't. You know how dreams do that?"

I nodded.

"It came from a lamp, one that I recognized. It used to sit in our living room. It was the strangest lamp I've ever seen, that's why I remember it. The bulb hung upside down inside a cage made of stained glass, so that the top of it poked out at the bottom." She motioned with her hands to show how the bulb used to hang. "I used to spend hours walking from one direction to the other, seeing how the light changed when it shined through different parts of that glass. So I saw that lamp, but it looked giant to me, almost like the sun hung upside down in the cage. It was our old house, but God lived there now and had made it the size of the galaxy."

"The mind playing tricks on itself," Sam said.

I shook my head. "More like drugs playing tricks on the mind."

She shrugged. "Last thing I remember is a big shadow falling over everything. When I turned around, this big black figure stood over me. I screamed, and my body started convulsing. Next thing I knew, I woke up here, choking on water."

I looked at Sam. "What do you think all that means?"

Sam frowned. He hid it well, but I had never seen him so frustrated and confused in my time at the Khesnaa. "How am *I* to know? I am the help, little more. I do not believe in what they are doing to you. It is needlessly cruel and pointless. I want nothing to do with these...*experiments*." His lip curled on that last word.

Lots of questions came to mind, but I didn't want to ask them just then. Questions about his presence there. Questions about what he wanted out of the whole thing. He looked at me out of the corner of his eye. I think he could sense the wheels grinding in my head and didn't want me to push him. Easy choice. I decided to wait.

Carla didn't share my compunctions. "So why *are* you here?"

"I would prefer not to discuss that. Not now," he said.

I winced, expecting her to push him the way she'd pushed me, but she either didn't care or didn't have the energy to keep it going. "Fine. Of course. One more mystery. Why not? But tell me at least one thing, will you?"

"What?" we said, at the same time.

"Does the name Tal'ia mean anything to either of you?"

Sam jumped, and his eyes went wide. "How do you know my wife's name?"

Now there was a nasty little surprise. But should it have been? He had pulled his hand away from mine so quickly. I wondered if he had been thinking of her. I turned to him, my mouth open wide. "Since when do you have a wife?"

He blinked. "Since long before my arrival." He waved a hand. "This is not important."

"No, this is important. Why didn't you tell me?"

"It was never any of your concern."

"Maybe not, but I thought we were friends," I said.

"We are *not* friends. Friendly, perhaps –"

Like a kick in the teeth. It put some fire in my words. "Well, that's great to know. I'm sure glad I shared about my life with you, then. Good to know you can't reciprocate now before…"

"Before what?" he said.

Carla's eyes swung back and forth between the two of us. I worried she might get the wrong idea about us, that we were falling for each other or something. Heaven *forbid* that.

I waved a hand. "Guess what? It's not important."

He looked at me a moment longer. I wanted him to burn up inside, to know the irritation that scratched the back of my mind.

He just looked to Carla. "How do you know that name?"

"That thing that came up behind me in the vision said it, right before I woke up."

The same old questions popped up in my head about the nature of the visions, and I remembered Gina's insistence that we were visiting another world. Were they so crazy? "What does that mean?" I said.

Sam stroked his chin. "I do not know. Did you see anything more of this shadow?"

She shook her head. "I was too busy being scared out of my mind. Sorry about that."

"Are you sure they kidnapped you from...outside?"

"Outside where? Here?"

He nodded.

"They took me from my apartment. What does it matter?"

Good question – what *did* it matter? What was he getting at? More importantly, was he holding out on something vital?

He continued. "I am wondering whether they took you anywhere else before they brought you here. Possibly another facility."

Hold up. "What do you mean, 'facility'? Are there other places like this?" I said.

"There must be, but I have never heard them speak of these locations."

"How do you know that?"

He grimaced. "I would rather not say."

All right, enough was enough. "Uh uh. You don't get to do that. You tell me right now why you think there are other places like this one."

He turned on me, eyes wild. It was the most emotion I'd ever seen in his face. "Do you think this is easy?"

I chuckled and shook my head. "It's a lot easier for you than us. Unless they've been putting you in that room."

He said nothing.

"Exactly," I said.

He gave me a withering look, a look that suggested he might not be completely averse to bodily harm if it came to that. Maybe he wasn't the pussycat that I'd been led to believe. His voice came out as a harsh whisper. "You fail to understand, or perhaps you do not wish to understand. I am as much a captive as you."

"That's bullshit," I said.

I wondered if he would explode. He had to stomp across the room, most likely to avoid doing some bodily harm. When he turned, his eyes were alight. "You do not know my story. Do not presume to –"

Carla snapped her fingers. "They kidnapped your wife, didn't they?"

I turned on her. "Say what now?"

"That's it, isn't it? They kidnapped her. That's why you want to know if they took me anywhere else. I might have seen her."

The fire drained from him all at once, and his body went limp. He hung his head. It was answer enough, and the whole thing bit into my heart in a way I hadn't quite expected.

Carla kept her voice soft when she spoke again. "You're scared they took her to a place like this, aren't you?"

He raised his head at that. "That or worse." His voice softened, almost a whisper. "They have my daughter, as well."

"Oh God. I'm so sorry, Sam, I didn't mean to –"

"You had no way of knowing. Perhaps I should have told

you, who can say." He sighed and made for the door. "I must leave you now. I should not be doing this."

I grabbed him by the bicep. Damn, those things were *solid.* "Come on. Stay. Who's going to find out?"

"They will. They have ways of knowing."

"Never stopped you from talking to me before."

"We never spoke about this. This is dangerous."

Carla made a noise from the bed. "I think he's right. Besides, I could use some sleep. Real sleep. Not the coma kind."

I let go of Sam's arm and he walked toward the door. I followed close behind, leaning near his ear. "Can I talk to you outside for just a second?" I said.

He considered it. "I do not think it safe. Not tonight." He gazed at me for a long second, eyes cutting right through me. "I will be in the front room should you require anything else."

I put a hand on my hip. "What do you do out there all night?"

"I watch television. I enjoy it." The corner of his mouth turned up a bit.

Now, I have a theory. I think you can tell a lot about a person by what they watch, listen to, or read. One of my favorite opening questions with a person is finding that sort of information out - it can help you read their emotional temperature. I had never asked Sam because the idea of him even watching TV was odd, but why not, right? "What's your favorite show?"

He looked a little embarrassed. "Seinfeld."

I couldn't help it. I laughed at the poor guy. "Of course." Then I asked him a question that had been plaguing me for ages. "Where *are* you from?"

That gentle smirk vanished. "I can't answer that, either.

It's...safer that way."

"That's a goddamned shame."

"It is," he said.

I thought I understood my emotions toward the guy, complex as they were, but that opened up something new inside me: a touch of disappointment that he couldn't open up. "Fair enough. I think I'm going to work some tonight."

"Very good." He started to turn away, hesitated, and turned back. "By the way, you have beautiful hair."

By God, I think he had tried to be charming; clumsy as hell, but sweet. A thrill ran through me, from my head down to my toes, taking a brief detour somewhere else to the south. I touched my hair. "Ah, yeah, thanks."

He averted his eyes. Cute on a big guy like him. "Have a good night." He let that hang for a second before he turned and went, leaving me alone with that little thrill.

Kind of cute.

Good lord, you are losing your mind. Really, crushing on someone who might as well be your kidnapper?

But come on, could I really be to blame if I got lost in those eyes? Was it my fault that he smelled so damn good? I don't think so. I did my best to resist.

I closed the door and wandered back across the room, floating on a cloud.

Carla's voice jarred me. "So what's the deal with you two?"

"Thought you were going to sleep." I crossed the room and sat at the Korg, facing her.

"I am. But if you think I can sleep without knowing the story between you two, you're crazy."

"There's no story to tell. He's the only decent one of the lot. He was there when Gina died, and we've been friendly ever since."

She scoffed. "You don't look at him like a friend. He didn't exactly look at you like one, either."

"I don't follow you."

"Right. Tell me another lie."

"Your choice whether you believe me. I can't prove a negative." Her questions hit on the nose, as usual, and her persistence was going to drive me crazy. I turned to the keyboard, hoping she'd shut up.

Alas, no such luck. "I don't think it's messed up or anything. It's not like he kidnapped us. My old man used to tell me, 'you see something you want, you need to go grab it'. I figure that goes double here."

I didn't look back at her. "That your inspirational speech?"

"I guess so."

"Well, thanks, Oprah. It means a lot. Gayle here has to do some work now." I plunked a few keys. "Am I going to bother you?"

"I don't think so. Way I feel, I could sleep through a war."

"Good. Get some rest. We can talk more in the morning."

As she settled in, I played the keys. I summoned up something new, a piece that came from my soul, from the feelings that had taken hold there that night. I wondered how it must have felt for Sam, to have his family taken from him. I remembered my own reaction to learning about it, and my feelings about another layer of reality peeling back in this strange new world. It all poured out in a song that I wish I could have recorded. Call me conceited, but I think it would have been a hit.

April 16th

This morning I woke up ready to commit acts of atrocity just for a fresh omelet and orange juice instead of the stale Power Bar and bottle water that Sam had left for me. I couldn't take the motel room anymore, and I couldn't see how it was much different than wasting away in Room 2. This isn't living. Living is going out, seeing the sky, and soaking in the sun. I just wanted to feel like a real human being, if only for a few minutes.

My conscience argued with me: Sam would kill me, *they* could find me and kill me, *they* could kill Sam. I paced for a long, long time.

I had a granola bar. Not bad, but not an omelet.

I had a banana. Intriguing, but still not enough. My conscience began to wear down, and the seductive arguments crept in.

It didn't take much more to convince me to put on my hat and glasses and head out the door.

Screw it. I'll deal with the consequences.

Guess what? Not a single problem all day. In fact, it was a damned *good* day. I started out by hitting the café right next door for an omelet (ham and cheese, thank you very much). I was feeling so chipper after that that I figured a run at the park would be a good idea. My stomach's getting flabby and I'm not getting any younger. By the time I had finished, it was lunchtime, so I stopped at DQ and got a Blizzard on the way back here.

So now I have an answer for my conscience: fuck off. Just

this once. Today gave me everything that I had ever hoped for from a "normal" life; for a few hours I even forgot myself and what happened to us.

Not that it could last. My troubles waited for me all along, right here, in the pages of this journal. I had sworn to myself that I wouldn't write today – my brain needed the time off and besides, who wanted a reminder of what we'd been through after a day like today?

Unfortunately, I couldn't focus on anything else *but* my story. It had gotten stuck on the roof of my mouth, and I had to work it out.

So here I am. Time to pick up where I left. With Zito.

You know, it starts with Zito way too much.

=======

"Hey Foster, think fast," he said.

I turned to face him and right at that moment something thick and soft, wrapped in paper, smacked into my forehead. It didn't hurt, but it sure surprised me. I yelped.

He couldn't control his laughter. It must have been a real gut-buster. He slapped his thigh, head rocking back and forth. "The look on your face," he said.

Maple slid up behind him and cleared her throat. Zito glanced back at her, and I saw my opening. I picked up the wrapped bagel and crossed the room, shoving it in his face. "You do that again, I'm going to cram whatever you throw at me up your ass."

His face went white, and I felt him reaching for the pistol.

I raised one knee to his crotch. "Uh uh. One more move and

you get this."

The side of my face exploded in pain as Maple slapped me and then grabbed my forearm, wrenching me away from Zito. One push and I went stumbling backwards. I hit Carla's bed and almost fell back onto her with a cry.

That wasn't enough for Zito. He already had his hand in his pocket, and whipped the pistol out in the next moment. Maple blocked his hand, twisted his wrist in one direction, and shook her head. "You are supposed to be my security, not the other way around."

"I didn't need you to help me," he said.

Maple sighed and shook her head. "Your childish antics are your own responsibility." She turned on me. Damn, the attack hadn't even knocked a stray hair out of place on her head. She leveled her crooked finger on me. "Do *not* try that again."

I sat down on the edge of Carla's bed, my head spinning. "Uh. Yeah. Noted," I said.

She looked to Carla, who had sat on her bed through all of this, clutching at one of the few books that they'd provided us, something called Imago's Forest. "Come, dear, it's time for your next session."

My mind boggled. Did they really think Carla could handle this? "Oh come on. Twice in two days?"

Maple's eyes snapped to me. "I don't recall asking for your opinion, Ms. Foster."

"It's just…you know. You never did that to me."

"Our friend is a special case," she said.

Carla cleared her throat. "I've thought about that, and I'm not who you think I am."

Maple put her hands on her hips. "Oh, really. "

"Nah. So you can just let me go."

Zito took a few steps toward her bed. "Now we *definitely* can't do that." He seemed to still be on edge, because he started to lift the pistol, and Maple had to stop him once again. He gave Maple an irritated look, and then kicked Carla's bed. "Come on, tub of guts. Drop the book and get moving."

I saw the fear in Carla's eyes, hiding somewhere behind her anger. Unlike me, I think she had already learned that resistance beat having them walk all over you. She stood up. "You know how to treat a lady," she said.

"Cry me a river. You might act tough, but you can't *fake* tough, girl. Take a look over there. That's a tough chick. The real deal," Zito said, and pointed at me.

I looked up from my bagel. "Don't be gross."

"Only as gross as you want me." Then, of all things, he dropped me a wink, angling his head so that Maple couldn't see.

My skin crawled. "Uh, no."

He grinned. "Maybe I'm wrong. Maybe you're not so tough after all." He pushed Carla forward a step. "Come on. I said move."

I considered intervening. No doubt they would break her. I didn't think Carla was weak, but two trips to Room 3 in less than 48 hours? I'd never done it, and couldn't imagine doing it and holding on to my sanity. I couldn't imagine the dosages building up in her body.

What could I do, though, with Zito holding that pistol? Not much. Not much at all.

They stumbled out of the room, leaving Maple and me alone again. I saw a pattern developing, but didn't understand it. Why did Maple want to talk to me so much? I took a bite of my bagel, trying not to meet her eyes, hoping she'd just leave.

"You can't save her," she said.

"I'm sorry, you must be confused. Did I even look like I was trying?"

"I saw the look in your eyes."

"I've seen you people kill. You're going to kill her, too. It's too much." I said it in such a matter-of-fact tone that it startled even me. My emotions had completely shut down. I didn't know if they had finished breaking me, but it sure felt that way.

She sniffed. "If sacrifices must be made for the great cause, then they *must* be made."

"What are you trying to tell me?"

"That you cannot rescue her, no matter how much you want to. I know it has to be going on somewhere in there, even if it's buried deep."

"Shows what you know. Why do you want to talk to me about this stuff? What is your 'great cause'?"

"I suppose I could educate you, but you might not understand."

This was unexpected. "Try me," I said.

She stood there studying me for a long time. "You're not ready," she said at last.

I met her eyes. "Nobody's ready for the shit you guys pull. Ever. What are you people playing at?"

She smirked and took hold of the door handle. "Have a restful day. We'll have a television for you very soon."

Another unexpected bomb. Maple was on fire. "Say what?" I said, but she had already exited, closing the door behind her.

I sat there, bagel in hand, wondering what just happened. It's crazy, but I felt like Zito and Maple had violated me, Maple even more so. I still feel that way, even though I can't point to anything to back that up - just the feeling that the whole encounter had put into me. I fought anger and sadness for a little while; eventually, the anger won out, and I jumped from the bed, charged the door, and slammed both fists against it.

Couldn't tell you if they heard me. If they did, they sure didn't care. I kicked the door and leaned back against it, breathing hard. I couldn't do anything about it. Not then. But I vowed to myself that things had to change – no, they *would* change – and we would find a way out of there together. Even if we had our differences, I wasn't going to watch them turn that woman into a vegetable.

======

"Good evening, dear," Maple said, her breath laboring as she pushed the door open. I didn't know how long it had been since they left – hours, at least.

I turned from where I sat at the keyboard, raising one eyebrow. She had managed to one-up even her earlier surprises by bringing Carla back on her own, balancing the larger woman on one shoulder. My surprise must have been written on my face because she gave me a smug look before she let the door slam shut behind her.

I played along. "Why are *you* bringing that girl back?"

The smirk faded as she started moving Carla. She huffed, dragging her for a step. "Part of the job."

"That's a pretty quick job change."

She gave me a look, but just kept on dragging. "Don't just sit there. Do come help me."

I hesitated. I wanted to help her – no, to help Carla, not *her,* but would doing so mean giving her approval to treat me the same way? I sighed at last and got up, joining her.

I wrapped one of Carla's arms around my back. "Seriously. Why are *you* bringing her in here? Where's Zito?"

"Do you think I would tell you?"

"Of course not."

She chuckled. "I don't know why you bother."

"It's better than beating me down."

"I suppose." We lowered Carla onto the bed.

I put my hands on my hips and leaned backward, cracking my back. "She doesn't look good. Why's she so pale?"

She wiped her forehead. "It is a temporary side effect, nothing to concern yourself about."

"Come on; don't treat me like an idiot. I've never had these kinds of side effects."

"Haven't you, though? How long was your previous recovery?"

"That's not the same at all. You kicked up my dosage, and I still wasn't completely knocked out. You've been knocking her out for –"

Maple raised a hand, cutting me off. "We are quite aware of what we're doing here."

"Were you aware of what you were doing with Gina?"

She bit her lip hard. I got the impression she'd like to smack me, but held herself back. "I strongly suggest that you back off. Now."

It could have been defiance, idiocy, or just plain self-destructiveness that made me want to push her. "So you were, and you're just a murderer?"

The slap came hard and fast. I stumbled backward, clutching at the stinging spot on my cheek.

"I warned you," she said, but she lacked the conviction of her words and her slap. The look on her face – a tired, haggard quality – and a stray hair falling down into her face, showed me a hint of the woman underneath the role. She knew abuse was part of her job, and accepted it without a fight.

She might not even know *how* to fight anymore.

"You did," I said.

She left, and I sat on my bed, bent over, hands dangling between my legs. My face still stung from the slap, but it made me proud. Still, the question hung in my head:

Now what?

Carla moaned in her sleep, or coma, or whatever it was. I went to her and wiped some drool from the corner of her mouth. She twitched, and I sighed.

"This has to change, girl," I said, hoping that, somewhere, deep down inside, she could hear me, and you know what? She just might have; she moaned and turned a little bit toward me.

"I haven't been fair to you, but you're right. We've got to stick together or we're never getting out of here. We'll figure something out when you're awake. Get some rest now."

Something in my words or my tone made her ease her body back into the bed, and I felt okay stepping away from her for a few minutes.

You've taken care of her, but what about you?

Yeah, what about me? I couldn't ignore a nagging voice in the back of my brain that told me I couldn't afford to delay any longer, that I had to pick up something, *anything*, beat the door down, and run for my life. To hell with the consequences.

My shaky memories told me that my childhood had been marked with instances of doing just this thing – running when I couldn't handle a situation. I had an impression of a time when I'd run out of a classroom and cowered in a stall after some girls picked on me, but I couldn't be sure if that had ever happened.

Another memory told me that there had been therapists; many of them. Men and women in darkened rooms asking me questions that I didn't want to hear and couldn't possibly deal with. I tried to remember what those therapists told me to do when I felt that way.

Occupy your brain. Do something – anything – else. Try to get your focus back.

Of course. Occupy my brain. I had the perfect way to do it, too. I went to the keyboard and sat down. I closed my eyes, resting my fingers on the keys.

I asked myself what I should play, but there should have been no question at all. I had to play the one that had always been somewhere in my heart. I started playing, letting it flow through me, the notes moving from my chest to my arms right down into my fingers, escaping in cascades, my emotions ready and raw, floating near the surface. I let the song scrape them off and cast them aside, reveling in the purity that flowed through me.

Something moved behind me, and a weak voice croaked: "Kelli?"

Carla. I stopped playing and swiveled around in the chair. "What the hell? When did you wake up?"

She lay on one side, her head plastered to her pillow, eyes slit. "Just now. What are you playing?"

I motioned at the keyboard. "Oh, this old thing. My Momma wrote it. I learned when I was little."

"It sounds like death."

I laughed. "Can't say that I've ever heard that. It's supposed to be played at parties, if you can believe that."

She rolled onto her back. "It's about as festive as a funeral."

"I suppose so."

"I'm being mean. It might just be me. Maybe I'm thinking of

death."

"What do you mean?"

She turned her head toward me. It took me a little off-guard, because her eyes looked like deep black sockets, where no light ever escaped. "Have you ever seen somebody die?"

I thought of Gina. "I might have, yeah."

She looked back to the ceiling. "When I was about 21, I lived in this little townhouse just outside DC. Southern Alexandria. Not the nicest place, at least in those days, but I took what I could get. Anyway, one day I went out with one of my roommates, I don't remember why, probably to get groceries, something like that, and there was this little hill that you had to go up near where we lived. As we were going up the hill, we heard a weird sound, and saw a shower of sparks a few cars ahead of us."

"Uh huh?" I said.

"The car pulled off the side of the road, and the sparks died down, but something rolled off from the back of the car. Couldn't quite tell what it was. We were far enough away that it just looked like a blur." She sighed. "When we drove by, we saw that the sparks had come from a guy on a motorcycle who had gotten hooked underneath the back of the car. I guess he was driving along and this old woman cut him off without even realizing it. When he hit his brakes, he slid up under her bumper and got stuck there."

I put a hand to my mouth. "Jesus H. Christ."

"Dragged him about 200 feet. We had to get out and try to help, but what could we do, other than call 911? Car was off in the grass on the side of the road, and the motorcycle was on its side, looking like something big had chewed on it. I remember the gas cap had come off at some point, because you could smell gas pouring out onto the grass. It was a bad sight, but my eyes were drawn to the guy who had been driving the motorcycle. You know how you can't just look away?"

"I can imagine."

"Yeah. He was lying down in the grass, arms up over his head, just breathing heavy. Not saying a word. When I got close, I could see that the bottom part of his right leg, from his knee down, was gone. It was nothing but ripped-up jeans. No blood, no bone. That bothered me the most, for some reason. My brain kept picking at that one thing - why was there no blood? My roommate told me later that it meant he was bleeding internally, and it must have been pretty bad."

My stomach flopped over. "Good God, girl."

"It took him a couple of minutes to die. I guess the internal injuries were too much for him or something. But you could see when he died. I never believed in souls or anything like that, but…his body shook and he went limp, and it was like, I don't know, something beyond just electrical impulses left his body." She shivered and wrapped her arms around her chest. "I'll never forget it."

Let me tell you, it was quite the conversational upper. I had all the joy that I might feel if I'd been hit by a freight train. "I'm sorry you had to see that, but why are you telling me this?"

"Because I saw all that again in Room 3. Only he was conscious. He kept looking at me with these hazel eyes and asking why I didn't save him, where was the ambulance, how could I let another person die like that." She looked at me. "But by the time he was talking to me, we were back in the room, and he was standing up, right behind Barren."

That was a first. I'd never heard of a vision bleeding over like that. "Say what?"

"You heard me. Barren shot me up, I re-lived the accident,

and when I got to his body, something hit me, like a slap. I woke up and was back in the room with Barren, like I'd teleported instead of waking up. That's when I noticed the guy standing there." She waved a hand. "I think I screamed. Barren didn't see him. He gave me another shot, and...I don't know what happened after that. I woke up here, with you playing that song."

"I've never heard of anything like that," I said. I didn't like it either.

"Have you seen the dead here before?"

"Can't say I have."

She bit her lip. "What do you think it means?"

"I have no idea." I paused, and then asked the question on the tip of my tongue. "What are you?"

She looked away. "I wish I knew."

April 17th

The last entry ended abruptly. I know this. I wanted to write for longer, but by the end I just couldn't. I was - I am - worried. I probably shouldn't be, but when you've lived the last year of my life, small things take on a more sinister meaning.

The thing is, Sam didn't show up last night. It's not the first time and it wouldn't be that big of a deal, but he's also not answering the phone in his room. Damn it, I've told him a hundred times: I understand that he doesn't want to use cell phones because they could track us, but we need a way to stay in touch. I'm going to kick his ass when I see him again.

God, let me see him again. Please?

It's not like I can just go look for him, either. I have problems of my own, like my "visitor" from last night.

Let me back up a little. I didn't stop writing last night because I was worried. I stopped because someone knocked on my door at one in the morning. I jumped up, excited to see Sam, but stopped cold just a foot from the floor.

This couldn't be Sam; Sam would have used one of our codes to let me know what was going on. This guy just knocked hard and fast, five times, and then stopped.

I put my eye to the cloudy peephole, trying to be as quiet as I could. From what I could tell, the guy outside wore a black suit and a red tie, with his dark hair slicked back, shining from the meager light outside my room.

Not exactly the kind of guy you'd expect to see at the door

of your seedy motel room. Especially not after midnight.

"Ma'am," he said.

I jumped and my chest tightened. He knew I was in here. And he knew I was a ma'am. "What do you want?"

"I'm with…the front desk. Your credit card didn't run through tonight."

My mind raced. Already he'd told two lies – no way was this guy with the front desk; the guy who checked us in wore a Hawaiian shirt and a perpetually stoned look. I couldn't see him sharing a job with the Junior G Man. I'd also paid in cash, so no credit card to run. Did he even care to try to get that right, or just think I was that stupid?

What to do? If I called him on the lie, he might try to break down the door, and I sure didn't want him to do that. Then again, I wasn't about to open the door for him. I decided to try a different approach. "I think you have the wrong room."

He frowned, clasping his hands at his waist. "I don't believe so. What's your name?"

"I don't have to tell you that."

"Look, I'd prefer not to call the cops. I just want to get this taken care of," he said.

"Right. If anybody should call the cops, it's me." I swallowed hard.

"What does that mean?"

"You know what it means, smart guy. I paid in cash. If you *really* think you've got the right room, you're not with the front office."

If that bothered the guy, he didn't show it. Didn't so much as unclasp his hands. "Maybe you're right. Maybe I have the wrong door."

"I think so. You should probably just move on."

Creepy as hell – the guy's face remained totally emotionless as he walked off, not sparing me with any more words.

When I was sure that he'd left, I leaned against the door, allowing myself to breathe.

That was a message.

I touched my forehead, my hand coming away covered in sweat.

When did I start sweating? I looked around the room, trying to figure out how quickly I could pack up and get out, if it came to that.

Pretty damned quickly, as it turned out. I had condensed my life into a few small bags and only removed items as I needed them. Five minutes? Maybe less, if I left behind non-essentials. Thing is, I didn't know if I needed to do it then. Would the guy come back that night? No way to know for sure.

I went to the phone and dialed Sam's number. Six rings, and it dropped to voice mail. I called back, and got voice mail again. I put the phone back in the cradle, my head spinning. Had the guy in the suit already gotten him? Should I call back and have the front desk at his motel look in on him?

No, that might raise more suspicions. Besides, he's probably on his way over here. Best to wait.

That was it – he would be here soon, if he wasn't already on the way up. He usually shows up around two or three, depending on if he's had to start making arrangements for our next move. So I waited; not like I could do much more. I wasn't going back to sleep, and I couldn't sit down and write after my little visit. I wished for the Korg for about the millionth time.

But like I already wrote, nothing. Not a sign of him all night, and no call this morning. I've gone from worry to almost sheer panic. Thank God I wrote about those therapy sessions last night, though, because they helped me remember how to cope with the panic. It's the only reason I'm writing again - I have to distract myself or I'm going to go crazy.

Am I worried? Of course I am. I'm going crazy. I can't lose him now, not after all that we've gone through. To have faced death and come out on the other side, only to have things end like this...it just can't. I can't accept that.

But I wonder - am I relying on him way too much? If he's gone, where does that leave me? Devastated, alone, and without a way to get around in a world I just barely understand.

Suddenly going out for a Blizzard doesn't sound so bad. Unless...

Unless that's how they found us.

No, no. That can't be. I only saw a handful of people, and they couldn't know about us, could they? The Organization couldn't have its fingers *everywhere,* could it?

I think I know the answer to that one, and I *know* I don't like it. God, I feel sick.

I don't dare to move, especially not during the day. I'm going to wait until tonight to see if Sam shows up. If he doesn't, I'll have to make a run for it in the morning. Somehow. Maybe I can get a bus ticket to the middle of nowhere.

In the meantime, I might as well keep on telling my story. I can't concentrate on anything else.

======

That visit reminds me of the night that Momma came to visit me at the Khesnaa.

I'd never managed to get a night of sound sleep in the cabin without the aid of their drugs. The slightest sound and I'd wake up, heart pounding, ready to make a run for it. That night was different. I popped awake, and I couldn't tell you why. There hadn't been a thump, or even a shuffle. I strained my ears, and couldn't even hear Sam making a peep in the front room, so he was probably out of it too.

I rolled over and stared at the ceiling. *So why am I awake?*

Because someone was watching me. I could feel it. I glanced over at Carla, but she was a dark, motionless lump in her bed. My heart beating in my throat, I look in the other direction, very slowly, afraid of what I'd see.

I'd have screamed if Momma hadn't put her hand over my mouth at just that moment.

"Shush, honey. You have to be quiet," she whispered, her face close to mine.

I'm sure my eyes were bulging out of their sockets in a comical fashion as I tried to process just what the hell I was seeing. I think I must have been screaming, too, but I can't remember fully. If I did, her hand stifled it.

She hissed at me. "Shush now. You stop that foolishness."

I heard Carla's voice in the back of my head: *Have you seen the dead here before?*

I shuddered. Dreaming. Yeah, that's it. I've got to be dreaming. Just play it cool. Maybe you'll learn something. That helped me calm down. I would be just fine. What was it Scrooge had said?

An undigested bit of beef. That's all that Momma was. No worries.

"You going to stop?" she said.

I nodded, and she took the hand away.

"What are you doing here?" I whispered.

"Now isn't that a fine way to greet me. I come all this way, and you talk to me like that."

"I just don't understand."

She put her hands on her hips. "Understand this: I'm here to help you."

I sat up, glancing at Carla. "What help can you give me? Can you help me get out of here?"

"You watch your language." She sat down on the chair next to the bed, spreading out her dark blue dress as she did so. Had she been wearing that dress when we buried her? I think so.

"I know you're not here. There's no way. I know this is a dream."

"You keep on lying to yourself. You always did. Why don't you go ahead and pinch yourself if you think that. Go on." I could tell by the way her tight mouth was set that she just *wanted* me to pinch myself.

I went ahead and did it. It hurt. But she was still there. I didn't think it proved anything, but maybe it would shut her up. "I don't get it. We buried you. I saw your body."

"Act like you never heard of a ghost." I realized that I'd forgotten just how husky her voice was - had been. I wondered how I'd avoided inheriting that.

She pulled a Pall Mall from inside the top of her dress - no doubt in her bra, like she used to keep them - and lit it up. The spark from her match temporarily lit up the room and I saw now that she had a waxy, unnatural looking complexion. Dead giveaway if I'd seen her in the light.

Oh. Yeah. Now I remember why I didn't get that voice.

"Never heard of a ghost smoking," I said.

She winked. "Guess you can write what you know about ghosts on your pinkie then, huh?"

I smiled in spite of myself. "Yeah, you're Momma, all right."

She blew smoke from her mouth, or at least, she should have, but nothing came out. "What's that supposed to mean, child?"

"Means you're still stubborn. And mean."

She chuckled. "You get it honest, don't you?"

I stuck my tongue out at her.

"I come all the way back from the grave and you can't give me some sugar? You don't want a hug or anything?"

I hadn't seen her in years. I hadn't even imagined I would see her again. I should have wanted to grab her and never let her go. Only problem was that just the idea of touching her set my teeth on edge. I decided to change the subject. "Can't you get me out of here?"

She sat back, shaking her head. "How is a ghost supposed to get you out of here? Use your head, girl."

"Then how am I supposed to hug you?"

She pondered this, rubbing her chin. "I guess you can't."

"Well, then."

"All right. But I'm here to help anyway," she said.

I frowned. "If you can't get me out of here, then what can you do?"

"You've been thinking about getting that girl out of here, right?"

"Both of us. They're going to kill us."

She gave a slow nod. "They just might. You've got to protect yourself, sure enough, but you also got to worry about keeping that girl safe and sane. She's your ticket out of here."

"Sam is my ticket out of here." The words just came out of my mouth without me even thinking them. Deep inside, I knew they were the truth.

She raised an eyebrow. "That the big, pale guy?"

"Yeah. He takes care of me."

She shifted on her seat, adjusting her dress under her. "Mm. Good. You trust that big man now, you hear me? Do whatever you need to do to be with him."

I slapped my hands on my legs. "I am not making googly eyes at a man just because you told me to."

"I can see in your eyes that I don't have to tell you. Sweet on him, aren't you?"

I didn't say anything.

She snorted. "Thought so. But I still know my girl. You're scared of him."

"I'm scared of no man."

She laughed. "I know that's a lie. But you don't have to worry, honey. He's not who you think he is – or might be."

"Clearly. I just found out he's got a wife and child."

She pursed her lips.

"Oh, what now?"

She leaned forward, clasping her hands in front of her. "Things aren't so good on that front."

My stomach flip-flopped. "Are they dead?"

"I can't say for sure. I'm not allowed to talk about certain things."

"Says who?"

"That'd be another thing I'm not allowed to talk about."

I waved my hand at her. "Oh, whatever. What a load of bullshit."

"Watch that mouth."

I smiled; it was an old joke between us. "I can't turn my eyes around."

She returned the smile. "That's my girl. Listen, he's a good man. You could do a lot worse."

"Because you did such a good job picking out 'good' men."

She pointed at me. "You're an adult, so I'll let you get away with some things, but don't you backtalk me, girl. Death taught me a lot of things, and I know I'm right about this one. He's got his eye on you and he's an honorable man."

Death. Right. I wanted to ask her who - or what - had brought her back, but I suspected that I knew the answer, or rather, the non-answer, so I took a different approach. "Who's telling you this stuff? Who sent you here?"

"Can't answer that."

Come on, you saw that one coming. I shook my head. "I couldn't tell you if I'm going to do it for myself or for her. I only just met her, but I can't watch what they're doing to her, not after Gina. I can't watch them fuck up another person."

She exhaled an invisible cloud of smoke. "Told you to watch that mouth. God doesn't approve."

I reached some tipping point in my mind where the surreal nature of this visit outweighed my own practicality and happiness at seeing my mother for the first time in ten years. Something gave in my mind, and I no longer felt like the little girl called on the carpet. I felt like a woman facing down a stranger. A familiar-looking stranger, but a stranger nonetheless. "So you came back after all this time to tell me shi - *stuff* I already know? And to scold me for cursing?"

"Well, when you put it that way, I could be nicer."

I crossed my arms over my chest and looked away. "You could."

"Aw, pumpkin. I'm sorry. You're right. Said a lot of things I regret on that dock, and then I show up here like this."

My head swiveled back to her of its own volition. Maybe

that sensation of talking to a stranger had been warranted after all. "Dock? I never saw you on a dock. What are you thinking of?"

She sat back in the chair and frowned. "You know, the dock? That time, with your father?" My memory had always been somewhat shaky, but I felt absolutely correct about this. She had to be mistaken.

I shook my head. "No, Momma. The three of us never went out on a dock together."

"How do you figure?"

"I figure because it's the truth. The last time you saw me…well, alive anyway, was when my ass - backside - was storming out of your…*crappy*…little apartment with Barry." I decided that the no-cussing thing might just kill me.

She put a hand to her forehead. "Oh. Right. Don't know what I was thinking. I guess my brain is scrambled."

There might well be some unforeseen side effects to returning from the dead. I wouldn't doubt that, but still, something just wasn't adding up here. I knew my Momma. She held a grudge like nobody's business and would never forget the last time we saw each other. No way. She had threatened to get a restraining order on me, for God's sake. "Where were you before?"

"Heaven, of course. With the angels and God," she said.

"Oh, really."

"Of course. You never did believe in that stuff, did you?" she said.

"That's just the thing, Momma. Neither did you."

She smiled. "Death has a way of changing your mind."

I shook my head. "No. You were a suicide, Momma. I thought God didn't let suicides into heaven."

That look of doubt crossed her face for a moment, and then

vanished. She dropped the cigarette to the floor and crushed it out beneath her heel. When she took it away, the remains had vanished. "You thought wrong, didn't you? See, you've got to stop being so bull-headed. You know very little."

This whole thing reeked. Floating around in Heaven with the angels after she took a whole bottle of Xanax? In the context of some of the things I'd seen in Room 3, it wasn't completely crazy, but still… "So you show up out of the blue, tell me to save the girl here, and romance the big guy?"

She exhaled the invisible smoke again. "That's about the long and short of it."

"Well thank you for nothing. Why don't you get on out of here? Nobody invited you. You're not offering me any real help, anyway."

She sniffed, but I knew that act. "This wasn't easy, you know. I'm just trying to look after you…"

"You never did before. Why the sudden concern now that you're dead? Did God send you?"

She gave me a pained look. "Honey…"

I thought about the last time I had seen her. The look of utter disgust on her face as I had walked away, knowing that she'd chosen my stepfather over me. "You showing up here doesn't mean that all is forgiven. Last time we talked, you called me every name in the book. You never even apologized." She started to speak, and I held my hand up. "Don't tell me you didn't have a chance. You had years left when I walked out that door."

She leaned forward, cradling her head in her hands, staring at the floor. "You're right. I never could let things go."

"She sees the light," I said.

I heard stirring from Carla's bed. "Who are you talking to?"

My head swiveled toward her, my mouth open, panic

tightening my throat. "I…uh."

She must have woken up at some point during our discussion, because she had rolled over to face me. She leaned on one arm, her eyes scanning the gloom. "Is it Sam? Didn't sound like him, but…"

I followed her eyes. Momma had vanished. Had she ever been there? She must have. Carla heard somebody, or some*thing*. "Uh. No," I said.

"Who was it?"

"Nobody. I guess." I rubbed the back of my head, wondering what just happened to me. "Talking to myself."

I couldn't see much of her face other than her eyes, but I could tell that she looked at me for a long time. At last she said, "Can you please keep your talking to nobody down? I'm trying to sleep here."

"I –"

A familiar pattern of knocks at the door cut me off.

Thank God. I hadn't been sure *what* that answer might have been. My right brain had taken control and my left brain was still trying to process the events of the last few minutes.

Carla groaned and turned over, covering her head with her pillow. "Let me get some goddamn sleep, *please,*" she said.

"Yeah, sure." I rose and shuffled across the darkened room. When I cracked the door, Sam's big head leaned up against it without a word. His eyes met mine, a beseeching look buried somewhere in there.

"What is it?" I said. I'd run out of patience for indirect people.

He exhaled. "My apologies. I heard you speaking, and I became concerned. Is all well?"

"Oh, peachy-keen. Just being held hostage by a bunch of

maniacs trying to brainwash me. No biggie."

His face went slack. By God, he might even be concerned for my well-being. "I apologize. Is there anything I can do to help? Are you not sleeping well?"

"Haven't slept well the whole time I've been here."

"Fair enough. Can I help you get to sleep?"

He was too much sometimes. I believe he had no idea how that sounded. I could have embarrassed him, but I decided against it. "Listen, can I come out there for a minute?"

He looked over his shoulder, then back to me. "I am not supposed to."

I touched his arm through the crack in the door. "Sam. Please. Can we forget about 'supposed to's for one night?" I pulled my hand back though and clasped my hands at my chest, begging him. "Let's just act like a normal man and woman for one night."

He ran a hand over his smooth head. "I do not know…"

"Let me guess. You're not supposed to let me out unless you're taking me to that room," I said.

"Essentially, yes."

"We need to talk. You know I don't bite - unless you ask me to." I grinned. "I promise I won't run away on you, tempting though it might be."

He nodded. "I appreciate that. Very well." He opened the door wider and took a step back, extending a hand.

I slipped through.

Surreal is the only way to describe the Khesnaa's front room. Removed from its threatening context, I found it almost laughable; it was mostly cedar - cedar armchairs, cedar couch, cedar chest by the door. The walls were covered with wood paneling, and the floor underneath was a cheap hardwood floor.

The real hilarity – and terror – lay in the equipment that they'd set up in the place. Gina had described it as a hillbilly war room, and I think that's just about as apt as it gets. What must have been a 100-inch TV dominated the far wall. They hadn't stopped there, though. They had set 20 other small screens around it, their flat bodies recessed into the wall. A rack of computers sat below and just off to the right of the screens, their red and green lights blinking as they hummed along.

The front door was a big steel piece of work with a keypad and card reader. The last line of defense, the place that had occupied many a discussion with Gina. We had decided that the timing for any escape would have to be just right, so that we could either get the pistol and blow the mechanism to hell, or slide past someone as they came out. We could threaten someone into doing it, but that seemed the least likely of paths.

I looked at the screens now, and recognized the scene in a few of them. One was Room 3; it was dark, but they had that green night vision thing on the camera. Another must have been somewhere in the front room, because I saw the back of our heads, standing there, gazing at it like a couple of dumb asses. I swiveled my head, trying to find the camera, when my brain spoke up.

Hold on. Back up. Take a second look.

I looked back to the screens. Specifically, the screen on the bottom.

Is that…?

I leaned forward. "Are you *kidding* me?"

"What?"

"You have a camera in our bathroom?"

I felt him tense up beside me. "I…uh, well." He took a step back. "I never watched it. I promise you."

"Why should I believe you?"

His eyes went wide, and he held one finger up. "If you mean my wife, that was not a lie. I simply had no reason to tell you."

I actually believed him, but I wasn't letting him off that easily. I circled him, enjoying his misery. It felt good to have the upper hand, even if I had every intention of giving it back to him. "What about now? You have any reason to lie to me now?"

His hands floated at his side, and I swear he started to blush. "I have never lied to you. Honesty is everything. Without honesty, we have nothing else."

I stopped in front of him, hands on my hips, cocking my head. "You're an interesting fellow, Samarta."

"I think of myself as the opposite. But thank you." He cleared his throat. "You said we needed to speak…?"

"Oh, you're no fun. Right down to business, huh?"

"I, uhm, suppose that is the best." He shifted.

"Have you seen anything weird around here?" I said.

He walked over to the old wooden couch that sat before the monitors and plopped down on one of the ratty plaid cushions. He dangled one arm over the side. "Everything about this place is strange. You will need to narrow this down for me."

I sighed. "I don't know how to ask you without sounding crazy."

He rubbed his chin. "Interesting."

I walked to his side. "What's that supposed to mean?"

"All of this –" He swept his arm across the room – "And you worry about appearing insane."

Yeah, why was that?

Could be that you care what he thinks. Could be. That sounded a lot like Momma's voice, floating around in my head. That was just what I needed.

"I've got a reputation to protect. Can't have word getting around, you know?" I said.

He smiled. At that moment, I couldn't remember if I'd seen him smile before, but it made me a little light-headed. "Of course. I would never harm a good woman's reputation. Please. Tell me your concerns."

"First, you have to promise that you won't think I'm crazy."

He waved a hand. "Of course. I would never think you crazy."

I bit my lip. *All right. Here goes.* "Have you…seen people who shouldn't be here?"

His body went rigid, his expression turning very serious. "What have you seen? Intruders?"

I held up my hands. "Whoa, calm down, chief. I don't mean I've seen people like that. I mean…you know…"

He raised his eyebrows. "I am afraid I do not understand."

Damn it, he just couldn't make it easy, could he? Fine. I'd go out on that limb. "*Dead* people."

There was a moment of silence as he studied me, a moment where I was convinced that he thought me completely out of my gourd. I wondered if I could melt right into the floor and flow away from him.

At last he broke the silence. "You are seeing dead people."

"I didn't say that. I was asking if you did."

"I have not. However –"

"Oh God, I must sound like a complete jackass." I turned on my heels and headed for Room 1.

I didn't realize the dude could move so quickly. In an instant, he was on his feet, touching my arm, pulling me back. "You do not. And I did not say I disbelieve you. Nor do I find you crazy."

"So what do you think? You're killing me here," I said.

"In my tribe, we have people who can see the dead."

"Wait. Back up. 'Tribe'? Are you telling me you're an American Indian?"

He shook his head. "I know of them, but no. It is rather complicated to explain and not relevant. The ones who see the dead…they are relevant."

"Do they only see them?"

"No. They speak to them, as well. In fact, the dead chose them at birth and granted them their abilities at the turn of adulthood. That is, following a journey into the wilderness, with little to defend themselves."

I crossed my arms over my chest. "So you guys psychologically scarred them, threw them out into the wood with no protection, and thought it was the dead making them see ghosts?"

His cheeks flushed red. "That is not it at all."

"Sounds like it to me. Sounds like abuse."

"Nonsense, it was the opposite. We revered our Deadspeakers. Their initiation was not an easy one. Many died during the process."

"Gee, that doesn't sound like abuse at all."

His eyes flared. "It was necessary for their survival and ours. You have no idea what we faced every day, with your beds and your flat screen TVs –"

I held out my hands. "Okay, back up. We got off on the wrong foot here. It's okay. We're very calm."

"Do not patronize me."

I remembered my dad, who had shouted down any attempt to lighten the mood during a crisis. I put my hands on my hips. "I'm sorry, big guy. I was trying to fix things. I fucked it up, I guess."

He sighed and gazed the floor. "I apologize."

"It's not your place to apologize. I'm the one who talked out of turn. You're right; I don't understand what your people dealt with. I don't even know who they were."

He looked up, and I wondered if it had really been my dad who flew off the handle after all. I had a weird doubling sensation in my head, like I was in two places at once.

"I appreciate that. Please, do not do that again. My people deserve respect for their loss."

I patted his shoulder. "They do. I agree. Now tell me, how did speaking to dead people protect the Tribe?"

He came to life as the last remains of his sadness melted away. Here was a topic he *really* loved. "Perhaps you are familiar with the concept of Spirit Guides? I understand there is a similar concept from where you come."

I put a hand on my hip. "You know, now that you mention it, where are you from anyway?"

"We are not discussing me."

"Hey, you're the one who brought up your heritage. You can't do that and not answer that question, at least."

"That is fair, but I do not wish to discuss it further right now. You will find out when the time is right. At the moment, we are discussing you." He took a step closer to me. "As I said, I do not disbelieve that you have spoken to the dead. Would I rather see the proof with my own eyes?" He spread his hands. "Of course. I may appear simple to you –"

"I never said you were simple."

"That does not mean that I do not appear as such. Regardless. Our people were highly sophisticated," he said.

"You keep saying 'were'. What does that mean?"

"It relates to why I am here. I have no wish to discuss it further at this moment."

The man was relentless. I threw my hands in the air. "Fine. I get it. Just get to your point."

"I have not seen dead people here, but I believe that you have. This either means that you are a powerful spiritual being, which frankly would not surprise me, or that something else is going on here."

"Like what?"

He rubbed his chin. "I do not know. This is a very strange place. I do not think the dead rest easy here. Could I tell you why? No. Our captors do not share that information with me. But I believe that they selected this strange place for a purpose."

"And that purpose?" I said.

"Again, I do not know. But if you were going to tinker with the mind of others, perhaps the best place to do so would be a place of power."

"So maybe the worlds are bleeding together here or something?" I completely pulled it out of my ass, but what did I know about talking to the dead in the first place?

"I will not speculate. Let it be enough that I believe you, and that I will keep my eyes and my ears open. I will let you know what I hear."

I sized him up. "Isn't that a pretty big risk for you to take? I don't imagine Maple would like it."

"It is indeed a risk, but it is a worthwhile one."

I didn't know what he meant by that, but I was pretty sure that I liked it. I couldn't remember the last time a man had said such a thing to me. I may never have heard such a thing, in fact: my memory was a little hazy on the subject. Shocker there.

We stood there for a few moments, eyes connecting along

with something deeper, something in our souls. I knew he felt it just the same as I did. "It means a lot to me," I said at last, trying to pull myself out of that trance.

He flushed and cleared his throat, looking away. "It is simply the right thing to do."

I grinned and patted his shoulder. "All right. I'll go back to my pen here in a second, but one other thing. Do you know what they're doing to her? Is it any different from what they're doing to me?"

He shook his head slowly. "I wish that I had more to tell you, but truly, I have no idea. Maple keeps a tight grip on her handling. It is a wonder I am able to interact with her at all. Why do you ask?"

"I know it's crazy, I barely know her, but I'm worried that they're going to break her. I can't live with it after what happened to Gina. They're pushing her a lot harder than they ever did me, and you know how crazy *I* was in the early days."

He smiled. "I believe you tried to slash me with your sharpened fingernails."

I laughed. "Good times, huh?"

"Something like that. Perhaps I can learn more. If nothing else, I will do what I can to protect you both. I do not want either of you to suffer an undue fate, especially after what happened to your friend. That cannot be allowed again."

It touched me to hear that. I had known the big guy didn't like what happened, but I hadn't heard him put it in quite those terms. "Thank you," I said, and walked back toward the room.

He spoke again. "Do you require anything else? Something that I could perhaps find, or give you?"

I turned and looked at him. "Other than freedom?"

"Except that, for now."

I stopped just in front of the door, turning to face him, rotating on the ball of one foot, trying to look coy. I wasn't sure if I could pull it off, but it was worth a shot. "Actually, I could use one thing," I said, the unspoken end of that sentence being *you big, strong man you.*

=======

I have to stop here. I think Sam just knocked on the door. More next time.

April 19th

I'm lucky to be alive. I know that. I shouldn't even be sitting here writing this. That was Sam at the door last time, but he was almost too late.

We were in the middle of packing my bags (I was a little off - we were around the seven minute mark and had a way to go) when we heard the rumble of a car pulling up outside the motel. Sure, people checked in late there from time to time, but given that Sam had spent two days dodging what he thought were members of the Organization, we were on guard. Sam had me stay back on the other side of the room while he went to the window and peeked out.

He glanced back at me. "You said that the man wore a suit?"

"Yeah, why?"

He closed the curtain and came back to the bed, scooping a dress into a bag and zipping it up. "I believe they are here."

"'They'?"

He slung the bag over his shoulder. "Three men. Dressed identically. We must hurry."

"Shit," I said.

He pointed at the bags at my feet. "Grab what is already packed. We will have to replace what does not make the trip."

"But the food –"

"Replaceable. We, however, are not." He pulled a pistol from his pocket and went to stand by the door.

I slung two bags onto my back and made for the door,

stopping only to pick up this journal. Sam opened his mouth to say something when he saw that, but he must have re-considered it. He waved me toward the door as I stuffed the journal into a bag.

We slid out the door, trying to remain as quiet as possible. The room was on the second floor, looking down on the parking lot, with stairs at either end of the landing. I wondered if that might be a good thing, right up until we heard different sets of footsteps coming from both directions.

I tugged on the shoulder of Sam's T-shirt and nodded toward the stairs on our left-hand side. With three guys, I guess that they had split up to try and catch us from both sides. Thing is, that left them with a lone man on one of the stairs, and I was pretty sure I only heard one set of footfalls coming from our left.

Sam understood the implications right away and headed in that direction, taking the lead and keeping that pistol ready.

The guy ahead of us had a head-start, though, and reached the top of the stairs, smirking. "There you are, Ms. Foster. We really need to settle up with you on your debt."

Sam stepped between the two of us, raising the pistol. "If you value your life, you will step aside."

The guy smiled. "Very amusing. Do you really believe that I wouldn't give my life for the cause?"

Sam glanced over his shoulder at the two men topping the stairs behind us.

"Sam," I said, as the guy before us made his move.

Sam turned back just in time. The guy in the suit tried to grab the pistol, but Sam was a little too fast and strong for him. He pushed him back with one hand, throwing him off balance for a second. Sam swung the pistol, slamming the butt into his head.

He went down fast and hard.

One of the guys at the other end of the hall shouted, but we were on the steps before our friend had finished collapsing. We heard the rush of the two conscious guys behind us, but I couldn't tell if they were going for their pal or heading after us. Maybe they split up, but it didn't matter. All that mattered was getting down those stairs to Sam's jeep and getting the hell out of there.

If I had to guess, I'd say that took about 40 seconds, tops. One of them had just appeared at the halfway point of the stairs about the time we tore out of the parking lot, tires squealing in protest.

"What are you doing?" I said.

Sam grimaced, looking in the rearview mirror. "If nothing else will bring the cops calling, that will. Perhaps they can slow those two down."

Headlights flashed on behind us, jittering and bumping as their car jumped the curb onto the street behind us.

"So much for that," I said.

He looked into the mirror again, and then looked to me as I tossed one of the bags into the back. "Don't be too fast to unpack. We need to switch vehicles."

"Yeah, you think?"

The squeal of tires again and their dusty blue sedan pulled up beside us. Sam slammed on the brakes, making the Jeep fishtail, but they anticipated that move, dropping back in time with us. The passenger side window began to roll down. I couldn't tell if anything or anyone was poking out just yet.

"Hold on," Sam said, and jerked the wheel, ramming the Jeep into the sedan, almost broadside. Metal screeched, and the sedan bounced up on the sidewalk, narrowly missing a hydrant as it bounced back onto the street beside us. Sam pulled the Jeep back and then moved again, slamming into the sedan and sending it all the way up onto the curb.

The guy behind the wheel of the sedan tried to jerk the car back onto the road again, but he overcompensated and the sedan fishtailed on the sidewalk. He managed to miss the corner of an old brick building, but that toppled the car onto its side. It kept right on sliding, going off of the sidewalk and into a nearby yard. It slid for a few more feet before it stopped abruptly. Well, that's not quite accurate: a *porch* stopped it abruptly, right before it collapsed onto the sedan.

"Damn, where'd you learn to drive like that?" I said.

"Television." He tightened his lips. "We must find another vehicle."

I sat back in my seat, cocking an eyebrow. "How are we going to manage that?"

"Contacts in the Underground."

I grabbed onto the bar over the window, looking out onto the small town for the last time. It didn't appear so sleepy all of a sudden; lights had gone on in almost every house up and down the block. "Ah, the mysterious Underground."

"They are a group of like-minded individuals..."

"Whoa, hold up. I thought you didn't want to tell me this stuff. Thought it was 'best for me not to know'?" To be fair, this was only the second time that he had mentioned the Underground. I had grilled him the first time, with the same results that I always got from him: not the right time, too soon, not safe.

"Things have changed. This is more direct action."

"So? Maybe I agree with you now. Sam, I'm not ready to be a revolutionary, for you or anyone else. I just want to live my life."

He looked at me, hard, and then back to the road. "I could have died last night. Where would you have been then?"

"Don't think that didn't cross my mind."

"Well, then."

We drove in silence for a few minutes. Sam knew the line; if I wanted the information now, I would ask for it. He knew better than to push me. At last, necessity won out over my stubborn need to "teach him a lesson". "All right, fine. I'll bite. How do we contact them?" I said.

He glanced at me, raising one eyebrow. "You really want to know?"

"I do."

He smiled. "Sometimes, you do surprise me."

"I try."

Then he told me. Simple, as it should be, but hidden enough to operate just beneath the surface of everyday life. I don't dare write it down in case I don't manage to grab the journal next time, but I know in case something happens to him. I don't want to think about it, but reality is reality. I know, and that's all that matters.

We swapped cars just before sunrise, boosting our next ride at a used dealership a few hundred miles South of where we started. From there we took a twisting route East, hoping that it might throw any pursuers off the course. We finally crashed at a goofy tourist trap motel based on a TV show set in the boonies. The place was distant enough to maybe be a good hiding place, but also known enough to throw them off the scent a bit. That was the idea. I have no idea what state we were in at that point.

We crashed around mid-morning, and I had the dream again, for the first time since leaving the Khesnaa. You know, the one with Mimi and the tree. This time I didn't need to play the music. It had already been played, and the tree stood cracked open and empty, devoid of its terrifying contents. That wasn't the crux of the dream at all. This time, it was something, or somebody, coming through the corn, and the scent of blood. It reminded me of a few different scenarios, but I've promised myself I'm not going to over think what that means. It's probably just a stress dream.

We got up with the setting sun and headed West this time, not exactly doubling back over our old path, but making it circuitous enough to confuse the trail even further. By the end of that night, we had stopped at the biggest dump we'd found yet.

"Please tell me we're not stopping here," I said, as he pulled us into the gravel parking lot. "Tell me this is just another stopover."

He suppressed a smile, the son of a bitch. "I am afraid we do have to stop here. I have determined this to be the safest location, for now."

"How did you do that?"

"That is a question that involves the Underground. Do you wish to know more?"

I considered it, but I decided that one might be too dangerous to handle. "Nah. Just tell me why they can't set us up with a cushy place instead of this dump."

"There are no Underground members in this area. *Yet.* We have to make do for now."

"Fine." I didn't like it, but I didn't have any other solid suggestions. Maybe I do need to get more information on this Underground, get to know their people. Get them to find us a place at the Hilton or something like that.

At least a Motel 6.

So that's where I'm at: sitting on a broken bed in a run-down dump in the middle of nowhere, trying to get my head on straight and get used to the eerie silence in this place. I have to wonder – is this the shape of the rest of my life, this stop-start, push-pull? I hope not. Death might actually be preferable.

That dream from yesterday won't let go. I keep seeing that empty tree trunk, and remembering where the dreams and visions started going off the rails. Right before we tried to escape.

======

Mimi spoke to me, but it took me a second to register her words. "You have a voice like an angel," she said.

I laughed, both at the words and how my head swam. Pleasant, pretty. "Hardly. I wish."

She clasped her hands together, looking like the most earnest thing to ever walk the Earth. Or wherever we were. "No, when you sing, it's like angels, singing right to my ears."

I put a hand on the girl's shoulder. "I appreciate it. You're full of it, but I appreciate it."

She didn't take it the way that I might have hoped. Her eyes got wide and rolled toward the sky.

"What?" I said.

"Look." She pointed to the sky. I followed her finger, and as I did so, I saw the blue in the sky rolling up from the horizon like someone rolling up a carpet. As it went, its absence revealed a black abyss hiding just behind reality.

I followed the track of the event, turning in a circle as the horizon expanded into nothingness, all of the points converging directly overhead. "My God," I said.

Mimi tugged at my jeans. I only just managed to clamp down on a surprised shout. I looked down to her; the terror in her eyes was a jab to an already-beaten mind.

"What is it?" she said.

I pulled the little girl close to me. I could feel her heart jackhammering against my hip. "I don't know," I said.

"You said you'd seen all of this before."

"I've never seen anything like *this*."

I didn't think her eyes could get any wider, but they did. "I'm scared," she whispered.

The blue overhead had completely vanished, leaving us floating in a darkness that felt like way more than outer space – it felt alive, waiting to push its fingers over the ground and pick us up, dropping us into its gaping maw. "I'm scared, too."

She pointed again. "Look."

A speck of light appeared in the center of the sky. It wasn't much bigger than a distant star, but it shone brighter than I had ever seen.

"What is that?" I said.

Her only answer was to cling to my leg.

I noticed that the light was getting bigger, bit by bit. I got the impression of a star approaching the Earth at full force: a giant ball of flame, dead-set on wiping out all life. Maybe I didn't need to worry about the black maw. Maybe that thing would take care of the job on its own.

Mimi buried her face against my body. "Don't let it get us," she said, her voice muffled.

"I –" I what? What do you say to that? I couldn't stop an entire star from destroying us.

"You have to," she said.

It took all of my will to tear my eyes away from the approaching light, but I did it. I knelt down and took her hands, looking into her eyes. "I'm going to do my best, okay? I'll try." I also had no idea how I was going to do it, but you don't tell kids that, right?

"You promise?"

"I promise, as much as I can."

She started to say something, but the organ inside the tree decided to speak then, letting out a loud, flat blast.

We both whirled in its direction. The tree caught and reflected the light from the approaching fireball, its surface appearing to catch fire. Red and yellow light curled up from the bottom toward the leaves, playing across the surface of the giant lock.

"Good God," I said, and the organ let out another one of those blasts. I flinched.

Mimi pointed at the keys. "What is that?"

It took me a second to pick it out in the strange, shifting light: a thick liquid had started oozing out from the space between the keys. In the semi-darkness I couldn't tell if that was sap or blood, but it might as well have been the same thing.

Mimi screamed and tried to say something that I couldn't understand.

I looked back over my shoulder toward the growing fireball, now the size of the moon. Flames danced across its surface and exploded in bright yellow and red geysers.

Mimi groaned. "Oh, no."

"What?"

"He's coming."

"Who's coming?"

She pointed toward the corn. It, too, had taken on the red and yellow cast, its stalks waving as a wind started to kick up around us. "The Bad Man," she said.

I wrapped an arm around her. "What bad man?"

"There!"

As she said it, the corn rustled. I recoiled, pulling her with me. Someone - or something - was most definitely out there, and it didn't like us one bit. A white, gloved hand emerged from between the rows, clawing at the ground. A second hand followed it, and Mimi moaned, pressing against me, trying to disappear into my body.

When the helmeted head appeared, I had no doubt about the identity of the monster being reborn, inch-by-inch, within that cornfield: Carla's cyclist. I didn't need to see his face under that helmet. My brain filled in the details: rotting flesh and a skull, with empty eye sockets that would eat your soul as soon as look at you.

The star had brought it. I didn't know how or why, but the star had revived it, and it would kill us before unending fire consumed it.

The cyclist pulled itself forward, gasping and heaving with wet breaths. My stomach clenched.

"Come back." Its thick, wet voice should have vanished into the maelstrom around us, but somehow I heard it the same as if he had been standing beside me.

I didn't know where this thing was asking us to go, but it didn't matter; its intent was clear. "You can't have us. We're not going anywhere," I said.

"Come back," it said again, and the ground began to shake. "You must come back."

I turned to run and -

Found myself sitting as upright as I could in Room 3's chair. For a moment it seemed that the ground had grabbed ahold of me and was waiting for the cyclist; these were the chair's restraints, pulling at my arms, trying to drag me back down.

I gasped and gazed at Barren. I imagine my eyes looked

ready to pop out of their sockets. "What the fuck?"

He put a hand to his chest. "Thank God you're back."

"It was you," I said. "You were the one telling me to come back."

He cocked his head. "You heard that? Did it intrude into your vision?"

"It did."

"Amazing. And you're…not in pain?"

I lay back, putting a hand to my forehead. "No. Just got the shit scared out of me is all."

"I've never seen a reaction like that. There was pain a few weeks ago, yes, but…oh, dear." He nodded at my crotch.

"What are you looking at?" I said, but felt like an idiot as soon as the words were out. Something was warm and wet down there. Guess I had been more scared than I realized. I wanted to disappear into the chair. I laid back and closed my eyes, listening to the pounding in my head and wishing he would just go away.

"*Are* you okay?"

"Told you I'm fine," I said.

"You don't seem that way."

I supposed I wasn't fine, at that. My brain refused to let go of the vision; anytime I lowered my guard and tried to just *be,* I would see the star streaking through the sky, or the cyclist creeping out of the corn. I sighed. "I'm not sure what's real or a vision anymore. Am I really here?"

He touched my shoulder with one gentle hand. "Do you feel that?"

I pulled away and looked at him. "Yes, but what's that supposed to prove?"

"Just that you're here, now. Tell me what happened. You have to tell me," he said

"I don't have to tell you a damned thing."

He got closer, resting a hand on the top of the chair. "Just between us. None of the others have to know."

"Why should I care whether they know?"

"They might want to keep going in this direction, see just how hard they can push you."

I hadn't considered that. Christ. "Why would you do that? Isn't your job to get results?"

He studied his nails. "It's entirely within my discretion to choose relevant data. Perhaps there's a therapeutic need for me to understand."

"You don't like them much, do you?"

He pulled back, crossing his arms over his chest. "I like my job. No…I like knowledge. I don't like torturing you."

"Could have fooled me."

"The information is vital, but there *must* be more humane ways to get this information. I've tried to plead with them, but my hands are tied. Please. Tell me what you saw. It might help with dosage decisions that go over my head."

I could see he wasn't going to give up, so I took a deep breath, and did what I had to do: I lied. I told him the same old story about the little girl and the organ, with the tree catching fire. Only this time it was so much more real. So real that I lost sight of where I was. It wasn't a whole lie, after all. Momma always told me that if I was going to lie, I should at least bury the truth somewhere in there.

He gave me a weird look once all was said and done, but he didn't push. He just started undoing my straps – or at least trying to undo them. He frowned, yanking at them, pulling my arm.

"Don't touch me," I said. "Please."

He gave me a weird look. "I had thought that trusting me

with that information might help you trust me."

"You thought wrong. Why don't you just get Samarta in here to free me right now?"

He frowned. "It's his night off. You're stuck with me, I'm afraid. I have no choice but to touch you, unless you want to spend the night in that chair."

"All right. When you put it that way, how can a girl resist?"

He went to one of the small tables and picked up a box cutter, flipping it open. "Please, hold still, and I won't hurt you."

"Don't have to tell me twice," I said.

He pulled the restraint off of my arm, putting the blade against the edge. A few motions, and he had freed me. He closed the cutter, dropping it onto the table beside him. "I'm going to free you now. Don't think you can fight me and get out of here. Mr. Zito is waiting on the other side of this door with a Taser just for you."

"How chivalrous of you."

He loosened the bonds, freeing me. When I started to get up, he reached out to put his arm around my side and hoist me out, but I pushed him away.

"Told you not to touch me," I said.

He held his hands up. "Fine. I can see chivalry is wasted on you anyway."

I stood, rubbing at my wrists. "Chivalry isn't worth a damn when you're sticking needles in a girl. Now get me back to my room."

======

Fast forward to the next week, or maybe a few weeks later. I can't remember exactly – the old memory, you know? After that scary little trip, things improved for Carla and me. I don't know what Barren told them; I'm not sure I want to know, but within a few nights we got that TV, and they started serving us something other than crappy, flattened sandwiches and water.

Like hamburger, for instance. I had no idea that a Z-grade hamburger could taste so damned good, but it sure did, even if it left a weird chemical aftertaste in my mouth.

I read somewhere that TV was supposed to work like a drug, and while the TV hadn't made me sedate, per se, it helped to be able to watch Law and Order in my prison cell, or whatever you'd call it. Of course, that also didn't mean we were happy. We were just…waiting.

After a few mouthfuls, I looked to Carla. "What do you think is in these?"

She muted the TV. "I'm trying not to think about it. It's delicious. That's all that matters."

"You have a point, but I'm not sure I want to be eating rat." I lifted the bun and looked at the meat: gray. With a splotch of ketchup to brighten the presentation. "Or some other drugs that Barren dreamed up."

She chuckled and turned the volume back up on the TV. "I don't think its rat."

I shook my head and squished the burger back together. "I hope you're right."

"I'm right," she said.

I glanced at her from the corner of my eye. We definitely weren't happy, but some of us were more present than others. Something had changed in Carla since the night that her visions had started creeping into mine. She'd closed herself off, retreating farther into her own head. She hadn't exactly pushed me away, but she also hadn't invited me into her life any further.

I put the burger down and looked right at her. "Has anything changed in your visions?"

She kept her eyes locked on the TV. "Nah. No changes."

"But it's always one of those things you told me about, right? You haven't seen anything…different?" I said.

She considered it. "I've been seeing more of the light."

I leaned forward. "What do you mean?"

"It's there longer?" She took a bite, her eyes still not leaving the screen.

I resisted the very strong urge to run across the room, grab her by her shoulders, and shake her. "I don't understand you."

"You know, it's in my old house. The light stays on longer, so I see a little bit more of the house." She finally looked at me. "Listen, I'm trying to watch the show, do you mind?"

"Please, excuse me," I mumbled, and looked at the screen, where Ice T shook down some guy in a boardroom. I tried to be quiet. I promise you that. I just couldn't let it go. "So…the guy in the motorcycle is from a real experience. The room is from your life. What about the shadow?"

She tightened her jaw and looked at me again. "What do you want from me?"

My anger became too much to contain. "I want some information, so we understand what we're both experiencing."

She looked back to the TV and shook her head. "I don't see why it matters. Let's just try to get on with our lives."

"It matters because we can't stay here forever."

"Whatever."

I took a big hunk of the burger, my jaws working hard, and nearly choked trying to get it down. I drank some water and coughed, hitting myself in the middle of the chest, twice.

She did nothing, and said nothing.

When I'd gotten my composure back, I pressed on. I figured if she could push me, I could give it back in kind. "So listen, is the shadow something that happened in real life? Like when you were little. Maybe it's coming up in the visions, all sideways."

She looked at me again, her eyes on fire. "Why would you ask me that?"

"Because I want to know. Because you're hiding shit, and you're driving me crazy. What's wrong with you?"

"Nothing's wrong with me."

"You don't talk."

She snorted. "That's rich, coming from Ms. 'I-don't-want-to-talk-about-that'"

That stung, but it was true. What could I say? Nothing.

She went on. "That's what I thought. I just don't want to talk about it. Don't I have that right?"

"I'm sorry. You're right. I just want to know, and I'll shut up. I think you're reliving a memory. The shadow has to be somebody, right?"

"Doesn't have to be anybody. Not all dreams are literal. Did you ever play an organ made out of a tree?"

"Well…no," I said.

"There you go. Could just represent my fear left over from the kidnapping or something I didn't digest correctly." She put her burger down. "This isn't just about getting away. What else is going on?"

I sighed. "I've started seeing things from your visions in *my* visions."

That got her full attention. She muted the TV and turned toward me. "Come again?"

"I saw your motorcycle man. I saw your light."

"You're full of it."

"No. Really," I said, and I shared my vision. All of it, including the sky rolling up, the evil darkness reaching for us – and the man in the corn.

When I'd finished, she sat there for a long time, not saying anything.

The woman was driving me crazy. I threw my hands in the air. "Well? Don't you have anything to say about that?"

She chuckled again, but this time, the chuckling stank of desperation and lunacy. It had something to do with the look in her eyes, the way they reflected the dull overhead light.

I didn't like that laughter, and I didn't like that look at all.

"What's so damned funny?" I said.

"I don't know," she said, but she kept right on laughing.

I started to panic, but I laid my plate on the bed, trying to stay calm. "You're scaring me."

She shook her head and snorted. "I'm scaring myself." That didn't stop her from laughing, though. She just kept on, louder and louder, harder and harder.

I slid to the edge of the bed. "Don't you go crazy on me now. We're the only two we got here."

She threw her plate down and stood on the bed, her laughter turning into something that sounded a lot more like screaming.

"What–?"

Before I could say any more, she picked up her burger and threw it at me. I didn't have time to react; it just splattered against my forehead and hit the floor. I reached up and felt where the ketchup had spread, leaving a long smear down toward my nose.

Carla pointed at me and cackled.

In other circumstances, I suppose I might have laughed

along with her, but I wasn't exactly in the laughing mood. "Goddammit," I snarled.

She clapped her hands. "The Bad Man is coming. The Bad Man is coming."

Mimi's words. A chill ran down my spine.

The door slammed open and Zito stood there, eyes wide. "What the sweet Christ is going on in here?"

"She's lost her mind," I said.

"Son of a bitch," he said, and snapped his fingers at her. "You. Get down from there. Come on"

She pointed at him and cackled again, like Zito was the funniest thing she'd ever seen.

"I mean it," he said.

"You're the big man. Stop her now," I said. I couldn't take that laughing anymore; it felt like it was scraping against my brain.

"You out of your mind? *You* talk her down," he said.

I shook my head, extending my palms. "How am I supposed to do that?"

"The Bad Man, the Bad Man," Carla cried.

Maple appeared at the door, wearing a pair of red silk pajamas. "What is the meaning of this? Mr. Zito, get her down right now."

He glared at her. "Fine." He stalked toward her and grappled with her, trying to get hold of her arm as she clapped her hands. It took him a few tries, but he finally got his meat hook around her forearm and wrenched her down to the bed. She squealed, but at least she sounded like herself instead of that half-crazed woman-child.

"Good God, get her out of here. Get her a sedative or something," I said.

Zito wrangled her toward the door. She had fallen quiet, but she kept struggling against him, bucking and kicking.

"Christ, she's like an animal," he said.

"We will deal with her." Maple stepped aside and looked to me. "In future, please do take care not to upset her. She's a very fragile girl."

I put a hand on my chest. "Me? Are you kidding me? I didn't do anything."

"This didn't just happen."

"Yeah, it did. We were just –"

She cut me off with one hand. "I don't care to hear your stories. Simply be more careful."

"Oh, whatever. Goodbye. Get out."

"Do keep this in mind, or there will be repercussions," she said.

"Repercussions my ass."

She left without another word. Crazy. They were all crazy, I decided, and Sam and I were the last sane people in that cabin. I shook my head and picked up the rest of my burger. I didn't need any further proof that they were pushing her too hard, and at some point she wouldn't be able to come back from one of these fits. It was only a matter of time.

I stared at the silent TV and began to plan our escape.

April 20th

I did something that might have been stupid today. Really stupid. As in, I-don't-know-what-I-was-thinking stupid. I should have learned after what went down last time, but holing up in a motel 24/7 isn't as easy as you think. At least this time when I went out I hid my identity pretty well and stayed away from populated areas. Not that there *are* that many populated areas in this hellhole.

It sounds like a dumb justification, but it's true. I went for a walk on a back road, collected a handful of flowers for the motel room, and picked up a few books at a thrift store. I figure if I'm going to end up writing something like a book, I might as well get an idea of what memoirs look like. I also picked up a new journal. I've already almost filled this one up. I'm going to go through these things in no time with how much of my story I still have to tell.

Speaking of which, I might as well get on with the next part. I need to talk about the escape - or what was supposed to be the escape. It might bring me down, but I'm compelled to talk about it. Besides, it changed everything. Without the attempt, I might still be stuck in that room. As much as I bitch about living life on the run, I'd much rather be here than there.

======

I wiped the blood from Carla's forehead and leaned close to her. "Can you hear me?"

She coughed, but she didn't open her eyes. "Sure."

"What did they do to you?" I dabbed a bit more blood from the place where her hair and her forehead met. The bleeding had slowed to an ooze, and I could see the serrated skin of a nasty little knock just above her hairline. It made quite a match for the rising purple bruise on her cheek.

"I don't remember all of it," she said.

"Tell me what you can."

She opened her eyes, gazing off to her right, toward the floor. "I remember you and me talking about my visions. Somewhere in there, my emotions just turned off. It was weird, but hard to panic when you're not feeling much of anything. The next thing to shut off was my brain in general. I was having a hard time even forming words. Then I almost floated up out of my body, but still held on to it."

"What do you mean?"

She met my eyes. "You know. Like someone else was controlling me, or I only had partial control. I watched myself from a distance doing crazy shit. I was jumping up and down, I think?"

I nodded.

"I remember Zito grabbing hold of me."

"He wrestled you down on the bed. You screamed," I said.

"Was I jumping on the bed?"

"Uh huh."

"Why would I do that?" she said.

"Damned if I know."

"Right." She rolled over and tried to sit up, but winced and grabbed her head when she was halfway up.

I put a hand on her chest and pushed her back down. "Don't rush yourself."

She punched the bed with the back of both fists. "I'm losing my goddamn mind. But who wouldn't?"

"How much are they giving you in your sessions now?"

"No idea. A lot." She touched the bruise on her cheek. "They got me good, huh?"

"Do you remember how that happened?"

"I remember throwing myself around, trying to claw his eyes out. I must have been a lot more aware than before, but I still couldn't pull myself together. I kept telling my limbs to do stuff, to calm down and just *be*, but they kept flailing. Anyway, Zito hauled off and slapped me. I probably deserved it," she said.

"How are you going to deserve something like that?"

"I *did* try to maim the man."

I couldn't hold back the smile. "Well, yeah. But I think that should get you a medal."

She smiled, too. "Too bad I didn't succeed, huh?"

I stood, stretching my legs. "We could use a win."

She sighed. "Yeah, well, I don't know how much of a win it really is. He hit me hard, you know?" she said, and rubbed her cheek.

"I'm sorry."

"Not your fault. Anyway, he slapped me, I fell on the couch, and Maple was there. Just, there. I didn't know she could move that fast. She had her hands on her hips and…did you see her PJs?"

I laughed. "Good Lord, yes. You know those were sex clothes." I put a hand on my mouth. "You think Zito's tapping that?"

She waved her hands. "Oh God, I don't even want to think

about it. I'm going to be sick."

I whipped the chair around and sat down, resting my arms on the high back. "Tell me now. We've already got to cut Zito's balls off for that," I said, pointing at the bruise, "but what else did they do?"

"I think Maple sent Zito into Room 3, and he came out with a syringe."

My eyes widened. "The shit that makes you see stuff?"

She waved a hand. "Nah, more like a sedative. They shot me full of it, and after a while I felt myself calming down, you know, settling into my body. My arms and legs started listening to me. I had full control of my body for about a minute, then I started going limp. I had no clue what they'd shot me full of, you know, so I panicked. It was like a nightmare; I told my body to get up and run, but it refused to obey. So I tried to talk and tell them that it was too much, but that came out all slushy. Hell, Zito laughed at me." She pulled her blanket up over her body.

My heart wrenched a bit at the pain I saw in her eyes. "Prick."

She looked away. "Where was Sam?"

"Barren told me it was his night off, whatever that means. Where else can he go?"

"I might know. I saw something."

"What?" I said.

She took a heavy breath. "I woke up, in the middle of the night. Who knows for sure? They leave those damned lights on all the time out there."

"Can't have us sneaking out under shadow of dark," I said.

"I guess. Anyway, Zito and Maple were mumbling to each other, and I noticed they were standing right outside Room 2, and staying there, like they had a purpose in there."

I straightened up, clutching the chair. "Room 2?"

"Yeah. I couldn't understand what they were saying - I wasn't fully there. I fell asleep for a bit, but I woke up when she opened the door."

I had my own theories about Room 2. It didn't consume me, but I thought about it from time to time - how could I not? I'd never seen - or even more importantly *heard* - anyone go in there. I figured that, at some point, I should have heard them fetching a box of Wheaties or what have you from in there if they stored our food there. So I'd developed my theory: it was a monitoring station for what they were doing to us, the place where they compiled both the information from the front room and Barren's reports, though I didn't buy for a second that those reports were enough for what they needed. You don't spend that much money and not have a way to capture the data.

But if she had seen the inside of Room 2...even some crazy impression? I might be able to work with that.

I leaned forward. "What did you see?"

"You're going to think I'm crazy. You probably already do, but you could think I'm even crazier."

I waved a hand. "Worst case, you were tripping off whatever they gave you, so come on. You have to tell me."

"She opened the door, and I saw this shining blue light."

"Say what?"

"Like I said, blue light. But not super-bright light, like Christmas lights or anything. It was dark blue. It...it looked like a net of blue lights hanging inside the door."

I tried to process this. Could they have just hung lights over the door? If so, why would they do it? "What does that mean?"

She shrugged. "At first I thought it might just be strands of lights, but Maple stepped through the lights, and just vanished. I don't know where she went, but..." She put her fist to her mouth, blew, and opened her hand. "Poof. Gone. Like she went to another world."

I cocked an eyebrow. "Another world." Gina's theories came to mind. Could she have been right, without knowing it?

"I know it sounds crazy, and I can't be completely sure that it happened, but..."

"But you think she really left."

She nodded.

"What makes you think it's another world?" I said.

"That's what my gut tells me. Told me. Deep down, I know it's true."

I studied her for a long time. Crazy she might be, but my own gut told me that she was telling the truth, or at least the truth as it felt to her. "Go on."

"Not much more to say. She was gone. Zito closed the door, and that was that. She didn't come back last night."

"Did Zito stay out there?"

"I think so. I remember waking up at one point and him sitting on the end of the couch, wide awake, staring out into space."

"So wait, if he only slapped you, then how did you hit your head?"

She rolled her eyes. "Oh. That. I rolled off the couch when I woke up this morning. Hit the floor hard. That's when Zito picked me up and dragged me in here. Next thing I knew, you were cleaning off my forehead like a mother hen."

"Speaking of which," I said, and took another chance to swipe at her forehead, but she batted me away, laughing.

This was an attempt to lighten the mood, but also to steal a moment and gather my thoughts. She throws a screw loose, they take her out there, dope her up. She wakes up in the middle of the night and sees Maple going into Room 2, only it's some sort of Christmas display into another world. Then she goes back to sleep, wakes up in the morning, falls, and hits her head.

Something seemed off, but I couldn't figure out exactly what. If I had felt that we had more time, I would have taken it to Sam, but our hand had been forced. We couldn't wait for me to figure it all out.

"Penny for your thoughts," she said.

"Thinking about how we've got to get out of here. They're going to kill one of us if this keeps up."

She looked toward the door and lowered her voice. "You think they can hear us?"

"If they can, they would've done something about it already."

"I suppose you're right. When?"

I could answer that question, no problem. "Now. Like, right now. Within the next hour, at least. Maple's going to be here soon. Zito has to be worn out from being up all night. It might be the only window we get."

"You think we can use our plan?"

As smart as she seemed, she could still surprise me with her stupidity – or naiveté. Not sure which that was. "It's got to be that one. No time to come up with something else. You need to go over it again?"

She rubbed her forehead. "No. I've been thinking about it for the last two weeks."

"You think you can handle it?"

"My head hurts, but I'm not going to break, if that's what you mean."

"All right, then." I rose and went to the sink. I took a good long moment to rinse and wring the blood from the washcloth. I didn't so much have to build up my courage as prepare myself for the inevitability of my own death should we fail. I wouldn't call it a feeling of fear, but more resignation - and the resignation made me want to sit down and do nothing. Not easy to overcome when you're about to stare down the lion.

But I had to do it. No, *we* had to do it. This couldn't go on. I laid the washcloth on the sink. It was time to set the stage.

======

Nausea crept up on me when we got about halfway through our preparations, but I didn't think much of it at the time; hell, I don't even remember what I attributed it to. Nerves, probably. I definitely didn't connect it to Maple's arrival, but within a few minutes of getting that feeling in the depths of my gut I heard her voice in the front room, saying something to Zito in snappy tones.

Carla and I locked eyes. I could see the fear in there, so I mouthed at her: "It'll be okay." Then I whispered: "remember the original plan."

She nodded.

We had noticed a pattern, and had counted on it that morning: every time they arrived, Zito entered the room first, a few steps ahead of Maple. I presume his job was to ensure that we weren't going to pull a fast one. Once Zito thought things were clear, Maple strolled in, imperious as ever.

The original plan accounted for this pattern. We'd switched it up just a little when we believed Zito to be their first line of defense. Maple's arrival screwed with those plans, but we thought we might be okay. Just go with the original plan and things would work out.

Of course, life never works that way for me.

For the first time, they deviated from the pattern. Maybe you could blame Zito's exhaustion. Maybe you could blame Maple's bloodlust; either way, Maple bounced in first, her face lit up and ready for battle.

She had a half a second or so to squeak when she saw our empty beds.

A step behind her, Zito started moving first. It could have been bad if he hadn't been so tired. He got the pistol out of his pocket just before I appeared from behind the door, holding the TV aloft. Maple reached for one of my arms, trying to arrest my movement. She didn't have the strength to stop me, but she probably saved Zito's life. She did just enough to push the TV sideways. It clipped the side of his head; he cried out and fell back into the door with a thud.

My sideways motion knocked me into the door beside him, and I lost all control of the TV. Zito hit the floor just about the same time that the TV hit my foot. I screamed and went backwards, tripping over Zito and falling ass-first onto the floor.

Maple made a break for it, trying to jump over him and get to the relative safety of the front room.

Carla appeared from behind the dresser, swinging a pillow case full of soap bars that we'd hidden over the last two weeks. Her first shot missed and smacked into the door.

I kicked one foot out, catching Maple's heel.

She waved her arms, trying to keep her balance, but I'd gotten her good. Carla pushed her, sending her backwards. She hit Carla's bed, falling right into it with a thump and a snarl.

Carla followed her with the pillowcase. One sick, heavy smack and Maple stopped moving.

I stumbled to my feet and pushed Zito into the bedroom before picking up his pistol. "Did you just kill her?"

Carla dropped the pillowcase and came to join me, her eyes wide. "No, you can't kill a demon."

"That could have been really bad," I said, and closed the door behind us, making sure that the lock latched behind us.

"The one time…"

"Right. Let's move." We reached the big front door in moments. I cocked the pistol and aimed it at the complicated lock above the door handle.

A familiar voice spoke from behind us. "I wouldn't do that if I were you."

Bloch. "Yeah, and what if I –" I glanced over my shoulder, and the words died in my mouth.

Bloch sneered at me as he held Carla against his chest, both arms wrapped around her - one for her neck, one for her head.

"You wouldn't dare," I said.

"Why don't you shoot that lock and find out?"

I swiveled the gun and aimed it at him instead.

Being the gentlemen that he was, he pulled at her neck, putting her right in the path of my pistol.

"Come on now, that's not fair. This is between us," I said.

"I think Zito and Maple would disagree. What about you?"

I didn't know what to say. I wasn't ready to give up. Not yet.

He pushed her forward. "Drop the pistol. You shoot me and I'll break this fat bitch's neck."

I cocked my head, looking at him around the pistol. "Now, see, I know that's not true. You're not vindictive like that."

"Who said anything about vindictive? The word is practical. Right now it isn't *practical* for you to ventilate my head."

I steadied the gun. I wasn't a complete newbie at this; my

father had taken me shooting a few times (at least, I think he did), teaching me trigger discipline and the proper shooting stance. I *might* be able to get a shot off and hit the side of his face, at the very least, but I didn't want to take the risk unless things got really desperate. "Let her go. I've got an eye, I've got a finger, and I can use both."

"Think you can hit me before I snap her neck in two?"

Carla tried to say something, but she had the issue of contending with a slab of beef crushing her windpipe.

"The lady speaks." He looked at her. "Trying to decide if you want to live or die?"

"Leave her alone," I said.

"Put the gun down and everything goes back to…well, close to normal. You go back to your rooms, and research continues as planned. Things will never be the same if you shoot me, or I kill her. Even if you escape, you'll never be safe. We have people everywhere. You could hide on a remote island or at the top of a mountain. We would find you."

"You're bluffing."

He raised an eyebrow. "How did we find you in the first place, then? How did we pick her out of all the people on Earth? Think about it."

I wanted to be stronger than I felt, but my bowels complained and my legs shook.

He went on. "I'm not saying there won't be repercussions, but even beyond these walls there's no such thing as freedom for you."

My hand shook, the barrel trembling.

He grinned and tightened his grip on Carla; she made another choking sound and started to turn blue in the face. "Got to choose soon."

I lowered the hammer on the pistol and held my hands in the air. "All right I'm going to put the gun down. When I do, you let her go?"

Carla tried to choke something out, I'm guessing she wanted to tell me not to do it, but I wouldn't listen even if I could understand.

"Deal," I said. I knelt and laid the pistol on the floor, keeping my free hand open for him to see. "I'm unarmed. Let her go."

He loosened his grip and pushed her toward me, hard. She stumbled across the room and I tried to catch her, but I wasn't strong enough. We bounced into the front door, giving him time to snatch the pistol from the floor.

He leveled the pistol at us. "I knew you could be reasonable." He backed toward the door to Room 1, keeping his eyes trained on us. At last he turned the knob, and Zito almost spilled out, blood gushing from the side of his head.

"Wuzza fuck?" he murmured.

"Room 3. Now," Bloch said without looking at him.

Zito couldn't object even if he wanted to. He just stumbled across the room while Bloch kept the pistol on us. He almost fell through the door to Room 3, slamming it closed behind him.

Bloch looked from the door back to us. "Get in your room. Now. No debate."

Carla rubbed her throat and shook her head. "Son of a bitch. I ought to kill you now."

"Wouldn't be the smartest move you've ever made," he said.

I stepped in front of her. "Not now. They've got us beat." I met his eyes. "*This* time." Don't get me wrong, the failure had left me heartbroken and a little sick to my stomach, but I wasn't ready to back down yet. There would be another chance.

Bloch kept the pistol on us as we shuffled into Room 1. "Good girl. You're learning."

We both jumped as Maple croaked, "you have no idea." She appeared from behind the door, fists on her hips, nostrils flaring. We froze, pinned to the spot by her glare. A beat, and she slapped Carla across the face. It sounded almost as loud as the sound that I had expected from the pistol.

Maple was far from done. "How dare you? I've done nothing but protect you. Who do you think fought for that television? Who do you think protected you? You have no idea what you've unleashed. But you will. You will find out. Your days as a guest are over."

We began to back away from her.

Bloch pressed up against us, stopping our progress. "I told you you were giving them too much leeway, but did you listen to me?" I could hear the smirk in his voice.

"Duly noted, Mr. Bloch." Her eyes never left us. "I think I'll listen to you more in the future. How about we start with a night in the restraints for our friends here?"

"Sounds like a start." Bloch closed one of his slab-of-ham hands around my upper arm, and pushed me into the room.

April 22nd

Obviously, I didn't write yesterday. Nothing major happened; no life-or-death chases, no disappearances, not even a Dairy Queen in sight. I just didn't want to write, so I spent most of the day with my good friends vodka and orange juice.

I refuse to apologize for missing a day, or even care about it. I've had enough caring for a while. In fact, I've decided that since I'm to the end of this journal, this is where it ends. I might as well throw away the empty journal because there's no way in Hell I can finish telling this story. It just hurts too much. I was probably naïve to expect this thing to help me instead of hurting me, but there you go. That's me, the babe in the woods, having to learn *everything* the hard way.

Damn it, it's so easy now to see where we went wrong. Little things we could have done differently, signs that Bloch might have been there.

Let me get the story of our failed escape over with and never write about this whole miserable mess again. I've had enough.

======

The door cracked open, letting the pale light into our room. It spilled across Carla's bed and onto my own, illuminating my bruised legs. The torn muscles in my shoulder screamed at me as I turned my head, looking at the large form that stood there.

I sighed. "Oh. You. Get out of here."

The shadow at the door didn't say anything for a long time. At last he said, "I am sorry".

"I don't care, Sam. Get out."

"You don't mean that." He stepped inside, turning on the overhead light.

I cried out, my eyes exploding in pain. "Asshole."

He turned off the lights. "I apologize. Your hostility is understandable, but I am here to help."

Carla stirred. "Sam. Can you get us loose?" She lifted her right arm as much as she could, which wasn't a whole lot.

He looked away. "It would not be safe for any of us."

"Not safe for you, you mean," I said.

Carla wasn't about to give up on our "savior", though she had to know he was nothing of the sort. It irritated me. The guy had been MIA for days now, and he shows up expecting a hero's welcome?

Well, fuck him, I thought.

Carla, though… "How about food? Can you do that? Please? They haven't given us anything since last night."

I heard the hint of a smile in his voice, and I wanted to smile in response, despite myself. "Yes," he said, "I can do that. One moment." He held up one finger and disappeared back into the front room.

"You're crazy. We can't trust that man," I said.

"Do you see many other choices?"

I didn't have an answer for that, so we waited for him in silence. My stomach had shut up a long time before, but the very concept of food got it growling again. I couldn't imagine what he might bring. Sandwiches? Chips? Hamburgers? My head spun.

After what seemed like an eternity, the door opened again,

and he slipped inside.

"I must turn on the light again," he said, and flipped the switch. He carried two small plates, both stacked with large sandwiches. He laid them on the dresser and crossed the room to us.

He stopped in front of me as he produced a key from his pocket. "If I undo one of your hands, will you harm me?"

The son of a bitch had a key. "Tempting. But no. This is where violence got us." I rattled the handcuff.

"I am capable of defending myself, of course." He leaned over me, working on the handcuff. Heat rolled off his body in waves, and I was suddenly aware of just how close his flesh was to mine. I wondered what it would be like to have him lying on top of me, his warmth consuming me…

Cut it out. This guy isn't helping you. He's doing what he has to do.

He freed my wrist.

His blue eyes met mine. "I apologize. I can only free one hand for each of you, and please understand –"

I grabbed hold of one of his lapels with my free hand, twisting it in my fist. "Why?"

He slowly removed my hand and took a step back. "Please understand that even this is technically breaking the rules." He saw the look in my eyes, and went on. "I wish that I could take you away from all of this tonight. Please believe me. I cannot."

"Why not?"

He said nothing and instead went to free Carla. Leaning close to her, breathing on her…

I closed my eyes. Stop this nonsense. Now.

A click, and Carla held her freed wrist. "Thanks for caring. Seriously."

He got this weird expression: his mouth tightened, and his eyes narrowed. I didn't get it then, but I think I do now. I'd hurt him more than I realized, and was having trouble thinking of himself as anything but an evil asshole. I've seen that look since then. "It is all that one could be expected to do."

He went to the dresser, picked up one of the plates, and approached me, keeping his eyes averted. "I do not agree with their methods, but it *is* difficult to see why they would continue to afford you with your previous accommodations after you attacked them."

I took the plate from him. "If that's your way of saying we fucked up, then I agree." I lifted a slice of bread. "What is this?"

"It is all that they will allow me to feed you."

"Stale bread and old bologna?"

Carla spoke up. "Oh, don't bitch. Better than nothing."

Sam didn't join in. He didn't say anything, in fact. He just picked up the other plate and took it to Carla.

"I asked you a question," I said.

He turned toward me. "They call it 'conditioning."

"Conditioning for what?" Carla said.

"What they think of as respect. They equate respect with fear." He glanced at me, and I saw that weird look again. He went to the wall by the door and leaned against it, arms crossed over his chest.

I picked up the stale sandwich, jamming it into my mouth. "Where were you, anyway?" I asked, spewing crumbs of the nasty bread.

"I cannot answer that. Not now."

Carla looked up to Sam. "What have you been doing?"

He held up a hand. For a second, with the way he was standing, the way he looked…something felt familiar about it, as if he channeled someone.

Gina. Gina used to stand like that.

If he did it on purpose, he didn't say anything about it. "I was working on freeing you. Both of you, but you moved too quickly and endangered yourselves. Now, things are more difficult. I do not believe that this 'conditioning' will be permanent, but you could have destroyed everything for which I have been working."

"How about you give us a hint of what you're trying to do?" I said.

"I will tell you when the time is right."

"Oh, cut the bullshit, Sam. I'm sick of hearing it."

"I do not blame either of you for hating me."

"We don't hate you," Carla said, and looked to me.

I didn't want to admit it. I wanted to hate him, but I just couldn't. "Fine. We don't hate you."

"Thank you," he said. "I do what I must, but it is not always the *right* thing."

Carla snorted. "Like I give a shit. Where did doing the right thing ever get me, except having needles jabbed into me and getting my brains scrambled?"

He sighed. "Things will worsen. You are no longer favored."

"I'm fine with that. About time we got some equality in treatment here."

"Are you crazy? They're pushing you harder than me. If they push you any harder…"

Sam nodded. "Your monitoring will also become stricter. They are about to plant listening devices in this room. Frankly, I was surprised to learn that they have not already installed them."

Carla finished off her sandwich and laid the plate on the bed. "Shocker. Are we only supposed to talk about ponies and rainbows now?"

Sam scooped the plate from the bed, taking it to the dresser. "Communication is the least of your worries. If they feel that they cannot trust you, then they must rush their project."

I extended a hand toward her. "See? Just like I said. Isn't that a bundle of joy?" I said.

Carla crossed her arms over her chest. "I'm just going to have to kill one of them when they take me in there."

"How?" I said.

"Slug Zito in the mouth, grab a needle? *Something.*"

"You think I haven't tried that?"

Sam held his hands out. "It is frightening, yes, but you must be patient. There is a great power at work here, and I do not entirely think that you will be allowed to die."

I cocked my head. "What does that mean? What do you know?"

"Not much. Rumors, whispers. They say that you cannot die."

I exchanged a glance with Carla. "I don't get it."

Carla snapped her fingers. "This has something to do with Room 2. I just know it."

"How do you figure that?"

"I…I don't know. Something in the back of my mind. Like something I used to know."

Sam spoke. "What do you know of Room 2?"

"Well, we know that there are more than supplies in there," I said.

His face remained impassive. He might as well have written *I know a lot more than that* on his forehead. "Indeed."

Carla glared at him. "You know something. What's in there? You can tell us. I saw the blue light one night when they took me out there."

He chuckled. "They wondered if you had witnessed it. I am glad to hear that you did."

"That's all well and good, but are you going to tell us what it means?" I said.

"I have no answer."

I tried to jump out of the bed after him, but the remaining handcuff kept me locked in place. "Damn you, I'm sick of this inscrutable sage shit. I thought you cared. You're playing with our lives."

His face fell. "I do care. Of course I care. I…I am sorry. I do not mean to play games with you. I only understand things imperfectly."

I bit back my anger. The light had dawned on me: anger just wasn't going to get me anywhere with him. "Look, Sam. We're friends, right?"

"I like to believe so."

"Then listen. We need more information about what's going on here. If we'd known more about, say, Room 2, then we wouldn't have gotten caught out with our pants down. Agreed?"

He shook his head. "I do not agree. Room 2 would have been inaccessible regardless of your plans."

I slapped my hand on the bed, but kept my tone even. "Do you understand how powerless we are?"

He put a hand over his eyes. "Of course I do. I just fear that if you know, and they discover that you have that knowledge, it will mean that your life is forfeit. I can't lose you, too. Not after all this, and I will do everything in my power to protect you."

Carla nodded. "That sucks, but it makes sense, you know. Not like we could do anything with the information, anyway."

I didn't like it, I didn't want to hear it, but it was the truth. I crossed my arms over my chest. "I don't want you to forget the situation here, buddy."

He turned his head, gazing right into my eyes. "I would never do such a thing. Ever."

I met his eyes, and my defenses dropped. Everything faded away, including Carla's presence. "I want to believe you."

"You can."

"I'll try."

Electricity passed between us; at the time I had no idea if it was good or bad, but it was *something.* We stayed that way for a long, long moment, sharing in each others' concern and fear. As angry as he had made me, I still cared about the guy. It didn't make sense to me at the time, but of course anger was not the opposite of what I felt for him, and maybe that anger helped me realize it.

We had been friends up to that point, even with the rocky nature of the power imbalance in our relationship. At that moment, we became something more that I didn't understand but was willing to take on faith, at least for a little while.

Carla cleared her throat, and the moment passed. "This is all great, and I'm happy for you, don't get me wrong – but there's still the matter of what we're going to do now."

Sam took my empty plate and carried it to the dresser. "We wait. There is nothing more to be done."

She rolled on her back and pushed up on her knees, sliding herself into a sitting position with one hand. "You know we're going to go crazy waiting."

He faced us. "I will do my best to avoid this. To help you. But know that my hands are also tied."

Carla sighed. "As long as we'll make a move at some point. That's all I ask."

"We will," I said.

That spark had given me something more than a connection to Sam. It had given me trust in him - no matter if I liked the choices that he had made. I *knew* that he would follow through this time, even if he had to die doing it. The guy didn't exactly hide his feelings well. It was written in the way he stood, in the way he moved his arms. "Kelli speaks the truth. The signs will reveal themselves when the time is right. For now, you must trust me. I have to put the cuffs back in place."

Carla groaned. "Oh no."

Those saucer eyes pled with us. "I am sorry. I have no choice. If they know what has happened here, I will not be able to help you any further, and it could well get worse for you."

I would have found it hard to imagine it getting much worse, but an image of being cuffed to a spot on the floor popped into my head. It could definitely get worse. "How long will we be cuffed up here?"

"No more than a week."

Carla gave a shocked little gasp. "A goddamned week?" I looked over to her and saw that she had hidden her free arm inside of her shirt.

Sharp thinking, girl. I almost laughed.

"Again, I apologize," he said, and approached me, motioning with one hand.

"No way around this, huh? Don't suppose I could offer you something to change your mind?"

He just shook his head.

"Fine." I extended my hand toward him. "You're going to make this worth our while, right?"

"Of course." He took my wrist, pulling it into place in the handcuff. "They have provided…facilities. Correct?"

"Chamber pots aren't exactly the lady's choice."

"I never meant...I...just wanted to be certain that they had provided for your needs."

"It could be better," I said, and I think we both noticed that he still held my hand at the same time. We gazed at our entwined fingers, and I tightened my grip, hoping that I could hold on to him just a bit longer.

He pulled his hand away. "I will do what I can."

I wondered if I was blushing. "If they feed us more than bread and water, I think we'll be all right."

"I will speak to them." He went to Carla and held his hand out.

She shook her head, pressing her arm tighter against her body. "I don't want to."

"You must."

"Come on," I said. "It's only for a while."

Resigned, she pulled her arm out of her shirt. "You'd better make this worth it, Lurch."

"I will do my best." He clamped her into the handcuff.

"TV's out of the question?"

He frowned. "You mean the one that you destroyed?"

She gave a sheepish grin. "Well, Kelli destroyed it, but...yeah."

He stared at her for a long, long time without saying anything. He didn't need to say much.

Carla buckled. "All right, all right. Stop staring. You've got bug eyes."

He went to the door and turned back to look at us. "Do not breathe a word of this after tonight. By the time you wake up, the changes will likely be finished."

"And after that?" I said.

"As I said, we wait. Once you are free, we will plan our next move." He gave a gentle nod. "Good night. Try to remain strong." With that, he was gone.

Carla allowed herself to slide back down to a lying position. Once she was down, she scoffed. "Remain strong. Has to sound so easy from his point of view."

How quickly our points of view had switched. I wondered if the connection that had changed my mind had done the same thing for Carla, then dismissed the thought. "Give the guy a break. He's doing the best he can."

"The best he can do is to get us out of here."

"No argument here," I said, and a silence fell between us. I felt a shift in our already-fragile alliance, and I didn't like the idea of where that might lead. I just hoped that Sam could get us out of here before the whole thing went upside-down.

=======

And that's enough. I can't do this anymore. I need to spend more time remembering why I loved him in the first place and less time focusing on this. I want my life to be a living document, not these painful fossils, so I'm burying this thing in my bag and that's the end of it.

May: Knock my Head Against the Sky

May 4th

Of course that wasn't the end of it. Not by a long shot. Oh, I believed I might be ready to move on with things – it seemed to just be the right time. If I couldn't escape the hell of our life these days, I could at least walk away from the story and not be haunted by the lingering emotions or dream. So, mea culpa. I admit it: I got it all wrong. Guess I had even more to learn about myself. Hey, it only took me a few weeks of solid boozing to figure it out, which might mean I'm improving on the "getting to know me" scale.

This is a long way of saying that I'm trying this again.

No, I have to do this again. Because I see Carla in my dreams.

As I write this, we're holed up in a safe house somewhere near the border. We hooked up with the Underground in the last place, and they gave us a warning: the noose was closing in on us again.

It made no sense. How could they know where we had gotten to? In the end, it didn't matter. Strange men showed up in town just the same.

We had to go with the Underground. At least they have a plan.

Now the Underground is taking us somewhere. This is the first step in something much bigger. They haven't given us many details on that and that's how I like it. Sure, I'd like to have some control over our destiny. Who wouldn't? We just can't have that right now – the last few stops have proven that. This thing is just too big for us.

At least now we can hide in plain sight.

We got here a few days ago, and since then it's been a case of hurry-up-and-wait. I keep reminding myself that it's almost over. We'll cross over in the next few days, once we've met up with the local cell and gotten our bona fides. The less said, the better, so that's all I'm going to write about that here. I can only imagine how the folks in the Underground would react if they saw this.

I've been having trouble focusing. I keep wondering what might happen when we cross that border. Sam keeps telling me that we're walking into a war zone. The soldiers think that the war is about drugs and power, and it is, partially. It's something else, too: something to do with why we're here in the first place. He either doesn't know the full story, or won't elaborate. That gets my mind going all over again.

This isn't what I need to write about. I need to pick up the story again.

I think I'm finally ready.

======

"Wake up, kid."

The voice sounded like gravel, scratching my skin, sinking into the depths of my dreams.

"I said wake up, kid."

It sounded like…

I sat up in bed. "Gina?"

Sure enough. Gina stood by the doorway like she'd never

left. She leaned against the wall, arms crossed over her chest, her jaw jutting out defiantly. "Surprised?" she said, and uncrossed her arms.

"You could say that." I was stalling for time, my mind trying to grasp this. First Mom, now Gina? What was going on here?

I looked toward Carla's bed and saw that her body rose and fell in slow breaths. Asleep. Just like the last time the dead had come calling, though I shouldn't have been so surprised; she'd been sleeping a lot since they'd finally let us out of the restraints. You'd think she was trying to find a way to restrain *herself.*

"She's out cold, and she's not waking up any time soon," Gina said.

"How do you know?"

She winked. "There are *some* perks to being dead."

That sent a jolt of adrenaline through me. "So you are dead."

"Only explanation that makes sense to me. What do you think?"

"I think I'm losing my mind."

She smiled. "Normally, seeing your second ghost might help you realize it's not about you, but you were never good at getting that."

"I guess not." Surreal. I should have been crawling out of my skin at this point, yet my mind kept coming back to the point that this was *Gina*. The same Gina who had held my hair back when they'd given me a little too much in Room 3 and I had to puke in the sink. The one who'd talked me down from slicing my wrists more than a few times in those early days.

In the flesh. Well, sort of.

I shook my head. "How did you get here?"

She shrugged. "One minute I'm watching my body from outside as they try to revive me, next I'm standing here in front of you."

"No tunnel? No pearly gates?"

"If there was, I don't remember it."

"So you didn't learn anything from dying?" I said.

She scratched her head. "I learned it sucked. I learned there's a reason people are so afraid of it." She crossed the room and sat on the chair before the keyboard. I couldn't tell if her weight affected the chair at all. Was she even there? Did that question mean anything?

She went on. "You know, I *must* have learned something, because I do know a lot more than I ever did before. Like your friend over there sleeping."

"What else?"

"Well, why we're showing up." She saw my eyes light up and held her hand toward me to calm me down. "I haven't pieced together all the particulars, but we're here for a reason." She glanced at Carla and then back to me, running her tongue around the inside of her mouth.

"Does it have something to do with her?" I asked.

"I think so, yeah."

"Is she bringing you people here?"

"In a manner of speaking. I can't explain it all – I get this *vibe* from her, like she's pulling me toward her at all times. I couldn't tell you why, though."

I sighed. "All right, fine. Do you at least know why you're here?"

She smiled. "Finally, an easy one. You've turned into quite the ball buster."

"Times have changed. I had to watch out for myself."

"So they have. That's why I'm here, too, because things have changed, and you're not as safe as you think you are, no matter how insecure you feel."

That put me in mind of the cameras and microphones that must surround us. "I shouldn't even be talking to you."

She might have been able to read my mind. "They won't hear me."

"Oh even better. They'll think I'm batshit crazy."

She smiled, and I saw an echo of the woman that had fought for me on that first night: protective and aloof at the same time. "Maybe they already think that. That can be an advantage, you know, even when they watch you so closely because they don't know *what* you're going to do."

"Sure doesn't feel like an advantage. Anyway, did you really come all this way just to tell me things have changed? I know that, thank you very much."

"I'm not talking about the same thing you're talking about, honey. Yes, your life is shit right now. Nobody would deny it. I'm trying to keep it from getting worse."

My turn to cross my arms over my chest. "How you going to make that happen?"

"By putting you on your guard. Your last visitor told you to watch out for Carla and make sure she's safe," she said.

I shifted in the bed, inclining my head to one side. I didn't want to meet her eyes. "I screwed that up. I tried to get her out, and...well, you know. Things changed. But I tried." I raised my head, trying to beg her forgiveness with just my eyes.

"You being good was never the problem, and it still isn't. You just had to toughen up."

I remembered the scared girl who'd offered to do anything for them if they just wouldn't hurt her. How far I'd come since that night. "I think I went too far in the wrong direction."

"That might be, but the hard-ass thing can be sorted out

later. You need that right now. You need to protect yourself, especially from that girl."

My head snapped toward Carla. I could only really see the back of her head. "Things *have* gone sideways since she got here."

"You know why, deep down."

"I know something's not right, and what they're doing to her isn't helping matters."

She made her finger into a pistol, pointed at me. "You got it. Think of her like uranium. She could be used for good, or she could be used to blow everything around you to hell and gone."

I glanced at Carla. Innocent or not, I sensed the truth in Gina's words. "I take it what they're doing isn't exactly Atoms for Peace?"

"That's one way of putting it. Mark my words; she's going to destroy everything you hold dear."

"How? I don't hold much dear anymore."

Gina cocked her head. "Don't you?"

It occurred to me in a flash. I think I blushed. "I don't know what you're talking about."

"Of course you don't."

I wasn't going to take that bait. Why would I discuss my relationship with Sam – if it even was that – with a dead person? Even if Gina did happen to be that dead person. "I don't see how she would take that away from me."

"You read the tea leaves, sugar. She's hiding *something* from you, and I think you know it."

I did. I'd sensed it all along. Then again, wasn't I hiding things from her? "Well…" I said.

"It's something that will change everything. You'll understand things in a whole different light when you find out."

"What is it?"

She sighed and spread her hands: *haven't a clue.* "That's the damned thing. I just know that she is, and that I'm here to tell you this." She glanced at Carla, and something passed over her face. Resentment? Jealousy? I wasn't sure.

I pondered this. Maybe Gina's message had more to do with Carla's power than her knowledge, but if even she didn't know for sure, what could I do? "You think I should grab her and make her tell me?"

"Nah. I don't think that would do you any good. I don't think she's admitted it to herself yet, so no way she's telling you. You might as well try to reach oil by digging with a spoon. It's going to have to come up on its own."

I ran a frustrated hand through my hair. "So why tell me? Why come all this way and spook the shit out of me to tell me something that I can't do anything about?"

She stood up. "If you really think there's nothing you can do with that info, you're not as smart as I guessed." She went for the door.

"Amuse me, then. Fill in the idiot."

She bent forward, her eyes intense. "You can *protect* yourself. Don't you dare believe everything she says. I should know. I was the queen of denial." She tapped her chest.

"Right. You're right. I'm wrong. I can protect myself. Like you said."

She sniffed. "Exactly."

I met her eyes, trying to push some anger out at her and instead just finding myself feeling so *sad.* "Damn you. Why'd you have to leave me? We were supposed to look out for each other."

"You think I wanted to leave? Like maybe death was an enjoyable little side-trip? Because I'll tell you, it wasn't."

"No, that's not what I mean. I just wish you were still here."

"I'm here now."

I shook my head. "But you're going to go and leave me alone with her."

"Listen, that's the way shit goes sometimes, kid. Besides, you had to figure out how to stand on your own."

"By shriveling up inside?"

"It won't last, I can promise you that. You're not like me. You're too pure."

"Whatever."

She crossed the room, going for the door.

"Where are you going?" I said.

She looked over her shoulder at me, frowning. "Sorry, kid. I can't stay for long."

"Important appointment?"

"Something's pulling me away... or maybe pushing." She looked at Carla again. "Doesn't matter. I've got to go either way. You remember what I said. We'll see each other again soon enough. Don't worry."

The handle turned in her hand, but it didn't: I saw it in both the open and closed state. I wondered what the world looked like to her.

"Hey, listen. I loved...love you," I said.

She smiled. "Thank you for that. Love you too, kid. See you later." She pulled open a phantom version of the door and walked through, vanishing.

I stared at the door for a moment, willing her to come back through, maybe to take me out of there and with her. A stupid idea, but could the Other Side really be as bad as this place?

Stirring from Carla's bed broke the spell. I glanced over and met her eye as she rolled over.

"Who was that?" she said.

"Who was who?"

She pushed herself up on her elbows. "The woman who just walked out of here."

She knew. Somehow. I began to tell her, but Gina's words pulled me up short: *don't trust her*. "I thought you were asleep."

"I was, up until she opened the door. Then I realized I'd been hearing her talking for a little bit, in my dreams. Who was that?"

Decision time. Was I ready to take the plunge and tell her, especially after I'd learned that she had been holding back on me?

Wait. Who's been holding back on who here? Did you tell her about your mom?

Ugh. No I had not. Could I really judge her when I'd been doing the same? "That was Gina," I said.

She sat up straight in the bed. "Gina, as in your old roommate? The one who died?"

I slid to the side of the bed, dangling my legs over the edge. "Correct."

Carla scratched the back of her head. "You're not bullshitting me?"

"No ma'am."

She stared at me for what felt like an eternity, and then shrugged. "What am I going to say? Maybe we're both losing our minds, or maybe there's some weird shit going on. Between the two, it's not that much different than what we're already dealing with, is it?"

"I guess not."

She climbed from under the covers and sat on her bed, facing me, hands on her legs. "Listen, can we agree that it's time to stop acting like everything's normal here?"

Maybe this was the way to get at what she hid from me.

Maybe this was what the ghost had meant to happen all along. I nodded. "Time to put the cards on the table. You got something you want to say?"

She lowered her head. "My brain's not doing as good as I try to make you think. Even with my freak-out the other day. It's worse than that."

Was this it? Couldn't be. I had already suspected *that* much. "I understand. You looked like you were going to die when Bloch was choking you. It's only natural."

"Right, no, see, it's not just stress or PTSD. It's like…I've been seeing things too." She held one hand up when I started to speak. "Not dead people. I have some questions for you about that, don't get me wrong."

"Wouldn't dream of it."

"It's more like I've been to…places. *Other* places."

"What sort of other places?" I said.

"Dark rooms. I don't know where they are, but I think they're hidden from everybody. I guess almost everybody, anyway. Black, nasty places, full of things you couldn't even imagine. I see those things, but I don't really understand what I'm looking at, you know? The main thing though, is that when they're closing in on me I get an image of myself, surrounded by this glowing green armor." She moved her hands across her body, showing me where the armor would go. "It's not quite real, but not quite fake. When I'm wearing that, it feels like I could do anything. Kill anyone, and no one could stop me." She trailed off, staring at the wall, her expression slack.

Good lord, she's gone psycho. "What do you do when you're in the armor?"

"I don't remember." Her voice had a dreamy quality, and I could almost see the vision along with her. Sure, she probably lied to me about her visions. Didn't matter. I got the picture. She shook her head and looked back to me. "It's only in visions and dreams and stuff so far. Just half-glanced, so there probably hasn't been much to do."

I knew that was bullshit. I didn't press.

She shifted on the bed. "It's like when you see something out of the corner of your eye, only when I shift, I can see it…her. *Me.* Standing there, just waiting on something."

"I'm not following you. You're not directly seeing the armor, or the person?"

"Neither…both." She put her hands on her head. "I have no idea what I mean. I think the armor is part of me. Jesus, what are they doing to me?"

A deep voice spoke from the door. "It's known as echoing."

I jumped. "Jesus Christ, Sam. How long have you been there?"

"Long enough. Is all well?" He crossed the room, sliding a piece of paper into my hand. He widened his eyes and nodded at the paper before he nodded at me.

Everything was all right – or it had to be.

Well, well. It gets more and more interesting.

"We're just peachy-keen," I said.

"Very good." He raised his eyebrows. "If that's all, I'll be going now."

"Yeah. Thank you."

Carla watched him go, mouth hanging open. Her head snapped back to me when he was gone. "What the hell?"

I held a finger to my lips and showed her the piece of paper before I unfolded it. I began reading it, but Carla interrupted, snapping her fingers. I held up one finger as I read it, and then turned it around so she could see it.

It read:

I am leaving the door open.

Meet me in the front room so we can discuss this further.

Say nothing. They are listening.

Carla nodded.

I stood, tiptoeing toward the door. "Not much we can do about it. May as well sleep on it and talk about it in the morning."

Carla gave me the okay sign with her fingers and stood up, coming along behind me. I folded up the paper and slid it into the hip pocket of my pajamas.

He had wedged a fork in the door's gap, propping it open just enough that it hadn't locked behind him. I removed the fork and motioned to Carla before slipping through the crack.

May 5th

Got around to meeting with the Underground folks today. Sam's still not crazy about the idea of me being so visible with them. I'm a little tired of hearing it, so I reminded him of how I got out in the first place and pointed out that I wasn't exactly a delicate flower. I may have thrown in some more choice, firm words. I think he got the picture, because he backed off and let me go with him.

I didn't expect their place to be so grimy. Sure, our safe house isn't in the fanciest part of town, but at least it's clean and furnished. Their house, on the other hand, wouldn't have been out of place in a warzone. The front door hung on one hinge and almost fell off when Sam pushed it to one side for me to enter. The inside was a cave, decorated with graffiti of genitals, gang signs, and vague warnings.

I still don't know how they hide their operations from the Organization, but locations like that have to help. I wanted to immediately turn tail and run, but I didn't dare.

The Underground folks looked just as ratty as their house, maybe even more so. Some looked like they would have been more at home in an isolated cabin in the mountains, refining their theories about the government. These guys had long, scruffy beards and eyes hostile to the intrusions of outsiders. Others looked more like accountants gone wrong - dressed in office casual, worn for about a month too long, sleeves pushed up to reveal fresh tattoos.

Their leader, a muscular, tattooed Latino who called himself only Araña, said very little as he took our money and handed over the envelope containing our passports and other identification papers (birth certificates, that sort of thing). I didn't understand why a guy like that needed so many people on his side for just the two of us. I guess it had something to do with the Organization's way of infiltration.

The exchange only took a couple of minutes, and we were back on our way. Eager for a change of pace, I drove us back to the house while Sam opened the envelope and went through its contents. In addition to all the identity papers we could need, they had included a note with directions to another safe house over the border, where we're supposed to get our next set of instructions.

Like I said in my last entry, not looking forward to going there, but we do have to, right? I just wish I had any idea of where this is all going, or who in the Underground might have taken an interest in our well-being. I am grateful, don't get me wrong. A question just lingers in the back of my head: is someone gaining off of all this, and if so, what do they want from us?

Probably cynical of me, but none of my experience leads me to trust in the goodness of humanity.

Tomorrow morning we make our move over the border. I'm anxious, and Sam's watching Seinfeld again. The guy is obsessed. I tried to tune out like him, but I just don't work that way. After a while I started feeling the pull to write, and I'm grateful to be able to spill my guts again.

======

Samarta stood at the bank of monitors, his back turned to us. When he heard me slip through the door, he twisted, putting one finger to his lips. He motioned us toward his side with one hand and then looked back to the screens. He pressed a few buttons at the bottom of one of the screens and the image froze, showing us our own backs. He reached up and touched the screen, swiping from right to left in one motion.

The video rolled back; we watched ourselves walk backwards out of the room, and then Samarta walking backwards, away from the monitor.

He made a motion at the bottom of the screen, and the image froze on the empty room.

"What are you…?" I said.

He turned and put a finger against my lips. He shook his head, gazing around the room.

Can't talk. They'll hear, the motion said. He inclined his head toward the couch and took his finger off my lips. We followed him in that direction, watching as he picked up the remote. A few button presses that I didn't understand tuned the big, central monitor to a TV show.

Seinfeld, of course.

He cranked the volume up and gave an unnatural laugh. He met our eyes, a strange fire in his own as he gave that weird cackle.

Everybody's just going out of their minds.

After a few more laughs, he put a finger to his own lips and approached us, walking gingerly. He put his arms around Carla and me, pulling us into a huddle. "I had to ensure that they could not see or hear us. We may speak now, but stay as quiet as you can."

How stupid did I feel? Of course Sam had been up to his super-secret spy shit.

Carla leaned forward, her voice a dramatic whisper. "So tell me, what is 'echoing'?"

He sighed. "I am not sure how to explain it."

"Give it a try," I said.

"Very well, but this will take some explanation."

"Do you think we have anywhere else to go?"

Sam frowned. "I suppose not. You must first understand that our tribe had a select few that were granted extraordinary abilities when they came of age. They were known as the Initiates. The Initiates were guardians of our people, given a sacred trust to protect the community. From those Initiates we voted to choose an Inner Council, who decided the best course of action."

I put a hand on his shoulder. "Sam. I don't think we need a lesson on your political system."

"If you wish to understand Echoing, then you must understand how exceptional such a thing is."

I waved a hand. "Fine. Go on."

He watched me for a moment, waiting for another objection, and then carried on. "The greatest of all initiates was the Kellik'at - you would call him a shaman," he added, catching the questioning look in Carla's eyes. "The Kellik'at's powers far exceeded that of an Initiate. He was our spiritual leader, but also a doctor, a warrior, and the equivalent of your priests. Every year at High Moon, he would mix the correct herbs to visit the 'other worlds'. When the planets aligned, our shaman would retreat into a cave with the herbs –"

"And trip balls," I said.

He smiled, just a little. "If that is how you wish to put it. He saw things in the cave - visions of the future, the past, things that had never come to be. When he emerged, he told the Inner Council of these visions, and they used those to determine the correct path for the next cycle. The process was straightforward, for what it was. Or so it would seem. Unfortunately for the Kellik'at, at times those visions refused to stay in the cave. Once he left, he would continue to see those visions, overlying everyday life. It drove some mad. *That* is Echoing."

Neither of us said anything for a long time. Did that really explain Carla's increasingly tenuous hold on sanity? Was she that special?

Carla spoke first. "It sounds like acid flashbacks."

Maybe the answer laid there. It wasn't about being special, it was about the drugs. "You think Carla's flashbacking because of the drugs?"

He bit his lip. "I am not familiar with the concept, but is it possible?" He shrugged. "Perhaps. I only tell you this so that you understand: Echoing is of a prophetic nature. Your vision of the armor may prove to be symbolic, but I believe it is quite literal."

My hand went right back to his shoulder. "Wait, hold up. What do you mean 'literal'? Like, the armor is going to appear out of thin air on top of her? How would that happen?"

"That I cannot tell you. I can simply relay the meaning of such Echoes."

I considered it. I had the traits of a Deadspeaker. Carla had the traits of a Kellik'at. Could it really be coincidence that we both were developing those powers under Sam's watch? "Do you think they're trying to recreate the conditions in your tribe?" I said.

"That I cannot say, but it would be foolish to say that I have not noticed certain parallels. This is why I wished for you to wait - I needed to explore and research."

"They let you do that?" Carla said.

"'Let' is a questionable word. Not all of my people's ways are known to them. We are crafty."

She went into a squat, rubbing her legs.

"You okay?" I said.

"Just fine. Listen, you keep saying that, 'my people', but it doesn't sound like any tribe I've ever heard of before. Who are they?"

Sam's turn to be quiet. I wondered what was going through his mind, but I'm not sure I could understand it even now. At last he said, "By now you must know that I am not from your world."

In retrospect, it really shouldn't have shocked me, but it did all the same. Sam, an alien? My brain couldn't compute it. I guess all along I had told myself that he was just some weird Eastern European, or maybe Russian. What did I know about their nomads, or if they even had them? It seemed so obvious now that I had been in denial, but I was…well, not *in love with* an alien, but possibly – maybe – headed that way.

It didn't horrify me, though; in fact, I felt more interested in him than ever. I only understand it now as I write it: we had some things in common right from the start. We were both misfits, in places we didn't fully understand, trying to survive the best that we could. No wonder he had felt protective on the night that Gina died.

"If you're not from our world, then where *are* you from?" Carla said, wincing as she shifted her legs.

"I have no idea where it was in relation to your world. There may not have been a relation. We called our home Abshir, and we never left it. Abshir sat atop a mountain, a sacred place. We were tasked to protect it from outsiders who would use it for harm. We were the greatest warriors of our world. No one had ever surprised us." He looked me in the eye. "No one."

I had a bad feeling about that one. "But they did," I said.

He nodded. "They attacked in the middle of the night. I still don't know how they caught us off guard." He went to the couch, shoulders slumped, and sat on the arm, his eyes staring at some empty spot on the far wall. We followed him, Carla groaning a bit as she straightened up.

"You don't have to talk about this," I said.

"I appreciate that. I know. And yet, I must. I have told no one of this, and the time is right."

Carla sat on the couch behind Sam, staring up at the TV. She looked back toward us. "Don't take this the wrong way, but what does it have to do with Echoing?"

I shot her an angry look. "Jesus, Carla."

She held up her hands. "Sorry, I just don't get it, that's all."

I put my hands on my hips. "Does everything have to be about you?"

"God, no, I'm sorry. Let me just shut up and listen."

Sam interrupted us. "You will come to understand. You will know the pain and grief that these people can cause. I wished to tell you about Echoing so that you might understand what is happening to you. That your mind might not be unraveling. That you see a great and terrible thing coming. Once you have experienced that, you will understand the need for your armor."

"Gee, sounds swell, but it's not much comfort."

"But it is. They will not stop you from trying to gain this power in your visions. In fact, it is their end goal. We need to discuss how you can use this power once you have gained it. We need to destroy this place. We need to destroy these people."

"Not going to get an argument from me," she said.

"Yeah, that's fair enough," she said, and looked away, putting her hand on her chin.

Sam frowned at me. We shared something there: a low opinion of the Woman-Child Who Would Be Queen. He carried on. "The screaming awoke me. It should not have been the first thing that I heard that night and yet..." He held up his hands, helpless. "When I came out of my home, two of our greatest warriors – my best friends – had been eviscerated. Strung up on their huts as those huts burned."

"Jesus."

"They slaughtered all of our warriors, and most of the women and children. They held me in place and made me watch as they butchered my people and burned the village. They left my wife and child alive. Rode off with them into the night. These are the people that I 'work for'."

"My God," Carla said.

He chuckled. "If such a thing exists, I see no evidence for it. They told me that my family would be freed if I went with them and did what they told me. I grasped at that, and did not listen when they told me that the land would also be spared. It was simply a barb to slip under my skin. Now…" He patted his legs. "I am not so sure I believe either now. I cannot feel my family any longer. Nothing resonates in my heart of hearts. I fear they are dead."

I put a hand on his arm. "I'm sorry, but you can't know that."

He looked down at my hand, but he didn't take it away. "Of course I can. Hope blinded me to stark reality. Why *would* they leave them alive? They serve no purpose. Best to do away with them and save the resources that you might have spent on them. I cannot help these people to conquer the world, or the universe, or whatever it is that they seek. We are pawns. Nothing more."

Carla had skipped the class on Leaving Well Enough Alone. "Doesn't sound like a husband and father to me."

His cheeks went red. He rose and faced her, his voice a barely-controlled hiss. "Do not dare judge me, woman, you who have been the center of their attentions, you who have ensured my continued slavery."

She held up her hands. "Easy. I didn't mean it that way. I was trying to help."

"Help? Are you mad?"

She looked to me, her eyes pleading, and I got it now. She really hadn't been trying to be nasty, but had the social skills of a life-long shut-in. I shook my head. I was pretty sure I couldn't help her with the big guy.

"I meant that you shouldn't be willing to give up so easily," she said.

He raised an eyebrow. "How is that better?"

I put a hand on his shoulder. "Sam, maybe you should –"

He shrugged off the hand and glared at me. "Would you say the same? Would you not understand the living Hell that I have faced, wondering every day if they would return to me?"

"I'm sorry for your family, but we've been through our own Hell too, buddy. Back up, cool down, and get yourself in check."

His face fell. "Yes. Yes, of course, you are right. She…" he looked at Carla. "I love my family more than life itself. I have surrendered my own will, the one thing I swore I would never do, in order to protect them. And for what, that you might accuse me of giving up?"

"I'm sorry. I didn't mean it that way."

I patted his back. "See there, she didn't mean it. We're all under a lot of stress," I said, but I wasn't completely with the two of them. Something had gone off in my head – a strange ping. As I concentrated on it, I realized that it had been there from the moment I walked out and it had only grown more insistent. Maybe the argument had pushed it to a new level; I have no idea. I knew its source, though: a door just off to Sam's left, between our bedroom and the kitchen. Solid wood, like ours, but without a number at all.

Back on Planet Weird, Sam was in the middle of another monologue. "…in my heart, I know it is true: they are lost. I can feel this." He looked at the floor.

I willed myself back into the moment. "I am so sorry." I ran my hand down his shoulder to his hand.

He took my hand and squeezed. It felt right, like little else in that damned place ever had or ever would. "When you asked me for your favor, I gave you my word. I did not know if I could live up to that word, but I would die trying."

"You asked him for a favor?" Carla said.

I let go of his hand and rubbed the back of my neck, acutely aware of her eyes drilling right into the two of us. "I figured if he couldn't get us out, he could at least look into why we were here, you know, give us a hint."

He smiled. "You also asked for the television."

I glanced away. "Yeah, that, too. You have to admit that wasn't a bad idea."

"Not at all. Not bad. For both," Carla said.

He nodded. "She is smarter than she appears to be."

"Fuck you both." I said it, but I smiled.

Sam carried on. "I knew that I could find some information, but it would require ingenuity. After some time of puzzling over the problem, I decided to request supervised trips to my homeland."

"They let you do that?" I said, honestly surprised.

"Well, of course they balked at first, but I pointed out that I had no way of knowing whether they had protected my homelands. They have to maintain that illusion, if nothing else, so they agreed."

How did he get this lucky? "So let me get this straight. They let you out of here, took you back to your hometown, let you mix up some acid, waltz into a cave, and trip your ass off?"

"Not…precisely. I informed them that I wished to commune with nature. They did not know what that meant, which allowed me to do much more than they would have liked." He smirked. "They observed me as I prepared a ritual, one that they did not, and could not, understand. Much was revealed to me during my meditation."

"Tell us what you saw," I said.

"I saw a vision of her summoning the dead."

Carla made a sound. "I don't…Gina?"

Sam's brow furrowed. "How do you know her?"

"Gina visited me tonight," I said.

Sam put one hand to his forehead. He looked a bit shaken. I wasn't used to seeing the guy taken so much off guard. It made me a little uneasy. "I did not see Gina. I saw others…those that I knew and loved. My people. But this makes much more sense."

I shook my head. "What does it mean?"

He looked to Carla, who had risen and walked a few steps from both of us. I wondered if she was going back to our room.

"I believe you are a natural shaman," Sam said, "Born to your calling. This is why they have used you, to push your natural talent to their own ends. Echoing, communing with the dead – these are the tools of the Kellik'at."

I spoke up. "Does that mean…I guess I'm wondering, isn't there usually some rite of passage or something for a Kellik'at? Before they get whatever powers they're supposed to have, or smoke the peace pipe, or whatever?"

"Yes. Hence her instability."

Carla paused outside our door and turned to look at us, one hand on her chest, her face pale. "That's impossible," she whispered.

"Is it? These people kidnapped you and brought you here to exploit your potential. I am still not 100% certain what this testing means, but I do believe it is an attempt to enhance your abilities. Tell me, before you arrived here, did you ever notice odd…*things* happening around you? Have you ever seen ghosts?"

If I had to use one word to describe Carla in that moment, *trapped* would be a damn good one. I didn't know what part of the discussion had done it to her, but she looked ready to bolt from the room.

Then she did it. She didn't go for Room 1, though. Instead she went for that unmarked door, the same one I had noticed earlier. She grabbed hold of the doorknob and twisted.

Sam choked and made a move for her. "No, wait," he cried, but she had already descended the stairs behind the door into a pale, blue-green light that rose up like steam from the basement.

I ran for the door, a few steps ahead of Sam, hoping I could catch up with her before she stumbled into something dangerous. She was out of her damned mind; you didn't just open up any random door around the Khesnaa. She should have known better, but she might not have been thinking much at all.

"Carla, stop," I said.

If she had an answer for me, it got lost somewhere in the strangled noise that came from her lips as she reached the bottom of the stairs.

"Carla?"

Sam let out a hiss of air behind me. "Damn fool woman. Exactly what I feared."

"What is it?" I rounded the landing near the bottom of the stairs. I had a vision of myself rushing forward and jumping on to whatever had grabbed her, beating the shit out of it and pulling her out of the fire.

Then I actually saw what had her and came to a dead stop.

I didn't think I could do a damn thing.

Carla's toes dragged the ground, her feet kicking and trying to get hold of something that would free her. No luck, though, because the thing holding her by the neck and draining her life out was a Golem.

Now, I'm not talking about the slimy guy in the Lord of the Rings; no, I'm talking about the monsters that holy people could apparently bring to life from nothing more than mud. I'd first heard about them in Sunday school. I think it had been a discussion about Psalms. I remember it - or at least think I remember it - so vividly because the concept had grabbed something primal in my gut. Not such a surprise, I guess, but even with what I know now, it's a twisted memory.

This golem looked a little more human than I'd expected, more like a sculpture turned to life than a lump of mud, but I had no doubt of exactly what it was, all weird angles and unseeing eyes.

Did I actually think I could hurt the thing? Of course not. But I also couldn't just stand by and watch somebody die, so I ran toward the thing and threw my right shoulder into its side. Sounds crazy as I write it, but I wasn't thinking at the time. Personal safety never even crossed my mind - I just had to get that monster off of Carla.

Samarta made some sound that I'm sure was supposed to stop me, but he was seconds too late. Not that it mattered: I found out why he tried to stop me right quick when I bounced off of it and landed on my ass a few feet away, knocking my hip.

The thing turned and "looked" at me, its horrible, unmoving face studying me. I realized now that it had been the source of the buzzing in my head, and probably had something to do with the pain in Carla's legs. I wondered if it had been trying to talk to us, and if so, why.

Sam stepped off the bottom step, getting between the golem and me.

"Help," Carla choked.

The sound nauseated me. I couldn't watch her be choked again. I couldn't watch somebody else die. I tried to get to one knee and cried out as pain ripped through my left side.

Sam spread his legs, expanding his whole body so that he blocked the thing from approaching me. He extended both of his hands outward. "Enliel."

The thing cocked its head at him.

"Let her go."

The thing must have loosened its grip on Carla, because her choking and kicking at the air slowed. She whimpered, but went quiet, letting Sam do his thing.

I wasn't so easily contained. "You'd better not have killed her, you son of a –" I said, but Sam cut me off with a hand extended behind his back, his eyes never leaving the monster's face.

"She is not a threat. Put her down," he said.

It gazed upon him for a long, long time. My nerves were on edge, waiting for it to finish its job on Carla. At last, it lowered its head and opened its hand. Carla rolled out and hit the floor, knocked unconscious by the drop.

I skittered towards her and put my head down over her mouth, listening for any signs of breathing. When I heard a choking gasp from the back of her throat, I closed my eyes.

Thank you, God.

"Is she well?" Sam said.

I stood, wincing at the pain, and wiped the dust from the

floor off my hands. "Yeah. Damn it, Sam, she just got over what Bloch did to her. She didn't need this."

The golem stirred, and I eyed it, giving it a wide berth as I went to stand beside Sam. Just being near the thing set my nerves on edge.

"Why did she do this?" Sam said.

"You really don't get it?"

He shook his head. Typical man.

"You scared her. You pushed her too hard too fast with *way* too much information."

"I only hoped to comfort her, to help her understand what was really happening."

"Too much too soon," I said, but I had gotten distracted. I had noticed our surroundings for the first time and didn't know what to make of them. The walls were cinder block, about what you'd expect from a basement in a place like this, but the rest...well, I'd never seen anything like it. A steel table ran the length of the room, its gleaming surface piled with scalpels, pliers, and assorted other tools that looked like they could turn your guts inside out.

Yet that wasn't the real strange part of the room. Oh no, that would be the big tubes full of glowing, green-blue water. Inside those? Big brown masses of the stuff that must have been used to create Enliel.

Strange, yeah, but at the same time something about the tubes felt familiar. I tried, but I couldn't connect them up with any specific memory. I wandered over to the table and ran my hand over it. "Jesus Christ, Sam, where are we?"

Sam didn't answer. Instead, he leaned down and checked on Carla, no doubt hoping that I'd let it go.

Not happening. I faced him. "I asked you a question. What

is this? Obviously you knew about it if you knew about the walking hunk of shit over here."

Give him credit; once he'd made a plan, he stuck to it: he just kept right on not answering me. He picked Carla up by her shoulders and started dragging her to the stairs.

I crossed the room and grabbed his shoulder, making him look up into my eyes. "Answer my question."

His eyes were big O's – the guy was legit scared. "We have to get her out of here. They could return at any moment."

"I'm not leaving until you answer me. What is this? And if you know about this, what else do you know that you're not telling us?"

"Please. I have told you everything that you needed to know."

"Oh, thank you so much. I'm glad you're deciding what we need to know."

"Very well. Help me, and I will tell you."

"Fine." I went to her feet and picked them up, helping him get her up to the landing. It was slow going; she might have been even heavier than I had originally suspected. Once we'd gotten her to the landing we lowered her, panting.

Sam shook his head. "You will be disappointed in my knowledge. All I know is that this is part of the project. Somehow related to what you do. I am sorry that you believe I am part of their conspiracy, but I am not."

"Don't play stupid. You know I don't think that. I just think you've been holding back on us." I sensed a pattern here. How could we work together as a team when none of us were allowing our true selves to show? "They're golems, right?"

"That is what they call them, yes." He bent over, picking Carla up by her armpits.

I picked up Carla's feet and we started taking her up the stairs, one agonizing step at a time. "How do they make them?" I said between gasps.

"I do not know. It is involved with the project, but I have not been able to uncover it."

"How do you know about Enliel, then?"

Sam winced as we struggled to get her up another step. "He is one of my charges. When I watch over you, I also watch over him."

"How did you not mention –"

Like his name had summoned him, I felt the monster's big, hard hand close around the back of my neck, its stone fingers sinking deep into my flesh. It made a quick motion and pulled me backward off the stairs, lifting me into the air. Carla's body slammed against the stairs and slid back down to the landing, but that was the least of my concerns; the biggest one was the feeling that my head would separate from my shoulders if I didn't do something quick.

I started beating at the monster's hand, shrieking. "Let me go."

Sam let go of Carla and came at us. "Enliel. She is not a threat. She is like you and me. Captive." He put his hands together, trying to show the thing chains or cuffs.

The monster pointed at him with its free hand.

"Little help here," I said, trying to get my hands between my neck and the inside of its fist.

Sam offered the monster his hands, open. "We are trying to help the woman who came down here."

The thing pointed at me.

"She is frightened. Think about how you felt when you awakened here."

The monster didn't move for a moment, and then eased me back down to the floor, releasing me.

I turned around and tried to kick it, missed, and fell on my ass again. Not exactly my finest moment. I rubbed my neck and stared up at Sam.

"What was that all about?"

Sam stepped between us. "He thinks that we're trying to steal Carla. He thinks that he's hers, for some reason." He knelt beside me, looking at my neck. "Are you okay?"

Part of me wanted to push him away. The other part wanted him to take me in his arms and comfort me. That part won. I took my hands away and showed him the flesh, hoping he'd take the cue. "It's sore. But I'll be okay, I guess."

He ran his fingers over my skin, careful not to press too hard. I hoped he didn't notice the goose bumps popping up on my arm.

He put his hand on my shoulder; it helped distract me from the pain, at least a bit. "I think you will be okay. I cannot say whether they will notice this, however."

I dared to meet his eyes. "They gave me a couple of turtlenecks. I can wear them for a few days."

He took one of my hands, closing both of his hands over it. "I am sorry. I should have warned you both about this place."

I squeezed his hands. "What's done is done. We'd better get her out of here so you can clean up."

He nodded and let go, rising. "You know everything now. Everything that I discover from now on will be yours, as well. I promise."

I stood up. "I know. I trust you. I have to be out of my mind, but I do."

He chuckled and went to the stairs. "We should get her

upstairs."

It only took a year or so to get her up those damned stairs and into bed. We pulled it off, though, and even managed to answer a few of her completely senseless questions with reassurances. Not bad, right? Just required every bit of effort we could expend, no biggie.

By the time we had tucked her in, we stood on either side of her bed, gazing at each other as we tried to catch our breath. A thousand words came to mind, but none of those went to my lips. The moment was beyond words, and for the first time it occurred to me just why I liked him so much: it was the little things. He was absolutely terrible with words and had the social skills of a turtle, but even when he frustrated the hell out of me and hid things, I still knew he had my back 100%. I can see now that it wasn't the best foundation for a relationship, but that seemed a lot more important in a place like that.

Something passed between us, and I don't know if his defenses were down or if he was just ready to take things to the next level, but he was around the bed in an instant, grabbing hold of me, his lips moving in for mine.

I wanted to back away and tell him no, but I also wanted that kiss so bad. Just a little kiss – some comfort – it wouldn't be so bad, right?

It was better than not so bad. My chest and head exploded when his lips touched mine, the electric shock of his skin traveling down my arms and my spine, making my knees weak. My hands slid up to caress his pale, bald head, running down the back and cupping it.

So this is what Fireworks feels like, I thought. When we finally broke off, we embraced for a long moment, lost in one another's' eyes.

He broke the silence, his voice gentler than I had ever heard it. "I will come for you – and only you – very soon. We have much to discuss."

I nodded. "There's more about her, isn't there?"

"Yes." He tore his eyes away with a very clear effort just before he broke the embrace.

I reached for him for a moment before I lowered my arms. It sucked, but it was the right thing to do.

He went for the door, trying to keep his head trained on his destination, but I think it just got to be too much. He turned back at the last minute, gazing at me. "Stay safe."

My heart fluttered. "I'll do my best." It felt corny, but what else could I say?

Then he walked out, leaving me with Carla, my thoughts, and the tingling remains of his lips on mine.

May 6th

We crossed the border yesterday, and it was suspiciously easy. I'm not sure what I expected, exactly, but it would have involved more of an ordeal, or at least something to justify all the churning that my gut had been doing. Maybe it should have been more like the movies - a couple of jackbooted thugs examining our papers, digging through our bags, suspicious of our very existence. The Underground had warned us that we might run into that, given how weird Sam can look in the light of the day.

Fortunately, it wasn't like that at all. Handed over our passports to the guy, he glanced over our stuff, asked us a couple of the questions (the Underground had fed us answers to these) and we were on our way. Is it possible that the Underground had a man on the inside? Maybe. I'm sure the makeup job to help Sam's skin tone didn't hurt, either.

The border guard directed us to take a certain path through the checkpoint and sent us on our way. By that point we had both collapsed into our seats, letting out a silent sigh of relief. The Organization might have its claws in most of the world, but thank God the good guys have their own ways to get things done.

A few more minutes and we were over the border. Relief gave way to anxiety as we watched the strange, sterile world of the U.S. roll into the distance and the more dangerous world of this corner of Mexico unfolded before us. What a place they chose for us; the city's a complete dump, and dangerous enough that I had heard of its problems long before I learned that we'd be coming here.

Araña had told us to go straight to this little dive bar in the center of the city and "Look at no one, say nothing."

As we climbed out of the car and approached the bar, a chubby, grinning man in a loose-fitting green Hawaiian tee and mirror shades intercepted us.

"Bienvenidos, gringos," he said, and slapped Sam on the shoulder, drawing us close.

I figured this had to be Carlos, Araña's hand-picked guide to the city.

Sam stumbled to find the correct word. At last he mumbled, "Hola," and Carlos laughed.

He leaned in close and gave us the pass question that Araña had arranged. When we provided the correct response, he laughed again and rubbed Sam's back. "Good to meet you, my friends. Why don't we go in back and enjoy the sun?"

I wondered whether I should protest his whole 'my friends' shtick, but what would be the point? It was probably some Underground affectation. "If there's a drink involved," I said.

He removed the mirror shades and bumped Sam. "A good woman. I understand. Come." He moved a little ahead of us, leading us around the corner of the bar. On the other side laid a small open café, where a few white men - who were most definitely not tourists - drowsed in the mid-day sun, nursing their *cerveza.*

The Underground, I hoped.

Carlos gave these men a significant glance as he tucked his shades into his shirt pocket. "Come," he said, and led us to the farthest table, positioning us so that he could watch them over our backs. Once we had all settled, he rubbed his hands together, giving a fake, toothy grin. "So. Your crossing was uneventful, I take it?"

Sam shrugged, a hint of just how eager he was to get to know the real Carlos. Not that I was much more eager; the contradiction between the guy's grin and demeanor versus what I saw in his eyes put my nerves on edge. The sooner we were finished here, the better.

He got it, and he didn't protest. "Right. I am glad you are safe." He reached in his pocket and slid a set of keys across the table, glancing at the drowsing men from the corner of his sad, dark eyes. He told us the street name and number of the safe house.

Sam swiped the keys and slid them into his pocket. We rose together, but Carlos had other plans. He touched our wrists and looked down toward our seats "Please. Just one more moment."

"We need to get out of here," I said.

"Please. In time."

We sat.

He leaned even closer to us, his arms hugging the tabletop. "Listen, friends. You must take the warnings seriously. The deaths in this city, some are from the drugs, yes, but our mutual friends wage wars for the souls of humanity with us as their pawns. Even you are expendable."

Something about the way he said it… "We're not the first people to pass through on your watch, are we?"

He tightened his mouth, and shook his head.

"Not all of them got where they were going, either?"

He shook his head again.

Sam put his hand on mine. "We will be cautious."

Carlos kept his eyes on me. "Especially you, you must be careful. No offense. It's just, a beautiful woman…"

Ooookay. Sam made a noise and I held up one hand. "None

taken. This wouldn't exactly be a vacation destination for me."

"May we leave?" Sam said.

Carlos nodded, his eyes softening just a little. "You know where to go?"

Sam rose, adjusting the collar of his Smashing Pumpkins tee. I don't think I'll ever get used to seeing him in T-shirts. I do know that it will never stop being funny. "We can find it."

By the time we reached the safe house, the combination of Carlos's words (yes, just those few words) and the paltry amount of luggage that we brought had gotten me down. Hell, I'm still not over it - is this really me, then? All this time and my entire existence can be packed into two small suitcases? If the Organization does find us, or if we get caught in the crossfire of the war in the streets, I don't think anything would remain to say we've ever been here at all. I've figured out that I can't ever have the picket fence and family in this world, and I think I might be okay with it, but I also damn sure don't want anonymity as an epitaph. Part of me wanted to be a star at one point, and now look at me: running from one anonymous place to another, my only real goal to stay one step ahead of death. It's not living. It's barely surviving.

Sam could tell I was down. Once we'd unpacked everything (took all of five minutes), he led me to the tiny living room, sat down on the threadbare couch, and patted the seat next to him.

"Come. Let us talk," he said.

I had an idea what was coming, but I slid in beside him anyway, cuddling up against his strong body. "I don't want to die like this."

"It is hardly ideal conditions, I admit, and I wish that I could give you more stability, but we live the warrior's life."

"I'm not a warrior."

"I know." He ran a hand through my hair, twisting a curl around his finger. "Is it the surroundings? I could ask the Underground for a more fitting place."

I sat up and his finger caught in a curl. I winced, and we took a moment for him to extract his hand. Once he was freed, I laid my head on my hand, considering the question. "No. It's not about material things…well, not entirely, anyway. It's just…this. All of this." I waved my hand at the shabby room.

He raised his eyebrows. "I am not sure I understand."

I struggled to get out what I meant. No, to even *understand* what I meant. "Okay, yeah, it's not about material things, but at the same time I don't want to die some nobody in a ditch, with nothing to my name. Look at what we brought in, Sam. We have nothing. We are nothing. Who wants something like that?"

He straightened up, turning to face me, arms on his thighs. "I understand you are upset, but that is far from the truth. We have one another. We are sought after by those in power within the Underground."

I slapped the couch. "That's not what I mean and you know it."

"I am afraid I do not. I am not playing games."

"I mean that…" He was right, though. We did have each other. We were in a position of importance, at least in our little world. What was my problem again?

Oh, yeah, that whole leaving-nothing-behind thing. But didn't everyone do that, in their own way. I put a hand to my forehead. "You're probably right. I shouldn't let stuff control me. I just hate having so little to show for my time here, I guess."

"So it is the lack of material possessions."

All that dancing around to get to the heart of the matter: I did care about the possessions after all. I didn't like what it implied about me, but truth is truth. "Yeah." I touched his chest, just once, quick, but enough to give us a connection. "I'm sorry. Sometimes you seem so much like a normal guy that…well, not *normal*, I don't mean that. I just mean that I lose sight of who you really are."

He took my hand. "I apologize. I failed to understand you, as well. To me, dying a warrior's death with very few possessions is a great honor. The Elders taught us from a young age that an excess of personal possessions spoke to something lacking in a person's soul."

Just the kind of thing that scared me about myself. Did I even *have* a soul? I wasn't ready to share that little fear with him. "You really like all this?"

"Of course not. I simply view it as a matter of course – what must be done."

I sighed and turned around, allowing myself to settle back into his chest. He pulled me close, wrapping his arms around my body. I closed my eyes and tried to let the sensation consume my anxiety.

It didn't work.

"Will everything be all right?" I said, saying a silent prayer that he would just answer me, no debate, no word games. A comfortable lie, I guess.

"I believe so. Yes." I felt the rumble of the words in his chest against my back, and the vibrations melted some of my fears. Nowhere near all of them – but good enough.

I laid my own arms on his. With the anxiety draining out of me, I felt the exhaustion that had lurked just outside the door. I nuzzled my head into his chest. "Good. I think I need some rest."

Sam's body tightened as he began to speak, but he never got to complete the thought, as two pops filled the air outside the house.

Those were shots.

We both froze. I felt the pounding of his heart against my back, the surge of his blood beneath his skin. A few shouts followed the pops, and some feet ran by our front door.

"Jesus," I whispered.

He held me tighter.

"Everything will be all right," I said.

"Yes."

May 7th

The Dark Thing loomed somewhere behind me, and my world had become corn. Corn as far as I could see, anyway: backwards, forwards, sideways. Tight rows, marching off into the distance no matter which way I looked. Had I needed to slow down and figure out how to get out, I might have panicked. As it was, I knew that the thing at my back would not relent. I had to move forward as fast as I could and hope the destination took care of itself.

But what is it?

I had only caught vague flashes of the thing through the rows of something large and dark, drawing in the scant red light that traced through the field. It looked a lot like the shadow Carla saw in her visions.

And it was on my tail, snarling as it pounded the ground.

"Help me," I yelled. No help to be had out there, but it was a reflex.

Glad I turned out to be wrong, as Momma spoke to me from somewhere off to my right. "No one is going to help you. Got to help yourself."

I whipped my head in that direction, but I didn't see her. I didn't see anything but that low-level red light that swirled toward the beast at my back and more corn.

"You keep on moving girl," Gina said from my left.

That had the opposite effect: I stumbled and caught a knot in the ground. It grabbed hold of my bare toes, sending me sprawling face-first into the corn stalks and dirt. I shrieked as the sharp edge of one of the stalks sliced my right cheek open, blood pouring down that side of my face.

The Dark Thing behind me snarled in triumph and something cold touched my calf, seeping into the layers of flesh beneath my skin. I shrieked again and scrambled to my feet, moving forward, shoving the corn out of the way as hard as I could. I tried to ignore my bruised and bleeding skin. It wouldn't do me a damn bit of good to listen if that thing sucked my soul out.

Just stop. There is no hope, the Dark Thing said - or maybe thought – to me. Probably thought, because in an instant it felt like something cold and nasty started climbing around in my skull, trying to pick out the juicy parts.

Nothing is hopeless, Momma answered in my head.

I looked up and saw she told the truth: the corn had started to thin out, and after a few more steps I rolled out into a clearing. As I went down again, I saw Carla's dead sun hanging overhead, turning everything - the sky, the ground, and my skin - blood red.

"She's here," a familiar voice chirped.

I didn't have time to place it. I scrambled to my knees and cried, "Oh God, help me."

That's when I saw Mimi (the source of the familiar voice) and Samarta, standing together, next to the soaring tree. I knew right where I had arrived then: the intersection between my purgatory and Carla's Hell.

Mimi bounced around, grabbing at Sam's hand. She wore a black hood and robe and held a tiny scythe in her right hand, like Death's youngest daughter. If she represented death, though, it sure was a gleeful version of it. The scythe bounced with her as she moved, just missing the top of her head as she gyrated. "Tell her," she said, tugging on Sam's sleeve.

He didn't even bother to glance at her. "The pursuer will not hurt you."

Mimi nodded, her hood bouncing on her head. "Yes, yes, but he can't even come here, so it doesn't matter. We matter. We've been waiting for you."

I pushed myself backwards a bit, even though I made myself closer to the beast. "For what? What do you want from me?"

They each stepped to one side and pointed at the organ in the tree.

"You've got to play," Mimi said, pushing the hood back from her forehead.

I shook my head. "Not now. I can't. I've got to get away."

Samarta stepped forward and helped me to my feet with one strong hand. "I told you. It will not harm you, and cannot."

"You don't know that for sure."

"I do," he said.

"Besides, if it does, we know how to kill it, don't we, Sam?" Mimi said.

He nodded and circled me, standing at my back. I could feel him back there gazing into the rows, his eyes on fire.

Mimi took my hand with her free one. "Come on. You've got to do this. It's time. She needs to be free."

"She…?" I said, but any further words died when music strained through the air around us. I exhaled and closed my eyes, singing under my breath:

Stars shining bright above you…

Oh yeah, you bet I knew that song. Dream a Little Dream of Me. The song that Momma used to love so much.

You've got to be kidding me.

"You know, don't you?" Mimi said.

I opened my eyes and gazed at the dark sun looming overhead. "I don't know if it's good or not, but yeah, I know your song."

"It's good, I totally promise. You have to use it to free my friend from the tree."

"Your friend?"

She nodded. "She can save us from the pursuer."

"You said the pursuer couldn't come in here."

She waved a hand. "We've all got to leave some time, right? It's not safe out there."

"Right." I stepped before the keys, closed my eyes, and stretched my hands. I had no idea what playing the song would do, but if this wacked-out version of Mimi said it would save us…well, I didn't see too many other options.

I had never played the song in my life, but that didn't have to stop me. It was never a precise science, but I might be able to fake my way through it, if I could only figure out whether the damn thing was looking for me to play a note in a certain configuration. It was an important point, and could mean life or death.

For that matter, is it looking for the piano part or the vocal part? I pondered it, and decided that the vocals had been way more prominent than the music itself. That had to be it. Hey, only instant death if I got any of these elements wrong. No pressure, right?

I let the lyrics run through my head, envisioning the keys that should match up to the notes. At last I put my hands on the keys and started to play, keeping time with the lyrics in my head.

The song from the organ entangled with the few remaining

notes that hung in the air. As I played and the sounds blended, the notes got lighter and tinnier, until they sounded almost brittle. The sound filled our space and expanded outwards, wafting out over the corn like a force of light, pushing the pursuer further back into the rows.

At last I opened my eyes. The music had an even greater effect than chasing the pursuer away: it had also washed the red light from the sky, turning the blood red sun into a bright, shining disc. It turned the color and quality of the clearing into a faded Polaroid, its colors washed out but at least existing in some spectrum other than red.

I kept playing. When I hit the chorus:

Dream a little dream of me…

Things began to really change. The next note that I hit made no noise. My fingers kept moving over the keys, but the keys themselves dried up, shriveling back into the tree bark. Something cracked overhead and I withdrew my fingers, gazing up into the canopy. I knew how this went: flames appeared, my body cooked, agony. I flinched.

It wasn't that at all; instead, the lock embedded in the tree had cracked and begun to wither.

"I'll be damned…" I said, putting a hand to my chin.

The lock groaned then shattered into a rain of sawdust that fell on Mimi and me. I covered my face, but the girl held her own hands out, giggling as it drifted onto her skin.

I wished I could be so gleeful. I didn't like the sound or sight of it. My heart grabbed hold of my gut and twisted it in knots as a split appeared at the center of the tree, beginning just above the keys and ripping its way skyward.

I took a step back, breathless, terrified out of my mind. "What is this?"

Mimi clapped her hands. "The Dreamer is awakening."

The split widened, becoming a black maw in the center of the tree. Smoke came from the hole, roiling across the blistered bark and oozing down the trunk. This wasn't the smoke that had come from the tree when it burned in my other visions; this smelled sweeter, like fine incense. It stung my eyes, and I waved my hands, trying to push it away.

Mimi grabbed my arm and shook me. "Thank you thank you thank you. She's free," she said, and pointed toward the top of the tree.

"Who?" I looked up, trying to see through the smoke. Something bulky moved in there, its shape pushing aside the smoke…

Oh my God.

"Cici," Mimi cried.

The thing that appeared from the thick haze? The Dreamer, Mimi's friend?

Carla. Carla was the Dreamer.

"What…the…hell?" I said.

Carla struggled against something that kept her suspended inside the tree. Her skin was two shades paler than usual, her cheeks burned red, and she wore a fiery dress that matched the hue on her face, all sequins and clinginess.

I took a step backward. "Carla?"

I had mistaken the lids of her eyes for blank white pupils, but got corrected very quickly when she opened her eyes. What appeared didn't look like any eyes I had ever seen. She *had* no pupils, no lenses – just two glowing green holes. She opened her mouth to speak and her hair came alive, transformed into orange flames that licked around her head without burning her skin or the tree itself. Real biblical shit. She grinned, and the flames flashed off of the gold stumps in her mouth.

I touched my chest without thinking; a holy terror grew somewhere deep inside me. "My God."

Carla moved slowly, grabbing hold of each side of the trunk with her gnarled fingers. The tree cracked, and she had pulled herself free, her shoulders clearing the crack's jagged edges. She had turned into something other than Carla, more like a terrible, ancient goddess than any human I'd met.

The dead lamps of her eye sockets connected with my own eyes and my body went numb.

She spoke, her voice a hallway full of metallic echoes: "Use the knife."

Instinct seized me and I opened my mouth to scream, but nothing came.

Next thing I knew, I was snapping awake in Room 1, a scream ready to roar from my lungs. Sam clamped a hand over my mouth, his breath pulsing in my ears as he held me close. Thank God he did it; things might have gotten ugly if I'd let loose. I'm sure my eyes were ready to crawl out of their sockets to get free of my head. I tried to scream again, but his hand tightened over my mouth.

He whispered in my ear. "We must be silent. Can you do that?"

I nodded, and he released me, taking a step back.

I sat up, balancing myself on my elbows. "What do you want?"

"It is time to talk," he whispered, and motioned toward the door.

May 9th

We saw a man murdered in broad daylight today.

What else can you say really about something like that? We watched a man die in the street, and no one tried to save him, not even us. It's quite a sentence to write.

The day started with the Underground folks' utter failure to deliver our weekly batch of food. Our *first* weekly batch. Not the best of signs. I've been trying not to torture myself with what that might mean for our overall security, but it's tough to stop the questions from bouncing around in your skull.

In the end, what it really means is that we have no choice but to try to fend for ourselves - not exactly new territory. A little search turned up the disguises that they had promised us before we crossed the border. They had been tucked into a small blue bag and hidden under the bed. Nothing dramatic, just a selection of wigs for the both of us and a cheesy black Fu Manchu mustache for Sam.

Oh, and pistols. Loaded pistols. Neither of us was crazy about taking them.

"Isn't this asking for trouble?" I said.

He nodded. "Perhaps. But going without them is suicide."

I wasn't going to argue. We put them in the back of our pants, "just in case".

People filled the narrow street - a lot more than I'd expected on a Friday morning in a virtual warzone, but needs still have to be met some way, I suppose. Their presence would be a blessing, though, as it made it that much easier to blend in. We took a few pushes and shoves, but it only took us a few minutes to make our way to the grimy market on the corner, pick out some "fresh" fruit and a few other staples, and start walking back.

I admit it. I let my guard down on the way back. It's just…it felt so damn good to be out with other people, like I had been granted access to the world that other people took for granted. Fuck suitcases full of stuff; *this* was what I needed to feel alive. I hadn't felt it since I had visited the Dairy Queen, and even then hadn't fully understood why it energized me. I allowed my identity to blend in with the people around me; in my mind's eye I tried on their faces, their sounds, and their smells just as easily as a little girl trying on her mother's clothes. Nothing had been like this during the span of memory that I could trust, and I felt ecstatic.

I'm sure it started with a couple of men started arguing on the other side of the street, the side that never seems to get sunlight. Could the deaths on that street have marked it? It sounds superstitious to talk about it that way, but I have to wonder after all that I've seen.

I didn't hear the beginning of the argument; Kelli didn't really exist in that moment. She had disappeared into the people around her. I probably should have noticed Sam's body tensing at my side, but my identity – and my mind – had been consumed by the dazzling world.

Reality. What a trip.

The first pop from the guy's gun drove me right back into my head. One of the women behind us, whose face I had borrowed for a few moments, screamed and dropped her groceries. As a group, we all took a few steps back, the street echoing with gasps, sighs, and screams. Some of us looked wary, some frightened, and some blank, with glazed expressions. The latter had seen this before, no doubt about that.

Working on raw instinct, Sam dropped the bag of groceries and stood between the murderer and me. He laid his hand on the pistol pushed down into the back of his pants, no doubt ready to do some damage. Thank God I had the presence of mind to step forward and block the other people on the street from seeing the gun's butt.

I heard two more shots, and the murderer ran off in the direction of the market, slamming into an old woman before the crowd parted, letting him slip between. Not one person said a word or moved to stop him; not even us. For us it was the right call, though. Imagine us getting wrapped up in a murder investigation.

Yeah, now try telling my conscience that and getting it to actually believe it.

A few moments of silence followed the guy down the street, but once he had disappeared, the market came back to life. Some people went to the dead man's side, cell phones in hand for both calls and pictures and a few collapsed, but the vast majority just went back to their business. Just another murder. Nothing that they hadn't seen before. Sirens sounded in the distance, no doubt grinding their way through the city.

Sam took his hand from his pistol and stepped to one side. He touched my fingers, and our eyes met. Neither of us opened our mouths, but we communicated all the same:

We should do something, my eyes said.

A slight headshake. We can't get involved.

As much as it killed me, I nodded. He was right, no matter how much I wanted him to be wrong. We really couldn't do anything for the man, and I had never even gotten a good look at his murderer. Besides, our safety had to come first – there were larger things at stake than even the poor guy bleeding out on the pavement.

We picked up our bags, our shoulders bowed, and started making our way down the street. I fought the temptation to glance back at the man's body. I'm only human; or at least I think I am, anyway. *Just keep walking,* I told myself. I didn't need another dead body – another life lost – haunting the back of my mind. I have enough already.

So now I sit here, trying to push the sound of those shots out of my head. Trying not to see the blank stares of the people who had seen it all before, or think about that man's last thoughts. Did he leave anything of substance behind, or would his existence be removed from the human record as soon as they removed his body from that cold street?

The world can't be this. I refuse to accept it. Yet…

I have a lot of evidence to the contrary. A trail of broken and destroyed people in my wake. I didn't kill them, but I served as final witness. Each one of them lived on in me, but did my memory even count, in the final toll? I couldn't say. Maybe in the end, none of us leave much behind.

Can't push this out of my skull. I wish I could get back some of the glory that I felt out on the street this morning. Reading what I've written here, I feel a hollow echo, words on the page, no emotion. Maybe my guilt is wiping out the positive, I can't say for sure.

I guess it doesn't matter. Time to escape to the past, to a rare, happy moment.

======

Sam slipped his big hand over mine as we left Room 1. It was as nice as it was unexpected. His hand felt nice and warm in mine, the palm hard and soft at the same time. Just the way I liked my men to feel. My heart did a few flip flops, and I had to steady myself.

My brain piped up, as it loves to do. Just keep in mind that he hid a lot of stuff from you. You don't know what he wants.

I stopped, releasing his hand. He reached for me again, but I took a step forward, removing my hand without making it too obvious. I took in the front room, hands on my hips. He had tuned all of the monitors to a silenced TV show that I didn't recognize; not a single camera. "How did you do this?"

"Magic."

I looked back at him. "Uh huh. If I were paranoid, I'd say you didn't want anyone to see what you're going to do."

He blushed. "In a manner of speaking, but nothing sinister, I assure you."

"So what is this all about, big guy?"

He put a gentle hand on my right shoulder and gave me a gentle push toward the front door. "I thought that you might enjoy a night out."

I hesitated, pushing back against his hand. "Wait. What do you mean?"

"*Out.*" He nodded toward the door.

I knew I didn't hear that. He couldn't mean really leaving the Khesnaa. Surely not. "What's the trick here?"

He raised an eyebrow. "Trick? Why would I trick you?"

"I don't know what you're up to. All of a sudden everything's okay for me to go outside?"

He let go of my hand and crossed his arms over his chest. "This is not 'all of a sudden'. I worked very hard to make this happen."

I felt a twinge of guilt at that. He had to be telling the truth – none of this could have been easy. "I'm sorry, big guy. Didn't mean to offend you. I just wanted to make sure I'm safe."

"Do you really think I would harm you?"

"Well, no." Not a lie at all. I just wasn't sure whether I could trust my gut.

"Well, then. You know that I would not risk your life without proper precaution."

I sighed. I had legitimate reasons not to trust him fully, but doing the same safe things would continue to get me the same results, and they were just not acceptable. "I'm sorry. I just don't get why you need to take me outside."

He shook his head. "I simply would prefer not to discuss some of these manners in this…place." He went to the front door, punching a code into the keypad. "Outside, it is safe. Safer than here, at any rate."

I got tired of arguing. *No risk, no reward,* I told myself. I got close to him, enjoying that incense-and-spice smell of his. "You can't do that."

He put a finger to his lips and opened the door.

The cold night air hit me, and the last bit of resistance melted from my body. I didn't know just how much I missed fresh air until that moment; giddiness filled me. I grinned at Sam.

"Go ahead," he whispered, ushering me out with one hand.

I hesitated as I stepped over the threshold, feeling something like a child taking its first steps into the world. Then I felt the ground beneath my bare feet, and the hesitation got buried in the same grave as the resistance. The dirt felt cool and soft, rising to support me in ways that I had forgotten a long time ago. I closed my eyes and soaked in the sensation.

He stepped close, leaving a crack in the door. His body radiated heat onto my back. "Do you like it?"

I opened my eyes. "It's amazing." I noticed what looked like a black wall surrounding the cabin, standing in an unbroken circle that hemmed in the tiny cabin.

No – not a wall.

Those were rows of corn stalks, tall and forbidding, their tops framed by the strained moonlight breaking through the gloomy clouds.

I felt ill. "What is this place?"

"I do not know. I have never been told. What troubles you?"

I faced him. "Is there a tree here? Or was there ever?"

"Uh…no. Not since I have been here. Why?"

I wrapped my arms around my chest. "This place looks way too much like my dreams and visions, but how could I know that?" I turned away and stared into the field.

"I do not know," he said, and then he waited – I guess he knew something was coming. I appreciated that. Another man might have rushed to break the silence, or question what bounced around in my skull. Not Sam. That might have been the first time that I realized just how in synch our emotions could be.

That gave me the courage to start. "I had a dream tonight." I turned to face him, lacing my fingers with his. I opened up, sharing that night's dream; the pursuer, the strange Mimi, even Carla coming out of that tree and becoming a crazed goddess. His patience helped me let go.

When I'd finished, he whispered two words, "the signs." His eyes were distant, looking at some point over the horizon

"Is that it? The signs?"

He blinked a few times, rapid, and looked at me. "My senses tell me that it is true. You see places that you cannot know. You speak to the dead. You visit her visions, or perhaps she lives in yours."

"Maybe both?" I said.

"All I can tell you for sure is that the time draws very close."

Those words made me shudder. "Do you know something secret about her?"

"Your dream suggests that you know more than even me. Whatever it is, it is something more powerful than we can understand."

"I don't get it. If these mystical signs are here, why aren't we leaving right now?"

His eyes shined as the moon came out from behind the clouds. "It is not as simple as just 'leaving'. Even if we find a way out, we must do it in the correct fashion."

"You always say that. The right time. The 'Correct Way'. What does that mean?"

He pointed to the sky. "Look. Do you see?"

I followed his finger. "Don't try to change the –"

The sight of the stars in the night sky shut me up. For a moment I was a little girl again, lying in our backyard in Norwalk. The tall grass would tickle my legs as I laid there staring into the void, reveling in my insignificance. It should have been terrifying, but my mind tells me that I found it freeing, and that sounds about right: no matter how bad things got on Earth, much bigger things were afoot elsewhere. I tried to hold on to that: no matter what they were doing to us, there was an even bigger picture where it made no difference whatsoever.

That feeling evaporated within seconds as a whole new emotion took over: confusion.

I glanced back at him. "That doesn't look right."

"Indeed."

"The constellations are all wrong. I don't even recognize them."

He pointed over my shoulder. "Look at the moon."

I admit that my mind had glossed over the moon at the first glance. It had always been there, steady, unworthy of the same notice as the stars, but something was wrong here, too. The light bouncing off of it looked right, like it *could* be our moon, but it had a different landscape. No craters. No dark spots. Not a hint of imperfection. Someone might as well have sanded it down.

"When they brought you here, your captors crossed the threshold between your world and another," Sam said.

The truth was obvious. Sam came from another world. Room 2 took people elsewhere. Of course this was another world. "I guess not. It's fascinating, and I love that you brought me out here, but why show me this? It's not like I can do anything about it."

"I tell you these things so that you understand: we cannot simply walk out the door and return to existence as either you or I knew it."

"But –"

"No 'buts'. There are rules for moving between worlds. Making the wrong move would leave us vulnerable *and* trapped. We must have the upper hand."

My last remaining internal defense crumpled under the weight of reality. In a moment it had finished crushing my soul. "So I've been…somewhere else this whole time?"

"Where better to hide you than somewhere where you never existed?"

"Room 2. That has to be the only gateway. Can we use it?"

He shook his head. "It cannot simply be accessed. The rules for access are very important. It is something that must be experienced to be understood."

"You know the rules then."

"No. Any time that I leave, I must do so under strict supervision. I have never gone through on my own."

I clasped his hands. "Come on, throw me a bone. Tell me what we have to do. I can't die here."

He sighed, releasing my hands. "I wish that I could tell you more, but I honestly do not understand the mechanism yet."

I restrained a bitter response: how could he understand what we were going through if he was leaving on a daily basis while I wasn't?

That's not fair. He's probably lost his wife and kid. My mind went to another question instead. "Why didn't you tell us this earlier?"

He cocked his head. "Note that I still have not told both of you. But surely you can understand that this is dangerous information. I had to know that I could trust you just as much you trusted me."

It occurred to me then how short-sighted and selfish I had been: always my level of trust and respect, always what was hidden from me. Not a thought for his own needs. But then... "What choice do I have *but* to keep your secret? You hold all the cards."

"Not true. You could very well have traded the information for better accommodations, at the very least."

I wanted to sit down all of a sudden. I couldn't believe how self-centered I had been. "I'm...honored that you trust me."

He smiled. "Of course I do. Do not be too harsh on yourself. These circumstances are trying."

"You can say that again."

He took my hand, leading me back toward the cabin. "I

know, it is all a bit much, but I am open to you now. Anything that you want to know, should I know the answer, I will share it with you."

"Fine. What's your full name?"

He tensed. "That is not an easy question to ask."

I let go and crossed my arms over my chest. "Oh, so you immediately back down on your promise. Nice."

He raised a hand. "No such thing is true. You have to understand that words are power. We believed that knowing someone's full name gave them power over you. It would render me extremely vulnerable."

"What am I going to do, burn you in effigy?"

He considered it. "I suppose not. But you must not share it with *her*. We have no idea what she could do with such information."

"Fair enough."

He exhaled, his cheeks puffing out. "Very well. It is Ak'alil. Samarta Ak'alil."

I repeated it. It sounded good in my mouth.

I couldn't see whether he blushed, but I have a feeling he did. The idea made me warm all over.

"My tribal name marks me as a Kellik'at. I do not want anyone else here to know. Not even the Organization itself knows the true nature of my abilities."

"Get out of here, *you*'re a Kellik'at?"

He couldn't meet my eyes. "Not that I deserve such a title, but yes. I was."

His story echoed in my mind: the sudden attacks, the deaths. I could almost hear their screams in my head. What had he called his world?

Abshir; that had been it. To watch his entire tribe wiped

out... "I'm sorry."

"You have nothing to apologize for." He waved his hand at the cabin. "These people are to blame. And myself."

I put a hand on his shoulder. "Come on now, how can it be your fault? You're a victim, too."

"That night wasn't their first amongst us. They showed up about a standard month before that day, just wandered into our camp, looking like they had no business in our world. They demanded to see me, and so I agreed, with some...misgivings. Their leader, a large, dark man you might know as the Senior, presented an offer to me: they would buy the land from us in exchange for their gold. He would also throw in a nice bonus for me, so that I could continue to rule my people." He scoffed. "*Rule.*"

"So you turned him down?"

"Of course. We were not ignorant children, to be taken advantage of, and I told them so. I threatened their lives for such a sacrilege. They retreated, with threats of reprisal. I wondered then if I had made a mistake, but I could not simply give the land up – it was our charge," he said, his mouth tightening with anger. "We went on high alert for quite some time."

"I know what happens next," I said.

He looked at the moon. "It is impossible to maintain eternal vigilance. They took what they wanted, and when they were done, when I had witnessed their brutality, they held me in the dirt, and told me to show them our sacred ground."

"And you did."

"I had no choice."

I wrapped an arm around him. "What did you show them? What did you protect?"

He pushed closer to me, no doubt grateful for the contact.

"A cavern beneath our tribal lands, buried in the mountain itself. The worlds are thin there, and the dead can speak more freely. We hosted the trials of adulthood there, and I first connected with the dead there. We respected it and we guarded it."

"So they killed your entire tribe to get access to the land."

"What was under the land, but yes. If I had only accepted their offer…" He looked me right in the eyes. "What happened was my fault. I bear the shame."

"You didn't kill those people. They did."

He gave a bitter chuckle. "I gave them cause. Had I accepted their offer, my people would still be alive. I also betrayed the sacred trust that our people had held for generations."

"Come on, honey. They would have killed your family. You didn't have a choice." *Honey.* That one just slipped out, but it felt good. "You did what you had to. You're not to blame."

He ignored that. "I must atone and make their sacrifices worth something. So I protect you."

I didn't see the connection, but I let that one pass.

He went on. "After I showed them the cavern, they knocked me out, and I woke up in a small gray cell not much bigger than your closet. It is my cell when I am not here. My family has been the only thing that kept me sane. But now…

I squeezed him; his body tensed, and I wondered if I should pull away, but he loosened up in the next breath. I had to tell myself that he just didn't expect it. He wasn't repulsed. Right? "Now you just don't know."

His lips hovered near my ear, sending a tingle down my spine. "I cannot feel them any longer. Our connection is severed. Every day I think about the fact that I did not act to try to save them, and I think about betraying my people. I have had to live with that and control the anger beneath the surface. Every. Single.

Day."

"How do you look at them every day without wanting to kill them?"

He separated from me, rubbing his eyes. "I do not. I want to slaughter each and every one of them."

"Who are they? The Organization, I mean. Do you know more about them that you haven't told me?"

"No. I would not withhold such information. But I plan to find out more."

"How?"

"I will use their greed for my land against them." He crossed his arms over his chest. I'm sure he meant to look powerful or resolute, but he just looked cold.

I remembered the look in his eyes on the night that Gina died: shame and strength. *Patience,* he had said. I got it at that moment. "Hey, I never thanked you for holding me back the night that Gina died."

He shook his head. "I share the blame for what happened, and I could not see the same happen to you. I did what had to be done."

"Is that all of it?"

He clenched his jaw. "I might have seen something special in you."

"Ah," I said; there wasn't much else *to* say. "Why did you really bring us out here?"

"I believe you know the answer to that. Your friend."

I toed the ground again. I'd have to remember to clean my feet when I got back in. "Why's it so hard for you to call her by her name?"

"Just as my people believed that knowing a full name gave one control over that person, we also believed that saying that person's first name opened the door to their psyche. And I do not trust her. I am not convinced that she knows nothing of this project. Her capacity to read the minds of our captors should have exceeded my own meager abilities long ago. It is the logical progression of her initiation."

I held up a hand. "Hold up. Does that mean you can read minds?"

He cleared his throat. "At an extremely limited level. I can only sense feelings, but do not worry. I would never dare to peek inside your mind."

Part of me actually wanted that. "I believe you."

"Anyway. That is how I know of the signs. I can feel their undercurrent around us. It is why we speak now." He locked eyes with me. "You must understand. She may very well know what goes on in your mind. There is a connection between you that I cannot quite work out."

I suddenly itched all over. Could he be right? "Carla wouldn't read my mind. She's not like that." But I wasn't so sure. "When Gina visited me, she told me that Carla was hiding something. Do you think that could be it?"

"Possibly. I am quite sure that she has known a larger part of the picture of your visions for quite some time. I have never felt surprise from her when you told her of them. Not once."

"That bitch," I said.

He held his hands up, asking for patience. "She may not have a choice *but* to see these things. If she has not learned control, her mind could well be open at all times. I suspect that may be why she has withdrawn to such a degree."

I rubbed my chin. "Like she's trying to block out all the stuff coming into her brain?"

"Precisely my thought."

It would explain her weird meltdown. She kept trying to resist my prying, but she might also have been resisting all the other thoughts in the place that night. Maybe she'd gotten a whiff of what had been going on between Maple and Zito that night, too. "So now what?" I said.

"I brought you out here so that we could escape any recording, but I also wanted to be certain that she slept and was not nearby when we spoke. She might not be able to resist listening in."

More pieces fell into place. Carla had recognized me that first night, I *knew* it, I just didn't know how. It all connected up, but I couldn't make sense of the picture that it showed me. "How do you know all this? Sensing feelings?"

"I have also watched her very closely. I will not entrust my life to her, no matter how kind she may appear, although..."

"What?"

"I wonder if I am having difficulty separating my observations from my feelings about what she means to me."

I cocked my head. "Going to have to run that one by me again."

He put his hands behind his back and exhaled. "She is the final piece to the Organization's puzzle. The last piece of their collection. This change with my family – my loss of contact, and our captors' refusal to answer my questions – only began once she arrived."

"I'm so sorry. Shit. There I go again," I said.

If he noticed it, he didn't say anything. "But it is not just the threat to my family. It is the threat that she represents to you. I do not know if this makes sense. My mind has been clouded...confused. By new feelings." He met my eyes.

The butterflies started up in my gut again. "Why are you

telling me this?"

"Two reasons. One is that I believe they are closing in on me."

"What do you mean?"

He took a few steps toward the corn, hands behind his back, and looked at the ground. When he turned back to me, I couldn't really see his eyes in the darkness. "I believe that they know what we have been doing, and they do not approve. The Senior will likely show up soon. Perhaps as soon as tonight."

I walked toward him. "Who is this Senior, anyway?"

"He is the...*man*, for lack of a better word, who truly runs this project. One of the heads of the Organization, I believe, yet he does much of his own dirty work. Maple, Zito, Barren...they all report to him."

"He'd be the one to, you know, take care of you?"

"I would suspect so, yes."

I approached him. "But if they suspect what we're up to, why haven't they done anything to stop us before now?"

He cocked his head. "Have they not? They installed the cameras."

"I mean something more physical, like chaining us up."

"I do not know. It is a curious play for them. Perhaps they are waiting for one of us to reveal some secret, betray something that they do not know." He sighed. "Regardless, I do not think I will be here much longer. If my family is dead, I must follow soon after."

Gina came to mind again. They ripped her away right when I felt I could count on something in that godforsaken place. They couldn't take him away, too, not right when I allowed myself to trust him. "I'm not going to let them take you."

"You will not have a choice."

"I'll find a way. If I have to go to the other side and bring you back, I will."

"I appreciate the sentiment, but –"

I grabbed his shirt and shook him. "Damn you, you're a warrior. Act like one. You don't just lie down and quit."

His eyes lit up and he picked my hands off of his shirt, one at a time. "Being a warrior is not only about battle. Being a warrior is about understanding honor and sacrifice. Fighting now would only endanger you. It would be pointless."

I threw my hands in the air. "I don't know what to say to you, Sam. You give me hope, then take it away, deflect every little thing I say, and when I object, you give me these platitudes that mean nothing."

He tried to take one of my hands. "I just want you to accept what I am saying."

I shook his hand off. "No, you don't get to do that. I'm the one who chooses whether to accept it. You can't make me do that."

"You are right, of course." He squirmed, and my anger eased back for just a moment.

"Why are you really telling me all this?" I said.

"My feelings."

"What do you mean?" Stupid, stupid rhetorical question. I knew just what he meant. Hadn't I just been scolding myself for feeling that way? Adrenaline coursed through me. I might as well have been standing on a cloud now as much as standing in front of him. I didn't know if I wanted to punch him or kiss him.

He looked away. "I have become...*fond* of you. You surely have noticed this."

Yeah, the anger won. "Damn you. You tell me you're going to die and then you drop that on me?"

"I admit, I probably should not…"

I paced away from him, deliberately stomping my bare feet into the ground. "No, you shouldn't. It's not fair." I turned back and came to him. "Damn you, I feel the same way. I don't want to say it, but I do."

There. It was out at last. My knees quaked.

He lowered his voice. "I understand your conflict. I do not know if my family is alive or dead. Not really. As such, this brings shame upon me."

I huffed. "Oh, really? So I bring shame to you? You're just on a roll."

He held his hands up. "I am not saying what I mean to say. I apologize. I do not mean it that way. It is not you at all. You bring me joy, not shame. It is our…situation."

I crossed my arms over my chest. "Still not buying it. Still not helping."

"You do not understand. Our people mate for life. Having feelings for another is unthinkable. Forbidden. Punishable by the worst."

"The worst?"

He wrung his hands. "There are far worse things than death, but let us not talk about that now."

I remembered the portal under their village, and maybe I got the picture – where could that thing send you, after all?

He spoke again. "This does not bode well for you. Zito fancies you as his prize. He may sense your feelings."

I blinked, the anger finally draining out of me. Confusion filled the void. "Say what now?"

"Surely you have noticed how he watches you."

"Of course, but I figured that was because he…you know, hates my guts." I felt nauseated. Just the idea of Zito's paws on me…

"Oh, he loathes you, but he wants you all the same. Perhaps there is a connection. I do not know nor understand."

"What should we do about it, then?" I cringed inside when I caught what I'd said. I didn't really mean *we*. I had no idea how there could be a 'we', even if both of us felt the same. He could be gone at any moment.

"I will keep him from you as long as I can. I promise I will protect you." He wrapped his arm around my waist and pulled me close before I could figure out what he planned. Our faces were close, and I noticed a slight shine to his lips, a reflection of the moonlight. I wondered if he could feel my heart pounding against his chest.

He spoke again. "If I am right, and if I do not have much time left, then I want you to know these feelings."

"I don't want you to go."

"I assure you, I do not *want* to go."

"I'm not sure if I could go on without you. I'd be lost."

He shook his head. "No. You cannot feel that way."

I tried to pull away, but he kept me in place. I sighed. "Don't tell me how I should feel, Samarta."

"I did not intend to. Please, I am struggling. I only mean that you cannot allow your sanity to hinge upon me. You must have another reason to fight."

I looked down. "I suppose. I don't know what that reason could be, though. Can't trust Carla."

He touched my chin, making me look at him. "Freedom. That is your reason. Let it be your anchor."

"I'm sorry, but that doesn't cut it. I don't have the greatest record with men. I finally meet the right one, and he tells me he's going to die soon, but that's okay because I can think of freedom.

It's hard to hold on to some vague hope when you could lose something - someone - that could finally mean something to you."

He sighed. "I understand. Such words would tear the soul out of me."

"Then promise me you'll fight when the time comes."

He frowned. "Of *course* I will fight. I cannot lie down and let them take me, if that is what you think."

"I guess I did. You sounded so defeated."

"Resignation to one's fate is not the same as surrender. It is simply recognition of one's limits," he said.

"Oh, just shut up and kiss me."

His eyes got as big as headlights in the moonlight. "Oh. Uhm." He squirmed. "I. Well."

The man was impossible. "Sam..."

"Very well." He closed his eyes and leaned forward, locking his lips onto mine.

He rocked me backward for a second. I didn't expect him to be so ferocious. If it weren't for his daughter, I might have guessed he was asexual or scared of girls, or something like that. Now I saw that he had been holding back out of fear that he might break me. I mean it; I wondered if his lips meant to do mine harm.

My anxious energy, pushed back by confusion and revulsion, surged again. Heat rushed through my body, and my head swooned. That's when I decided to show him he wasn't the only warrior in this relationship. I could give just as good as I got, so I grabbed hold of the back of his head and drove my passion right back toward him.

I wouldn't call it a movie moment, but it was damn fine all the same. Everything I had hoped for? Quite possibly, yes. Whatever else you might say about it, it felt right, like no matter what else might happen, we were meant to be there at that moment. All my concerns and fears melted away, and for a second I allowed myself to believe that he just might stick around.

That's what I need to hold on to when I think about that guy in the street. As scared as I had been, my fear – the idea that I'd lose the only thing that mattered – melted away. It left just the two of us, kissing under that strange moon.

It was my last truly happy moment at the Khesnaa.

When we finally broke the kiss, I looked up into his eyes and said, "thank you."

"No. Thank you. You gave me the courage to do things that I might not have otherwise. To take risks again. I cannot tell you what that means. I can be the man that I once was."

"That's why you've accepted what's coming."

He nodded. "One way or another. Yes."

"Good, I –"

He held up one hand and cocked his head.

"What?"

"Do you not feel that?"

I did feel a little queasy, but I just chalked it up to my jittery nerves. "Maybe."

He grabbed my hand and pulled me toward the door. "There is no time to debate this. You must get back in your room this instant."

He had lulled me with that kiss; good thing, too, because I might have fought him. "What? Why?"

"The Senior is coming."

We stopped at the door and he entered the key code again.

"Wait, hold up. How do you know?"

"I can feel when the doors between worlds begin to open. I suspected that you might, as well." He looked to me. "I suppose you become more sensitive when you grow up on top of such a portal. Come on, move."

My head began to spin, my stomach lurching. "I don't feel so good," I said, and put a hand against the wall to support myself.

"You will be okay. Please. Move. For your own sake."

"Okay, okay." I let him put a hand on my back and push me through the front door without another word.

He followed me inside, closing the door behind him. I stumbled toward Room 1, using every ounce of willpower that I could summon to stay on my feet. I wanted to rush, but I felt like I'd been drugged.

"What's wrong with me?" I slurred at him.

He changed the picture on the monitors without looking back. "It is a side effect. They typically wait until you are asleep for just this reason."

"I…" I couldn't manage much more.

I heard him turn, and he got in front of me in two strides, unlocking our door and opening it in a breath.

His eyes pled with me. "Move."

I wanted to. God, I wanted to. I managed to stagger into the room, falling to the floor just as he closed the door behind me. I cried out, and whatever food had been lurking in my stomach came up to the back of my throat. I belched and put a hand to the top of my chest, fighting it back.

Then a whooshing noise came from Room 2, and the door between worlds swung open.

May 12th

I haven't written in a few days, and I couldn't even tell you why. We haven't left the house, haven't spoken much, and haven't really done much of anything. We're in a holding pattern, waiting for the Underground to make a move. It should be the perfect time to catch up on my story...but I haven't. Maybe I haven't been ready to face the Senior again. Just thinking of him makes me shudder.

I slept a lot the last few days; I wondered if it might even be depression. It had all the hallmarks that TV and books had told me to expect: listlessness, sadness, exhaustion...it had to be that, right?

That's when I realized something quite surprising: I wasn't even sure what depression really *feels* like. I could read you off that list of ingredients above, but I didn't know what those felt like together. Had I felt it right after Gina died? There had been a lot of sadness, sure, and we've established that the thing damn near broke me, but that's just it: I was broken, not depressed. There had been no listlessness, no exhaustion. I'd been filled with mean, spiteful purpose instead.

That epiphany gave me something of a panic attack. I didn't know something so basic on an emotional level. What did that mean for my psyche? I wondered if I really was just a wind-up toy that had been set in motion and became self-aware. It put my bellyaching about what I would leave behind in some new perspective: should I measure myself by the same yard-stick that everyone else used when I'm so clearly different in every way?

For that matter, would I even recognize happiness if I had it?

Nah, that's silly. Of course I would. I just wrote about it, didn't I? I've had it, even back there in the Khesnaa, in that moment with Sam. I think I'm just falling into a trap in my thinking. Maybe that's depression, constantly doubting yourself? It sounds damned close to what I've read and heard.

I'm writing here because things started changing last night. One of the folks from the Underground stopped by; he said he couldn't stay for long, but he dropped off some food and told us a little bit about what they're planning for us. I wish I felt safe saying more here, but remember that bigger picture that I mentioned when they first talked about bringing us here? There might be something to it after all.

They're working on getting us not just out of *this* country but off the continent altogether. The guy said one of the higher-ups wants to meet us, has some vested interest in our well-being. He didn't give us any clues, but all the same I think I might know what he's talking about.

I want to, but that's another thing that I don't dare write down here. Not until I know we're completely safe and it won't give us away.

The important thing is that we have to be ready to go at a moment's notice. I know, right? Like we haven't been ready to drop everything up to this point. Like we haven't lived our lives on this side in constant danger. I might have gotten a little lax before the murder the other day, but those instincts are alive and well now, thank you very much.

I want out. I just don't know what else I can do.

Write, I suppose. Face the Senior again. At least it beats

dying inch by inch.

======

After the portal opened, things got really quiet in the Khesnaa. I heard Carla stir in her bed, but even she could figure out that something big was going down, as she stayed completely silent. I couldn't imagine what Sam might be doing. Grabbing a sharp weapon? Getting ready to beat the guy over the head?

Kneeling?

It sounded a lot like that last when he said, "Senior. What a surprise. I am honored."

A man with a snooty, crisp English accent (with just an undertone of sinister bass) spoke. "Spare me the pleasantries. I know just what you think of me."

Carla began to speak, but I shushed her. I slid to the door, putting my ear against it so I could better hear the confrontation in the front room.

Sam cleared his throat. "Very well. This is true. I hope you do not find this impertinent, but is there something I can do for you?"

"I find it quite impertinent, and you can answer *my* questions, as that is what *you* do. You do not question me. Do you understand?"

"I understand."

At this point I got the picture, loud and clear, that this guy had to be the Senior that Sam had spoken of out in the corn field.

I heard heavy footsteps outside the door. Heavier than even Sam's feet. How big was this guy, anyway? "There's a good boy. I am here to determine just how this project is proceeding. It's been some time since I involved myself personally. Maple and her kind are good for only one thing, and that's keeping people like you in order."

"I see," Sam said. He wasn't doing a very good job of hiding his loathing for the guy. I couldn't blame him, but my nerves were on edge, worrying what the bastard might do to him.

"What is it you do here all night?" the Senior said.

"I keep watch over the Participants. I guard the Investment."

"That is not an answer."

"I watch television, mostly."

The Senior snorted. "Television. Yes. Perhaps we should revisit that arrangement. Tell me, do you go to the basement often?"

"Only when required, sir."

"Mm. To *guard* the Investment, of course, as you so eloquently put it. Did you disturb him?"

Sam hesitated. He wouldn't give us up, right? At last he spoke. "I am…afraid I might have. I have been clumsy. When I fed Enliel, he reacted strangely."

The Senior stopped pacing. "Strangely? Explain yourself."

I imagined a shrug. "He appeared not to care for the dish. Perhaps he is evolving."

"Hm. Yes. Perhaps. I have been told that you requested a trip to your homelands."

My stomach started twisting again, but this time it was nerves rather than nausea; that, thank God, seemed to have passed.

"You heard true," Sam said.

"What was the purpose of this trip?"

"I do not see why I have to tell you."

Two more heavy steps, and I think the Senior stood in front of Sam. "Of course you do not; you are a foolish primitive given a man's job. Simply answer the question as directed."

Some sounds. I was pretty sure that Sam had risen from his knees. I couldn't imagine the look on his face. "Very well. I have lost faith that you have protected my family. I have lost faith that you protected my lands. I have lost faith in any of your promises."

I wanted to scream at him, tell him to shut up; couldn't he hear how dangerous this guy could be? But of course I wouldn't. I couldn't. And if he did hear it, he didn't care.

"Perhaps you are wiser than you appear. Do you speak to the Participants very often?"

Participants. He means us. Something in his voice sounded like he knew *exactly* how often Samarta talked to us.

"Only so often as necessary. And never on friendly terms."

The Senior scoffed. "Perhaps it's my turn to lose faith in you. That is not my understanding of the situation here. There are some who question your commitment to your job."

"Perhaps they should address such concerns to my face, rather than running to others with their...*concerns.*"

The Senior sounded amused when he responded. "Perhaps. This *is* a spineless, cowardly lot, Samarta, be quite sure of that, but these Participants are not your friends. Do not forget that."

"I would never forget that."

A long silence. "Do you suspect that they are planning something?"

"If they are, does it really matter?"

Bold. Very bold.

"Explain yourself."

Sam hesitated again, but only for a beat. If you didn't know him, it might not even be perceptible, but it was there. "What can they possibly do to affect the Organization? They are locked down tight."

The Senior seemed to consider this. "Good point. No, I suppose their plans don't matter. Now please, take me to the basement, if you would be so kind."

"Uh…sir?"

"Yes, you. Take me."

"I'm sorry; I'm just not accustomed to-"

The Senior scoffed. "You are the one currently in charge, yes? No matter how unfortunate that may be."

"Well, yes," Sam said.

"Then take me downstairs. I wish to see how things are proceeding."

"Very well."

I closed my eyes and prayed that Sam would let the Senior into the basement, but not follow him down there. He wouldn't let himself be trapped down there, right? Sure, he said that he had accepted his death, but not like this.

I heard what I guessed was Sam pulling out his keychain, and not one but two sets of footfalls headed toward the basement door. The key clicked in a lock, and the door opened.

Don't go down there. Please. Don't.

If he really could sense my emotions, he either didn't care or didn't figure he had a choice. His footsteps followed the Senior down the stairs, and the door swung shut behind them.

I sighed and leaned my head against the door.

"What is going on?" Carla said behind me, her voice low.

I jumped. She stood over me, hands on her hips, her face just barely visible in the light bleeding from under the door.

"How did you get here without me hearing you?" I said.

"I'm a ninja, didn't you know? Now tell me what's going on.

Who *was* that?"

Feeling a little snarky, I tried to "push" a thought toward her: *you should have heard it and known.*

My head swam a bit when she said, "I only heard a little bit."

She'd heard my thoughts. She really could read my mind.

No, you're just on edge. That could have easily been a follow-up to what she said.

Yeah, sure. Maybe I could convince myself of that. "That would be the head honcho. The one that scares all the other little assholes around here," I said.

"The Senior."

"So you did hear it."

"No. I've heard them talk about him."

I rose, facing her. "When?"

"I don't remember. Probably in Room 3. Listen, was that him and Sam going downstairs?"

I sighed. "Yeah." I gave her an abridged version of the night's events, naturally leaving out the whole part where Sam and I went outside. In this version of reality, I just so happened to be awake when the door to Room 2 opened up, and so, naturally, I went down to lie by the door and listen to what happened. It could have happened.

She might have bought it, but I had my doubts. From what I could make out of her face, she didn't seem too sure. She must have heard (or whatever you want to call it) a lot more than she let on. Had her poker face always been that bad, or had I just not been looking for the signs?

She opened her mouth to say something, but the thump of the basement door opening cut her off.

Heavy footsteps followed, and we both leaned against the

door.

They stopped just outside our room, and the Senior spoke first. "Do we understand one another?"

"Perfectly."

"I am most pleased with the progress. Our latest acquisition has been very productive, has she not?"

"They do not keep me up-to-date on the project's progress. For obvious reasons."

More footsteps. I imagined the Senior circling Sam. "Hm. Yes, wise, I suppose. All the same, even you can see the progress."

"Of course," Sam said.

More silence. "May I see her?"

Those four words chilled me more than anything else that had come out of the Senior's mouth. It wasn't that he wanted to see either of us, though that idea did disturb the hell out of me. What *really* gave me the heebie-jeebies was the tone of his voice. He sounded like a kid on Christmas morning.

I could only imagine the war in Sam's heart. Would this be the right time to sacrifice himself, or would it be in vain? It's not like the guy couldn't just enter our room anyway. "It is your project," he said at last.

"An excellent point. Take me to their room. It *is* Room 1, correct?"

Carla and I exchanged a terrified glance a moment before we almost ran each other over trying to get back to our beds. I slid into the bed and pulled the covers over me, waiting for their approach. My heart pounded; the Senior *must* have heard us.

The door creaked open, and I closed my eyes, trying to will my heart to slow, my breathing to ease up. I didn't really succeed.

The two entered on quiet, cautious feet. At least, they tried; I don't think the Senior could be stealthy if he tried. I could hear now that the Senior snorted on every inhalation. Between that and the heavy feet, it sounded like a wild animal had entered the room. I tried to picture him in my head and found my imagination coming up short every time. All I could picture was this huge, snorting wreck of a guy, but I didn't think that could be quite right, either, as he had a sharp accent and was clearly intelligent. Maybe he was a suave demon.

A few scuffling steps and the two paused.

"They're more beautiful than I'd expected," the Senior said. I could hear that he stood close to Carla's bed. Like, *way* too close to Carla's bed. She must be shitting bricks at that point. I wondered if the Senior could pick up on us faking our sleep and didn't want to disturb us, or if he honestly couldn't tell the difference.

"I am sure you have seen photos, or video…?" Sam said.

"Of course, but it's nothing like the real thing, is it?" He snorted, and I imagined him sniffing Carla up close. "You will do such wonderful things. Such awful, wonderful things…" he said, almost to himself, his voice real low.

I ground my teeth. I wondered if she could see into his mind and the filthy, awful things that hid there.

Sam cleared his throat. "We should allow them their rest."

A sound; I think the Senior straightened up. He must have been leaning over Carla's still form. "Of course. I will let you get back to your…television. Please do keep an eye on them. Especially this one. She is a prized possession."

"Yes, sir," Sam said.

Without another word, the Senior turned and left the room. Sam took a long moment, no doubt gazing at me, before he followed. I heard the door close, and I dared to open one eye. I had to be cautious, just in case the Senior had laid a trap.

"Good God," Carla said, and I saw that she had sat up, her arms crossed over her chest.

"Did you get a look at him?"

"Are you out of your mind? I wasn't about to let him see me. But good God. His breath smelled like rotten meat."

"Oh, that's nasty."

A door shut in the front room and a wave of nausea spread over me. It didn't take a genius to figure out that the Senior had stepped through the Room 2 portal, going back to Hell, or wherever he lived.

I needed to know if she had read his mind. "Did you get anything else off of him? Like…a vibe or something?"

She shuddered. I don't think she meant to, and she recovered from it really quick, but she shuddered.

What are you hiding, Carla?

She spoke. "Nothing. I…I didn't get anything. Other than him being one spooky son of a bitch."

"I could hear that. Sounded like a pig."

She didn't answer that. Not directly, anyway. "You going back to sleep?"

"You think I can, after that?"

"I guess not. Think Sam would let us out there to watch some TV?"

I chuckled. "Call me crazy, but I have a feeling he might want to be alone after that thing came through here."

"Yeah. Crazy." She stared at the ceiling, wrapping her arms around her body.

Awkward silence followed. Oh, I didn't want to be quiet. I wanted to scream at her, tell her "I know that you know, you're a piss-poor liar and a bad actor, and I don't need you to go on playing and lying to me like I was one of *them*." I'd rage. I'd get in her face.

But…no. I couldn't do it. Not when I had lied to her. Not when I was hiding just as much from her.

It turned out to be quite the night. At different points, each of us tucked into bed, trying to get to sleep, but within minutes were awake again. Think we talked to each other, though? No. The space between us might as well have been a chasm. Our secrets divided us, and each had to wait for the other to play her hand.

I hated it. I wanted out, but I couldn't see a better way. Looking back, I wish that I had been the first to take that step, shown her my cards. Who knows how things would have turned out, but I should have known that keeping secrets would make things worse.

No. I hadn't been much more than a child; I had no way of knowing better without getting my ass kicked for it. That's how growth works.

My memory of the next morning is fuzzy, but I'm going to wring as many memories as I can. Let's just say that neither of us were at our best when Zito and Maple came knocking. It should have been a routine morning, but it sure didn't feel like it. Even then I remember feeling like we had been strapped to a live rocket and just had to see if they would fire us into the heavens or right into the ground.

The answer came quickly, as the two went for Carla without as much as a "good morning".

Carla looked from one to the other, her eyebrows raised. "What do you want?"

Maple fidgeted with something in her apron. "Simply to check on you."

"Yeah, just wanted to brighten up your morning," Zito said,

and winked at me.

"You aren't brightening shit," I said. If I'd had enough sleep the night before, I might have figured out what they were doing, but I had been reduced to simple reactions.

Zito shot me the finger.

You don't fool me, you little shit. In the cold light of day, after enduring the presence of the Senior, he seemed like a clown. I returned the finger.

Maple took advantage of the distraction. She moved fast, or at least it seemed that way at the time. It could have been the effect of a fit, alert woman moving on an exhausted, confused woman who hadn't slept, but before either of us knew what was happening, Maple had pulled a giant syringe from inside her apron and plunged the thing into Carla's arm.

A lot of things happened at once then; these are the few remaining things from that day that stand out in my mind, even if the order is a little confused. It started with Carla shrieking and throwing her arm out, knocking Maple backwards. I can still see the syringe sticking out of her skin when she did that, the needle tearing a bloody hole in her skin.

Maple fell into the chair beside Carla's bed and spilled over, bringing the chair with her.

Zito hollered and pulled the gun from his jacket as Maple tumbled. I made a choked noise and jumped from my bed, trying to grab him and stop whatever would happen next.

Problem was, *I* was what happened next, because Zito turned on me, raised the gun, and squeezed the trigger.

Pain exploded in my neck as the bullet sliced my jugular, opening my neck. I tried to scream, but I could only get raw gurgles through the new hole. Zito swore, and I think he ran for me. I might have had a millisecond to think that I was about to die, but it happened so fast that I can't remember. It took seconds for me to fall back onto the bed, back into the nothingness from which I'd come.

I wonder what would have happened if the safety had been on, like he no doubt expected it to be. Would I have ever gotten out and been here to tell you the story? I doubt it.

Try as I might, though, I can't quite muster a feeling of gratitude toward the man.

May 15th

This journal is becoming an incredibly irregular thing, but screw it, it's my journal and I'll do what I want. I **needed** a few days off after the last entry. It's not every day you write about your own death. You'd be surprised at what it can do to your head. I spent awhile just wandering around the house, not even sure what to do. To my credit, I didn't descend into the weird again, or sleep all day, or anything like that, not that I had much of a choice.

We knew something was off when someone knocked on our door. Yeah, he used the Underground pattern, but a visitor outside of the usual delivery schedule couldn't mean anything good for us. Sam left me at the table with my cold bowl of oatmeal, stumbling to the door, his eyes still red-rimmed and bleary.

When he opened the door, Carlos (yes, that Carlos) stood before him, hands together at his waist. He wore a stained white T-shirt and jeans, his hair sticking up at weird angles. He hid his eyes behind dark shades, his demeanor stiff and aggressive; he had basically become the polar opposite of the guy who greeted us when we arrived. Just the sight of him made my stomach feel funny.

He entered without a word, flopping down in the armchair by the door.

"Uhm, please, enter," Sam said, heading for the couch opposite of Carlos, flopping down against the arm rest.

I joined him quickly. Who wants cold oatmeal, anyway?

Neither of us said a word. The man's presence demanded silence and respect. If he hadn't scared the shit out of me, I might be impressed at how he could transform himself. I have a gut feeling that the *real* Carlos sat before us. I'm not sure that other guy could have lasted a week in this war.

He glanced around the room with an indifferent air. "We can do better."

I laughed, more from tension escaping my body than actual humor. "I've been saying that for days."

He didn't smile. "This is not a friendly visit. We should never have seen one another again, you understand, and yet here I am."

"Here you are," Sam agreed, running a hand over his head. I could tell he was nervous and trying not to show it.

Carlos sat forward, clasping his hands at his knees. "You remember what I told you when we first met. Between the lines, the clowning. That there is much more going on here."

We nodded, but said nothing.

"We are their pawns, yes. Nothing more. This battle is fought in many layers, and we can trust no one. I told you this." He sat back, pushing his glasses up on his nose. "There is no other way to say this. Your deliveryman, we caught him last night using an encrypted cell phone."

I raised an eyebrow. "Meaning?"

"This phone was unauthorized. No one could identify it. We believe it came from the bastardos, the Organization. He was their pawn."

Sam caught it first. "What do you mean 'was'?"

Carlos wagged a finger at him. "You are sharp. When we found him, he hid behind a dumpster. He tried to destroy the cell phone, but we got it first. We don't know what he used on himself, but within moments he was dead."

I put a hand to my mouth.

Carlos nodded. "You see what we face."

"We saw someone die in the street here," I blurted out. I still have no idea where that came from, but it felt appropriate at the moment. I'm still working on that whole filtering-what-comes-out-of-my-mouth thing.

He nodded. "This war. We did not ask for it and yet we are stuck in the middle. You are a casualty as much as that man in the street. It's why we must protect you. We won't allow them to use you."

I glanced at Sam. How much did this guy know? "You don't say."

"Yes. Your benefactor – the one at the top – has told us much about you. They have made it our goal to save you, so do not fear." He rose. "But we must move you now. Gather what you can. One of my men will show up in…" He glanced at his watch. "Five minutes. They will bring a truck. You will get into the bed and lie under the blankets."

Not another move. I thought I might go crazy. "We'll melt."

He held up a hand. "I know. I am sorry, truly, but this is what must be done." With that, he turned tail and left us to pack up our shit.

So yes, we got moved to a new location because someone in the Underground turned out to be a mole. Surprise!

I can't deny that it was a unique experience. There's nothing quite like hiding in the back of a creaky old Toyota, inhaling the odor of dog vomit from a wool blanket while you bounce around the streets of one of the most dangerous cities in North America. I recommend it to everyone. By the time we got out, we were on the south side of the city, as well. Yes, that's the most dangerous part of the most dangerous city. It just gets better and better. I suppose you just don't get many options when you're an inter-dimensional fugitive.

Credit where credit's due, though. The new place is a whole lot better than the last. Clean, with a nice firm king bed, a full kitchen, and a couch that has absolutely no springs poking through. Moving up in the world.

Where was I, though? Oh yes. My own death. Silly me, how could I forget?

======

When I awoke, my eyes sticky and heavy, I tried to raise a hand to shield myself from the multi-colored lights shining down from overhead. I groaned when I discovered that someone – not naming names here – had restrained me.

As my body came alive, a burning erupted at the right side of my neck and throat. It felt like someone had shoved a hot poker into there, melting right through my skin. I didn't know if I was alive, dying, or dead.

Momma's voice broke through the pain. *You're alive. And you're back in Room 3.*

Panic grabbed me by the chest. I wanted to jump up and run, or hell, even shout. I moved my head, trying to figure out how I could get myself out of the chair. The burning exploded into the rest of my head, and I cried out.

Don't do that. That wouldn't be any good idea, she said.

A man spoke from somewhere beyond the wall of pain. "Very wise. Remain still. Don't try to speak."

Barren. Even if I hated the guy, I had to admit that he had a soothing voice. It might have been the only thing that kept me from completely losing it. I moved my eyes to the left and caught him just on the edge of my vision.

He stepped closer, pushing his glasses up on his nose. "You are okay."

Zito spoke from somewhere behind him. "Tell her."

Barren looked over his shoulder. "You've *done* your job, let me do mine."

"I told you it was an accident."

"Maybe you should tell her that. She might forgive you," Barren said.

Zito didn't answer, but that was just as well. Call me old-fashioned, but I think shooting someone in the goddamn neck is a little beyond forgiving. Maybe that's just me.

Barren went on. "Listen carefully, Kelli. I've closed the wound on your neck, but it's a very bad one. You have to be as still as you possibly can."

I wondered about that. *Closed the wound.* Could you really do that when somebody had their neck sliced open like mine? I guess he had, or I wouldn't be there.

Still, something didn't seem right.

He pushed a pad into my left hand. "I'm going to free your hands."

"Are you crazy?" Zito said.

Barren rolled his eyes. "Do you want your answers from her?"

Zito sighed. "Yeah."

"Then how else would you suggest we get the information? Osmosis? Perhaps we could scoop her brains out?"

"I get it," Zito said. I'd never heard his voice so shaky. He sounded like he might be sick.

Good. Maybe you'll choke to death on your own puke.

Barren looked into my eyes. "I don't think your hatred for me is any mystery, but please do know that I care about your well-being, whether you believe it or not."

Zito hissed, and something clanked. He must have hit something. "Get on it with it, already."

Barren grit his teeth. Don't ask me how, but I actually started to feel a little sympathy for the guy. Yes, he'd tortured me, and much like Zito's little "stunt", I wasn't about to forgive him for it, but by God I think he actually did care about what had happened to me. It was a lot more than I could say about some of the other assholes in the Khesnaa.

He spoke again. "We have to ask you a few questions, for your own good. I'm going to free you, but please don't do anything rash. Your injury could kill you. Blink twice if you understand me."

I blinked twice.

"Good." I felt one of his hands close over my wrist, lifting it to give the rope some slack. He moved his hand. The restraint around my wrist loosened then slid away.

He disappeared for a moment and circled me. Zito emerged from the shadows one slow step at a time, his hands clenched at his waist.

He spoke. "Listen, I'm sorry. I know that's shit. I can't fix things the way I'd want to, but..." He lifted his hands. "I thought I had the safety on, like all those other times. I just didn't want you coming after us. I thought it was an attack, like last time. I guess I thought a lot of stuff."

I gave him the only answer I could: I lifted my hand and extended my middle finger.

Barren chuckled under his breath as he appeared at my right side. He started working on that wrist.

Zito scratched his head. "Fine. I deserve that. I don't expect you to accept that or anything. I just had to say it."

Barren pushed a pen into my right hand.

Okay, pen, paper. I can work with this. I picked up the pad and wrote the first thing that came to mind:

Fuck you asshole

That made Zito's face turn red, and he might have actually gone ahead and finished what he had started on me if Barren hadn't stepped between us.

Barren clapped his hands. "Very amusing." He looked to Zito. "Don't you think?"

"Laugh riot," Zito said, turning away.

I wrote again:

What do you need to know

Zito glanced back to read it. He nodded to Barren. "Ask her about her neck."

Barren spread his hands. "You ask her. You wanted to question her."

"All right, fine." He turned back to face both of us. "You got other bruises on your neck that got nothing to do with what I did. Where the hell did they come from?"

Enliel, of course, but he couldn't know that.

Shit. Think, girl. Think. If I told them the truth, they'd probably kill Sam. Of course, maybe they knew and already planned on killing Sam – they just needed my word to follow through.

I wrote:

Walked into the door

Barren narrowed his eyes. "I think not. These are indicative of choking trauma. Did someone choke you, Kelli? You can tell us."

Any sympathy I might have gotten for the asshole disappeared. He had me going for a little while, but he had turned it on a little *too* much. I wrote:

Fuck your good cop bad cop

Zito stepped forward. "Let me choke it out of her. I'll get it in less than a minute."

"I thought you cared for her?" Barren said.

There it was. Sam had been right.

Zito backed off. "Don't you bring that up now. Not when she's like that."

"Who put her in that state?"

Zito pushed him out of the way, standing over me again. "Tell us. Go ahead. We know already. You've always had something for that pasty asshole, haven't you? It's obvious he's been letting you out. You got to know that thing in the basement, didn't you?"

Suspicion confirmed. They knew more than even Sam suspected. Of course, it also didn't mean I had to give in to this asshole. I wrote:

Of course. He's got a bigger dick

Barren actually laughed out loud, and Zito turned a shade of red that I had never seen in a human being.

"Listen, you dirty cunt, I don't care what you say anymore. I'm going to wait for your boyfriend tonight, and I'm going to gut him like a fish. Maybe I'll paint your door with his blood," he said.

You don't have the balls

His eyes lit up. "Good idea. Maybe I should take his balls first. Wouldn't you like that?"

Barren reached across Zito's chest. "Okay, really, that's enough. She needs to-"

Zito pushed him away. "Don't touch me. Don't you ever touch me."

He looked back in time to see what I had started to write:

You'll never have me

He roared. I swear to God, he roared, just like a lion. Then he knocked the paper and pen out of my hand.

My whole body twisted, and I felt something give in my neck. I tried to scream again, but I only heard a gurgling noise, spilling out of the opened hole in the side of my throat. I reached for the hole, but that only made the pressure worse. Barren shouted something just before I disappeared again, down that dark hole.

May 17th

We're leaving soon. It's about time; I don't think I could take much more time in this godforsaken (and I mean that word in the most realistic sense) city. Carlos showed his face again this morning, this time wearing a plaid shirt and torn jeans. I'm done trying to figure the man out; it's a waste of time and I say let him be who-ever or whatever he wants.

I should back up, though. You see, we haven't left the place since we arrived. Who would dare to leave, and why should we, when we have everything we need? Neither of us had an idea of how long we would be here, other than expecting things to change soon – after all, once change becomes a way of life it stops pulling the rug out from under you.

So we weren't exactly shocked when Carlos showed up in the foyer this morning, standing there waiting for us to notice him. Surprised? Sure, I jumped about fifty feet in the air. I wouldn't call it shocked, though. The guy, or someone like him, had been bound to show up.

"Jesus, Carlos, can't you knock?" I glanced over my shoulder. Sam had appeared at the living room entranceway, a spatula in his hand.

Carlos shook his head. "Can't be risked." He extended his right hand. It held two yellow airline tickets, each tucked into their own baby-blue jackets.

I took them and studied them. Headed for England. Leaving in four days.

That's right. Four days. I can now count my days in this place on one hand.

Sam had been looking over my shoulder, and spoke now: "I assume transportation will be provided."

Carlos inclined his head. "You assume correctly, amigo." He gave us the details on when - and where - they would pick us up, but again, I'm not going to detail those here. There are still four days, and God only knows how close the Organization might be right now. I don't want any more deaths on my conscience if something happens to us.

My conscience, or, you know, my memory once I'm dead. Whichever.

Once he'd given us the information, he left without another word.

"He is desperate," Sam said, returning to the kitchen, where he was cooking some scrambled eggs and chorizo for both of us.

I followed him and hopped up on the counter by the sink, dangling my legs off of the edge. "Why do you think he's desperate?"

He raised an eyebrow. "He would not take such risks if he had many trusted lieutenants remaining. I fear what this means for the Underground."

Now that shut me up. Is the entire Underground at risk, or just operations in Mexico? I can't say for sure, but sending us away so soon seems like a bad sign either way.

So it's time to twiddle our thumbs, lay low, and wait for the 22nd to arrive. I have to admit, I'm excited but I'm also terrified. This is my first flight ever, as far as I can tell - the ones in my memory feel distant and hazy, disconnected from reality. Just thinking about it makes my knees shake a little, with images of the plane suddenly lurching and going into an uncontrollable nose dive into the ocean, all the passengers screaming in their final moments.

Knowing I'm going to die and having absolutely nothing to do about it.

Brrr. Best not to think about those kinds of things. Best to retreat into the past, I guess, though you know, it's a sad state of affairs when the Khesnaa is more comforting than my current situation.

======

I wasn't sure when I woke up again, but my brain had been set to full-on spin cycle. Wait, did I say spin? Spin is a little too easy a word. It was more like I had been on the Tilt-a-Whirl for about ten minutes, and then thrown off into my bed. Fighting back the need to spew, I peeled my eyes open, clinging to the edge of the bed with every bit of energy left inside my body.

Things weren't much better in the wide world; the scuffed wooden floor whirled in circles, refusing every attempt I made to stop it. On top of this, every few seconds the world decided that it might be fun to tilt over, spilling me out of the bed.

I closed my eyes and took a deep breath. All things considered, it could be worse. At least I knew where I was: my bed. Not that I could do much with the information, but I had some sort of grounding.

I remembered what happened in Room 3. That feeling of my skin bursting, the warmth trickling down my neck, and both hands went to my neck without me even telling them to do it. I felt my skin, looking for a bandage, a hole, a scar, *something*.

But I found nothing.

No pain; not even any soreness. Nothing. Like the whole thing had never happened.

"What the fuck?" I muttered.

That gave me the next clue that things had changed: I could talk. It didn't hurt. No hole in my throat.

Next order of business: Carla. I steadied myself and pushed myself up on my elbows. I looked toward her bed; it lay empty, the sheets flat, the pillows arranged. Somebody had made it, which meant she hadn't been in it since at least the night before.

Now if you could only figure out what day this is, you might be ahead of the game.

No light came through the cloudy windows, so I could tell that it was night-time, but I couldn't tell you what night that might be. Maybe hours had passed, maybe days, maybe years. I just had no way of telling. Somewhere in the middle of trying to figure all this stuff out, my head had stopped spinning, at least for a little bit. I figured it might be safe, so I tried to push up off my elbows, maybe even sit up.

My head exploded in pain, like someone had driven an ice pick right through my brain from above. I shouted and fell back on the pillow, holding my head in both hands. That set off a whole new wave of nausea.

Stupid. Stupid ass. You knew it was too soon.

I curled in the fetal position, moaning. I put a hand on my stomach, trying to keep whatever food might be in there down.

After a few moments, a shadow appeared over me.

A familiar voice spoke. "Are you okay?"

Sam. I reached out for him without even thinking about it, grabbing hold of one of his big hands.

Thank God, Zito hadn't gotten to him. Not yet. "You're all right," I said.

He knelt before me and smiled. "Of course I am all right. The question is whether *you* are all right."

I touched the top of my head. "Other than feeling like someone's trying to scoop my brains out? I've felt better. Where's Carla?"

He didn't say anything for a second, and then said, "Carla is…no longer with us."

I didn't like the sound of that. "What do you mean? Did she die?"

"No, no. Nothing like that. You should not worry about her." He touched my forehead, running a finger across it.

I smacked his hand away. "Don't condescend to me. Did they shoot me? Or did I imagine it?"

He cocked his head. "Why would they shoot you?"

"It was…I just…Zito said it was an accident." It couldn't just be a dream, could it? It had been too real. All of it, right down to Room 3. "Turn on the light and help me up. I want to see myself."

"I do not know that the light would be a great idea."

"Come on."

He sighed and walked toward the door.

I closed my eyes, preparing myself, but let's face it: nothing could really prepare me for what felt like a nuclear blast going off overhead. I shielded my face and moaned. "Goddamn."

"I warned you. Would you like me to turn it back off?"

"No. Come over here. Please."

I heard his footsteps, and I knew he stood in front of me again. I grabbed his hand, squeezing it. "I need your help. I can't sit up without feeling like my head's going to explode."

He took my hand and helped me to a sitting position. "What did they do to you?"

I touched my aching head. "Like I said…" What did I think?

What *had* happened? How could he not know about a shooting? "You said Carla's not with us anymore. What does that mean?"

He let go of my hand and moved forward, putting his hands under my back, supporting me with a gentle touch. He lifted my upper body inch by inch. I have no idea how he did it, but he managed to keep my head from hurting while he did it.

Once he had me standing up, he slipped in behind me, letting me rest against his side. He wrapped one arm around my stomach, keeping me in place.

God, yeah. That's what I need.

It felt better than any painkiller. I wanted to go to the bathroom, take a look at myself, but I needed to rest, even if just for a minute.

He spoke. "It is not very clear. Something occurred earlier today. They removed her from this location and took her to another. At least, this is what they have told me."

"We know how trustworthy they are. Did they tell you where they took her?"

"They did not."

"And no one said anything about me getting shot," I said.

"There was no mention of any such thing. They told me that you were not feeling well, and I must be careful with you."

"Yeah, let's. Come on. Let's get to the bathroom."

"Are you sure you can handle it?"

I forced myself to take a step forward, wincing as pain rose through my body from the soles of my feet. "Never better. Come on."

We crossed the room in dead silence, save for the occasional grunt as I moved too fast and the pain walloped me. At last he got me into the tiny bathroom; there wasn't enough room for him to stand beside me, but he kept one arm wrapped around my waist, steadying me as I leaned against the sink, staring into the mirror.

An almost entirely different woman stared out at me. Don't get me wrong, it was *me*, I wasn't that different, but someone had thoroughly combed out the tangles in my mop of hair, the bags under my eyes had vanished, and the blotches on my skin from their shitty diet were completely gone.

I ran a hand through my hair, wincing as my head got angry again, sending pain down my nerves into my arms. "Unreal," I said.

"What?"

I shook my head. "You didn't notice anything different about me?"

"Frankly, yes. You look well-rested and clean, but I figured they had allowed you to shower."

Boy, wouldn't that have been grand? "Not that I know of. Last thing I remember was them coming in and jabbing a needle in Carla's arm. Things went crazy after that, and my memory is just…poof."

He considered that. "Sedation *would* be the first step in moving her to another location. But what did they do to you?"

I touched my neck, right where the shot should have gone, right where I should have burst open and bled out. "My brain keeps telling me they shot me in the neck. Severed my jugular."

He leaned over, staring at my neck for a long, long time. "I see no sign of such a wound. Not even a bruise."

"Yeah, you think? Why do you think I'm so confused?"

Sam's eyebrows knitted up, his mouth tight. "I do not understand what has happened here. I do not like it."

"Me neither. Come on; help me back to the bed."

We hobbled together across the room, though the pain had begun easing, finally. Nothing like a little shock therapy to get the body right. Once he'd helped me down onto the edge of my bed, he sat beside me, damn near tipping the far end into the air. We both grabbed onto the comforter and adjusted ourselves, making sure that we didn't bite it.

Once we were settled, I spoke. "Well, I can tell you one thing about all this: Zito said he wants to kill you."

That eased his face a bit. He actually smiled. "Zito cannot harm me."

"He said he's going to gut you like a fish." Just saying it made me want to cry. How could he smile, especially when he acknowledged that he was already a dead man?

"He does not know how to harm me."

"You mean you don't...what *do* you mean?" I said.

"One cannot simply murder a Kellik'at. Even if I were to surrender to such treatment, it would take one with far more wisdom and ability to get past my inborn defenses. Zito is not such a person. They may be planning to burn this entire operation down, though, and you are the only 'asset' left."

I hadn't considered that Carla's disappearance might mean just that. What good was I to them if she was doing her thing? Nothing. I hadn't even solved their puzzle in Room 3, only in my dreams. "Then I guess I've got to protect myself, like you said. Right?"

"I –" he said.

I put a finger on his lips. I didn't want to hear another word of it. So what if he couldn't rescue me? So what if he wasn't my knight in shining armor? Those assholes were overrated, anyway. I leaned over and replaced my finger with my lips.

His lips were soft and moist, their touch electric. I grabbed the back of his head and pulled him deeper into the kiss. Our mouths opened, and our tongues twisted over one another. Fire ran from my tits right down to my groin, lighting it on fire. My need for him was heavy and physical, the hunger you get when you haven't eaten for days.

I think he felt it, too. One of his hands came up to my chest and caressed me there. I moaned around his mouth, ready for what came next.

At least, so I thought. It turned out what came next was me grabbing my head and falling back on the bed, shrieking. I might not have been quite so ready for it.

"Are you okay?" Sam cried, but I couldn't answer him. Something had starting ringing in my head, a bell twice as loud as any I had ever heard in the outside world. I couldn't take it. My body went limp, and my voice got thick and slurred.

I couldn't even ask why or how it was happening. I knew immediately. It was the portal in Room 2.

He figured it out and went even paler than he already was. It seemed impossible, but he managed it. He held out one hand. "Stay here."

I tried to reach for him, but I might as well have been trying to lift a car. "Please" was all I could get out, and even that sounded like I had severe brain damage.

"I will return. I promise. And…I love you."

I tried to answer. I *needed* to answer. But damn it, I just couldn't.

He nodded like he understood anyway and went for the door. He was gone before I could do anything more than roll off the bed, bumping my arm. I couldn't even yell and express the pain and anguish ripping me apart.

I dragged myself inch by inch, each movement something like trying to climb Everest. When it started to get easier, I moved foot by foot - anything to reach him before shit went down. The ringing in my head stopped, and the pain went with it.

The portal must have closed.

I pulled myself to my feet and ran for the door, slamming both fists against it.

That's when I heard the door to Room 2 hit the front room wall, and a bunch of heavy footsteps following it.

"Good evening, Senior," Sam said.

"Sam, no," I shouted, but he - and his enemies - were beyond me now.

May 22nd

I'm writing this in a 777 traveling somewhere over the Atlantic Ocean – I couldn't tell you whether we're in the middle of the ocean; geography is hardly my strong suit., but I know we're over a large body of water and I can't see a hint of land in sight, so close enough.

On the positive side, all that bitching about being forced to live a light-travel existence might have been a little…well, short-sighted. Turns out that's an advantage when you're traveling internationally. Thank God. This whole thing has been stressful enough. I can't imagine facing a more thorough search at the airport.

So yeah, I missed a few days in this journal because of my flight anxiety. Wait, did I just write *anxiety*? More like utter terror. I couldn't focus on anything but abject fear. I sat down a few times to try to pick up where I had left off, but before I knew it, the sun laid low across the back of the tiny house and I had been staring out the window, lost in thoughts of what it might feel like to live the last few minutes of your life in a doomed plane.

I gave myself a day. When I woke up the next morning, I took our shitty little laptop and dialed up to our even shittier Internet. Computers scare the shit out of me, but I had to do something, and the Underground sure wasn't offering therapy. I hit Google, looking for flight anxiety and ways to fix it. I found a whole lot of jack-shit. Oh, there were videos, lots of videos, but that does you no good on a slow modem connection. I learned a little bit about how planes work, which only served to heighten the fear, and some vague grounding techniques about looking at your surroundings and counting the things around you. Utter bullshit.

Next thing I knew, I was on airdisaster.com, and learning new and even more gruesome ways to die as nausea climbed the back of my throat.

I told myself, "Kelli, for God's sake, stop scaring the shit out of yourself," and tried to stop. It's just really hard to pull yourself out of the tailspin (get it, get it?) when your most reliable distraction (this journal) fails you. We had some cheap tequila, but would it have helped? I doubt it. I've been drinking since we got seated on this jet, thank you very much First Class and the Underground, and it's just ratcheted the fear up to new heights.

I just woke up a few minutes ago from an intense dream, where the plane had started making weird, terrifying noises just a few seconds before everything started to shake. I definitely screamed in the dream, not so sure if I screamed in real life, though. I did wake up to find that the plane *was* being shaken – and still is. Everybody on board seems relatively calm, but still… Someone said that we're going around some monster storm. All I know is that it's a load of fun with all that alcohol in my belly.

Unable to distract myself with the crap on the seat-back TV, I forced myself to pull the journal from my bag and start writing. I've used this thing to cope with just about everything else that life has thrown at me over the last few weeks, why not use it to deal with the terror, if not the need to vomit all over my seatmate? Oh, yeah, did I mention that they put Sam several seats back? They said they just couldn't get us seats together, but I don't buy that. Sure, he couldn't understand my fear, but he could have at least calmed me down if he sat by my side.

Oh, and while I'm writing, just by the way, Carlos died this morning, so there's that.

It's just as dramatic as it sounds, and the whole thing really makes me wonder about the Underground and whether they can tell shinola from that other stuff. See, here's the thing: they sent us back to that restaurant; you know, the one that we visited on that first day in Mexico? I didn't know how smart it might be to circle back like that, but far be it from me to question the Underground. We followed their instructions and waited for our contact. We wouldn't know the guy, but all we needed to do was grill him for the latest pass-phrase and all would be well.

We waited him out, sitting in the hot Mexican sun, bathing in our sweat, and downing endless gallons of Coke. I found it somewhat difficult to contain my anxiety, frustration, and anger. I tapped my hands on the table, doing the best I could, but I was afraid of where my mind might end up. Leaving me hanging in the middle of that place could quite easily push me over the edge.

At last, I couldn't take it anymore. "Where are they? We have a schedule to keep."

Sam sipped his third glass of Coke. "They said that we may have complications. I only fear that something bad has happened. It would hardly be the first time."

Not like I hadn't considered the idea about 2,000 times in the last 30 minutes, but I bit back a sarcastic reply. "Do you think we could make it to the airport on our own?"

"Not likely." He smacked his lips and put the glass back on the table, placing it right in its own condensation ring. "Would you feel safe taking a bus or a cab in this city?"

I shuddered. "When you put it that way, no, but what do you think we *should* do if they did get caught?"

"I have no idea."

"Well, maybe the cabs aren't such a bad idea. Beats the Organization finding us."

"Perhaps." He picked up the Coke again, opened his mouth, and then paused. "I believe our transportation has arrived."

I looked up to find a gleaming black Mustang idling at the curb, its engine rumbling with something like an idle threat. I made eye contact with the passenger, a lanky young Hispanic man with the mustache of a 15-year-old boy and he grinned. He popped the passenger side door open and bounded out, flashing that smile at both of us. Two gold teeth caught the sun, winking at us. "So good to see you. You are ready to go, yes?"

Our experience with Carlos had soured me somewhat on the whole "gregarious-Mexican-greeting-the-gringos" thing. I glanced at Sam, and could see that it had raised a flag in his head as well.

He cleared his throat. "Good to see you. Our apologies, but we have to ask - what is the pass phrase, 'amigo'?"

That stopped Milk Mustache dead in his tracks. The kid looked back toward the Mustang's driver. That guy didn't look much more savory than our new friend. He was a much stockier, middle-aged white man with a permanent scowl and a tangle of curls to rival my own.

The man shrugged and Milky looked back to us. "They didn't give us one. Things been crazy, you know?"

My turn. "I bet. You should probably call somebody and get it then, because we're not leaving until we hear it."

Anger flashed in Milky's eyes. He suppressed it almost as soon as it appeared, but he had made a rookie mistake. We had no doubt at that point that he wasn't with the Underground.

He gave us an *aw shucks* shrug. "I forgot my cell phone."

"Better go get it, then."

"We're in a hurry." He took a step toward us.

The next moment, an old brown Mercedes slammed into the back of the Mustang, driving it up onto the curb and into a light pole with a sickening crunch.

Carlos jumped from the passenger seat of the Mercedes, two silver pistols in his hands.

Milky reached for the back of his pants, twisting as he did. We could see the gleam of a pistol hidden back there, but he never had time to draw it. Carlos took care of him with a single shot to the head.

Carlos wheeled his arms at us. "Come on, get in," he cried, and we weren't about to debate him. We skittered past him and into the back seat, flinging our bags in ahead of our bodies.

He slammed the door shut behind us and slapped the windshield. Our driver, a chubby black guy in a Kangol hat, glanced over his shoulder and threw the car into reverse.

"Wait, what about Carlos?" I said.

The driver looked forward, slamming the car into drive. "Sorry lady. This is his fight."

"You have to go back."

Sam put a hand on my shoulder. "He is right. This battle belongs to Carlos now, not us."

I gazed out the window as Carlos pumped two rounds into the driver of the Mustang, who had dared to open his door. I swallowed a victory cry when I saw one of the café patrons, a heavy-set Hispanic woman, approach Carlos, lifting a small pistol. I slammed my fist on the passenger side window and shouted.

Carlos didn't hear me. The last thing he felt was the woman's gun at the back of his neck, right before she squeezed the trigger.

I slammed my fist against the window again. "Damn it," I cried.

The driver wasn't listening. He floored it, and Carlos' slumping body became little more than a receding shadow in the distance.

I started crying. I didn't have any deep connection to Carlos, mind you, but it was too much to add yet another person to the body count that was my continued existence. Back in the Khesnaa I had sworn that I would never let it happen again. And yet…

I know, naïve of me to think that way. I couldn't control Carlos any more than I could control my own anxiety on this godforsaken plane, but it didn't lessen the sting, did it?

Hey, speaking of which, I'm barely even noticing these bumps right now. How about that shit? Maybe there is something to writing as an escape.

Except that wasn't much of an escape at all. It was something, but hardly an escape. Maybe I should go back to the Khesnaa. Now where did I leave off?

Oh. Right. That.

Well, here goes…

======

I leaned against the door, listening to what I feared might be Sam's last moments. The portal in Room 2 had let out the Senior, but he had also brought a little goon squad with him. I could hear at least two other bodies out there, and possibly a third, though it was hard to tell with the Senior's heavy footsteps.

Zito was the first to speak. "Well, well. Look at this shit. Were you just in her room, buddy boy?"

Sam stood his ground. "What if I was? I have been charged with her well-being. It is only natural that I would be there."

The Senior sighed. "Do answer the question, Samarta, don't be tiresome."

"Of course I have. But you knew that already," Sam said.

Zito spoke. "Damn right we did, numb nuts."

"Yes, very disappointing. I do not appreciate lying, but then I can't imagine how you wouldn't know that," the Senior said.

Someone circled Sam; I think it was the Senior, as the footsteps punished the front room's floor. "How disappointing. You have been a model servant until now," he continued.

Sam spat. "Servant? Hell. I am a slave."

"Really, what is the difference? It is a matter of degrees, and a moot point now."

I banged on the door again. "Don't you touch him."

"Zito, see to the woman, please."

Silence followed, at least three to four seconds. I imagined Zito's face, twisting around. "You said I could –"

"Plans change. Do take care that she is silenced. There's a good lad."

Zito began to walk toward our room; I took a step backwards, without thinking, but Sam got between Zito and the door. "I will tear you apart with my bare hands before you touch her."

Zito laughed. "Look at this feisty bastard. You move, or I'll stomp your ass into the ground."

"You cannot harm me."

I imagined Zito getting up in Sam's face – well, as much as he could, anyway. "Why don't we just find out?"

"He's right, Zito. You cannot harm him," the Senior said. "Still, Samarta, *must* you be so difficult?"

"You wanted me to protect them. I am doing my job, *master*."

The Senior scoffed. "As if I would allow him to harm her. Harming her would, of course, be foolish. Please, let us be civil."

I could hear the frustration in Zito's voice. "Yeah, well –"

Two steps, and not the ones I wanted to hear. That was Sam stepping to one side.

Another few seconds, and Zito stomped toward my room. Something heavy smacked the door three times; I imagined it as the same gun that he had used to shoot me. "Shut up in there. Don't make me do something we'll both regret."

"Fuck you," I said.

The Senior clapped. "Oh, bravo, Zito. Surely none of us could have done that. You showed her."

"Listen, you," Zito said, and then fell silent. I could only imagine the look that the Senior gave him. When he spoke again, his voice was low and fragile. "I didn't want to take another risk with her."

"You are afraid of her. Afraid of more rejection," Sam said.

A scuffle followed. I think Zito got close to Sam with that damned pistol of his, and Sam did something, because Zito shouted in pain. The pistol must have fallen to the floor, because it clattered against the hard wood. Did Sam have his arm wrenched behind his back?

The Senior chuckled. "Very well done, Zito. I'm so glad I included you in this."

"I'm doing my best, boss," Zito pleaded, his voice strained. I'm sure he was giving the Senior his best ass-kissing face.

His charms didn't seem to work on the Senior. "Do release him, Samarta."

Zito hit the floor, heavy. The Senior approached both of them. "I suppose your best isn't good enough, then, is it? Remind me again why I employ you. Tell me again what I said during our first interview. You seem to have forgotten."

"Oh, right. My…uh…" Zito said.

"Your unerring loyalty in the face of brazen stupidity. Do you understand what that means?"

"That I'm brave no matter what?" He sounded so hopeful. I almost felt sorry for the bastard.

Almost.

The Senior clicked his tongue. "So very close. It means that you are a colossal idiot, but you are *my* colossal idiot. I know that you harbor delusions of grandeur in that dim mind of yours, but don't let them overstep my boundaries again. You will receive no other warning."

He sounded so cold it shook me right to my core. Zito might as well have been a toy that he didn't like anymore, and wouldn't mind tossing into the garbage. Zito had to be pissing himself.

"Yeah, boss. No problem," he said.

"Now Samarta. My friend. I've been informed that you let one of the assets out of the cabin. You know this is not acceptable."

"They are people, not assets, and they deserve some freedom," Sam said.

Yeah. You tell 'em.

"Humans, yes. Agreed there. Worthy of freedom? That's another discussion entirely, one that I won't share with you. Regardless, you owe your continued existence – and that of your family – to my good favor. Why would you make this sort of mistake? I believed you to be reasonable."

Sam must have decided that it was the right time to lay the cards on the table. "Do not feed me that lie. If you believe me to be reasonable, at least grant me the favor of the truth. My family is dead. You killed them."

The Senior exhaled. "Very well. Yes. They are dead."

I can't describe the sound that came out of Sam. I'd heard anguished cries before – made them myself. This came from an even deeper place, a place that maybe a normal human can't even visit. The Senior might as well have torn his chest open and ripped his beating heart out.

The asshole wasn't done. "It's regrettable, for sure, but I am not responsible. There was an accident when we transferred them from one location to another. A derailed train…"

"You lie," Sam roared, and I think he went for the Senior because a scuffle started again. It ended with a wet smack, and something hit the floor.

I picked up the chair from beside Carla's bed and spun with it, slamming it against the door. The door started giving way, shimmying in the frame. I yelled in triumph and swung back for an even bigger hit, but the door opened.

I went sprawling, dropping the chair as I went down on my side, the breath knocked out of me.

There had been a third person in the room: Bloch. He kicked the chair away from me and pointed a shotgun in my face. "Get inside. No more beating on your door."

I put one hand to the sore spot on my side, struggling to one knee. "You wouldn't dare hurt me."

He fingered the trigger. "Try me."

Bloch didn't see Sam coming. Good thing, because Sam slugged him in the mouth, knocking him to the floor like a ton of bricks. I yelled and fell backwards, supporting myself with both hands.

Sam followed right behind Bloch, falling to his knees as Zito knocked him in the back of the head with his pistol. It would have knocked out a normal man, and possibly caused lasting brain damage, but Sam just got his bell rung. He shook his head, putting his palm against his eyes.

Zito loomed behind him, placing the barrel against the back of his head. "Give me an excuse, cue ball. Come on."

A giant form, one that I hadn't even noticed in the middle of all that insanity, took two huge strides and had Bloch on his feet before I could even figure out what was happening.

That giant form? The Senior.

I craned my neck and looked up at the guy. Or…whatever he might be.

He couldn't have been shorter than eight feet tall. I couldn't even comprehend the height of the guy; he dwarfed even Sam, and looked like something out of your worst nightmares. If Sam's skin was pale, he might as well have been see-through, without even a hint of color, and that didn't even approach his most alien feature. That could have been the glowing yellow eyes, shot through with bright streaks of red, or his teeth, yellow, jagged mass of razor-sharp fangs.

"Boo," he said.

I scrambled backwards on the floor, legs kicking and sliding

He laughed and clapped his hands, his eyes wide. "Excellent to finally meet you, Ms. Foster."

"Leave her alone," Sam said. Bloch had him on the floor, locked in a headlock, while Zito kept the gun pointed at his head, but still he had the balls to stand up to the Senior.

I knew there was a reason that I loved him.

The Senior grinned. "Of course. How could I not see it? You have feelings for her, don't you?"

"I did not say that."

"There's no need." He laughed again. God, I wished he'd quit it. Tortured cats sounded more pleasant.

I got to my feet, holding out my hands. "Please don't hurt him. He's a good man."

He raised an eyebrow. "Oh, this is mutual? Absolutely incredible. Tell me just why you love a man who participated in holding you hostage. I'm quite fascinated."

"Do not say a word to him. He will use it against you," Sam said.

The Senior got near me. Up close, he smelled like hot, raw ass, something like Carla described. "You see? He has no problem telling you what to do."

I wanted to run and hide; anything to get away from the beast. "Instead of just torturing me, right?"

He sniffed. "I never claimed to be anything other than what I am. Unless you would like to learn more about what I am like as a lover? I promise you, it is quite the interesting experience, or so I have been told." He giggled.

I shuddered. "I'll pass, thanks."

He leaned close, his hot, smelly breath washing over me. "A pity. I could teach you many things. Many…enjoyable things."

Sam snarled. "Do not touch her."

The Senior's eyes narrowed in pleasure. He turned and strolled over to Sam, standing before him with his hands on his hips. "At last we get something interesting. Tell me, does it make you jealous? Enrage your heart?" He closed his eyes and inhaled. "Smell that anger. I wish I could bottle that smell. Impressive that even now it is stronger than your fear. Love truly *is* a many splendored thing."

"Kill me. Do it now and get it over with. Just leave her alone."

The Senior pouted. "Well now that just wouldn't be any fun, would it? Where's the harm in enjoying my job?" He nodded to

Zito, and the little bastard kicked Sam in the side.

Sam took it with a grunt, his eyes never leaving the Senior's face.

"Yes, give me more of that fight. Bloch, release him."

Bloch grunted, but he did what the Senior told him. Sam snorted and rose, putting himself face-to-face with the Senior.

Sam cocked his head and smiled. "I destroyed Enliel."

The smug look on the Senior's face dissolved. "Impossible. You could never."

"Are you so sure?"

The Senior's lip curled into a sneer. "I would have known."

"You have been traveling. You had never seen him before I showed you his cage."

The Senior's eyes flicked to Zito's face. Score a point for Sam; the beast actually looked uncertain for a moment.

Zito nodded and spoke to Bloch. "Go check it out."

Bloch went for the basement door as Zito grabbed my arm, squeezing the hell out of it.

I pushed against his body. He fell backwards, giving me a chance to wrench my arm free. I made a run for it. I had the line on beating Bloch to the basement door and hiding out down there, but Zito recovered faster than I had expected. He slammed his foot into my heel and sent me sprawling, my jaw slamming into the floor. I could only watch as Bloch slipped through the basement door, slamming it behind him.

Sam cried out and went for Zito, but the little bastard had one advantage over him. He cocked the pistol and pointed it at me. "You'd like it if I killed you, but I bet it wouldn't be the same if I plugged this little cooze, would it?"

Sam froze. "You wouldn't dare."

"Why wouldn't I? She's nothing to us now. Same as you."

The Senior cleared his throat. "Zito."

Zito sighed and lowered the hammer. "You're lucky."

I rose, my nerve endings screaming at me, my face already swelling. "Always a gentleman, aren't you?"

"Oh, just shut up."

Big, clumsy feet stomped up the basement steps and the door burst open. Bloch stepped through, his face pale.

The Senior barely contained the tension in his voice. "Well?"

Bloch shook his head. "It ain't good."

The Senior hissed and turned on Sam, grabbing his throat with one big mitt. Sam isn't a little guy, but the Senior had no problem lifting him in the air with that one hand.

Sam's face went an awful shade of purple. I ran for him and the Senior, ready to beat the big son of a bitch away with my bare hands if I had to, but Zito hooked an arm around my waist, pulling me back against him.

"Ah, ah. Not so fast, kitten," he said.

I felt something hard press against my lower back, and I wanted to vomit. Good God, the son of a bitch got off on this.

The Senior squeezed and Sam made an awful gurgling noise. When Sam looked like he was about to black out, the Senior relaxed his grip, the yellow in his eyes blazing bright enough that the color fell over Sam's face. "What have you done?" he said.

Sam grinned. It looked hideous in the middle of his purple face. "You should have spared my family. You failed."

The Senior snarled – I swear to God, he *snarled,* like a lion. "There is no failure. Not so long as the other lives. You couldn't protect or destroy her. *You* are the one who failed. Now, you die."

I screamed and fought against Zito, but he clamped tighter and took full advantage of the situation, grinding his crotch into me. "Let go of me, asshole," I said, trying to throw an elbow at his face.

He avoided it and pushed the pistol against my neck. "Never. You watch this. You caused it."

The Senior tightened his grip. Sam made that gurgling sound again and started to go blue.

I grabbed hold of Zito's arm and bit down as hard as I could. I tasted blood, and he shrieked, dropping the gun. A kick to the shins, and I turned, kneeing him in the groin, hoping I broke that dick of his.

All of my pain forgotten and operating on pure adrenaline, I sprang toward the Senior, ready to sacrifice myself if it meant wiping the bastard out.

I didn't get a chance, though. I managed to be fast, but again Bloch was faster. My face exploded in pain and I stumbled backwards as he laid a single, solid slap across my already-sore face.

That gave the Senior all the time he needed, ratcheting his grip up one more notch. No matter what happened after, and no matter how long I might live, I'll never forget the noise he made. I've heard of death rattles, but it went beyond that into the sound of pure agony.

He went limp in the Senior's arms.

I screamed and surged forward again, running right into Bloch's wall of a body. He tried to get his arms around me, but I slipped around him.

I never saw the Senior's fist coming, but I sure felt it when he knocked me to the floor once again. A moment later, the senior dropped Sam's body right beside me. Dazed, I stared into Sam's lifeless eyes. I think I screamed.

The Senior said something to the others that I couldn't process, and it got those two moving again. Zito hauled me to my feet, dragging me toward Room 1 as I sobbed, calling them every name that came to mind.

"I'm sorry," Zito said under his breath.

"Quiet," Bloch admonished him, and the two pushed me through the bedroom door. My arms pin wheeled, and I caught myself on the bed. The door slammed shut behind me, and I laid face-down on the bed, shoving my face into the pillow and screaming as loud as I could to shut out the agony rising in my chest, knowing that it wouldn't work. I wondered if anything would ever work for me again.

I don't remember much of the night past that.

June: The Grim Specter

June 5th

If you asked me a week ago, I would have told you that these things never happen, but I learned otherwise today: I got an honest-to-God makeover. You know, just like on TV, a whole team of women dedicated to making me look like a goddess, and even though it turned out to have some strings attached, I liked it. I could probably get used to it, in fact. They…well, I should probably back up and start with our arrival in London. This whole thing needs some context.

If I had to choose one word to describe our arrival (and I'm not sure why I would, but let's just go with this for the sake of argument), I'd probably choose Smooth. Funny that after all my jitters and nervous nights on the toilet, we didn't hit a single pocket of turbulence as we approached Heathrow. There were no terrifying lurches, no failure with the landing gear, and no problem getting through customs as Mr. and Mrs. Theodore Eisley, a well-to-do American couple who decided that their Mexican accommodations simply weren't up to par and they had to go to London at this time of the year, *darling.*

People crowded International Arrivals, but we didn't have too much trouble picking out the white guy in the black suit and sunglasses that waited for us. Of course, it helped that he held one of those little white signs like you see in the movies. He - or someone else - had written on the sign in black magic marker:

The Eisleys

I elbowed Sam as Black Suit nodded and began leading us through the crush of humanity. "Can you believe this? Why would they go to all this trouble for us? I feel like a celebrity."

Sam adjusted his horn-rimmed glasses and let his hand wander up to the brown rug on his head. I guess he had to reassure himself that it was, indeed, still plastered to his pale head. "I suppose we are celebrities on some level."

I narrowly avoided a screaming child, clicking my tongue. "What are you saying? Being in the Khesnaa made us into stars for the Underground?"

"You must admit that we are unusual specimens."

No denying that; I had just never seen my differences as something desirable. Why *would* I? They had only led to torture, terror, and heartache. For so long I had wanted nothing more than to be normal, but a voice had always whispered in my ear that it would never happen.

Well, suppose that wasn't such a bad thing? It wouldn't be the end of the world, I guess.

Black Suit took us to a sleek black limo idling just outside one of the quieter entranceways. He tucked us away in the back while he met up with an unseen second driver somewhere toward the front of the car. They exchanged a few words and Black Suit climbed in; we could just see his silhouette through the smoked glass separating us from the cabin.

We sped off.

To say that I know little about London would be such an understatement that it borders on the absurd. I'd never even seen the city in a movie or on TV, so I just watched the sights roll, my mouth hanging open. My memories had told me that I'd spent time in Boston, but, as always, those memories are incredibly unreliable; never more so than when I compared those memories to the real, breathing cityscape outside of the limo.

Rain began to fall as sunset began. The buildings looked

surreal, backlit by a blue and pink hue that pushed right up to the edge of the gray clouds that covered everything with a dark curtain. Lights went on in apartment buildings, shops, and offices and reality became a painting. I wished that I had a camera on hand; I needed to capture something that I would likely never see again. Instead, I tried to memorize every detail of the sights around me.

At last Black Suit took us to what Sam informed me was Soho. It baffled me that he knew it, but he said he'd seen enough BBC shows to pick the place out. I couldn't exactly question that wisdom, so I just savored the way the name sounded on my tongue.

Black Suit climbed out and opened the door, leading us to an awning attached to a non-descript brick building, its front streaked with white from years of rainfall. Black Suit took a moment fumbling with the keys to the place, so I closed my eyes and inhaled the earthy scent of the rain splattering on the city streets. For a moment, I really felt the miles of our journey from the Khesnaa to this point, and a nice sense of exhaustion settled onto my bones.

Black Suit finally got the front door open and led us into the gloom of a musty foyer lined by cracked and warped blue-and-black checked linoleum. The foyer extended down a short hallway to a few boarded-up doors, but the real centerpiece was an ugly set of concrete steps climbing into the darkness overhead.

Black Suit reached behind us and flipped a switch, lighting the foyer and revealing a woman standing at the top of the stairwell, no doubt just waiting for her cue to make a dramatic entrance.

We had plenty of time to ogle her as she slid down the stairs one at a time, throwing her back in what I'm sure she thought looked like an elegant maneuver. She was solid, made of pale flesh and a towering blond beehive, but I couldn't help admiring her purple-and-white polka dotted dress and matching black-and-purple Mary Janes.

She spread her arms when she reached the bottom of the stairs, grinning. "Ah, there is my canvas, and even more beautiful than I was informed." She might think herself elegant, but she wouldn't pass for it with her trashy accent. Still, I found it charming, in a woman-of-the-earth way.

"And you must be Sam," she said, and offered her hand.

Sam took it, pumping once. The look on his face was nothing short of amazing: he looked pained and enchanted, all at the same time. "Yes. And you are?"

"Just call me Iris." She pronounced it *Aye-Ris.* "I don't matter, not really. But come on now, they're waiting for us upstairs." Just like that, she turned and began gliding up the stairwell, her hands lifting the dress to free her knees.

Sam glanced at me. "'They'?"

"This is your party," I said, and began climbing the stairs.

Iris spared us a glance. "Not really a party so much as a welcoming committee, I'm betting you haven't seen one of those in quite some time? Anyway, and don't worry, we know you're worn so this won't take long. Just a few quick how-do-you-dos and we'll be out of your hair. For a while, anyway." She giggled, but the effect was something like a broken jack-in-the-box.

The woman amused me, but I had my principles. "Who is this 'welcoming committee'? Who are *you,* anyway?"

She stopped at the top of the stairs, putting her hands on her hips. "*We* are your personal team of handlers. We've been sent to get you settled, help you cool off a bit."

"Before?"

She waved a hand. "Oh, you know. Before you meet the folks upstairs. Not literally speaking, of course."

We joined her on the landing and looked back. It seemed Black Suit had returned to the limo and gotten our bags; now he was struggling up the stairs, huffing. Sam descended again, picking up two of the bags and helping the guy carry our meager possessions.

When Black Suit finally joined us, he set the bags down at my feet, gave us one curt nod, and turned, descending the stairs.

"Thank you sweetie. You're a dear," Iris called after him.

He grunted, and I realized that I'd blanked out for a second as I watched him go. I caught myself swaying on my feet, my mind completely blank.

Yeah, still a little out of it. A long flight does that to a person.

"All right then," Iris said, and pulled a ribbon from around her neck, revealing a small bronze key that must have been hidden in her bra. Classy woman.

Sam might have been staring at her chest, or he might have been doing the same bordering-on-dead thousand-yard stare; either way, we both caught his eyes focusing on her cleavage as she withdrew the key.

I elbowed him and she winked at me.

"No worries, love, happens to us all," she said, and slid the key home, twisting it. The door popped open, and she motioned toward it. "Please. You two first. It's your new home, after all."

We stepped inside and got hit in the face by a luxurious world that I'd never suspected could exist. No expenses spared. Marble floor. Chandeliers. Leather couches. Statues. All of it tastefully lit by a row of candelabras that formed an impromptu aisle leading us toward the center of the room, where four women stood grouped together.

Those women belonged as the centerpiece because boy, did they draw the eye. All four were the same size, with the same shade of brown hair, same makeup and the same *faces*.

My very own little clone army.

Sam made a noise at my elbow, no doubt as confused as me.

Iris circled us, wrapping her arm around me as she waved a hand at the women. "Quadruplets, loves. This is the Welcoming Committee. Cathy, Charlene, Caty, and Catriona. They're going to take care of you over the next few weeks. Ladies?"

The one named Cathy stepped forward, seizing my right hand in both of hers and pumping heartily. "Honored to finally meet you. We're going to do great things together," she said, with just a hint of a New England accent.

"American?" I said.

"Born and bred. All of us. We moved here a few years ago."

Catriona nodded and spoke in a voice identical to Cathy's voice. "Never going back. Especially now."

I'd never known quads could be so creepy. If I hadn't known better, I would have sworn something else was going on here, but I know that was just my lack of sleep and road grime coating my brain.

All the craziness I'd seen, and I could still be surprised.

The Cs, as I came to think of them, did a pretty good job of "assisting" us over the next few weeks. We needed rest, so they were there to clean up after us and cook. We needed entertainment, so they brought us Blu-Rays and books. We needed new clothes, so they replaced the ones we brought. We didn't want for anything. The catch?

They wanted my journals. All of them. And they wanted me to keep writing down my story. I fought the idea for a little while; the issue wasn't so much trust as not wanting to let the books out of my hands after protecting them for so long. Cathy – she was the head of what I've come to think of as The Journal Project, promised me that I'd get them back at some point. They just needed to make a few copies and read them so they could better understand the Organization. Didn't I want to help destroy the Organization?

Sure. Of course. I coughed up the first two marble notebooks on the 29th. I haven't seen them since.

Cathy's poked me a few times since then, trying to get me back onto writing the story, but once I'd handed those journals over, it got real tough to think about writing more. It's hard to see the point – I can't go back and re-read, and I was using them for distraction. Why would I need to distract myself at that point? I didn't see the point.

Someone at the top must have found my stonewalling unacceptable and figured that I just needed something exciting to get the creative juices flowing. They obviously hadn't read the journals yet and seen what really drove me to write, but I'd have to be crazy to object to even more perks, wouldn't I?

So they took us to Club Aquarium; VIP accommodations no less. Don't get me wrong, I had some fun, drank some booze, wandered out onto the dance floor a few times, but I couldn't have felt more out of place. Not to mention poor Sam, who put on a brave face even if he looked completely miserable. We were both wiped out and irritated by the time we convinced Black Suit to drive us back home.

Their second attempt involved a romantic dinner for the two of us at an upscale restaurant, followed by a walk in the city. That one turned out to be a lot more successful, and may have brought us closer for a little while. Sam looked ready to crawl out of his skin by the time our entrees arrived, but the moonlight stroll changed his tune.

They had to be going out of their minds; I couldn't imagine how much they were plunking down on us and I hadn't produced a single thing. Sure, I didn't owe them anything…and yet at the same time I kind of did. So I tried to write. I really did, but I got nowhere fast. It didn't take me too long to figure out what was missing, but I wasn't about to stop the flow of free gifts. Let them keep plying me, and eventually maybe, just *maybe*, my brain would cooperate.

That's where the makeover comes in: the Underground's third, and biggest, attempt to get my creative juices flowing. Iris and the four Cs knocked on our door around eleven this morning, Black Suit in tow. They had made the poor guy carry a pile of plastic-bagged clothing all the way up those stairs. He tried to stay professional, but his body shook and sweated as they stood on the landing.

"Good lord," I said. "Stop torturing the man and get in here." I took some of the clothes from Black Suit – he grunted and I caught the hint of an Irish accent – and helped him moved them to the bedroom.

Iris and the C's followed us, shooing poor Sam away from his breakfast cereal.

"We're here for the girl, and you don't get to watch," Iris said.

Sam began to object, but I caught his eye and shook my head as I emerged from the bedroom.

Black Suit smirked. "We'll do it one better, mate. Arsenal and Chelsea are on this afternoon, we can catch up with it down the pub."

I'm not sure Sam had ever watched soccer in his life, but he nodded. A few minutes to throw on a hoodie and jeans (still not used to the sight of Sam in a hoodie), and they were out of our hair for the rest of the day. I would feel bad, but until he had left, I hadn't realized just how much time we had been spending together and what that might have meant for him. He loves me, and I love him, but it still must be a huge relief to get out for a bit, especially for a guy who grew up the way he did.

With Sam gone, the ladies got to work on me. Iris led and the C's followed, beginning with my hair, which I had a feeling might be their One True Challenge. It took a lot of chemicals, ironing, brushing, and general abuse, but they managed to do the impossible: they straightened my hair. I barely recognized the woman in the mirror by the time they had finished, and they were only getting started.

Foundation, rouge, eyeliner, mascara, lipstick; not only did they apply them, but gave me handy lessons in what works with my skin tone and face shape. I soaked in every little bit of information, hungry for every morsel of knowledge they could offer. Me, a girly girl. I never would have guessed it.

Then we got to that pile of clothes that I had helped Black Suit carry through the apartment: a cute green miniskirt and blouse. We took a few pictures, and I changed. A slinky black dress. More photos. Change. A red-and-orange striped sweater with brown slacks. More photos. You get the idea. Once I'd changed into a sensible blue blouse and black slacks, the ladies put the camera away and promised me print copies of all of the pictures once they had been printed. I can't wait to see them. I think they'll go at the end of this entry once everything's said and done.

The thing about the makeover, the thing that really kicks my ass, is that I never knew I could feel this way. Feminine. Beautiful. Oh, of course I knew I could feel that way on a primal, I-am-woman-hear-me-roar level, sure, but not like this. I'm almost drunk on the feeling.

Now I wish they hadn't gotten Sam out of here. I wish he could have seen the whole thing, or at least the results. He'll have the pictures, but they're not the same. I glowed, for God's sake. I didn't even know it was possible, and that messes with my head for some reason.

Once they had finished, Iris helped them pack most of the stuff up (leaving the clothes and makeup, of course), and they filed out together. Well, except for Cathy. She volunteered to stay behind and help me sort through my new collection of nail polish.

Caty had nipped away at the beginning of the makeover, hanging a giant metal organizer in our walk-in closet with some enthusiasm; a few times I wondered if she would just knock the wall down and come on through. Once she'd hung it, she began putting the nail polish into rows in the organizer, but my hair had demanded her attention, so she'd joined us, leaving the work for Cathy and me.

We had worked our way up to the bright red of "I'm Not Really a Waitress" by the time Cathy gathered her courage, giving me a significant look.

I knew what was coming. I paused, holding the polish just short of its place on the rack, wondering whether I should acknowledge her. I could kick myself for agreeing that she should stay behind when I led the rest of them out of the apartment.

She cleared her throat.

I put the polish into the organizer and faced her, crossing my arms over my chest. "Something you need to say there?"

She nodded. "It's about the journals."

I sighed and smoothed down my skirt, unable to meet her eyes. "I'm trying. Really."

"You've tried everything?"

I left the walk-in closet and sat on the edge of the bed, delaying, trying to figure out what I could say.

Cathy followed and stopped before me, hands on her hips. I panicked and almost ran from the room, but when I realized what had triggered me, I could breathe deep. She wasn't Maple. This wasn't the Khesnaa. She wasn't going to jab needles into me.

If she noticed my panic, she didn't care. "I don't doubt you're having problems, you understand. We just need that story."

"Why? Why is it so damned important?"

"We need them to understand our enemy."

"The Organization," I said.

She inclined her head. "If that's what you call them, yes."

"Who are they?"

She sat on the bed beside me, crossing her legs as she gazed into the walk-in closet. "Their company is properly known as the United Watcher Corporation, and they have their hands in just about…oh…everything, as I understand you learned back in the New World."

New World. Did they really think of it that way? "What do they want?"

She hesitated just enough to tell me that she was hiding something. "All we really know are the stories of women like you, women who were taken to strange places and forced to do strange things. None of them, however, faced the…man…that you faced. At least, they never faced him and lived to tell the story."

The Senior. My stomach clenched. "You know about the Senior?"

"Of course. We also have a rough idea that something happened between the two of you, and yet here you are." She turned to face me. "We need to know what you did - what happened. You are the only one we know who has seen him and lived to tell the tale."

I hadn't even considered that my story led to that moment. There had been so many other things afterwards, but…well, what else *could* have been the logical ending?

I hedged. "I didn't do anything special."

"It's more than anyone else has managed."

I closed my eyes, remembering the Senior towering over me. The room felt a whole lot smaller. I opened my eyes again and stared deep into hers, trying to will my fear into her body so that she could understand what she asked of me. "I can't face him again."

She steepled her hands together at her chest. "Oh, dear. You don't have to. I don't think you understand. Your battle with the Senior - and the Corporation - is done for now, but the Underground is in extreme danger. They haven't traced us to London, but it's just a matter of time. Their spies are everywhere."

I put my head in my hands. "Got that." I hated it, but it *had* stirred me again. Danger. The threat of annihilation. That's what had been missing the whole time. I had gotten soft and comfortable, when I should have known better. The story had to be told. Lives were at stake. "All right. Fine. I'll write it."

I would have guessed that Cathy would be gleeful at the news, but instead she just gave a heavy sigh and let her arms dangle at her sides. "Thank you," she said.

"Nothing to thank me for. I need to finish things, and I can't have peoples' lives hanging over my head."

'You're right." She put a hand on my shoulder and squeezed. "I should go. Leave you to your business."

I chuckled. "Right. My business."

She squeezed my shoulder once more, tighter, and left the apartment without another word.

I sat on the end of the bed, alone for the first time since before Mexico. My thoughts rattled in my mind, and I briefly considered going in to finish with the nail polish, but it, and the makeover, had already started to recede into another world - the world where I might feel at ease in my body. I'd love another makeover sometime, and I'm not about to let myself go already, but that little chat smacked right in the face, let me know where all that stuff lies in the spectrum of my existence.

So I got up, dug out my journal, found a fancy metal pen in one of the kitchen drawers, and sat down at the great mahogany dinner table. I'd love to dive into the next part of my story, I would, but it's going to be quite the gut punch after all that happened today and even with my newfound "perspective" I'm not quite ready to surrender today's glow.

I'll push on tomorrow. Sam just got home and I think I need to talk some things over with him.

June 6th

"I am bored."

Three words. Three simple little words that I never expected to hear out of Sam's mouth and yet…

We had been watching TV, some reality show fluff about a guy who eats his own head (I may be misremembering that), when Sam switched off the TV, turned to me, and made his grand pronouncement:

"I am bored."

I blinked. It wasn't exactly a revelation – I could tell he hadn't been happy, but to hear him just *say it*? A whole different experience. "Say what now?"

"I believe you heard me."

"Oh, I heard you just fine. I don't understand, but I heard it."

"What is there to understand? This life is soft. Complacent."

I have to admit that irritated me a little, despite my own revelation last night. "So you'd much rather go back to being chased around, fearing for your life? Being shot at and nearly run off the road by a bunch of maniacs?"

He considered it. "If it prevents my spirit from rotting away in a velvet cage, then yes."

I laughed. "'A velvet cage'? Listen to you. When did you turn into F. Scott Fitzgerald?"

He cocked his head. "I do not know what you mean, but I assume it to be an insult, and I do not appreciate it."

"I'm sorry. I didn't mean to be snide." I put a hand on his chest. "This is the first chance we've had to live a normal life outside of the Khesnaa. You know what that means to me."

He gazed around at the apartment. "You call this a normal life? I confess that our previous life was hardly ideal, but this is simply another version of captivity."

"Okay, yeah, I don't get that. What captivity? We can leave any time we want."

"Can we?"

I hadn't considered it. Why would I? And for that matter, why would I want to leave? "Sure, I haven't asked, but why not?"

He stood up and began to pace. "That is precisely the problem. They would want to lull their captives into a sense of security, unwilling to consider whether this was even the right choice."

"Oh come on. How could this *not* be the right choice? They haven't exactly forced us to kill anyone."

"Yet. They knew that you would feel beholden to them. Anyone with a conscience would feel that they owe the Underground *something* in exchange for this lifestyle."

"Do I need to remind you that you were the one who found the Underground?"

He stopped, gazing at me. "Actually, they found me, shortly before you crossed back over."

"Why have I not heard this story before?"

He waved a hand. "I did not believe it relevant to our situation before now. They have been nothing but good to us."

"Exactly. What changed your mind?"

He snorted. "I do not like their tactics, and I do not trust them."

Something occurred to me. "Is this about last night? Did Black Suit tell you something?"

Sam crossed his arms over his chest. "His name is Seamus, and yes, as a matter of fact he did."

I picked up the remote and started fiddling with it. I found myself less annoyed at him and more nervous. "And what would that be?"

"The leaders of the Underground are former employees of the Corporation."

All his bluster over that? "And? It sounds like a good thing."

He leaned forward, closer to me, and lowered his voice. "Seamus doesn't think it's a good thing. He suspects ulterior motives."

"Like what? Getting our information and then handing us over?"

"I do not know, but when someone in his position expresses doubts, you would do well to listen. I know from first-hand experience."

He had a point. Had some of his information been much different? "I don't get it, though. If they were going to sell us out, why not do it before now?"

He extended his hands, palms out. "Is it not obvious? They need you to finish your journals."

"Bullshit. A little critical thinking, Sam. They show us their secrets, give us an idea of how things work, and then just hand us over to the Corporation?"

"What secrets have they shown us?"

Really? "The faces of six of their employees, for starters."

"Replaceable. Perhaps even expendable."

"Their locations in London."

He waved a hand around the room. "This is literally all we know. This could be gone tomorrow, and it hardly links them to us. Next?"

I didn't have an answer to that. What *did* we really know about the Underground? Everything in Mexico had been torched. Everything in London had been carefully controlled.

He went on. "You know that something is amiss. Look in your heart."

When he put it that way, yeah, and it embarrassed me that I had been so blind even with last night's discussion. It also amazed me that I'd so blithely accepted my little clone army without question. "Okay. Yeah. Something is weird, but it doesn't mean it's bad for us."

"Do you at least admit that there could be danger?"

"All right. Fine. There could be danger. But what are we going to do about it? Run off?"

"Perhaps."

I sighed. "Don't be ridiculous. There's no reason to run off."

He sat on the armchair, running a hand over his bald head as he stared at the floor. "I saw someone important yesterday. Or at least...I think I saw her."

I got closer, my curiosity piqued. "Who?"

He glanced at me, then back at the floor. "You would not believe it. We had arrived at the pub and, believe it or not, a crowd had already gotten there, waiting to see the match. Smoking, talking...the usual."

That *the usual* contained some venom. I knew Sam's feelings on such congregations, but I let him continue.

"Eventually they opened up, and we all started going in. I wasn't crazy about the idea - you know me - but what other choice did I have? I did not want to come back and ruin your happiness. So football it was, but when we were in the middle of that crowd, something caught my attention. Just a flash, you understand, but it grabbed me. I believe Seamus noticed as well.

He tried to distract me, but I cannot be certain about that, either. I slowed him down while I searched for the woman."

"And?"

He looked up at me. "And I believe I saw Carla."

Dead stop, full stunner. I sat down on the armchair next to him, my head spinning like he'd punched me in my ear. "But Carla's dead," I heard myself say.

"Hm. So you would believe."

"No, trust me. I saw her die with my own eyes."

He gave me a sad little smile. "You saw me die, and yet here I am. Do you not think something similar might have happened to her?"

"No. Really, she's the whole reason you're here, but it's impossible for her to have done the same thing for herself."

He rubbed his chin. "Perhaps. Or perhaps something else has happened here. Regardless, I believe that we should go back and look for her."

It seemed like an awful risk for a very small chance of finding something out. "You think she's just hanging out on the street?"

"No, but this is our only lead. Clearly she has been in the area. She may return. Whatever we do, it is better than sitting here, rotting away in this cage."

There it was: the real reason he wanted to do this. Boredom. Those three little words. "What do you think finding her will accomplish?"

"She must know more. She has to be connected to either the Underground or the Organization. I cannot surmise which, and I do not understand why she would not have contacted us."

I felt weary at the very idea of chasing ghosts through the streets of London. Would I have taken the risk fresh out of the

Khesnaa? Most likely, which made me wonder if I had been the one to change, not Sam. I didn't know what that meant for our relationship, but it didn't seem very good.

Did it change my mind? Did it make me want to gather my things and go charging off through the dark, rainy streets with no real endgame in sight?

No, and why *would* I after what I've been through? "Look, let's just sleep on it tonight and we can talk about it in the morning. Try to figure out what comes next."

His mouth tightened, and for a second, I wondered if he would fight me about it. Make me go out with him. Then it loosened, and he gave a gentle smile. "You are correct. You should get some rest and think about it."

"I think we both need some time to think."

He rose. "Perhaps. I believe I will go for a walk."

That made me pause. "A walk? At this time of night?"

"Correct. I need some fresh air. I need time to think."

I didn't like the sound of that. Did he mean time to think about chasing this ghost Carla down, or time to think about us? I stood between him and the door, hands on his chest. "You're acting weird. What's going on?"

He looked at me for a long moment. He had a chance to say something, to try to bring it back from the brink, but he just shook his head. "It is nothing. Please. Just allow me some time."

I didn't like it, but fear and sadness held me back. I didn't want to cage him. No, I *couldn't* cage him. Not anymore. If you love something, let it go, right? I stepped aside. "If I'm asleep when you get back, wake me up, okay? We need to talk."

He went for the door.

Somewhere deep inside, I knew this time was different; things would change forever the moment that he stepped through that door. It didn't make a bit of sense logically, but something important had shifted, and it would never go back to its original shape, no matter how much we did to repair it.

Sam paused, hand on the doorknob. He looked back at me. "I love you."

I tried not to show my fear. What right did I have to try to change him? "I love you, too."

Whatever his fears or misgivings, they weren't enough to stop him. He opened the door and left.

I sure as hell didn't feel like sleeping anymore. I thought it might be time to pick up where I left off, so I came in here, to the kitchen, and got out the journal.

No idea where things go from here. I just know that I don't like it.

======

What are you supposed to do when your sole reason for living is taken away from you? Once upon a time I might have gone back to my music, but the idea of creating music felt utterly pointless. Even after I'd recovered from what Maple told me must have been a concussion, I didn't – couldn't – see the point of doing much of anything.

The thing is, I couldn't get the visions of Sam out of my head. Those eyes. He had such beautiful eyes. It feels a little crazy writing about this now, after all that's happened, even after the argument earlier, but I think maybe I need to remember it. Maybe the timing fell this way for a reason.

I've read that there are five stages of grief. You don't experience them all in order, but they're all supposed to be the same, like climbing this ladder that leads you out of despair, even if you get knocked down a rung every now and then. It sounds great, but it's bullshit.

It felt a lot more like someone dropped me in the middle of the ocean and getting battered by wave after wave. During the weeks that followed Sam's death, I'd begin to think that I had my feet under me, that I might actually survive the whole thing, but it was only a matter of time before another wave knocked me over for good. Those were the days where I lay in bed staring at the ceiling, hoping that death would come get me soon.

I don't know how long I lived like that; it had to be weeks. Carla didn't return; neither did Zito, at least for a while. All trips to Room 3 stopped. Maple and I seemed to be all that remained of the Khesnaa's little shit show, and even her job had gone downhill. She seemed to have nothing else to do than cook and take care of me. I'll give her some credit. She took it seriously for a while. She could have easily left me to rot. She baked me cookies on the first day that I woke up and tried to get me to engage in conversation.

Of course, I wanted nothing to do with it or her. The longer I remained quiet, the more frustrated she got, and I wondered what might happen if the supplies dwindled to nothing or she reached the end of her rope.

That didn't happen, but we did reach a point where she stood over the bed, one hand on her hips, holding a bowl full of what looked like straight-up gruel in her hand. Until that moment, I hadn't even known that gruel still *existed.*

"When are you going to get out of that bed?" She said.

"What do you care?"

She put the bowl on the night stand and stood there, her bug eyes boring into my skull.

At last I just couldn't take it anymore. "What do you want from me? I don't have anything else to give you."

"I want you to eat."

"Why? We're both going to die here anyway. Don't see much point in prolonging the agony."

"You must at least try."

I grabbed the spoon. I lifted it, and the goop of the oatmeal inside, into the air. "This really the best you can do?"

Her face turned red. "Now listen, you know this isn't some resort –"

"No shit. They feed you better crap in prison." I dropped the spoon – and the oatmeal - back into the bowl. "What's the point in feeding me, anyway?"

She frowned, putting her hands on her hips. "The point is to sustain yourself."

"For what? Are they coming back to get us? We be free?"

She said nothing, but the red in her face drained. She knew the truth, even if she didn't want to admit it.

"That's what I thought," I said.

"Please. Eat."

I don't think I'd ever heard that tone from the woman. I could almost believe she cared. Almost. "Look, I'm sorry they took away whatever authority made you feel like a big woman. I'm even sorrier if we fucked things up for you. I'm sorry Samarta died. I'm sorry for all kinds of shit, I guess. But this isn't going to make your life mean anything. Might as well go volunteer in a cancer ward and get away from me."

She sat down beside me, smoothing out her skirt with both hands. "It's not about feeling like my life has meaning. Well, not entirely."

I rolled my eyes. "Do tell."

She looked at me. "I understand your hostility. I really do, but we're not so different. Once upon a time it might have killed me to admit that, but it's true."

I leaned on one elbow. "Now this I have to hear. Tell me, woman who holds me hostage, how are we so similar?"

She shook her head. "Your hostility grates on the ears and on the soul. Do you know that?"

"Maybe I have a reason to be hostile."

"I would never disagree, but I suspect you might also use it to keep others at arm's length, so you never have to get to know them," she said.

I snorted. "That's real rich coming from you."

"Your anger..." she began to speak, and then seemed to reconsider her words, knocking her palm on the night stand. "Of course you have a right to be angry. It's practically an obligation."

I laid on my back, staring at the ceiling. "I'm glad you get the picture."

"I do." She shook her head. "I hate what I have become."

Hard to accept self-pity coming from her, but I didn't have anywhere else to be or anything better to do. "And what have you become?"

"A kidnapper and a torturer aiding and abetting murderers. I wasn't always like this. In fact, when I first arrived, I was in your shoes."

That one made me think for a second. Maple in Room 3? Maple trying to clear those tests?

I saw her smile out of the corner of my eye. "Oh, yes, I took the injections. I had the visions. They didn't even need to take me by force, like you two ladies. Love was enough to draw me in."

Now she had my attention. I rolled over and sat up on the side of the bed, studying her hard. "What do you mean?"

"I assume Samarta told you the story of his family? Yes? Well, my story's not so different. Before I came here, I had a husband with a job in the civil service. Two beautiful boys. A house in Liverpool. I couldn't really want for much else. It was…a different time."

"How old *are* you, anyway?" I said.

She flushed. "A lady never tells her age."

"Cut the bullshit. You've seen just about everything there is to see about me. If you *really* want to put us on some even playing ground and make me even think that listening to your bellyaching is worthwhile, you're going to have to give a little bit."

She pursed her lips. I wondered if she would tear me a new asshole, but at last she nodded, adjusting her chestnut-colored hair. "You're right, of course. The last day that I recall living free in your world…my God, has it been so long?" She put a hand to her mouth.

"What? When?"

She shook her head. "1957."

Impossible. "That means you should be in your, what, your 70s?"

She snorted. "Please. Have some decorum. Time here moves differently. You're never older than the day you arrive."

Her accent slipped on that last sentence. Oh, she still sounded English, but not like an upper-crust snob at all.

You were a poor kid just like me, weren't you? I thought, but I didn't want to ask her. I wanted to hear her story. For the moment, I pushed aside the obvious questions about my own aging and focused on her. Yes, God help me, despite myself, I wanted to speak to Maple. "Did they kidnap your family?"

She winced, running her hands over her dress. She became a different woman as she spoke, dropping any hint of the accent and her affectations. She had most definitely been a poor kid like me. "Not precisely. It was the husband, right. Planned a holiday down to Rome; we'd never done that since we'd been married, trying to keep things together. It was a grand time, planning the thing. Got the children involved and all. Lucky us that Harry's job was providing the flight. I didn't think to question it, just figured it part of his job and us lucky is all."

"Only you didn't make it to Rome."

"Sharp girl. I'm not sure where we landed, but it didn't take long to figure out it wasn't Rome, right? They took the plane into a hangar and made us get off. Wondered what was going on when my legs went out under me and they dragged me the rest of the way off. Last time I saw the kids." She said it like you might talk about someone taking out your trash, but I saw a tear in the corner of her eye. She hadn't walled that part of herself off just yet.

"I'm sorry." I wasn't quite ready to touch her hand and try to comfort her, but I had some trouble accessing the rage that had burned toward her.

She nodded. "I don't let myself think about it. Kids are long gone and grown anyway so what's the use of crying, right?" She wiped at her eyes. "Anyway, passed out in the hangar, woke up here. Still don't know if they doped my drink or something else did it."

"Something like Room 2," I said.

"Yes. I woke up in this very room, with Harry standing over me, telling me I'm doing the right thing. 'We're helping the world, not just Downing Street,' he said, but he wouldn't answer any of my questions. He said they needed to see the inside of my psyche and the sooner I helped out the sooner I could get home and 'besides, love, isn't it best that you and the boys are safe from the people who'd harm us'?" She snarled that last sentence, wiping at her eyes again.

"Good God," I said.

She laughed. "I don't believe in such a foolish thing. If there is a God, He's not here, that's for sure."

My head swam with questions. How could I pick just one? "Where is 'here', anyway? I know we're somewhere…else. Another world, right?"

"Samarta told you that, I'm sure. He always thought small. This isn't just another world. Not even another dimension. Try another universe entirely."

A weird feeling spread over me. It felt like dread, but dread of a different stripe than the kind I felt when I faced Room 3. This was more like the dread you get when you consider that one day you'll simply cease to exist. "Another universe. How's that work?"

She shrugged. "They explained it to me as a 'pocket universe' that someone formed. I don't really understand it well. All I can tell you is that no government made this. I don't think anyone else on Earth made it either. You've seen the Senior, you know the kinds of things that exist now."

"Are we in Hell?"

"I doubt it. My understanding is that this place formed in the 1940s. Something to do with a test, but that I truly don't know. Of course, it might as well be Hell for all the suffering it's caused."

I sat forward. "What was it like then? If you want to talk about it."

"Don't see what difference talking about it would make."

"Wouldn't it bother you?"

She waved a hand. "I cried those tears long ago. You're not going to break me with some simple reminiscing. It should be funny, I'm sure, but so many faces are still the same. Harry's long gone, and who can blame him, with what I became. Barren and Bloch have been here since the day I arrived." She looked at me.

The implications staggered me. That made Barren and Bloch older than Maple. It seemed inconceivable. "Insane. Somebody could just come here and live forever?"

"So long as no one killed them, I suppose. But then you'd have to stay in the circle forever and I can't imagine anyone would like that. It plays with your head, the whole thing. I don't imagine we're meant to live like this. I admit I lost my mind for a little while at the beginning. I wanted to give up." She sighed. "Harry kept telling me that I'd see the boys again; it was just a matter of time to get through the tests. Just a few more tests, and I'd get home." She shook her head. "Of course the tests kept stretching on. Just one more. Then another. 'That one didn't go right, let's try again.'"

"Then the bastard walks out on you," I said.

She nodded. "Nice of him, wasn't it?"

"Why did he leave? What about your kids, did they not mean a thing?"

She gave a wan smile. "On the contrary, I imagine they meant a lot to him. He returned to them, I have no doubt of that." She sniffled. Hate her or not, I had to give her some credit. I don't think I would just be suffering a case of the sniffles if I'd been ripped away from my kids. More like World War III. "The boys never had a clue. The government told the world I was dead, that the plane had crashed. I'm told it was quite a fake. I think the boys even believe it, but I suppose I'll never know for sure."

"You haven't left the Khesnaa since then?" I said.

"Many times, but they have never allowed me to return to my - our - world. Even if they would, I don't know that I could dare see them. Dire circumstances, you see. Might not end well for me or them."

No wonder the woman had turned to stone. Would the same thing happen to me? "You still didn't say why Harry left," I said.

"Didn't, did I? Not much of a story there, I'm afraid. I got better at solving the puzzles, and he got a nice, fat promotion for finding me. A promotion took him away from here for weeks, and the weeks became months, and, after a while, years." She shrugged. "He was the least of my worries by that point. Oh, I could have torn his face off for a while there, but the love dies pretty quickly in such circumstances, you understand."

"I'd want to tear the asshole's balls off."

She giggled; it sounded weird, but not really unpleasant. I didn't think she had it in her. "Wouldn't lie and say that didn't occur to me, either. Anyway, I made my own way. Got promoted out of this room when I solved all their puzzles, put their little games together. Helped get this going proper," she said.

"What *is* all this, anyway? Why kidnap women - it is just women, right?"

She nodded.

"...And make them do these tests, if nothing ever moves forward?" I said.

"It moves forward. Fits and starts, yeah, but it moves. I'd think your friend was proof of that."

Carla. The first time she'd mentioned her in ages. "Where did they take her?"

"Haven't a clue. I know you don't believe me, but it's the truth. I swear." She put one hand on her heart and held the other up. "They don't tell me much that goes on beyond the circle. Sometimes not even that. I had no idea what they planned on doing to poor Samarta."

That made my anger flare again. *Poor Samarta.* As if she'd ever befriended him. "So they've taken away your power?"

"What little I had, and what small amount of good it did." She met my eyes. "I know you don't think I cared about Samarta, but I did. All the more pain that he betrayed my trust, but given his situation, I think I can forgive him."

"That's big-hearted of you."

She hung her head. "What else can I do? It's too late now."

"You can start by telling me what they're up to here. That would be an awfully big help."

She sat forward, elbows on her knees, and blew air out through her nose. At last she looked over at me. "They're using us – you – to build an army."

"To do what?" But as soon as I said it, I figured it out. "That thing in the basement."

She nodded. "They're immortal."

I shook my head. "That can't be right. Sam said he killed one. That's what pissed the Senior off so bad."

"Oh, yes, Enliel. Poor thing. Well, he *was* the first. Quite mortal, I'm afraid, if you knew how to get to him – spot in the back of the neck, you know," she said, and pointed at the base of her neck. "There are others, though. You can chop them up, cook them, drop a bomb on them…they'll come back."

I felt horrified. "You mean there are more downstairs?"

"Oh, no. This is simply a proving ground. Once they develop, they're moved elsewhere. I suppose that might be where they took Carla."

Now I understood why the Senior hadn't looked in on Enliel in so long. Of course it had been a pretext to see us. But then… "What do we have to do with them? Why do they need us if that's their goal?"

"No, we can't discuss that." Her voice reverted when she spoke those words, freezing into her affected upper-class accent. I could *see* her putting a wall back up around her ego.

Desperation seized me. It might have been the first thing I'd actually felt in days, and it made me clumsy. "You told me that you hated what you'd become."

She arched an eyebrow. "So what if I do? I must keep surviving."

Then I really screwed the pooch, so to speak: I tried to grab hold of her arm. "Please."

You would think I had thrown boiling oil on her. She snapped her arm back and stood up, her eyes wild. "Do *not* touch me. Do not plead with me."

"But I don't – what happened? It's your kids, isn't it?"

Her mouth tightened, and I genuinely wondered if she was going to take a swing at me. I even flinched, but she just said: "do not speak of my children to me again if you wish to keep eating."

Her voice froze me deep into my soul, taking every bit of fight out of me. "Yes, ma'am."

She picked up the bowl. "You're lucky you have survived as long as you have. I could quite easily have left you to starve."

"Might have been better for both of us," I said.

She snorted and turned on her heel, slamming the door behind her.

I sat back and leaned against the wall behind the bed, pulling my knees up to my chest. I remembered the look on Sam's face on that night that we'd shared in the corn.

Freedom. That is your reason.

I let go of the illusion that I would return to a magical life, or even the life I had known before they brought me there. I had no illusion that I would return to the same world that I thought I had left. Lord knows nothing about me would be the same.

I could do this, though. I could escape. I refused to believe that Maple had drawn me in only to shut me down and hurt me further. She had told me too much. I just had to figure out how to get through that armor of hers for good. I didn't know if it would be impossible, but it gave me a goal, and that had to be enough, at least in this new, Sam-less world.

My mind lingered on the ghosts of Gina and Momma. A fat lot of good they'd done me. *Protect her.* I had been the one who needed help all along, assholes, thank you very much.

"You're right. You were the one who needed help," said a voice from near the window.

I turned my head, my mouth dropping open. "Carla?"

"Hey, kid," Carla said.

"What are you doing here?" I said.

June 7th

I had a terrible moment this morning: for a few seconds, as I stared up into the dirty gray light streaming through the open cracks in the blinds, I could swear that I had returned to the Khesnaa. It felt so *real,* as if I might hear Maple stirring outside the door, or roll over and see Carla's dopey eyes staring back at me. Panic gripped me, and I grabbed hold of the sheet on Sam's side of the bed.

Pull it together, Momma said in my head.

The fuzziness in my head cleared, and I recognized the ceiling above me. Not the Khesnaa. Not my place back in Boston. No, the apartment in Soho. Back in the land of the living.

Here's the damned thing: I felt disappointed.

What is that all about? I sat on the edge of the bed.

At last I figured it out: things felt a little simpler back then, even if they weren't *good.* I had a purpose, as messed up as it might have been. Now? In some vague way, I hope that we're fighting the Organization, and of course Sam is important to me, but it's just not the same.

Isn't that fucked up? That's really fucked up, I think.

That's when something else registered: I had touched Sam's side of the bed, and it had been empty. Sam had either never come back, or he had come back and gotten up before I woke up. Hoping for the latter, I got out of bed and threw on a robe, heading out to the living room.

I felt some relief when I saw the back of someone's head on

the couch, but it didn't last long when I saw the pile of blonde hair rising from that head.

Iris.

Even at eight in the morning she had dressed for a 1960s runway, wearing a slinky green dress and black mod boots with large brass buckles on the sides. She sipped at a cup of tea as I entered the room, meeting my gaze with sad eyes that twinkled slightly in the low light sliding through the half-opened blinds.

I shook my head. "Iris? What's going on?"

She nodded. "Morning, love, good to see you." She trailed off, her tone leaving an unspoken *under the circumstances.*

I frowned and sat down in the armchair. "Where's Sam?"

"I was going to ask you the same thing."

"So you haven't seen him?"

She blew on her tea. "Afraid not. You?"

I shrugged, trying not to panic. "As far as I can tell, he's not here."

"Mmm." She nodded toward the kitchen. "You might want some tea. I've made plenty, and I brought some pastries for you."

"Sure, why not? It's not like a loved one completely vanished," I said, and stood up.

She sniffed and watched me as I wandered over to the kitchen, trying to gather my thoughts. "I assume you know he went out for a stroll last night."

Iris had left a cup for me, right by the stove, pre-loaded with a tea bag. I poured from the kettle, eyeing the pile of pastries by my side. "Yeah." I didn't know what else to say.

"Hmm." She took another sip as I returned to the living room with my cup and a cruller, sliding into the armchair.

"He said he'd be back," I said, and I actually believed it, but I've gone back and checked yesterday's journal and see no record of him ever actually saying that. I guess I assumed that his return should be implied. Shows what I know.

She nodded. "Well, we do know that he went for a walk last night. He left here and walked down the street a bit, we couldn't figure out what he was up to. Security said that he knew we were following him - no harm in that, I suppose, but he must have freaked out, you know. Kept looking back at him, then he turned a corner and vanished."

I raised an eyebrow. "I don't understand."

"Neither do we."

I held a hand out. "No, not that. Well, yeah, that, but...you were following him?"

"Of course, why not?"

"So you've been monitoring us?"

She shook her head. "Why wouldn't we? We have to make sure the Corporation doesn't harm you."

I stared into the cup, contemplating this and feeling like a complete jackass. Sam had been right all along: this was a Velvet Cage, cousin to the Khesnaa. "But...we didn't sign up for that."

"I'm sorry, I really am, but I assumed you would know. It's the nature of what we must do to protect you."

Unbelievable. "So you have no idea where he went?"

"None. That's why I'm here. What did he say?"

This shifted things. Would I be betraying Sam if I told her the whole story? He had been right about their surveillance and had most surely been right that something more was going on with the Underground.

But could I find him on my own? I didn't think so, especially not if they followed my every move. I had no idea which decision better protected him, or if he could be protected at all. Just no way of knowing, and it tore my heart apart, no matter how frustrated I had been with the man. At last I decided to give it up. "He said he saw somebody familiar near the pub where they went last night."

She perked up. "The pub?"

"You know. He went there with…what's his name?" I snapped my fingers. "Seamus. The driver."

"Aye, Seamus." I could be wrong, but I think I saw a wistful look pass over her. Something between the two of them?

Interesting.

"I assumed he was coming back. Sam, I mean," I said.

She considered it. "Did he tell you who he saw?"

I needed to hold that back. My instincts told me it was the smart thing to do. "No. He just said it was somebody he remembered and that he wanted to go look today."

She shook her head. "So that's it, then, he went to see if he could find her?"

"No. That's the thing. He was just going for a walk. Said he had some things to think about." I kicked myself. Once upon a time, I knew better than to trust people. Sam had been the one exception that had never caused me heartache - until now. Now I had no idea who I could trust.

She rose, setting her empty teacup and saucer on the mahogany end table. "Well, it's a start. We can start looking near the pub, maybe spread out. He didn't say anything about going anywhere else?"

I rose with her. "Not a word. Listen, take me with you when you go looking for him. If he is out there, he might not hide if you have me there."

She held both hands out. "No. We can't take that risk."

So it seemed to be official, then: they had decided that I would go crazy waiting for him. "I can't just sit waiting with my thumb up my ass."

She went for the door. "You can, and you will. Do I need to remind you of our true goal here?"

"Maybe you do, because I'm not sure I understand a thing you're doing and I know I'm not board with what I do see."

She turned to me and smiled. "No need to get huffy. We're just trying to save the world, aren't we? You're more important to bringing down the Corporation than any one of us, and that includes Sam." I started to say something, but she held her hands up again. "I know you love the man, that much is clear, and I understand it, but sometimes the world demands more of us."

I sat back down, hard. "What do you expect from me? I don't have any powers."

"No powers, no, but you're vitally important to taking the Corporation down. Please. I beg you. Just wait it out, and I promise all will make sense."

I hated it, but what other option did I have? "If he dies…"

"You'll want to kill me then, and maybe rightfully so, but we will not allow that to happen. Just trust me this once. We'll get your man back."

"What's to stop me from going out that door the moment you leave?"

She fished the key out from her cleavage, holding it aloft. "It can be locked from the outside, you know."

That was it. They could and would lock me up in here, just like the Organization had locked me into Room 1. "You wouldn't, not after what I went through."

She cocked her head and smirked. "I'm hoping it doesn't come to that. Just stay by the phone, work on your journal, and remain calm. We've pills in the cupboard that can beat the anxiety if you need them. Look for the Lorazepam." She winked. "It'll take care of all your ills."

I waved a hand at her. "Get out."

She had something more to say, but closed her mouth and nodded. She opened the door and exited without another word. I listened for the key in the lock, but she offered me the small mercy of not completing my imprisonment.

That should have calmed me, but instead rage at my situation seized me and I picked up a crystal vase from the end table, flinging it at the door. It exploded like a bomb, sending a hundred shards showering to the floor.

"Assholes. All of you, assholes," I said to the air, looking around for the cameras, microphones, or whatever else they might have hidden in the apartment. I looked at the remains of the vase and felt vaguely ashamed; they had put me in a glass cage like a monkey at the zoo and I had reacted in just the manner you might expect from a monkey.

Luxury has its price, as sure as being "special" has its price, and they were already exacting a heavy toll on my humanity.

I went to fetch some Lorazepam and a broom.

======

Carla strolled toward the bed, hands stuffed into the pockets of what looked like faded old jeans. Her shoulders slumped; she looked defeated. "I'm not exactly 'here'," she said.

Yes, I saw the truth of that pretty quickly: something about her seemed *off*, like a photograph of a photograph. Something had been lost in the colors of her clothing, the cast of her skin, and her movements. It put my nerves on edge. "Do you know where you really are?"

Her eyes took on a faraway, haunted look as she gazed into

a distance that I couldn't begin to understand. "I…don't know." She closed her eyes and shook her head. "It's dark. I can't tell if I'm inside something or if they just haven't turned on the lights."

"Can't you move?"

"No. Something is bound around me." She wrapped her arms around her chest. "It's like this, all the time."

"Did you wake up there?"

She opened her eyes and gazed at me. "Yes. My last memories of the Khesnaa are so hazy…"

I approached her. "How *did* you get here?"

"Same as your Mom and Gina, I guess." She sat at the end of the bed. "Only I'm not dead. At least, I don't think I'm dead yet."

Screwed up as it sounds, a happy, vindictive streak ran through me. Part of me had been afraid that they had whisked Carla away to even greater comfort, leaving the broken project to wither away in neglect.

I swallowed hard. "You think they ended the project?"

"I don't think so. They're doing something different, a new phase of some sort, but I can't read them like I did before."

Those words caught in my mind, and the vindictiveness rose to the surface again. "'Does that mean you actually understood the whole mess back here? Because you can feel free to fill me in on some of the details. You know, if you're feeling up to it."

She ran a hand over her face and looked at the floor.

I crossed my arms over my chest. "Gina *told* me you were hiding something, but I didn't want to believe it."

She raised one hand toward me. "Yes. All right. I know more than I let on. I'm not proud of it, but I did it." She met my eyes. "Things were screwed up."

"Oh, you bet they *are*," I said, and would have continued on, but I felt something weird dancing across the back of my mind; it distracted me, made me take a step back and touch my head.

Carla made a choked noise, putting her hand to her mouth.

"Oh my God. Did you just try to read my mind?" I said, my eyes boggling.

"I'm so sorry."

I took another step away. "What is wrong with you?"

"I didn't mean to. I can't help it sometimes."

I shook my head, trying to clear the fear that had grabbed me by the throat. I couldn't let her intimidate me; it might be the last chance I had with her. I had to get as much information as I could. I forced the words out. "What did you see in my head?"

"I saw what they did to Sam."

"Yeah? Did you see them shooting me when I tried to protect you?"

Her eyes widened. "I thought that was a dream."

I sat by the Korg. A headache had started to blossom behind my eyes. The shooting must have happened, which meant that the events in Room 3 afterwards might well be real. Did that mean I had died? Had we both gone to some sort of afterlife? "So you remember it too."

She frowned. "They stuck something in my arm and then I remember…a shot?"

"Yeah. Right to my neck. You knew what was going on. Tell me why they shot me. Tell me why they killed Sam. Tell the truth for once in your life."

"I don't know any of that," she said, and sighed. "If I did, I promise that I'd tell you."

I narrowed my eyes. "You know enough. You could guess."

She slid off the edge of the bed and walked toward me, but I threw my hands in the air.

"Don't you get close to me. I don't want you near me," I said.

"Please. I'm sorry."

"Ghost. Freak." I realized that my dazed, horrified brain had regressed to somewhere around the mental age of ten. For that minute, it felt like Carla might as well have pulled the trigger that killed me.

"Please," she said, and grabbed my arm.

I gagged at her touch. She *was* there…well, sort of. Her grip felt like one of those water snakes, you know, the plastic sleeves filled with water that can't sit still in your hand? Imagine that crossed with rotting flesh and you begin to get an idea of what her fingers felt like on my skin. "What are you?"

She pulled her hand away. "Sam called me Kellik'at. They have a term for it too: Class A Folder."

"The hell does that mean?" I said.

"I can fold reality. That might be how I got here."

"So wait, when you stuck your fingers in my head, did you see *everything* that's happened since you left?"

"How should I know?" she said.

"Did you see what Maple said?"

"About what?"

So she couldn't know all and see all. *Interesting.* Quick debate with my conscience, not too unlike the debate I had earlier today: should I spill Maple's abbreviated history of the Khesnaa? My personal history with folks like Bloch suggested that trusting her might not be the wisest thing, but at the same time she might be able to fill in the blanks.

Yes. I would tell her. I proceeded to unload on her, sparing only the identity of Maple's captor. I couldn't tell you exactly why I did that - only that it felt right. Some things are sacred, even between enemies. Maybe especially between them.

When I had finished, Carla sat quiet for a long time, to the point where I wondered if she had checked out. At last she spoke. "You're telling me we're in another universe. And the British Government knows about this."

"According to her. I suspect more people on our side know, too. Why wouldn't they?" I said.

"I don't even know what to say. It makes sense, but…"

"Yeah. I have thousands of questions. Did you…you know, 'hear' anything that might explain some of that?"

She rubbed her chin. I wondered if she faced the same decision over how much to share and felt a little sad that our trust had fallen apart.

She started it.

Then she surprised me. She said, "it might be easier for me to show you what I learned, rather than telling you."

"What does that mean?"

She didn't say anything. Not exactly. Instead, she raised her right hand and motioned toward the window, like summoning an animal.

"What are you –" I said, but the sight that answered her motion shut me right up.

I saw a shade of my Momma, fading into existence right by the window like an old TV tuning in a fuzzy station.

"Momma?" I said, standing up and taking a tentative step toward her.

Carla held up her left hand, a sign of silence. I stopped, watching her. She made the motion again, and I realized that I heard something – had heard it the first time, too. The kind of sound you hear when something small shifts behind a closed closet door. Like something being rearranged behind the scenes.

Gina appeared beside my Momma. She put an arm around the older woman's shoulder and winked at me. "Hey, kid."

I looked from them to Carla and back again. "Are you guys really here?"

"That's for you to decide," Momma said.

I glanced back at Carla. "How did you do that?"

She sighed. "They're part of me. Always were."

"That's impossible," I said.

Gina crossed her arms over her chest. "Wish I could tell you otherwise, but that's the truth."

I faced Carla. "How? You never met them."

"You got me. Those nights when they showed up, I saw them in my dreams. Well, didn't quite see them…I *was* them, but they were speaking through me, if that makes any sense at all. They were in control."

I gazed at them, wondering if they would have the same consistency as Carla's strange flesh. "No wonder you guys disappeared when she woke up."

Carla spoke. "Yeah."

"But she's gotten a lot better at it," Gina said.

Momma nodded. "She can move her consciousness."

Gina winked. "To either one of us. Ain't that some shit?"

I took a step back, horrified. "You're the general of their fucking army. They want you to control that thing in the basement. *That's* how we're connected." It made perfect sense. My visions, the Carla that came out of that tree, none of that had never been about myself. It had been my job to unlock Carla's true powers, and I'd performed like a good little soldier. I felt sick to my stomach.

Carla waved a hand. Gina and Momma vanished. "It doesn't matter what they want. I'm not going to do it."

"What if they make it so you don't have a choice?"

"They made Sam that way, yes, but he had something to lose. I don't."

"Bullshit. *Everybody* has a lever. They just haven't found yours yet." Something occurred to me. Something awful. "Or...maybe they have."

Her face darkened. "What are you trying to say?"

"Maybe *I'm* the lever. Maybe leaving me here with Maple and letting us waste away is their way of pushing you to do what they want." I took another step away from her.

"They never said anything about that. They never said anything at all. I just woke up in the dark."

"They didn't *have* to say anything. You're here, aren't you? Maybe they just needed to set things up so you could feel what was going on with me. See how you reacted."

She shook her head. "I wouldn't fall for that."

"Like I said, you're here. You came to help me, didn't you?"

She nodded. "And you –"

"I what? I led you right into a trap? Because that's what this is. A way to draw you out and see how you'll react."

"I was going to say that you attacked me. And fair enough, I did a lot of what you said. I can't defend not telling you some of that stuff." She turned in a circle, waving a hand to indicate the room. "But if it's a trap, where are they?"

"They're watching and listening," I said.

She closed in on me, and I fought not to back away again. "You know what I think? I think you've been alone too long here, and you're imagining things. This place is bad enough without jumping at shadows as well."

Maybe she was right, but I didn't get a chance to answer before something rolled overhead, like a plane taking off. We both jumped.

Thunder. What the hell?

I couldn't remember ever hearing thunder at the Khesnaa before. What could that mean? I opened my mouth to say something about it, but the door creaked open before I could speak.

We both turned to find Zito standing in the doorway, hands on hips, grinning. "So you get clear and you decide to come back here, huh? Well, good job on you."

Carla gasped and made a hand motion. She vanished like Mom and Gina, leaving me alone with Zito.

Zito leaned against the doorjamb. "Long time no see, girly. Lonely without your boyfriend?"

"Fuck you, Zito." The words came out of my mouth before I could think. He scared me. Something had changed about him. He looked like a big cat stalking its prey rather than the preening jackass I used to know.

He cocked his head. "Once upon a time, I'd have taken you up on that. But I've seen the light, Good Lord, Good Lord. I'm here to take you to see him one last time."

My stomach churned. "Who?"

He scratched his chin. "Barren. Senior wants you to go to Room 3. We know you solved the puzzle, pulled that out of Carla's head. We need to know the answer. You're going to give it to us," he said.

"Or what?" It should have sounded defiant, but it came out as just plain scared.

"There are worse things than death, sugar." He raised his eyebrows. "Now get over here, and let's strap you in one more time. What do you say?"

June 8th

Still no Sam. I spent this morning flipping through the channels trying to find something to distract me for a few hours. I blew past a few shitty reality shows, some crime procedural, and rugby until I found some Lifetime Channel piece of fluff, something about an evil man who threatened his wife unless she had his brother's baby, something like that.

It held me for all of half an hour before I started flipping again. I admit it: I got desperate, and downed another Lorazepam, but even that slowed me down a bit. I'm sure it didn't help that I had downed about a gallon of coffee that morning (might be exaggerating a bit there), but the only other thing I could think to do was write in this journal, and it seemed too soon.

Two nights without Sam – two nights in an empty bed. Sure, I've been on my own, but I also get used to things very easily, and he became my new norm. Besides, I miss the big lug, even if we were having problems. Seriously, I had thought *that* might be the end of our relationship? I had been sick on privilege and the illusion of wealth.

I'm not saying it's my fault he walked out and didn't come back. That's his own call, but I do wonder if I could have been more understanding, tried to draw him out on just why he had been so unhappy.

But I know his leaving didn't really have anything to do with us. It's Carla – or what he suspected was Carla, anyway. I didn't like to think about what might have happened if he started sniffing around for her. Maybe he had been right about the connection between the Underground and the Organization.

It might be best if I don't write about stuff like that. There's no way of knowing for sure unless I go out there and try to find him, and I admit, it crossed my mind. I even got to the point of taking a butcher knife out of a drawer and debating whether I should use it to force Seamus to drive me around the city until I found Sam.

In the end, it just didn't seem like the right thing to do. Suppose I went to all that risk and still couldn't find him?

I started to formulate another plan, and this plan started with using that knife to make Seamus a ham sandwich. I piled it on a plate with a bag of chips - sorry, packet of crisps - and a can of Coke. No reason not to talk to the guy, right?

He seemed to sense what I had been thinking as soon as he saw me at the top of the stairs. He stood up and started protesting, telling me that I knew I couldn't leave.

I told him "I understand that perfectly" and handed the plate over. "I was just thinking about you guarding me, all alone, and thought you might want something nice to eat." You know, being really slick.

He said he couldn't accept it, that it wouldn't be right, and that he could get in big trouble.

It took me less than two minutes to get him wolfing down the sandwich and crisps while I stood at the door, watching the rain gather in the gutters.

Once he had finished, I took the plate from him and placed it on the stairs. "You're a hungry man, aren't you?"

He nodded, sipping the Coke. "It's very kind of you. Lucky for me you don't want to poison me."

I smiled at him, running my hand over the railing. "Uh huh.

If you really thought I would poison you, you wouldn't have touched that food no matter how sweet I got."

"Sam said you're a smart one."

The mention of Sam took the wind out of my sails. I sat on the bottom stair, my hands on my knees. "Would he have been with me otherwise?" I tried to keep my voice light, but I don't think it worked.

"You're worried about him, aren't you?" he said.

I cocked my head at him, smirking. "Is it that obvious?"

"Oh, you're a smart mouth too, I see."

"Come on. You had to know that going in."

He nodded. "I reckon I did. I'm worried about him too. He's an awkward fellow, no doubt of that, but I can tell he's a good man."

"That he is. Did he say anything to you about why he would have walked off? Where he'd be going?"

Seamus sat forward in his seat, scanning the room from floor to ceiling. I followed his eyes, wondering what he might be after. When I came back to his eyes, he raised his brows and nodded. *Careful, girl.* "You're going to have to be a little more specific about that one," he said.

The walls had ears. "He mentioned that you had some issues with the…er…structure of this group."

He pulled a cigarette from his shirt pocket, lit up, and nodded as he exhaled. "I might have mentioned it."

"That's why I want to talk to you."

"I see. Is this about the bird that he saw outside the pub?"

I nodded.

He smiled. "Oh, don't worry. I pulled him away from *that* mess. Besides, I don't think your man is the cheating type."

I waved a hand. "I know that. He wasn't out to screw her or

anything like that."

"You don't pull your punches, do you?" he said, and took a drag.

"If you'd seen half of what I've seen, you'd understand that there's no point in pulling the punches."

He exhaled a dirty white cloud. "I reckon so. So he told you that he wanted to find her, then."

I rubbed my chin, a little surprised that he would have mentioned that to Seamus. I guess the guys really bonded after all. "That's right."

"So. I suppose that would be a place to start looking."

"Does the Underground know this?"

He tapped ash onto the floor. "They might have some ideas, but they don't know the entire situation. I didn't see a need to fill them in on every minute detail."

I didn't know what to think of that one. "Even if it meant they might not find him?"

He shrugged. "I gave them enough information to find him without giving away his secret. Don't worry about that." He studied me. "There's something you're looking for, why don't you just come out and ask instead of beating around the bloody hole?"

I sighed. "Do you think they would have harmed him?"

He scratched his arm and considered the question. "It's a good one. I wish I could tell you no, but I just can't know for certain. I'm sure he told you about the 'questionable' elements of the Underground, aside from my own issues."

"He mentioned it."

"Mm. Well, seeing the lady there…it might just have meant somebody listened in on our conversation."

I narrowed my eyes. "What do you mean?"

"I didn't recognize who he meant, but chances are if you see a stranger hanging around in this line of work…well." He extended a hand toward me. "You know."

I considered it. "What are you saying? That someone might have heard you and grabbed him?"

"It's a theory."

"If that's the case, then why are *you* still here?"

He waved a hand. "Please. I'm not going anywhere. I'm too important to their hierarchy. Besides, I know too much. They let me go and some of their…how do you put it…'organizational memory' goes away."

"What do you know?"

He put a finger to his lips as he dumped some more ash. "No more talk about that. But listen, do I think they'd kill him? It's possible. I don't think it's likely, though. Not exactly, anyway."

"What do you mean 'not exactly'?"

He took another drag and made me wait for him to exhale the smoke. "I think it's more likely they'd have taken him to get information out of him. Maybe information that's not coming quickly enough from your pen," he said, and arched an eyebrow at me.

Oh my God. "They wouldn't do that to get at the information I haven't written yet, would they?"

"Consider their perspective – that information could save humanity. What would you do?"

The stakes couldn't be that high, could they? "I wouldn't throw away my principles."

"Easy to say when you're on the other side of the fence. Of course, he seemed to believe the same. Let's just say he wasn't a willing participant in the questions that they asked him."

I didn't understand that one. "When did that happen?"

The look on Seamus's face said that he might have been trying to help me, but he clearly had *some* boundaries, and had overstepped one. "I guess he doesn't have to sleep as much as you. He was awake quite a bit more than you after your arrival from Mexico. Those times you were sleeping…well. Iris came to visit a few times."

I felt nauseated. "What do you mean?" I said, but I had a pretty good idea *just* what he meant.

"She tried the dab hand first. Shaking her arse at him, trying to convince him you'd never know the difference."

I slammed my first on the railing. "That slut."

He looked a bit angry at that. "Please, don't be unkind. Just part of the job, I'm *quite* sure she didn't enjoy it. We all have things to do that are distasteful. That's life." He ground out the first cigarette and lit a second one.

"Part of the job, huh?" I remembered the way he'd looked at her that first night. His eyes on her tits when she slid that key out. I closed my eyes.

He wouldn't, right?

Seamus could read that body language, all right. "Trust me. He didn't crack. Showed zero interest. Less than zero, in fact, pushed her away." He leaned forward. "But I understand how you feel. I'd likely want to kill her myself, even if it were just the job. Not productive to do so right now, however."

"How do you figure?" I said through clenched teeth.

"Supposing they do have him, huh? What then?"

I knew right away that this was the truth. Best to wait and strike when I knew he had gotten out safely. Or…well, I don't want to think about the alternative. "How do you know all this stuff? Were you involved?"

He sat back, one hand in his lap. "I am merely the

transportation, my dear. You'd be surprised what people talk about around their drivers."

I stood up, cracking my knuckles. Next time I saw Iris... "What else did you see them do? I mean, to question Sam."

"They pulled him aside a few times whenever your clone ladies came over. Nothing overt, mind you."

"He never said a word about it."

"He wasn't supposed to. There was a distinct threat associated with such behavior, if you catch my drift," he said.

My head spun. No wonder he didn't trust the Underground. No wonder he had been so miserable. Had he been trying to tell me this all along? "Have they bugged our place?"

He studied the ceiling again. "Knowing what you know now, would you doubt it?"

"No. Is there anything I can do about this?"

"You can keep writing in your journal. You can keep telling your stories. I know it might sound like this is all some way to pressure you into it, but I only care about Sam here. The sooner you finish it, the sooner you two will be free. Well...at least, you. I don't know what's going to happen with the big fellow."

I got closer, crouching in front of him and lowering my voice. "Seamus, if there's anything you can do to help him..."

His eyes were soft, his voice softer. "Trust me, I will if I can. But for now there's nothing. I can only surmise based on what I've witnessed to this point." He touched my hand. "Listen. You have to understand that they'll work out what we've discussed, no doubt about it. I'll have to play dumb about some of this, but I will do what I can."

I nodded and rose. "Why are you doing this? It's not just the sandwich."

He patted his belly. "And why wouldn't it be the sandwich?

It was a damn fine one."

I put a hand on my hip and raised one eyebrow.

He smiled. "Aye, okay, maybe not the best. Do you remember the makeover? When you helped me bring in the clothes?"

"Of course."

"I figure I owe you one. You're a good woman. I don't care what they say. Keep yourself safe, okay?"

I looked around. "No offense, but isn't that your job?"

He gave a weak smile. "Hard to say. Might not be, after today. If I find anything, I *will* figure out a way to let you know. I promise. Here," he said, and handed me the Coke can with a wink. "Can't have you thinking you have too much of an upper hand on me."

I chuckled. "No. Can't have that." I turned and went back up the stairs without another word.

So now I sit at this damned table, powerless to save the man I love, and wonder why I'm even committing this to paper. Why would I potentially bury myself? Why would I bury Seamus?

It's because I see two options at the end of this road:

One, I find out something happened to Sam. I hold on to these journals, and they never, ever see what I've written here.

Two, you assholes in the Underground read these journals and realize that you can't control us all. That what you're doing makes you no better than what we escaped in the Khesnaa.

We are not your dancing monkeys.

======

"Hello again," Barren said, leaning over me. I couldn't

remember ever seeing him so chipper, like someone had found a long-lost toy, cleaned it up, and presented it to him.

Ugh. I guess maybe that's what had happened, after all.

"Aren't you a happy one," I said, straining as he adjusted the straps holding me in the chair.

"I missed my favorite patient."

"Don't patronize me."

He held his hands up. "Wouldn't dream of it. I really did miss you. I'm glad to see you…whole."

I remembered my last time in the chair – the pain, the confusion, and…death? "Yeah, well, it won't stay that way if your people have anything to do with it."

"I…"

A boom rolled over the cabin, and he paused.

"That's thunder, isn't it?" I said.

He shook his head. "No clue."

"I don't ever remember hearing such a thing while I've been here. Any theories on why it would start now?"

"Not a one." He picked up a bottle and syringe from one of his tables and set it on the tray beside the chair.

"So what mind fuck am I in for today? Tell it to me straight, Doc," I said.

He glanced backward, toward one of the overhead cameras. "Can't really talk about it, but we need to extract something important." He swabbed my arm with alcohol.

"It's about Carla, right? How I got her powers working?"

He said nothing.

"All you people do is take. Haven't you taken enough from me?"

He looked at me over the top of his glasses. "This is a very important project. Universe-altering." He plunged the syringe into the bottle.

"You really buy that garbage, or do you *make* yourself buy it so you can keep doing this? Are you protecting some loved one?" I said.

He paused, needle still in the bottle. "What did you say?"

"You heard me. I know how these…whatever-the-hell-they-ares…work. I know what they did to Samarta."

He slid the needle into my arm. "My personal life is none of your concern."

"Ow. You're a…" I didn't get to finish the sentence. The colors and lights in the room started blurring together, sounds echoing off of one other.

He said something I didn't understand, very slow and drawn-out. He put a hand on my hand, and I disappeared down a dark tunnel, followed by the rumble of thunder.

======

I was very small. At least, it seemed that way to me. The living room around me – us – felt more like a cavern than somebody's house.

Did I say us? That would be the three of us: Carla, Mimi, and me. Friends forever, or so we said. I'd met the sisters down the street, playing jump rope. We'd stuck together ever since then. Momma insisted that I was lucky to have them as friends, as most kids wouldn't understand my sensitive nature. I had no clue what the crazy old woman meant, not fully, until the other kids began to laugh at my high, reedy voice and curly hair. The sisters hadn't cared, though. They'd stood up for me even when other kids threw rocks at us, so I guess Momma had known something.

Now we sat in front of a Sorry board and taking our turns, their mother's big old lamp shining down on us and casting our shadows on the board. I must have played last because Mimi was pulling the first card of her turn, but I had no memory of the move. In fact, I couldn't remember how I had gotten there in the first place.

I shook my head.

Carla glanced at me, her eyes veiled under her tight red curls. "You okay?"

"My head hurts," I said, and found myself surprised at the thin sound of my own voice. For some reason I had expected something else to come out of my mouth, something deeper and more womanly. A silly idea, right?

Something heavy dropped behind us, and we all jumped and turned around at the same time. Their mother, a wisp of a woman who always looked on the verge of tears (and that's saying something coming from a crybaby like me), stood behind us, one hand to her forehead, biting her lip. Their heavy yellow telephone lay at her feet, the receiver pointed toward us, its dark holes gazing into me.

"Everything okay momma?" Carla said.

Her mother nodded, her eyes closed. "I'm fine. Don't worry."

She sure didn't look fine, though. "Uncle" Dave, the family friend with the long hair and thick blond mustache, came up from behind her, putting an arm around her stomach. He whispered something in her ear, and she turned around.

Carla and Mimi insisted that Uncle Dave was not only safe, but a good man – he'd helped their mother through a lot of tough spots, and sometimes he took them out for ice cream. I wanted to believe them, but I saw something in his eyes that I didn't like. I'd had an uncle who Momma told me "just wasn't right" and wouldn't ever leave me alone in the same room with him. She'd made him into a boogeyman against my Poppa's will, but she'd been right; he ended up going to jail for hurting a girl, though Momma would never tell me how.

Dave reminded me of Uncle Steve. He moved like him. He looked at us like him

Carla and Mimi returned to the game, but I kept my eye on Uncle Dave. Whatever they were talking about, he must have convinced her of what she had to do, because she turned around, wiping a tear out of the corner of her eyes and clapping her hands. "Listen, girls, daddy's had a little accident."

Mimi and Carla gasped, and their mom held out her hands.

"He's going to be okay, but I've got to go pick him up. Uncle Dave's said he'll stay and look after you."

The sisters started crying right away and ran to their mom, who gathered them up against her.

"Daddy's really okay?" Mimi said; I could hear an edge of hysteria in her voice, though I wouldn't be able to identify that until much later.

"Of course. Mommy wouldn't lie to you, right?"

She sobbed. "I guess not."

Their mother looked at me with those sad eyes. "Kelli, if you want to call your mom to come get you, that's okay."

My stomach twisted. I sure didn't want to be alone with Uncle Dave, but Momma had also told me to never abandon my friends, no matter what I did. I struggled with it, and at last decided that I couldn't leave them alone with him. I shook my head. "I'll be all right."

Their mother nodded and turned her attention back to her little girls. She put up with a little more crying and a lot more begging to take them along, but she stood firm. I'm sure he had ended up in the ICU, which isn't exactly the place for little kids, but I had no way of knowing it at the time. Eventually the girls began to wear down, and their mother managed to free herself and grab her battered brown purse. She gave Uncle Dave a goodbye kiss (*gross,* I thought), and headed out the door.

The girls watched out the window as she backed out of the driveway. When she was gone at last, they rejoined me at the game board. We kept going, though what might have happened to their daddy took center stage as the topic of debate.

Uncle Dave allowed us about three minutes for discussion.

"Will you three shut up? You give me a headache with that pissing and moaning," he said.

I glanced over my shoulder at him. He sat on their ratty tartan couch, holding a can of beer against his forehead. It took me a moment to notice that he'd undone his belt. I didn't like the look of that. It usually meant a whipping, and I didn't like thinking about the kind of whipping Uncle Dave would give a girl.

He sneered. "What you looking at?"

I said nothing, turning back to the game as quickly as I could.

"That's right, don't you look at me," he said.

We lowered our volume from then on, trying to lose ourselves in the game. I had a hard time escaping a vision of their father, laid up in a hospital somewhere, with no idea if he would live or die; I can't imagine how the girls felt. They *needed* to talk about it, but none of us dared to invite Uncle Dave down on our heads.

As the game began to wind down, Uncle Dave turned off the TV and seemed to take notice of us again. "Carla. Why don't you come over here and sit on Uncle Dave's lap? We don't spend enough time together."

We all froze, our wide eyes meeting.

"I'm busy," Carla said.

He chuckled. "Come on, we can talk about your fat-ass daddy and why he don't do it for his old woman no more."

Carla and Mimi went red, and I could feel my heart ready to pound out of my chest. None of us said a thing.

"I was talking to you, girl. Don't disobey an adult," he said.

I could see insanity building behind Carla's eyes. She stared into space, looking beyond the world around her.

Uncle Dave lurched to his feet. "Are you listening to me, you little bitch?"

Unable to handle the strain anymore, Carla screeched, jumped to her feet, and made a run for the back door.

Uncle Dave roared at her, staggering and nearly tripping over the coffee table.

Mimi and I followed Carla into the back of the house, and the kitchen. All I could think was *hide hide hide* as Uncle Dave's shadow grew over us.

I spotted Carla at the back door. It was a sliding glass door, the kind that had been popular in the late 70s and early 80s. She worked at the stubborn latch, yanking on the door handle. I went to help her, but Mimi grabbed the sleeve of my Rainbow Brite shirt and nodded toward the kitchen sink.

Right. Under the sink. It would be perfect.

Mimi hissed at Carla, but she'd already gotten the lock undone and was working on pushing the heavy door out of the way.

Mimi and I crowded together to fit under the bottom of the sink. It stank to high heaven of bleach, but we managed to get the door closed (save for a sliver – had to make sure he wasn't coming) before Uncle Dave came thundering past us.

"You're not going nowhere. Your mom wanted me to watch you, and I'm watching you," he said. I saw the back of his head on the other side of the sink, and the glass door slammed shut.

"Please, Uncle Dave. I didn't mean to cause trouble," Carla said.

"Should've thought of that before you smarted off." Something cracked. I grabbed hold of Mimi's arm, thinking of that belt.

"We've got to help her," I whispered.

Mimi shook her head, her face buried in her hands, tears streaming down over them.

Uncle Dave continued to rage at her. "Just like your pops, fat and lazy. I should show you what a real man's like before you end up fucking a sad sack just like him."

I didn't understand all the words, but what I could understand made me sick to my stomach. I couldn't let it continue. "Come on," I said.

Mimi shook her head again. "You do it."

I swallowed hard. She *would* leave me alone to do this.

"No, what are you doing?" Carla said, and the terror in her voice wrenched at me. I heard Momma in my head, talking about how you take care of your friends, no matter what.

Enough.

I let go of Mimi and told her to stay there and be quiet. She nodded, and I pushed the cabinet door open quietly as I could.

Carla shrieked and I heard Uncle Dave push her up against the glass, making a weird noise that turned my stomach again.

It only took a second to spot what I wanted. I put my foot on one of the drawers by the sink, climbing up onto the counter far enough to reach for the wooden block of knives.

Carla kept on making noise, but I think Uncle Dave had put his hand over her mouth, because they came out as muffled cries. He had gone quiet too, save for a grunt here or there. This wasn't a good silence, though. This was the kind of silence that made my head buzz.

I slid the butcher knife from its hole in the block and sat it on the counter. Moving at double speed, I dropped back down to the floor. My heart pounded in my ears, but I kept telling myself to stay calm, that Carla needed me. I picked up the knife and crept to the edge of the wall between the sink and the sliding glass door.

The nausea hit me full force, and I almost threw up right there.

Uncle Dave pressed Carla's body against the glass door. His pants had crumpled down around his bent knees, moving with him as his body jerked. The rest? I didn't understand, and didn't *want* to understand. All I knew (and wanted to know) was that I had to move fast before he caught on to my presence.

It only took a few quick steps to get up close behind him. I had hoped to sneak up on him, but the act had made him more alert. He whirled on me, snarling. Desperate, I swung the knife, catching the side of his neck right before his arm swept around and knocked me backwards into the kitchen table, the knife sliding away under the fridge.

Blood everywhere, running down his neck, spurting onto the floor, and over his hands as he grabbed the wound.

He hit the floor, pants dropping to his ankles at last. Carla collapsed in a heap beside him, the blood spilling over her, too, as she cried out.

Mimi appeared from the cabinet, freezing when she ran smack into the scene, her hands clamped on her mouth as she made a sound that a human, and especially a little girl, should never make.

Carla stood up, hiking her shorts back up. We locked eyes, and I knew I'd never forget what I saw there. Terror, grief, gratitude. I got up to one knee and started to say something, but I didn't have time; the room vanished into darkness around me, and I disappeared down a black tunnel again.

June 9th

Still no Sam. I'm beginning to make plans.

======

I woke up screaming with Barren's hands clamped on my upper arms. I struggled against his grip, but he held me back, saying something I couldn't understand.

That couldn't be true. It just couldn't.

But it had to be. I remembered Carla's vision: the light. The shadow at her back.

Thunder rocked Room 3 as I bucked against Barren. He took a hesitant step backward, releasing me.

This is your shot. You've got to get out of here, girl.

I looked down at the restraints on my arms and legs, pushing against them. They gave a little more than usual, but I could tell I wouldn't be going anywhere.

At least, until some unseen force grabbed hold of them and ripped all four restraints open at once.

Moving like I'd moved in Carla's house (*couldn't be true*), quick and decisive, I grabbed the syringe next to the chair and drove it into Barren's neck. He screeched as I pushed the plunger down, giving him a full dose of the crap that he had been giving me.

I left the needle hanging in his skin. He clutched at it, his eyes wide. I swung around in the chair, planting both of my feet into his chest. I pushed as hard as I could, and he crashed into the table behind him, collapsing when it hit him right in the middle of the back.

He lay on the ground, twitching, groaning, and moaning.

I jumped out of the chair and went for the door.

"What the hell's going on in there?" Zito said.

I searched the room for a weapon - any weapon, and spotted the box cutter sitting on the table where Barren had left it all those nights before. I picked it up and opened it, sliding to the right side of the door.

Zito opened the door slowly, pushing the pistol ahead of him. I leaned away from him and extended my arm, hoping to get the drop on him. He saw the motion and shouted, but didn't have time to get the gun up before I jammed the sharp end of the cutter into the meat between his thumb and forefinger.

He shouted and dropped the pistol. Pocketing the box cutter, I swept the gun from the floor in one movement, leveling it at him.

"Give me a reason. Please," I said.

A moment hung between us then, him squeezing his hand and weighing his options, me ready to unload on him - no, *begging* to unload on him.

"All right,' he said at last, and backed away.

I pushed the door open, following him. "Where's Maple?"

"I'm here," she said, from my left.

I kept the gun on Zito and looked to her. "I'm getting out of here. Tell me how to use Room 2."

She stood at the back of the couch, hands crossed over her waist, head held high. She gave no facial reaction to my words. "Or what?"

"Or he gets it. Then you."

She laughed. "Do you really think death frightens me?"

"I don't care –"

"You should, if that's your sole threat."

I grit my teeth. "You know what this feels like. You have to help me."

"On the contrary, I have no such obligation."

Zito looked from me to her. "What's she talking about?"

"It's none of your concern," she said, her eyes never leaving mine. "She's going nowhere."

I cocked the pistol, aiming it at Zito's knees. "Last chance."

He turned his pained eyes on her. "Maple, come on. I'm begging you."

"This is not the way," she said.

I couldn't believe what I was hearing. "Really? You're one to talk."

Thunder boomed overhead again, and Maple flinched. She waved a panicked hand. "Fine. Just open the door."

I didn't move the pistol, or lower the hammer. "Why don't you open it for me?"

"I wish I could help you, but it doesn't work that way. It will only show you what you need to see."

I frowned at her. "What does that mean? Where would I go if you opened the door?"

"Likely nowhere good, given my feelings toward you at the moment."

I lowered the hammer; Zito gasped in relief. "Fine. That's the way you want it, that's the way it is. I'll just have to figure it out on my own," I said, and circled him, keeping him in front of me at all times. "

They didn't say a word or move, so I went to Room 2 and

grabbed the handle. A charge of electricity jumped through my body, something like sticking your tongue on a 9-volt battery.

You better be sure about this, Carla said in my head.

Was I? No, but I didn't see a better choice. I exhaled and turned the knob, opening the door.

I expected the flash of blue that Carla had told me about, followed by a glimpse of a different world. Just a step through the portal and I'd be on the other side, free from this nightmare at last. Instead, I saw a storage room. Shelves lined the walls, all filled with neatly labeled boxes. The boxes covered the floor as well, leaving only a thin path to a clearing in the center of the room. I followed the trail with my eyes, and gasped when they met the centerpiece of the room: three familiar corpses, wrapped in a plastic film of some sort.

The corpses belonged to Samarta, Carla, and me, with my throat laid open.

My head swam. "That's impossible."

Zito grabbed me from behind, pushing himself into me, and I screamed and spasmed. I couldn't help it; my mind had been far, far away, and it had been all he needed. He reached across my body, grabbing the pistol with his good left hand. I took way too long to recover, giving him just enough time to rip the pistol from my hand.

"Too bad so sad," he said, backing away from me, pointing the pistol right at my face.

"How...?" was about all I could get out.

Maple stepped to Zito's side, glancing into the room. "Oh. Pity. Would prefer you didn't see that. Cat's out of the bag, I suppose."

"What cat? What bag? I don't understand," I said.

"You don't have to," Zito said, and looked to Maple.

"Summon the Senior."

She tightened her lips. "I don't think that's very wise."

Zito's turn to be shocked. "What did you just say?"

"You heard me. The Senior will only make this situation worse."

"Well, then, how do you propose we get her back under control, ask her real nicely?"

I wanted to tell them something, but what? That I could go back in my room? That wouldn't be truthful. I'd rather die there after what I'd seen – both the vision and the room. And that room…what did it mean? Too many questions, no answers.

Maple got closer to both of us. "We can let her go."

"Let her go?" Zito said, incredulous. "You're out of your goddamned mind."

Yeah – let her go – that was a damned good idea.

"It doesn't matter. This project is over anyway, save for the crying. You've all been waiting for us to die," Maple said.

Zito narrowed his eyes, and his hand wavered a bit. "Oh, bullshit. You know I wouldn't have let that happen."

She put her hands on her hips. "Hardly. You're his puppet now, aren't you?"

Zito's face turned red, and he roared, "I'm no one's puppet. No one."

"I don't think you have a choice. You have to be his puppet, or he'll do to you what he did to me," she said.

He pointed the pistol at her now. "Don't you get high and mighty with me."

She laughed. "How the mighty have fallen. Remember when you were going to take his place? Turn the Organization back to human rule?"

"Things change," Zito said. "So are you on her side or

what?"

Maple studied me, eyebrows raised. She tried to be hard and cold, as always, but the softness in her eyes, betrayed something else back there: the woman who'd told me about her boys and wanted nothing more than to see them again.

Something inside me clicked, and I could push the sight of my corpse into the back of my head, at least for the moment.

Maple. She'd been the key once. She had to be the key again.

"Think about your boys," I said.

Might as well have slapped her. She recoiled, raising a hand.

"What boys?" Zito said.

I ignored him, keeping my eyes locked on her. "Tell me why my body's laying on the floor in there, Maple."

He pointed the gun back toward me. "What are you doing? Don't pull that voodoo bullshit on her."

"Reminding her of who she was. You guys took it away from her, but there's something more there. Deeper."

The room lit up as lightning struck outside, I guess in the cornfield, because the thunder came right after, shaking the cabin.

Zito started shaking. Blood dripped from the hand that he had wrapped in what looked like a wash cloth. "I don't like this. You shut up," he said, and looked to Maple, "and you summon the Senior. Now."

I smiled at Maple. "He doesn't have any power over us. Not anymore."

The sweat on her brow and her pallid face made Maple look like she might puke at any second. You could practically *see* the battle going on inside her; her eyes went from my face, to Zito, then back to the gun.

"I hold the gun, I hold the power," Zito said, but he didn't seem to really believe that.

Maple took advantage of it. She grabbed hold of his good hand and wrenched at the pistol.

I remembered the box cutter in my pocket, and slid it out in one motion, eyes on the spot on his neck where he'd shot me, right where I'd slashed Uncle Dave.

If anybody deserves it… Gina said in my head.

That's when the front door slammed open, pushed by the shrieking wind outside. We froze and turned in unison.

Bloch stepped over the threshold, shotgun in his hand.

June 11th

I got a nasty little surprise this afternoon; I had been sitting at the computer for a good portion of the day working on plans to…well, I'm not talking about it here, just in case. I'll just say that I had gotten to the point of resolving my main obstacle when a knock came at the front door. I must have jumped twenty feet into the air before I recovered and made my way to the door.

I paused outside the door, wondering whether this might be the right call. What if the Corporation had come calling?

No, Seamus is out there.

So it might be him. He could have taken the wrong message from my sandwich, and now he'd –

Another knock, and I jumped. All right, I'd just open it and take my chances. After a quick glance around for any handy weapons (a pyramid on an end table by the door seemed a likely candidate), I opened the door.

I believed that I had anticipated just about anyone who could be standing there when I opened that door. No problem. I had prepped myself.

I believed wrong.

There stood Iris, or someone who resembled Iris. She had let out her beehive and then tied it up into a severe bun. She had cleaned off her thick makeup, leaving a pale, familiar face behind. To complete the look, she had donned a conservative blue housedress with a red sash around her waist.

My jaw dropped. "Maple?" My stunned brain made the

connection at last. "Wait, Iris?"

She smiled, and in that long-lost snooty accent said, "let's try both. I don't suppose I could come in?"

"Uhm, uh...sure." I stepped aside, motioning with one hand.

She sauntered in, studying the place for a moment before heading to the armchair.

I closed the door and followed her. "You..."

She sniffed. "Yes, it's me. I'm sorry I had to deceive you. You, of all people, deserve better." She sat daintily in the armchair, dress spreading beneath her legs.

I closed the door and went to the couch, flopping onto it. So many questions fought in my mind. I had no idea which to pick first.

Maple flattened her dress against her legs and nodded at me. "I know you have many questions."

I laughed. It was more an expression of relief than humor. "That's an understatement."

"I will answer what I can, but I want you to understand some things. First, and most important, you must understand that the Underground had nothing to do with Sam's abduction. I know you suspect this, and it is simply not true."

"How can you be sure?"

She locked eyes with me. "Trust me. I am very, very certain."

"Okay...I guess first question is why you're here. What made you want to come talk to me?"

She ran a hand through her hair, considering the question. At last, she cocked her head at me. "Truth? I'm here because I could see the Underground slipping into the same mindset that resulted at the Khesnaa. I couldn't allow that to happen to you after you spared my life." She looked away. I wondered if she was ashamed of her behavior then or what had gone on since then.

"Does anyone else in the Underground know you're here? Other than Seamus."

Her hesitation told me that she weighed and chose each individual word. "Certain elements are aware that I am here, yes. Those that matter. I know you wish to escape. The fact that the very word applies to your situation indicates a grievous failure on our parts. You should not be a prisoner. Period."

I adjusted myself in my seat. "You think?"

She rose. "Would you like some tea?"

"Actually, I would," I said. I could use a little kick in the ass. It wasn't quite a nice dark cup of coffee, but it would do, under the circumstances.

Maple strolled to the kitchen, continuing to talk as she did. "The boys are doing quite well, just by the way."

It took me a moment to figure out what she meant. Then it clicked. "Oh, that's good to hear." I didn't know what she expected to hear. In other circumstances, the news might have warmed my heart, but I felt way too confused and betrayed for it to do much more than scratch the surface.

"Mm. Yes." She filled the tea kettle from the sink and put it on to boil. "As a matter of fact, you met one of their sons."

The conversation irritated me. Of all the things to talk about, why discuss this with me now? "I have?" I said, but didn't really care.

I heard the clanking of tea cups as she set them on the kitchen counter. "My oldest, Paul, married a lovely lass from Dublin, and they had two children. A daughter named Glynis and a son, Seamus. I believe you two had a lovely conversation just the other day."

Ah. Yes. Pieces began to fall into place. Iris was Maple. Seamus was her grandson. They had been the forces behind getting us here. It made a strange sense. "Did you create the Underground?"

She chuckled. "Heavens, no. I had no such ambitions. I would have been perfectly happy spending the rest of my days with my family, but the Underground approached me and explained a few things." The kettle began to whistle. She wrenched the burner off and took the kettle, pouring the hot water into the cups. "This all goes way back to well before our civilization was born, I suspect, but I can't tell you that for sure."

She emerged from the kitchen, handing me a cup and saucer.

"So why the deception? Couldn't you have just told us who you were up front?"

She sat down, balancing her own cup and plate between her hands. "Do you truly believe Samarta would have allowed me into your lives had he known otherwise?" She sipped her tea.

I sighed. "I guess not. He never bought that you'd turned over a new leaf. Said you'd just been using me."

She sat back. "That is why I felt the ruse a necessary evil, and I do apologize. I understand if you're angry."

"No. Not angry. Just curious and a little confused," I said.

"I would expect that. There is so much you still don't know."

I raised an eyebrow, picking up my tea cup. "I'm here. I have time. Start talking."

She smiled. "Very well. We need not worry about the distant past – the who, the what, the why. You need only know about the first World War."

"What about it?" I said.

======

We must have made quite the picture from Bloch's perspective: Maple wrestling with Zito, my hand frozen as I went for Zito's jugular.

"What's this happy horse shit?" Bloch said, lifting the shotgun.

Zito lit up. "Oh thank God you're here, buddy. You've got to help me."

Maple twisted and snatched the pistol from Zito's hand; he made a little yelp, but he didn't dare try to take it back.

She pointed the pistol at Bloch at about the same time that he managed to swing the shotgun on us. "Wheels are coming off the whole thing, love," she said.

"Don't want to do this, Maple," Bloch said.

She sneered. "Maybe I do. Maybe I owe it to you, for all the times you threatened me."

Zito's body tensed, prelude to making a move on her.

I pressed the blade tighter against his throat. "Uh uh. Don't even think about it."

The four of us stood like that for some time, considering our positions and the related possibilities that might unfold with the wrong move. I sat somewhere at the end of the chain; with a little twist I might be able to hide from that shotgun, but I didn't like the idea of taking that risk, either.

Bloch broke the silence at last. "The Senior's not going to let you live after this. You know that."

"What does it matter? This could be my only life or my fifth life. How many times have I died? I have no way of knowing," Maple said.

"Wait, what do you mean?" I said.

She risked a quick glance back at me. "I think you know."

Bloch took a step forward. "Don't say anything you can't take back."

She looked back to him and chuckled. "You're an authority on holding your tongue, aren't you? She deserves to know. I wouldn't be here if I had known up front."

"Know what?" I said.

Bloch took another step forward. "You tell her, I have to take the shot. That's out of my hands."

"Do it. You'll take his lapdog and her with you," Maple said, shifting her feet to a shooters position. "After what's happened over the last few weeks, I doubt you have enough Clay left."

Clay? "You mean that stuff in the basement?"

"Maple..." Bloch said.

She sniffed. "Yes. The material in the basement."

Zito struggled against my grasp, getting a drop of blood on his neck for his troubles. "Maple, what are you doing? Don't be an idiot."

"I wouldn't say you are any wiser, working for that...thing, enabling him to steal away lives and destroy our world."

"He's not going to destroy the world," Bloch said.

Zito glanced at me out of the corner of his eye. "Yeah, he's saving us all."

I held the box cutter steady. I'd seen exactly what the Senior could do with my own eyes. I wasn't about to buy into that propaganda.

Maple seemed to be done with it, too. "Tell me how this glorious new regime will solve all the inequities in the universe. We just need to hand them one more child, one more husband, one more wife. One more regrettable atrocity, and everything will be fine."

"You know it's the truth," Bloch said.

"How about I just tell her the truth? How about I tell her The Big Secret? Huh? Expose the Big Lie?"

Bloch shook his head. "Don't do it. Please."

"What big lie?" I said, looking from Zito to her, my hand wavering for the first time.

Maple sighed. "Carla made you."

Total inversion. I put my free hand against my forehead as visions began dancing through my mind: Carla inside the tree, the tree on fire, me slicing Uncle Dave's neck. "That's not true," I said. "Can't be. I have memories…"

"We put them there," Maple said.

Bloch looked ready to cry. I wouldn't have thought the man capable of such an emotion. "Please stop."

She didn't. "Oh, I'm sure there was a Kelli at one point. She might have even been in Carla's life. But you are not that woman."

I didn't know how many more shocks I could take. The hand holding the box cutter against Zito's neck dipped a bit. He tested it, shifting a little, and that brought me back to the moment, pressing against him and hissing. I told myself I'd do it if I had to - I'd done it before, right?

Right?

I didn't know. I had no way of knowing.

"That's impossible," I said, but that was nothing more than a bid to stall for time. I knew the truth after seeing Enliel and touching Carla's visions - and her touching mine. She knew all about my Momma, too - enough to create a version of her that talked about things we had never discussed. I connected the dots. If that part was true, then what else could be true?

I pushed the box cutter harder against Zito's neck, a spot of blood popping up at the tip. "You killed me," I said.

He went pale. "It was an accident. I swear. I didn't mean to hurt you. Not like that, anyway."

"I've lost count of how many times you've died," Maple said, and she almost sounded amused about it.

I glared at the back of her head. "You think this is funny?"

"On the contrary. It's tragic."

======

Maple ignored my question. "May, 1915. The Kaiser's zeppelins bomb the East End and the docks. Seven people lose their lives, but that's not our focus here. Our focus is on a small, unassuming church, where an errant bomb blew the roof off and tore the thing to pieces. The members couldn't go back for months as crews cleaned up the mess."

I interrupted. "What does this have to –?"

She held a hand up. "I think you'll understand in good time. When the crews reached the altar, they discovered that a hole had been blasted in the floor just below it. The hole was the size of a small boy." She used her hands to indicate the size before she went on. "They hired a local street child to climb in and see what they had discovered. Inside, he found a set of stairs that led to an old iron door, its face covered with some sort of writing. Unfortunately, the child was illiterate, so he couldn't tell them what it said when he came out – only that it said *something*. The church convened a meeting to decide whether they would cover the hole up or find out what else had been hidden down there. It could be pure evil, you understand."

"Oh, of course. Who wouldn't expect pure evil buried under a church? I think that's standard issue," I said.

She narrowed her eyes at me, and then carried on. "They contacted the proper authorities, a fellow by the name of Bryce – an archaeologist fresh out of Egypt, which was all the rage in certain circles in those days. He put together a team to widen the hole and go down there, ready to break into whatever had been hidden down there. Unfortunately, they found that the door would not yield." She paused, taking a sip of her tea.

I sat forward. "Did they at least figure out what the door said?"

"That was rather the crux of the problem. They had no idea what it said. They didn't recognize the language. After much studying and connections with numerous colleagues across the country, Bryce found one man who recognized it. It was known as the Angelic Language."

"As in…?"

"The language of the angels themselves." She saw the look on my face and waved a hand. "You know what you know, and still you balk at angels?"

I shrugged. "It's just… I don't know. Angels? You're really going to tell me that they exist?"

"I have no idea, though I rather suspect they might. The language might not have had anything to do with them. Modern man discovered it in the 15th Century, promptly forgot about it, and then re-discovered it in the 1880s. An order known as the Golden Dawn decoded it properly. Are you familiar with them?"

I shook my head. "It sounds familiar, but…no."

Another sip of tea, and she nodded. "They were magicians who used this language in their rituals. Bryce didn't need an archaeologist; he needed a magician." She chuckled. "They found one in an Irishman named Yeats; you might know a few of his poems?"

"No." The name sounded vaguely familiar, but poetry was not my thing.

"Hm. More's the pity. Anyway, he had once been a member of the Dawn and understood the language front to back. They say he was quite excited to get hold of a genuine example of the language and jumped at the chance."

"What did he find?" I said.

She finished her tea and set the cup and saucer back down. "Instructions. Two sets of instructions, actually. The first set was apparently quite worn or broken. It took them quite some time to even make them legible for Yeats. Eventually, however, they were able to provide him with the text. Yeats discovered that these were the instructions for opening the door. The second set of instructions, quite easy to read and much more recent than the first, told them to never open the door, lest their souls be lost."

She let that one settle on me for a bit. It doesn't get much more ominous than that, does it? "Let me guess. They opened the door."

She spread her arms. "Would we be here otherwise? They opened the door."

======

I felt the world caving in on me. "I remember dying. Why don't I remember dying any other time?"

"No clue. First time for everything, I guess," Bloch said. "Now we're going to end this little party nice and easy. Kelli, I want you to drop the cutter and step away from Zito. Maple, I want you to drop the gun. I'll put down the shotgun. We'll handle this like adults."

A thought occurred to me. The voices I'd been hearing in my head that night, Momma, Gina…all along it had seemed like my brain had conjured them up to help me out, but no. They had to be the result of my connection with Carla. "What about Gina? Carla make her too?" I asked Maple.

"Enough talk. We're getting out of here," Bloch said.

Maple raised an eyebrow. "Oh are we now? Did something change? Were you unable to contain Carla?" She cocked her head. "Is that why it's storming outside?"

The wind gusted, rocking the cabin.

Carla, if you can hear me, I think I understand. I could use your help.

Thunder cracked outside.

"I'm not telling you anything in front of her," Bloch said.

Then it happened. One second Bloch stood by himself on the other side of the room; the next, Carla stood beside him, but not the Carla I'd come to know. Nah, this was the Carla that came out of that tree, all fiery hair and death eyes.

"Sweet Jesus," Bloch said, and turned the shotgun on her, but he moved far too slowly.

She grabbed hold of the barrel and the end of the shotgun melted into a useless lump. Bloch dropped it and took a step back. "Mother of God."

"What have you people created?" Maple said.

"We didn't –" Bloch said, but got no more out. He grabbed hold of his chest and made a terrible howling noise, his eyes half-closed in agony. He went down to his knees, and looked up to Carla, his mouth a wide O.

She made a motion with one finger and he fell flat on his

face in front of her, rattling and kicking.

She turned to face us, and I realized with horror that she floated about a foot off of the ground. "Maple," she said. Her voice echoed and rang all on its own, like she spoke through some a voice distorter at the end of a tunnel.

Maple held up both hands, showing her the pistol. "I don't want trouble. I just want to get out of here, love."

Carla smiled a fiery grin. "I've seen in Kelli's heart. I won't harm you. Your children lived to be old men. One is a banker, the other a writer."

Maple gasped and lowered her hands, clasping them at her chest. "Are they happy?"

"There are holes in their hearts. But yes."

The door to Room 2 slammed shut all on its own, and we both jumped, turning to face it. A moment later it creaked open again, and the blue light that Carla had once told me about leaked out onto both of us. The light issued from a web of blue light that hung just inside the door, presenting a dark veil to a void that I couldn't quite make out.

The portal. Finally. Guess this was what Maple needed to see.

"Step inside, and be done with this," Carla said.

======

"Of course. What did they find inside the door?" I said.

Maple licked her lips. "You must understand that this church had been built upon what used to be a temple of some sort. It sounds sinister, but it's not so unusual. St. Peter's Basilica itself was likely built on a pagan Roman necropolis, after all. Bryce suspected all along that the door had some tie to the temple, but the language on the door threw most of his theories out the window. They made quite a show of opening the door at the time, inviting some local celebrities and authorities. I'm sure today it would have been quite the reality show," she said, and chuckled.

She went on. "When they opened the door, they discovered a small place of worship, not able to hold more than ten to fifteen people, or so history suggests. Not much information remains about the inside of the structure, but we do know that they found another altar inside, and that altar is where the story really gets interesting."

"What do you mean?"

"Well, the altar held only one thing: a sealed clay jar."

That sounded somewhat familiar. An image flashed through my head. "You mean like the Greeks made?"

"Very close. Of course, just about every ancient civilization worth knowing made them. This one was extra-special, though. It contained something very exotic and very dangerous."

I laughed. "What, like an ancient nuclear weapon?"

She rubbed her chin, contemplating the answer. At last she said, "yes, that's a very apt analogy, actually. They hesitated to break the wax seal, especially with so many people down in the temple, but Yeats apparently insisted on seeing what was inside before he returned to Ireland."

"Did everyone die or something?"

"No. They just found a thick, brown fluid inside." She looked at me, giving the words significance. "Does this sound familiar to you?"

I shook my head. "I don't…wait. The Clay?"

"Yes. They had no idea what they were looking at, of course. The entire thing was something of a minor sensation in the scholarly journals of the time, but very quickly dropped from the public eye when a certain 'moneyed interest' became aware of the discovery."

"The Organization?" I said.

She nodded. "Very smart. It's said that they once had a hand in creating the Clay, but we have no idea whether that's true. All we know is that they have a connection to the temple. We also know that they bought out Bryce and most of the men on his expedition. Those that wouldn't sell out?" She shrugged. "They saw to them, as well, and soon had exclusive rights to the Clay."

"And they knew how it worked," I said.

"Absolutely. They knew how it worked and they wanted it. Luckily for them, they had no opposition at the time, and so no one to document what happened next."

"So they had the Clay since World War I, but didn't do anything with it until much later? The Khesnaa wasn't *that* old," I said.

She nodded. "Of course not. The group disappeared from the public record for quite some time. We have no record of where they were, or what they had done with the Clay. Their trail only picked up again during World War II. A few known members of the group resurfaced, doing business with both the Axis and the Allies as the United Watcher Corporation. Those men are still alive today. Do you understand what I'm saying?"

These 'men' must have been very much like the Senior. "I think I get the picture."

"Good. We suspect that this is when they gained leverage over the apparatus of government."

It made sense. Withdraw until you have the means to take control, then re-emerge and worm your way into government. "And they convinced the government to create the Khesnaa and places like it."

"We believe so, yes. That's where I enter the picture. I imagine you can fill in the blanks. The group - reformed as a 'legitimate' company - sells the idea of the Clay to world governments, each one, individually. The tests make much more sense. The Corporation offered the perfect engine of war: they could, theoretically, create a perfect duplicate of a rival nation's bureaucrat. Think of the power that a government or company could wield over their rivals."

I nodded. "All the more reason to get in bed with them." I sat back. "I can figure out the rest. Kidnap women who have the potential to work with the Clay, experiment with them until you unlock their abilities, and keep refining the system until you have the perfect system."

"And here we are today." Maple picked up her tea cup, realized that it was empty, and frowned. She nodded toward my cup. "Would you like a refill?"

"I'd like some answers on the Underground's connection to all of this, actually."

======

Maple put the gun on the floor, and I noticed some moisture at the corner of her eyes. "I'm sorry. For everything," she said, bowing her head toward this new, intense version of Carla.

Carla nodded. "I understand. Now go. Be with your family. You've earned freedom, if not forgiveness."

"Thank you." Maple raised her head and looked to me. "And you. Without you…"

I waved a hand. "If I get out of this, we'll meet up on the

other side for a drink some time. We can talk about it then."

I could tell she wanted to say something more, but the time wasn't right. At last, she nodded and walked toward us, facing Zito. I moved around to his back, keeping the blade in place, so they could stand face-to-face one last time. It only seemed right to give her the chance.

"And you," she said.

He tensed. "What about me?"

She raised her hand to slap him and reconsidered it. Instead, she reared back and spat in his face. I let him wipe it from his face, and we both watched her saunter away from us, toward the doorway. She stopped right before the web of blue light, looking back one more time.

I nodded. *Get your ass in gear. We've got other fish to fry.*

She sighed and stepped through the web. The door swung closed on its own behind her.

Carla drew our attention. "You can take the blade away," she said and raised her hand.

Zito began to shake, and I did what she told me, closing the cutter and putting it back into my pocket. I stepped away from the asshole really quick, not wanting to get close to whatever she had in store for him.

He faced her, hands at his chest, pleading. "Come on. I was just doing my job."

She sneered. "Liar."

One word, but it hit him like Maple's spit. He took a step back; I had to stumble backwards so he wouldn't run into me. "I didn't mean to hurt you. Neither of you. You've got to believe me."

"Too bad I don't," she said. "I've remembered my lifetimes here. The beatings. The deprivation. The murders. Death is too good for you."

He moaned. "Oh, sweet Jesus."

My limbs became heavy, my movements slowing down, my head filling with sludge.

The portal. Again.

Carla raised her head, the lamps of her eyes flashing over the room. "Another is present," she said.

As soon as she said it, the door to Room 2 flew open, slamming against the wall.

Carla fixed her gaze on the large, shaggy form that stepped through the blue web: the Senior. He took his time coming through, putting through first one big foot, then the other. He pulled himself straight once he'd come through, his yellow eyes on fire as he swept the room, studying us like we were his bratty kids, ready for discipline.

Finally, he shook his head. "Well, well. I see you have run to ground. A pity."

"You have no dominion over us. Not any longer," Carla said, clenching her fists.

He chuckled. "Silly woman. Of course I do." He motioned with one hand.

Her eyes widened and she fell to the floor, grabbing at her throat and gasping.

He took a few steps forward. "I have always had dominion over you. Over all of you." He looked at Zito and me, then back to her. "So long as you pumped out the members of my army. So long as you remained docile."

"Like…hell," she choked out.

He snarled. "You were to rule my army, not destroy it. You could have been my queen." He kicked her in the side.

She cried out, and some sort of wave of light bounced off of her, sending the Senior crashing to the floor.

Zito had seen enough. He grabbed the pistol that Maple had laid on the floor and ran for Room 1, closing the door behind him. I imagined him barricading himself in there, pushing every chair and piece of furniture he could grab up against the door.

Carla got to one knee, her green-fire eyes coming back to life. "Better an honest death than a lifetime of servitude."

He mirrored her move, getting to his knee, snarling at her. "Things would have improved. The Multiverse would have improved."

Carla gathered her strength and rose into the air again, soaring higher than before, her hair flickering just below the ceiling. "Nothing will improve under your watch." She motioned with one finger, throwing a line of fire at the Senior.

He moved a lot more quickly than a guy that big should and the fire hit the floor, spreading like someone had thrown gasoline onto the flames. In seconds a bonfire stood between them and me, the smoke already beginning to choke me out.

"A pity your twisted morals stood in the way of making things better," he said.

Her eyes flared, and he flew back across the room, slamming into the wall right beside me, opening a path to the front door.

Now, Carla said in my head.

No need for debate on that one. Fight or flight kicked in and told me to get out of there. Maybe I had been supposed to take care of Carla, but I couldn't be the one to take the Senior down. Time to save myself.

Thank God, Bloch *had* broken that door; it hung from its hinges and took a slight effort for me to slip through and into the screaming night.

======

Maple put the cup back down. "That is the question, isn't it, the connection between the Underground and all of this?" She rose and went to one of the windows, gazing out on the rain-slicked street below. "I told you that I would answer what I can, and I will keep that promise, but some of those details are still unknown even to me. Only the leader of the Underground knows most of those facts."

Ah, yes. The mysterious benefactor. "Your leader?"

She smiled. "She's the one who identified the potential in both of you. She's also the one who returned Sam to life and sent him to rescue you."

That stirred a stray memory. "*She* did that?" Sam had told me about it shortly after I arrived in this world; when he awakened in that hotel room, after what the Senior did to him, he had sensed a presence that retreated as he became conscious.

"Absolutely. Anything for you. The information that you hold could make all the difference in the world in defeating the Corporation. Many attempts have been made on the life of the beast that founded the Corporation. None have succeeded. None have even wounded him. Save for you."

"The Senior?" I said.

"Indeed, and Samarta alone, of all of us, had the strength to stand against that beast. Both are incredibly valuable."

A shiver ran through me. Such immense forces aligned against us... "How does the Underground even have a prayer against something like that?"

She sighed. "I wish I knew. I wouldn't be here, begging you not to leave us. Please. Don't run. Your aid is literally the difference between life and death for thousands, if not millions, of people. We can figure this out together."

I raised an eyebrow. "And if I don't want to be your slave?"

"You are not our slave. I told you, I will not allow that. I have no desire to cage you. That is the way of the Corporation. It is not my - *our* - way."

I wasn't crazy about the answer, but I didn't see too many other options. My plans had always been seat-of-the-pants. Worst case, I could listen to their offer, pretend to play along, and devise new plans based on the new information that I gathered in that meeting. I sat forward. "All right. So what do we do now? Where do we go from here?"

She strode back toward the living area, and I could see that *this* was her real reason for the visit. She'd been waiting for just this question. "Our leader wishes to see you tomorrow. I'm trying to convince her that there's no need to hold you - we can make you an active partner in our leadership. I need you on board with that."

"So this is your way of repaying what you think you owe me?"

That slowed her down a little, but she nodded.

"What about freedom?"

She swallowed hard. "You'll have it. I will not allow her to stop you. I just ask that you meet her first. I believe it will be a revelation."

Before I could hold them back, words began to pour out of me, scratching an itch at the back of my mind. I uttered the name that had hovered over the conversation since we'd begun. "Carla. Carla's your leader. I don't know how it could be her, but it is. She was tailing him that day."

She clicked her tongue. "Oh, dear. I'm afraid not. The woman he saw is an employee of the Underground. I assure you that she is not Carla, but you'll see that for yourself."

"Fine. I'll meet her. What's to lose?"

She smiled. "That's the spirit. Seamus and I will be here at ten in the morning sharp." She began to exit, but paused, and then glanced back at me. "You know what Carla was capable of. Imagine an army full of men and women just like her, sweeping down upon any human city. How long do you think we'd last?"

I pondered that. The Carla I'd seen had been terrifying, but good-natured. What if the woman who possessed those powers had nothing but malice? It made me shudder. "You helped make that happen, you know," I said.

She sighed. "I have to live with that for the rest of my life, but I'm trying to correct it now."

"By using me?"

"Call it what you will. Just don't let dogmatic belief blind you. I did it once. It's not worth it," she said, and left without another word.

June 12th

And so it comes to this: I met the Leader. Well, "Mistress" is the official term, I think. Mistress Marie. Lady of the Underground. Oh, and a few other momentous events happened, including the destruction of a good portion of London, but I'll get to that in a bit. I'm tired, and all things in due time. Obviously, things have changed, and not just because I met her, but why don't I write some about that meeting?

The term "Underground HQ" is somewhat misleading, as the place was anything but underground. In fact, it occupied one of the tallest buildings in London, a monument to human greed and willful ignorance. Some days, I'm glad that I don't call this species my own.

Seamus, Maple, and I rode the elevator to the 44th floor in absolute silence. We had nothing left to say to one another. This day belonged to the Mistress, not Maple or her grandson.

At last we reached the 44th floor and the elevator doors slid open to reveal a small, marble-floored foyer dominated by a mahogany reception desk. A tasteful tin art installation hung on the dark red wall behind the desk, spelling out the letters Servi Lumen in an archaic font. Below those letters waited a familiar face: a broad face, framed by red ringlets that hung to her shoulders.

Carla's face. Only…not exactly. The nose didn't look quite right, and the light in her eyes seemed different, as well.

"You," I said.

Maple stepped between us. "Yes, this is Cayla."

Cayla put a hand to her chest, her eyebrows knitted. "I am so sorry. I never wanted any of this to happen. I mean, with your boyfriend. They told me that he saw me. I didn't want to cause him trouble."

I contained my anxiety, but just barely. "Do you know something about what happened to him?"

She shook her head. "No. I didn't have anything to do with it, I promise. I *was* at the pub, but Seamus only had me watching out for anyone who would try to get them."

Interesting. Seamus had asked her to be there. But he hadn't indicated anything like that to me. I wondered what it meant. "Let's just get on with this," I said. I had tired of the whole thing. Tired of their denials. Tired of their subterfuge. I just wanted this over with.

Cayla tightened her lips and looked off to one side, cringing a little. "Right. I'm sorry; it's just...such an honor to meet you. You're so important to what we do here." She scurried to the lone frosted-glass door on the right-hand side of the foyer, the only sign that anything laid beyond Cayla's domain. "She's waiting for you," she said, and punched a series of numbers into the keypad on the door handle.

I'm surprised she didn't curtsey.

Maple took the first steps toward the door. "You notified her of our arrival, I trust?"

"Absolutely." She stepped to one side, pulling the door open and motioning with one hand. "Please. After you."

We all went inside, with Cayla close behind.

On the other side of the door laid a huge...well, office isn't the right word. More like a multi-purpose meeting room. There must have been more to the floor, but I saw no other entrance or exit. The wall on the left side of the room had been covered with faded yellow maps, photocopies of old documents, and mugshots of several individuals that I didn't recognize. Below that sat two mahogany tables stacked high with old books, ancient manuscripts, and a plethora of journals.

To the right laid the library that had produced these works: four mahogany bookcases crammed full of the same kind of material, books bearing titles like *The Sword of Moses, The Book of St. Cyprian,* and *The Magus.*

All this paled in comparison to the low-rise dais that dominated the west side of the room. A small mahogany desk sat off to the right side of the dais, seemingly forgotten in the glorious view that shone through the window. That window must have stretched across that entire side of the building, or damned close to it, and faced the west side of the city, past the hospital and cathedral and on to Soho itself. A lone woman with curly black hair stood at the window, her hands clasped behind her back as she surveyed her domain.

Cayla went ahead of us, taking two steps up onto the dais. "Excuse me, Mistress Marie? They've arrived."

The woman stirred and raised her head. Her long dark locks bounced with the movement. She turned to face us, and her appearance stunned me. I knew this woman. I had to. But…I couldn't place her. Something felt familiar…was it the blue eyes, the hair, or something else? I couldn't place it. "Greetings," she said. "It's so good to finally meet you."

======

If the storm above the cornfield sounded like a hurricane

from inside the cabin, it became the voices of all the demons of Hell outside, unleashing Armageddon on us poor little flyspecks. Two steps out of the cabin and the best I could do was hold tight to the door handle, dodging the rotten corn cobs that slammed into the side of the cabin.

God, if you're going to help me, now would be the time, I thought, crouching away from another corn cob, feeling my feet sinking into the wet mud of the front yard.

Something heavy hit the side of the cabin from the inside and almost knocked me off my feet. I lost my grip on the handle for a second and screamed as the wind got hold of me, trying to push me off the side of the building.

I lunged with all my strength, hoping I could get hold of the door handle again before the wind pushed me into the open and lifted me off my feet like Dorothy, slinging me into the night. My fingers closed around the handle and I closed my eyes, exhaling. I wouldn't last much longer out here if I couldn't reach Carla.

You there? I thought.

Nothing for a few seconds. The wind continued to batter me, and I tried to prepare myself for the moment when I peeled off the building. I wondered where I'd end up. Did the corn field just run off into blank nothingness after a while?

Little busy, came Carla's voice in my head.

I know, but can you dial the storm down a touch, maybe? For little old me?

I'm not in control, but I'll do what I can.

My shoulder began screaming. I wondered what it would feel like when it popped out of its socket.

Then the wind began to ease, transforming into a raging thunderstorm rather than a full-on hurricane. At least I could work with that. I let go of the handle and stood up, rubbing my shoulder.

Something crashed, and it wasn't thunder. It took my confused mind a second to figure out just what might cause such a loud sound, but the sound of splintering wood cleared it right up for me: someone had gotten thrown through a wall inside the cabin.

That had the desired effect of shocking me into motion. I headed for the corn rows, fighting for each step as the mud clung to my legs, trying to pull me under.

The cabin door blew open – and I mean *blew open* literally; it slammed off the side of the cabin then broke what remained of its hinges with a shriek. I shouted as it went cart wheeling past me just a few feet to my right. I felt the effect it had on the wind as it skipped off the top of the mud, leaving divots in the ground right before it slammed a hole in the corn wall.

I shuddered. A few steps to the right and I'd be paste.

Jesus Christ.

The Senior bellowed behind me, sounding like a wounded bear.

Panicking, I whirled and fell right on my ass in the mud as he appeared at the door, those eyes burning right through the darkness between us. I shouldn't have been able to see him grin through all that rain, but I did anyway.

He said something, but the wind stole it away. Didn't matter. Some vague threat. It took a second to figure out why he might be coming for me, but it clicked. He couldn't kill her, so he'd get me first, and she'd have to back down.

Can't let that happen, I thought. I had to get into the field as fast as I could. I backpedaled, fighting the mud, eyes locked with his as he took his first step down into the mud –

And sank up to his thighs in the muck, shouting in

frustration.

======

The Mistress left the window and approached us, her eyes locked on mine. She knew me, no question of that, but my mind still struggled to figure her out. Her nose, maybe? No.

"Kelli," she said, and opened her arms. Before I could react, she pulled me into a tight embrace, resting her head on my shoulder. "It's time you came home," she whispered in my ear.

After a moment's hesitation, I put one arm around her, clapping her back. The effect might have been worse than a total stranger hugging me right off of the street; my brain had gone completely out of whack trying to figure out who she might be and her touch made my skin crawl.

At last she broke the embrace and smiled at me. "You don't remember me, do you?"

Relieved to have permission to speak the truth, I shook my head. "I'm afraid I don't. I'm sorry."

She must have expected it. No hesitation at all. "No worries. We'll get to that, but first, let's discuss business." She led us to the twin tables on the other side of the room, pushing aside a stack of journals as she sat down. Among those journals were two very familiar marble notebooks. She picked them up and leafed through the pages as we joined her.

When we had settled, she closed them, laid them on the tabletop, and pushed them toward me. "You can have these back, I think. I trust all is going well on the third edition."

I took the notebooks. "They're…uh, they're fine."

Maple cleared her throat. "Oh, now don't be coy, Mistress."

I glanced at her, and then at Marie. "What is she talking about?"

Marie narrowed her eyes at Maple, a look of pure disdain, but it passed in a moment as she turned her attention back to me. She held her hands in the air. "Guilty as charged. I'm afraid I've been peeking at your work in progress."

It baffled me. "What? How? I've had it under my pillow."

"Cameras," Maple said. She impressed me, despite my own frustration and confusion. Maybe she really did mean to work as my advocate here.

I sat forward. "You put cameras in our apartment?"

Marie shrugged, pouting. "Oops. I'm sorry, but we really couldn't take the risk that you wouldn't hand those journals over. I know that Iris has *explained* –" At this, another nasty look toward the older woman, then back to me. "– What is at stake here, so I'm not going to give you a sales pitch. We're both smarter than that."

I sat back, crossing my arms over my chest. "What are you going to give me, exactly? My lover? My freedom?"

"I really don't know what happened to Samarta. I wish I did; chances are this conversation would be very different were he still around. But I can offer you what you've always wanted to know. I think it's been somewhere in the back of your mind, nagging you."

"Yeah? What's that?"

She smiled. "I'm going to tell you where you really come from."

======

I chuckled as I turned away from the Senior, heading for the corn.

This might not be so bad after all, I thought.

One day I'd learn not to think things like that. But not that day.

A deafening sound pushed through the wind and a big chunk of the front side of the cabin splintered into a thousand pieces, the roof sagging and threatening to collapse the whole thing.

Least of my concerns, though. My biggest concern had to be those pieces catching the wind and turning into a million flying needles, all headed our way.

The Senior roared in agony, and I had just enough time to cover my face with one muddy arm, stings screaming out as the splinters dug in, tearing my skin to shreds.

When the assault died, I lowered my arm and saw the Senior.

I might have been bleeding from a thousand little cuts, my arm full of splinters, shrieking at me, but he proved it could have been worse. He clutched at a hundred different places on his body at once, where the worst of the splinters had cut right through the armor he wore. Some pieces as big as bricks stuck out of his back and chest, twisting and turning as the pain shot through him.

Couldn't happen to a better guy.

Flames began to crawl through the hole in the cabin, licking the side of the building and crawling toward the roof, moving faster than the rain could douse them. My brain told me I still had to run, but I couldn't. I couldn't do anything but watch the flames, emotions numb, my body already shutting down.

It's shock, girl. Fight it, Carla said in my head.

The Senior shook off the pain and took a huge step, his other leg sinking into the mud. He might have been moving slowly, but it would only take a few of those strides for him to reach me.

Move!

Can't. Can't do anything, I thought. That was the truth, too; I had become more like Enliel, my limbs in slow motion, and this time I couldn't blame the portal.

Carla didn't reply. Instead she appeared through that hole, her head wrapped in a wreath of awful light, eyes cutting right through the storm.

The Senior stopped mid-stride, straightening up, his eyes narrowing. He turned as best as he could, grunting at the pain. He had a second to get one hand up before she flattened him with one motion of her hands, driving him deep into the mud.

"Get him girl," I shouted. I didn't know if she could hear me.

======

Impossible. I knew my heritage, even if I didn't like it. She had to know that. I tapped a finger on the notebooks. "Maybe you need to do some studying. I know already. If you're going to try to sucker me in with some grand revelation, you need to think again."

She gave me an enigmatic smile, studying me. I didn't know what she meant to communicate with that look, but it irritated me. "Who are you really?" I said.

She nodded toward the marble books. "Why don't you pick up the first book? I've marked the section you want to read."

"Just come out and say it in plain English," I said.

Seamus laughed. "I'm afraid this is how it is. She has quite an eye for the theatrical, this one."

Cayla glared at him from across the table. "Seamus..."

Marie held a hand up, a look of mischief in her eyes. "No, he's quite right, I do, but I'd rather she figure this out on her own. There's no better way to learn. It means something *more.* Go ahead. We'll wait." She sat back and mirrored my earlier position, crossing her arms over her chest.

"Fine. Whatever," I said, and picked up the first marble notebook. I flipped it open and found that she had stuck a yellow Post-It Note within the first half of the book. I flipped to the page and found that she had highlighted the passage that she wanted me to read – a part of my vision in the corn field.

I read, and as I did, the tumblers in my mind clicked. Of course. I immediately knew her true identity. No wonder she had looked so familiar. "You're Mimi?"

Mistress Marie – Mimi – spread her arms. "In the flesh. Finally. You had to wonder what happened to me."

I felt shame. I had never even considered her; I had pushed her down along with the visions, buried both deep inside of me in a place that I never visited.

She lowered her arms. "Oh. I see. You believe that I never existed."

"No, that's not it."

She chuckled. "It's okay. It's kind of the opposite. Carla is the one who never existed. The Carla you met, the one who undid the straps on your chair that night? She definitely existed, but only because of one person." She hiked her thumbs toward herself. "The big kahuna."

Such a simple statement, but it yanked away my identity yet again. You can't imagine my horror to learn that I'm nothing more than a copy of a copy. "But the vision. Carla was..."

"In the past with us? Uncle Dave attacked her, right?" She

shook her head. "Your memories play tricks on you. That night happened, but there was no girl in the cabinet with you. I know. I created that version of the truth for the Corporation," she said, some of her humor finally draining.

But if Carla wasn't there… "You're the one who got attacked," I said.

She glanced at the others. I'm sure she didn't want to discuss this in front of them, but she'd opened the door, so she had no other option. "Yes. You're the girl who saved me, too. Well…a copy of the girl who saved me, anyway. I don't know what happened to the real Kelli. Sometimes I imagine that she grew up to have a sweet, happy life. You know, two-and-a-half kids, house in the suburbs. I doubt it after what happened that night, but it's a nice little fantasy." She gazed at her fingernails, no doubt unable to meet my eyes.

I stood up. I didn't know what I would do, but I couldn't stay in the room and listen to this story any more. "This is bullshit."

Maple sighed. "I'm sorry," she said, her voice gentle. "It's quite true."

Marie raised an eyebrow. "Is it that hard to believe? You know Carla made you using the Clay. Why would none of this other stuff be true?"

Because I didn't *want* it to be true. I didn't want to know that someone else out there had my face and had even a shot at living a normal, happy life, blissfully unaware of the United Watcher Corporation, the Khesnaa, and the Clay. That should be my life, not hers. "Because it just can't be."

======

The Senior sat up. He had been covered in mud; his only distinguishing feature, those burning eyes, cut through the darkness. He grunted and began to rise.

Carla made another motion with her hands, but he managed to get one hand up, I guess blocking whatever she'd done. She circled around him, getting between the two of us.

"You must move. Into the corn," she said.

"I can't –"

You must, she thought at me.

The Senior staggered to one knee and clenched his fists. They looked like they caught fire, baby blue flames wrapping around them.

"You can't protect her forever," he snarled.

She said nothing. She just steadied herself, lowering her hands to her sides. Enough for him, I guess. He lunged after her, swinging those fists right at her head.

She ducked one swing, but a second one caught her shoulder, swinging her around. She faced me, her wild eyes losing their light again. Another punch and she went flying over my head and into the cornfield.

Nothing stood between us now, save an expanse of mud and a curtain of rain. The flames destroying the cabin cast a long red light over his armor, and he grinned a death's-head grin. He looked like a mud-covered demon that had dragged himself out of Hell just to find me. "She's strong. But not strong enough. Perhaps your death will open her eyes."

My stomach tensed and the spell that held me in place broke. "Like hell," I said, and scrambled out of the mud, running for the space in the corn that had been opened by the flying door.

He laughed. "You only delay the inevitable."

Lightning sizzled somewhere off to my left, connecting the

cornfield with the sky. The roar of thunder just about deafened me, but it wouldn't stop me. Neither would the fire that began to rise from that strike. I clambered over the door, almost sliding off into the mud again.

I'll hold him off as long as I can, Carla said in my head.

I got to my feet and pushed a stalk out of the way. *Are you okay?* I thought.

Don't worry about me. I was never getting out of here anyway.

That last part sounded a lot more like the Carla I'd known than the raging goddess of fire that had killed Bloch.

I'm going to save you somehow, I thought, and climbed into the denser part of the field.

I received no reply to that one.

Behind me, the Senior had reached the door. Rather than climbing over it, he picked it up. In the next second it landed in the corn behind me, the force making the ground shake under my feet. I cut toward the right, hoping a zigzag pattern might save me.

"You know that I can find you no matter where you run," he said. He sounded more amused than angry.

Probably the truth, but nothing I could do about it. I just kept zigzagging, and he stormed after me, the dark presence at my back.

======

Marie sat forward, her elbows on the table, hands folded beneath her chin. "I'm sorry. I truly am. I wish I could give you that life, but I can't right now. We have to finish off the

Corporation first. Nobody can be safe with them still around."

The same answer as always. Later. Some undefined time in the future, so long as I did exactly what *they* wanted. I waved a hand. "Fine. I don't see what other choice I have. But tell me one thing."

"What?"

"Why...why all this? The Underground, you, Maple...what's your connection? Why do you care?"

She sat back and sighed.

Maple spoke first. "She was once in Carla's position."

"That true?" I said.

Marie nodded. "You can't imagine life after...well, you know. They sent Kelli – the real Kelli – away. I never found out where they sent her. My family was torn apart. My father wanted nothing to do with me. I went to live with my grandparents. You met them once. One of those memories might still be bouncing around in that head of yours."

I felt something familiar, but it didn't amount to much more than a phantom in the back of my mind.

She went on. "I pulled things together, but life was never really the same. I did the best I could. High school honors. MIT."

I interrupted. "I don't want to sound like a jackass here, but..."

She gave me an irritated look. "Is this going somewhere? Of course. Would I waste my time otherwise? I studied genetics. Had a promising career ahead of me, too; I got a lot of offers from researchers and biotech companies, but the most promising came from the United Watcher Corporation."

Now we were getting somewhere. "You *worked* for them?"

"Oh, yes. They promised all the research funds, equipment, and employees that I could want as long as I put them toward researching cloning. Not really a hard sell, since I'd been interested in it from the beginning. This was the early 90s, so it was still cutting-edge stuff – anyone who got there first would get their name in lights. How could I turn it down? Yeah, well, you know how things that are too good to be true often are. They didn't want my biology skills at all. They wanted my brain itself."

Of course. "They knew you were a folder."

She nodded. "They knew that I could use the Clay, even if I didn't know it myself. Damned thing is, I liked it. Sure, I'd rather have been carrying out my research, but I couldn't resist creating my own forms of life. What geneticist wouldn't want that power? Besides, they let me poke and prod the creations so I could figure out how to make them better, smarter, and more human."

This sounded familiar. "Like Enliel."

"You know, I laughed when I read about your first encounter with him. What a clumsy creation. I'd never make that mistake. But then Carla was never quite me."

She talked a good game, but I had a feeling it hid the pain that still lurked somewhere in her heart. "Did you know what they were planning?"

"Not a clue at first. By the time I figured out where they wanted to go with it all, it had gotten much too late. I asked to be transferred, and they refused. I tried to quit, and they said it wasn't that simple. I finally tried to walk off of the campus, but security caught me and chained me in a basement in their facility. They gave me the bare minimum of food and water and forced me to start creating their grand general so she could pump out the clones. I stalled on purpose, because I knew what they'd do with me once Carla had arrived. I created women with…diminished capacities."

It explained a lot. This was about much more than just

Carla. "The Four Cs?"

"Yes."

I glanced at Cayla; our eyes met, and I saw fear and shame.

"Yes. Cayla was another attempt," Marie said, her voice soft. No matter what the outcome, she seemed fond of the woman.

Cayla looked at her hands where they rested in her lap. My heart went out to her for that moment.

Marie went on. "After Cayla they knew that I was stalling. They threatened what remained of my family if I didn't produce their general. So…Carla." She shrugged. "Once they had her, they didn't need me anymore. They had their nuke. They could get rid of Oppenheimer."

"Too much knowledge in her head," Seamus said, his voice strangely subdued. "To all our good fortune, the Underground refused to allow her execution."

"Wait," I said, looking from him to Marie. "You didn't found the Underground?"

She shook her head. "Not exactly. The Underground started as a group of Corporation employees who didn't approve of the company's methods." She glanced at Maple with that, but said nothing. "They had enough time to rescue me and my children. They gave us a small amount of the Clay and held off security while we made a run for it."

"They helped you build things up once you were out?" I said, but I thought I knew the answer.

"No. The showdown with Security didn't go well. They lived on, though. I recreated them, and we did what we had to do to stop the Corporation in the name of the people who died rescuing me that night."

======

I didn't care where the cornfield led me, even if I turned up at the edge of the world, ready to fall into the void. Anything was better than letting the Senior get hold of me. It meant death at best; at worst, it meant going to whatever other facility might remain now that the Khesnaa had been wrecked.

I felt a pang of loss at that. Prison or not, it had been my birthplace, and as screwed-up as it might have been, I still had a connection to it.

Carla's voice spoke up in my head. ***Don't worry about that now. You got to save yourself.***

"Got you," a harsh voice said from behind me.

I panicked, trying to jump away, but I hadn't moved in time. The Senior's hand clamped down on my calf, battering my head against the corn stalks before I fell face-down into the mud.

You got out of this once, girl, you've got to do it again.

He dragged me toward him, and I turned over, staring up into that terrifying face of his. I grabbed two stalks of corn, holding tight and kicking at him with my free hand. I think I found one of the chunks of wood that had embedded in his body, because he howled and let go. I got to my feet, ready to run off, when I felt something heavy pressing against my leg.

The box cutter.

I pulled it out of my pocket and reversed direction, rushing toward him.

One shot at this, I thought, and caught a lucky break: he had been bending over, clutching the chunk of wood sticking out of his wrist.

I drew my arm back and thrust forward, unsheathing the blade in a smooth motion. He shrieked as the cutter sank into his left eye, bursting it with a thick spray of yellow jelly.

As much as I wanted to give him a one-liner and act like an

action hero, adrenaline had taken over, making me into a bundle of movements and nerves. I gave the wood on his wrist another kick and ran off into the rows again, his shrieks filling the air behind me, the wind carrying them right to my ears.

Of course, the wind also carried the sizzle of lightning and the burst of thunder that followed, hitting the spot where he stood, setting those rows aflame.

Run, Carla said in my head. ***Go straight. I'll meet you there.***

I did as she told me.

======

I cleared my throat. "There's just one thing that I don't get. After all that - after what they did to you - you had no problem with turning us back into prisoners? Even knowing what you know about those…people?"

Maple cleared her throat. "Yes, I believe I made that point as well."

Marie kept her eyes on the table before her, picking at a spot on its surface. "I told you. I did what I had to. The same thing you did to Uncle Dave."

A burst of rage burnt through me. "Don't throw that back in my face. I…or Kelli…saved your life."

"What did you think I did for you? Do you think you would have lasted two minutes in London without me?" She looked at me now, trying to stare me down, but it fell flat. No amount of intimidation that she threw at me could supersede the image of her in the arms of Uncle Dave, completely under his control.

That's what this is really all about, I thought. She had trusted the Corporation and they used that trust against her, reducing her again to that powerless child. I don't doubt that she wished to destroy the Corporation for good and noble reasons, but she also saw this as a personal battle. "That look might work with your 'employees', but not with me. I'm sorry you had to go through all that shit, and I'm happy to help you out, but let's get something clear: we're equals here. I'm not going to be your pawn."

Her discomfort at the idea showed in a slight twitch in her bearing, in the curve of her shoulder. At last she nodded. "I guess I shouldn't expect anything less. I think Kelli would have been the same. Maybe we can be friends."

"We'll see. Why don't we talk about what you want me to do first?"

She opened her mouth to speak, but didn't get the chance, as a muffled series of thumps began to sound from outside. I wish I could have heard her plan. I would have loved to have helped her put it in motion.

Unfortunately, the words would never pass from her lips. The Corporation would see to that.

June 15th

The last entry turned out to be a race between finishing my dinner and finishing the entry. Dinner won, and I couldn't delay any longer, not safely, anyway. I haven't had a break since then; I had to stay on the move and once I'd finally stopped, I needed a lot of rest. I seem to have found the right time and place to finish this at last. I don't think the Organization can find me now, but I can't know that for sure.

I have to finish this, even if no one ever reads these last few entries. Closure. I need closure, more than anything else.

Now where did I leave off in London? Oh, yes…

======

"What the hell?" Marie said. The woman could move with speed and grace; she made it up onto the dais in a few strides and stared down at the city, her fists wrapped into tight little balls. We had begun to mount the dais when she moaned and put a hand to her mouth. "My god."

Maple paused, her brow creased with worry. "What is it?"

Another thump from outside; the building rattled this time. It hadn't been enough to throw us off our stride, but it set our nerves on edge. We arrayed just behind her, staring out the window with a sense of dread.

A cloud of dark gray smoke rose into the blue morning sky,

obscuring much of our view of the city. We could see enough, though: the smoke originated from various points in Soho, with red-orange licks of flame following just behind the explosions that had generated both.

Maple gasped. "Are those…?"

Marie nodded. "Those locations all belong to the Underground." The words spurred her into action. She turned and went for her desk, her face knitted into a look of determination. I wondered if she was going to send out a rally cry, pulling the troops together.

That cry, like her plans for me, would go unspoken.

Seamus stepped forward without a word, producing something from his pants pocket. I saw a glint of steel for just a moment before he drove it forward twice, creating two bleeding holes in Marie's back.

She cried out and reached for the wounds, but Seamus didn't give her time to react. He wrapped an arm around her chest and raised his arm, making a large incision in her throat.

She gasped and gurgled, going down to her knees. He watched her, all emotion washed out of his face, the blade in his right hand dripping with Marie's blood. It felt like we stood there for an eternity, unable to comprehend what he had just done.

Then Cayla screamed and rushed at him, fists swinging.

That same blank look on his face, he whirled and buried the knife in the center of her chest, right between her breasts. She gave a shocked look of surprise and dropped to the floor.

Maple took two steps forward and paused, thinking better of approaching him. "My God, Seamus, what are you doing?"

He looked up at her, his jaw slack. He licked his lips, and I saw that sweat had broken out on his forehead. "How did she put it? Ah, yes, I'm doing what must be done."

I circled him, and though he glanced at me, he didn't make a move. I gambled on the idea that the Corporation would want me intact. It might have been a stupid gamble and even stupider assumption, but Seamus's clouded head worked to my advantage either way.

======

It felt like I ran all night through the corn as the storm slowed and lost power overhead. Impossible, of course. It could only have been a few minutes, but I think we've established that time in that world flowed very differently than it did elsewhere. So much of my memory of the rest of that night is corn stalks and panic, but at some point I came out on the other end, panting and gasping, ready to collapse.

I found myself on my knees, facing the back of the burning cabin.

I didn't know if I'd gotten turned around, or if –

"It all works like this," Carla said, and I jumped, damn near falling on my side again.

She came around the edge of the burning cabin as she spoke. Her feet touched the ground as she walked; her flaming hair had been extinguished and her body slumped. The Senior's attack must have done a number on her.

"What do you mean?" I said. I tried to stand up, but my tired legs protested and I went back down on my knees.

She limped toward me. "Save your energy."

"Answer my question." I clenched my fists against the tops of my thighs.

"It all works like this." She waved a hand around her head.

"This universe. The corn is the beginning and ending."

Pain seared my chest. "But it's all burning down."

She nodded. "It's a good thing."

"But the Khesnaa. Room 2." I pointed, as if she couldn't see the thing burning at her back.

She nodded again. "Gone."

"You don't understand me. How am I supposed to get out?"

"You'll find a way. Don't worry."

I couldn't understand. I looked around at the corn rows, shaking my head. "How?"

She held up one hand. "Just trust me. You're going to be fine."

I didn't want to trust her, but she'd kept me relatively safe to that point. "Are you going to be okay?"

She chuckled, and then coughed, wincing. "I doubt it. But don't worry about me, either. It's time I got out of this race."

I had to know something for sure. "Did you make me?"

"Yes. I didn't mean to, and I wasn't aware of it when I did it. I was just so scared and lonely, and one night, a few lifetimes back, I guess I dreamed about the girl who saved my life when I was little. After the drugs killed me that time, Gina disappeared, and you showed up."

I felt strong enough to stand up now, and I did, taking a step closer to her. "So Gina was a real woman? You didn't create her?"

She shook her head. "No. I created Gina too. I guess they figured you'd be a better prototype, what with you once being a real person and all, so they 'disappeared' Gina. You never actually met her."

"That's impossible. I remember Bloch grabbing me off the street in Boston. I remember Gina helping me through things…"

"No. That's all an illusion."

Fear and anger blazed in my chest. I stumbled toward her. "You don't know that. You can't."

"I do. I put her there. Didn't mean to, but I did."

I prepared to protest, to insist that my memories with Gina had to be true - I had this bit of proof or that bit of proof - but all the proof in the Khesnaa had burned up.

She swayed on her feet a bit, and then spoke. "Listen. I don't think there's a word for what we are. We're the same person, and we're not. But I'm glad I got to know you. And I'm glad I got to pay you back for saving me."

I embraced her, allowing her to rest against my body. "I'm glad, too."

======

Catching on to my plan, Maple took a quick step to the side, heading for the tables piled high with books.

It had its intended effect: Seamus faced her, brandishing the knife. "Don't make me. Please."

She froze at the bottom step of the dais, extending her hands toward him. "You don't have to do this."

"I do, though. You don't get it, do you? I'm not going to stab the Underground in the back for money or power. They have Glynis. We were so busy on our wonderful crusade that we didn't bother to protect the family."

I inched closer to Marie's desk, wondering if he would turn on me and rush me with that knife. I wouldn't have much of a chance if he got an idea like that, but Maple had frozen in place, holding his attention.

"That can't be true," she whispered.

He cocked his head. "No? And why not?" He approached her. "We never had a prayer against these people. You wanted to take back control of the world, but all of you, even the goddamned genetic genius over there, failed to realize one thing: they *are* the world you're seeking to control."

Maple shook her head. "You've gone mad."

"No. I'm quite sane. I'm just seeing things for the first time – things you tried to hide from me. I'm going to make sure Glynis is safe. I don't want to hurt you... Seanmháthair..." he said, and took a step closer to her. I heard tears in his voice. "But I will if I have to."

I wondered if he had forgotten me. It gave me time to reach Marie's desk and search it for a weapon. At last I found a small glass paperweight and hefted it in my right hand.

Seamus raised his head. "If you're thinking of making a move on me, missy, you'd better be ready."

I froze, staring at his hair. "What makes you think I'd do that?"

He turned sideways so that he could look at both Maple and me. "I don't suppose that chunk of glass in your hand has something to do with it? I'm not daft, you know, and if you kill me, you lose your shot at finding Sam."

I almost dropped the paperweight right there. "You know what happened to Sam?"

He gave a solemn nod. "I'm not proud of it, but did you never wonder at the timing of it all? He spends one day with me and disappears right after. Cayla just gave them the excuse they needed."

And you sent Cayla there in the first place. I felt sick to my stomach. "Where is he?" I said, my voice low. I saw Maple moving on the other side of the room, but I couldn't focus. Sam occupied my thoughts – Sam and our last moments together.

He tried hard to look nonchalant, but he came across as queasy. Betrayal didn't suit him. "If I tell you that, then I lose all my leverage, don't I?"

"What if I promise not to hurt you?"

He laughed. "And I can trust that, then."

I didn't know what to say.

"I thought not. I'm sorry, but I can't risk my sister's life. She's family. She comes first."

I considered pointing out that he'd just threatened his own grandmother, but I didn't want to turn his attention toward Maple in any way. I went for Plan B: I surrendered to the pain surrounding Sam, letting the tears flow. I let the paperweight tumble from my hand. Yes, I wanted to distract him, but I also wanted him to see the pain he'd caused. "You helped them get what they wanted."

His face fell, his eyes turning into saucers. He approached me, the knife lowered. "I'm sorry. I didn't want to do this, but…just imagine the pain if I'd lost my sister."

"Son of a bitch," I said, and slapped him when he had gotten close enough. No need to fake that one.

I didn't see too much difference between the look on his face and the look on Cayla's face when he'd driven the knife into her chest. He touched the place where I'd slapped him and nodded. "I earned that, but do it again, and I'll be forced to do unpleasant things."

"Seamus," Maple said from behind him.

He turned, and she hit him across the face with one of the heavy books from the table. He cried out and raised his hands, trying to catch the book.

It didn't work. Another shot from her and the blade tumbled

from his hands. Dazed, he bent down to pick the knife up, but I kicked it away from him.

Maple took one more shot at him, nailing him in the back of the head. He went down in a heap.

I picked up the knife and passed it to her. She fumbled with it for a moment, and then put it against the back of his head. "Seamus…I don't want to kill you, Lord help me, but I will if I have to."

I thought of Sam. "Please, don't. He could –"

He cried out. "You're going to kill Glynis."

She leaned close. "Not if I can help it."

"You don't know where she is."

"First tell her where Sam is. At least do her that courtesy."

He considered it for a moment, no doubt stalling for time. She wouldn't allow it, though. She pressed the blade closer against his neck. He whined and began to speak. "They took him to your apartment," he choked out. "The one that just blew up."

======

I hugged Carla tight, letting her presence ease some of the tension that still hung on in my body.

She patted my back. "Good. Something good came from this shit, huh?"

I stepped away and smirked. "I wouldn't say I'm *good.*"

"Better than average?"

"That'll work. So what's next?" I said.

"You have to wait for the cabin to burn down. I think. And then we'll –"

I would never find out Carla's plans, either. Fate is such a funny thing…echoes inside of echoes. It makes me wonder if there's a larger creator with His or Her fingerprints all over these things. It wouldn't be comforting, because this God works through violence as well as love: a shot rang out and blood sprayed from the side of Carla's head. Some of the blood spattered me moments before she fell to the ground, dead. I didn't even have time to register what had happened before Zito came out of the shadows and fell to the ground, the pistol skittering away from him.

It's a miracle that he managed to make it that far: his body was pink and shredded, skin hanging off from where the fire had got hold of him.

Shock taking over, I watched myself walk over to him and pick up the pistol, kicking his hand away as he reached for it. I leaned over him and put the pistol against his head. "Why did you do it?"

He said something, his voice raspy.

I bent down. "Say what?"

"Bitch deserved it," he said.

I squeezed the trigger. Then I did it again and again until no more bullets remained and his melted body lay still at my feet.

======

Sam couldn't be dead.

I kept repeating that, but it didn't keep my head from spinning. I only just made it to the edge of Marie's desk, falling onto it. Papers scattered and fell, some landing on Marie's fresh corpse at the foot of the desk. So much death. So much loss.

Maple glanced back at me and then turned back to her

grandson. "Tell me their plans."

He didn't hesitate this time. "They're on their way here. They want the girl."

She looked back at me, eyes wide. "You have to get out of here. I will deal with the Corporation and the Senior."

I shook my head. "I'm not leaving you here to face those assholes."

"I'm not giving you the choice. Listen carefully. Go down to the third garage floor. Once you leave the elevator, take two rights. There's a car parked down there. Are you listening?"

I strained to focus. Third garage. Two rights. My brain kept spacing out, but I *would* remember. "I'm trying."

"You'd best do it. The car is an Acura, in Spot 36. The code to the door lock is 4573. Do you understand?"

"Yes."

"Repeat it," she said.

"4573." I glanced out the window toward the growing fires in the distance and what might once have been our apartment.

Sam…

She wouldn't allow me a moment's reverie. "Go. Now. They're coming."

I looked back to her. "What about your granddaughter?"

"That's my concern, not yours. Your involvement in this drama ends here. Now get downstairs. Look under the passenger seat. There's a GPS."

"What's a GPS?"

Seamus laughed. "Are you kidding me?"

Maple put her foot against his neck. "Not a word," she said, and looked back to me. "Plug it into the cigarette lighter and turn it on. It will give you directions right to where you need to be." A look passed over her face, as if something occurred to her. "You *have* driven, right?"

"I…uh…Sam showed me some."

She closed her eyes and shook her head. "Fine. It will have to do. You have to go now."

"But…"

"Just go," she roared.

I climbed down from the dais, going for the tables and my two marble notebooks. I scooped them up and glanced back as Maple hauled Seamus to his feet.

"Now, then, Shea. Let's see how much the Corporation values you. Maybe we can talk our way out of this and get to Glynis despite your pigheadedness," she said.

I fought an urge to return and stand with her. I knew I wouldn't see her again for a long time, if ever again, and it made for quite the scene. She stood with a knife pressed against her grandson's neck, one foot in a puddle of blood spreading from Cayla's body. Behind them I saw Marie – Mimi. Her calf stuck out from behind the desk, disappearing behind their tangled forms.

Cayla, Mimi, and Carla gone. Did that make me the last of my line? What about the Four Cs? Had they been caught in the blasts? I had no way of knowing, and no way to rescue them.

So powerless. So goddamn powerless. Then and now.

I sighed and made for the glass door, and the elevator beyond.

======

Shock began to settle on my bones at last. I took a few staggering steps backward before I fell into a sitting position, watching the cabin burn. I grabbed my head with both hands and tried to push back the darkness closing in around me, but this time it wouldn't be denied.

If I could just lie down for a bit, everything would be fine. Yeah. That's it. Just lie down.

I lay back, staring up into the night sky. The rain had stopped sometime after Zito shot Carla, and the clouds had begun to depart as well. The remaining cloud cover had been painted with streaks of red and orange from the spreading fire. It might be the most beautiful thing that I'd ever seen.

Would the fires close in and take me too? Probably, but I didn't care. I didn't care about anything but that beautiful sky.

And then nothing.

For a long time, or what seemed like a long time.

My next memory is someone - or something - large and strong picking me up from the ground and carrying me close to his - or its - chest. At first I thought it had to be the Senior, and tried to break out of my daze, but I couldn't even open my eyes, let alone start swinging my arms and kicking.

Might as well let them do what they're going to do. We're both dead anyway. No escape.

So I let the man, or thing, carry me. I may have convinced myself that it was the right thing to do, and that I felt comfortable in its arms. It's all so hazy. Oh, sure, I felt some heat, no doubt from one of the fires, but I think whatever was carrying me stood between the flames and my body.

Sam never confirmed whether he had been the one to save me, but I saw a light in his eye that told me all I needed to know. Of course, it didn't occur to me at the time. I just accepted his presence and clung as hard as I could, whether man, beast, or Senior. I remember a big field of blue washing over the both of us, and him trying to say something.

I don't remember whether I understood what he said. He lifted me up, pushing me forward and through the bright blue light.

I blacked out again when I passed into the light.

======

The trip out of London isn't much more than a blur, though I'm writing this only a few days after the fact. Oh, sure, I remember stopping for fish and chips and writing the entry on the 12th, and I remember moments here and there. I saw smoke and fire, a mass of confusion on the streets, and emergency units heading deeper into the city and away from my own path and the tower. The emergency made travel near-impossible. It took a few hours to get clear of the city, but once I passed places like Hatfield the English countryside opened up, and my stress levels dropped.

The calm, collected voice of the GPS kept me company on my drive. Incredible machine, and something Carla must never have encountered because I have absolutely no memory of such a thing. I also found a few pleasant surprises as I embarked; Maple neglected to mention the hundred-pound note tucked into the ashtray and an apple and protein shake hidden under the driver's side seat. Those kept me sated for a while.

The GPS took me on a roundabout loop, no doubt intended to throw the Organization off of my tail, if they had ever had it in the first place. I'm not sure about the latter, as I never saw a sign of anyone following me, and it should have been obvious inside the city limits, given my intense paranoia and anxiety.

Eventually I felt confident enough to make the stop for fish and chips. I saw no suspicious types hanging around. Not even the odd stranger who stared at me. I might as well have been invisible. It's an odd freedom - not quite the one I'd dreamed about, or the one that Mimi had been discussing, but freedom just the same.

It took about eight hours to get from the tower to the front door of my new home. I passed through a small town on the way east, a cozy little place that just appeared out of nowhere. The GPS told me that I had drawn close to my destination, and so I wondered: could this be my new hometown? It seemed pretty likely.

Just past town, I caught the coast and headed North for another mile or two before the GPS had me pull off into an unpaved road just before I crossed over one of the old viaducts. The path led me into the wilds of a small forest, and as the darkness of the trees' shade closed in on me, I felt exhaustion settle on my bones at last. Safety. Anonymity.

Whatever this place might be, I'd need a good day's sleep once I got there.

At last a cottage appeared out of the woods at the end of this path. I pulled to a stop in the soft grass off to its right and began to climb out of the car. I stopped, though, as the cottage door popped open and four very familiar women stepped out.

The Four Cs.

======

I woke up, but I had no idea how much time had passed. Light filled whatever room I occupied. I opened my eyes and saw that a set of bright fuchsia curtains had been thrown open over a pair of cheap, streaked windows. I grunted and rolled over on the worn-out mattress, my bare feet hitting the red shag carpet.

I looked down and found them - and myself - still caked in mud, though it had dried up on my skin. I looked back to discover that the bedspread had been covered in my filth. I shuddered. I'd never needed a shower more in my life. I stood up, ready to wash off and figure it all out later, when I spotted a note on a table by the door.

It had just two words, written in a familiar handwriting:

Wait here.

No problem, I thought, and went to the bathroom.

I never had a more glorious shower, let me tell you. I had mud in some strange places, and I had to stop a couple of times to push the crap down through the drain as it clogged the works up. The Motel 6's shampoo and soap didn't quite have the oomph to get my hair as clean as I wanted it, but it had to do. It more than did the job. I felt *human* when I stepped out of that shower, for the first time in ages.

I paused at the bathroom mirror, scrubbing my ears with the towel. I stopped when I spotted something brown by the foot of the double-bed. A suitcase. I tied the towel around my body and retrieved it, laying it out on the bed.

I opened it with a bit of trepidation, but I didn't need to worry after all. It might as well have been a care package from some long-lost relative: clothes in my size, a brush, the right kind of shampoo and conditioner (wouldn't that have been nice), a handheld radio, a marble notebook (that one might come in handy), and a bag of treats - right down to my favorite: biscuits. Somebody knew me.

Beneath all that I found a copy of a beat-up paperback. Its cover showed a cabin in the woods, and its title gave me the creeps.

Imago's Forest by Regina Tolleson.

I sat down on the bed and turned over the book, shaking my head. Sure enough, I recognized the face staring at me from the back cover: Gina.

======

I received hugs all around from the Four Cs. I'm not good enough of a writer to explain the sensation that I got when I embraced those women. It went way beyond relief into a deep, soul-cleansing warmth.

After that brief moment of bliss, we broke and stood in a semi-circle, staring at one another, sharing the emotions of five orphans in the storm.

Cathy spoke first. "You met her, didn't you? You wouldn't be here otherwise."

I rubbed my neck, wondering how I'd handle this one. "Yeah. That's right."

"She's dead, isn't she?"

I closed my eyes, wondering how to put it, and instead just nodded.

They let out a collective sigh and the world felt a bit smaller for a moment.

"We felt it," Catriona said, studying the floorboards of the cottage porch.

Ugh. I hated sharing this with them, but they had to know. "That's not all." I took a deep breath and proceeded to tell them the story of what happened in the tower, of Seamus's betrayal and the detonations in Soho.

Once I had finished, the whole group might as well have been utterly defeated. Cathy stared at the ground, her eyes focused on some point far away. Catriona hung her head. Charlene looked ready to vomit. Caty went to the edge of the porch and crouched, head in hands.

"That's it. The Underground is finished," Catriona said.

Cathy looked up, blinking away the cobwebs. "No way. We're still here, aren't we?"

"What are we supposed to do, fight the Corporation on our own? Five sad little artificial women?"

"Hey, that's not fair," I said, and Catriona looked away.

She murmured under her breath. "It's the truth."

"Shape it up, Catriona. Priorities," Cathy said, and nodded at me. "First we help Ms. Kelli recover. Nothing else can happen until she's well. If Iris survived, and I think she did, she'll come for us when the time is right."

I wanted to protest. What did I need to recover from? I wanted to get back out there and take on the Corporation with my bare hands, if I had to. I wanted to join up with Maple and find Glynis.

Then a wave of lightheadedness passed through me, and I knew just what they meant about recovery. I swayed for a moment, and said, "what do I do in the meantime?"

Cathy put a hand on my shoulder. "You slow down. We have enough food to last for months. We'll figure this thing out."

Catriona rolled her eyes and Caty rose, turning toward us. "You're always the optimist, aren't you? What if we're the last ones? What then?"

Cathy turned on her. "Do you have any other suggestions? I'd be happy to hear them. I just refuse to lie down and die. Sorry if that inconveniences you."

My wooziness intensified and I took a stumbling step forward. I tried to regain my balance, but there was none to be had. Moments before I did a face plant into the porch, Catriona, Cathy, and Charlene all caught me in their arms.

Cathy clicked her tongue. "Now you see, she needs to go rest. We'll discuss this later."

Another wave of lightheadedness made me gasp. "Sam," I said, and I didn't know why.

"I know," Cathy said, and slipped her hand inside mine, helping the others lead me to the cottage. "All in good time."

"We have to save Sam," I think I said. I'm not sure on this.

"Of course we do." Even more unclear on that. Think it might have been Caty.

My last memory from that morning is the four of them leading me over the threshold.

======

I sighed and shook my head. Gina's face on that book meant so little and so much at the same time. It meant that I had truly been born into the Khesnaa. It meant that I couldn't be truly human, not really, and not ever.

And now I'd been born into a world I only knew through second-hand memories of stories, TV, and music.

But music might just be enough. I picked up the radio from inside the suitcase and clicked it on, dialing through the stations. Lots of talk and lots of country music, the like of which I'd never really heard (they informed me that this station was 96.3, KLL, Lubbock's Country Leader). Some hip hop - that sounded interesting - and then a familiar song broke through the static somewhere between 101.1 and 103.5, like a ghost on the airwaves.

Dream a Little Dream of Me.

Maybe not all my memories had been created. And if they had, then so what? They still made me feel warm. They made me feel enough to hug that little radio to my chest. They didn't have to be "authentic", they just had to mean something to me, and they did.

So what if I didn't come from this world the same as everyone else? I existed, and that was all that really mattered. All those other things, when you got right down it, didn't really matter. I mattered. Just like those "false" memories.

I gripped the radio tighter and began to plan what came next.

======

My next memory is waking up in bed yesterday morning, nearly 24 hours after the scene on the cottage porch. I guess I needed so much sleep after all that that happened in London, but I still felt a pang at all that lost time. What could have happened in London while I'd slept? The Corporation could be drawing closer. Maple could be dead. The Underground could well and truly be wiped from the face of the Earth.

You can't do anything about it, and couldn't if you were awake. Just breathe for now, I told myself.

I readied myself and made my way out to the rest of the cottage, where the Four Cs laid in wait. They fussed about me for a while, made me breakfast, and promised that they would replace my wardrobe. Those women sure do love to shop, but I'm not going to object given that I'm down to the blouse, slacks, and pumps that I wore to the tower that morning.

Their words passed through my mind for the most part, making the faintest of impressions as they did. I found myself consumed by other, more serious, matters. Visions of the past. London in flames. The sound that Mimi made when Seamus slit her throat. Sam.

But not Sam dying or dead. No flames. Instead, I saw Sam tied up somewhere in a dark room, looking for a way out. I didn't know if that was delusion, wishful thinking, or something more legitimate. Not then.

Around noon I insisted on visiting the beach, no matter how reckless they found it. They all wanted to go along given my condition. I fought the idea, but at last compromised and accepted Cathy as my sole companion. Besides, I argued, didn't they want to go buy some clothes? At last, they consented, and Cathy and I departed.

We had a bit of a hike through the woods, across a field, and down the Cliffside to the beach below. Thankfully, Cathy knew the safest path, as the four women had gone to the beach more than once since they'd arrived a few days before my arrival. If it hadn't been for Cathy, I don't know what might have happened. I might well have killed myself on the rocks in my weakened state.

I sat down on the beach with the last marble notebook and a sturdy fountain pen. The ink doesn't match my earlier entries, but screw it. It just seems appropriate to finish this thing up at the edge of the sea, so far away from the world that the Khesnaa represented. It seemed time to gather my thoughts about not only what happened on the 12th, but the last few months on this side of the veil. The crashing waves on the rocks perfectly complimented the melancholy that resided behind my eyes when I sat down here. So much death. So much loss. And for what?

For the bad guys to win? To become little more than an exile?

I suppose on one level I got my wish. Haven't I dreamed of going to the beach? To walk with relative freedom in the world?

What a price to pay, though. I've been an idiot. Freedom is important - scratch that - freedom is *essential,* but I wonder if I've paid *too* high a price. Things seemed so much simpler in the Khesnaa. I'd pay anything, *do* anything to be free. But now, without Sam, without the support system that had popped up around me - whether tangible or intangible - I wasn't so sure.

What's freedom without hope?

But that's ridiculous. I'm not the one who kidnapped Sam. I'm not responsible for that collapse. I'm only responsible for my own choices. I think I've gotten so used to bearing the weight that others have put on me - the Organization, the Underground, even Sam (though he never meant to) - that I internalize every catastrophe as the price of my continued existence.

That's bullshit. It has to end. Right here and now. I draw the line and walk forward taking responsibility only for my own choices.

Besides, I haven't told them, haven't even admitted it to myself until this moment, but I know that hope is still alive.

You see, I'm pretty sure Sam is still alive. I thought about it on the walk to the beach, and even more as I wrote this. The Sam that's been with me for the last three months is not the Sam that I knew in the Khesnaa. Oh, the consciousness might be essentially the same, somehow drawn from either his dead body or my memories (I suspect the latter but may never know), but unlike the original Sam, this one's body had been shaped by my own creator.

We have a tie, much like Carla and I had a tie. Like that tie with Carla, in moments of extreme stress, I think it opens up and tells me something about him. I'm pretty sure I feel him. I think that's what the vision meant.

I think it's why I feel him now, when I close my eyes. His heart is so close to mine that I could reach out and touch it. That connection…that's the thing that everyone wants and so few get. Maybe in some ways it's better to be what I am. In some ways, it's even more human.

It kills me, but I know that I can't do anything about Sam right now. I have to bide my time, recover, and figure out where things are going. Then, when the time is right, Maple will either re-appear or we'll begin to plan again. We will pick up the pieces and carry on, one way or another.

This isn't finished.

ABOUT THE AUTHOR

Born and raised in the rural Shenandoah Valley of Virginia, Jonathan wrote his first fantasy/sci-fi novel at the age of 13. After studying writing and communication at James Madison University, Jonathan turned his passion for writing into a full-time technical writing career in the DC Metro area. He may have drifted away from fiction at times, but it was always his first love - and he always returned to it. Since returning, he has authored works such as *The Kayson Cycle* and *The Corridors of the Dead* and *The Station,* both part of the Among the Dead cycle.

Now living in Bethesda with his wife, two cats, and two quirky guinea pigs for whom his publishing company is named, he crafts the kinds of stories that he had always hoped to read but just couldn't quite find.

Mr. Allen is currently working on the sequel to The Corridors of the Dead, the City of the Dead.